PR

Al

"Loved *Alchemystic*. Every girl needs her own Stanis!"
—Jeanne C. Stein, national bestselling author of *Blood Bond*

"Like being strapped to a wrecking ball of urban fantasy fun.
Hang on and enjoy the mayhem."
—Mario Acevedo, author of *Werewolf Smackdown*

"Just when I thought Mr. Strout couldn't do any better than his
Simon Canderous series, I was proven wrong! I couldn't put *Alchemystic* down. It was nonstop action and tension, a bit of romance
but not overdone, and all sorts of twists and turns . . . The magical
elements will keep you riveted, and I guarantee you'll be begging
for more." —*Night Owl Reviews*

"This is a heartfelt look into the human nature that is intertwined
with magical elements. Metaphysics, romance, humanity, compassion, action, and humor all meshed into a wonderful masterpiece
of writing splendor." —*Earth's Book Nook*

"The magic behind *Alchemystic* was incredibly intriguing . . . All
in all, *Alchemystic* was a very solid start to a new series that will
definitely be on my radar for future releases."
—*A Book Obsession*

"Strout has come up with an even more fantastic story than before.
Alchemystic is a fun and exciting start to a promising new urban
fantasy series. With plenty of adventure, mystery, suspense, and
magic—this was impossible to put down. Fast-paced, fresh, and
surprising, there is never a dull moment. Urban fantasy fans will
definitely want to check out this new series (as well as Strout's
previous Simon Canderous series)." —*SciFiChick.com*

"*Alchemystic* has a unique story with delightful characters and
plenty of mystery to keep you interested." —*Rabid Reads*

continued . . .

"*Alchemystic* is thrilling, funny, and eerie—all the elements that make Strout books such irreverent fun!" —*RT Book Reviews*

"Excellent character development. The ending leaves this whole world open in a great way . . . My favorite part of this is the use of magic . . . It feels organic and interesting." —*Nerdist*

PRAISE FOR ANTON STROUT AND HIS SIMON CANDEROUS NOVELS

Dead Matter

"Strout's . . . great sense of humor, combined with vivid characters, a complex mystery, and plenty of danger, makes for a fantastic read. Urban fantasy fans should not miss this exciting series." —*SciFiChick.com*

"Strout's good-hearted, bat-carrying hero is once again faced with extraordinary peril from both bureaucratic paperwork and things that go bump in the night. His skillful blending of the creepy and the wacky gives his series an original appeal. Don't miss out!" —*RT Book Reviews* (top pick)

Deader Still

"Such a fast-paced, engaging, entertaining book that the pages seemed to fly by far too quickly. Take the New York of *Men in Black* and *Ghostbusters*, inject the same pop-culture awareness and irreverence of *Buffy the Vampire Slayer* or *The Middleman*, toss in a little *Thomas Crown Affair*, shake and stir, and you've got something fairly close to this book." —*The Green Man Review*

"It has a *Men in Black* flavor mixed with *NYPD Blue*'s more gritty realism . . . if you think of the detectives as working the night shift in *The Twilight Zone*." —*SFRevu*

Dead to Me

BOOK TWO OF
The Spellmason Chronicles

Stonecast

ANTON STROUT

ACE BOOKS, NEW YORK

THE BERKLEY PUBLISHING GROUP
Published by the Penguin Group
Penguin Group (USA) LLC
375 Hudson Street, New York, New York 10014, USA

USA | Canada | UK | Ireland | Australia | New Zealand | India | South Africa | China

Penguin Books Ltd., Registered Offices: 80 Strand, London WC2R 0RL, England
For more information about the Penguin Group, visit penguin.com.

STONECAST

An Ace Book / published by arrangement with the author

Ace Books are published by The Berkley Publishing Group.
ACE and the "A" design are trademarks of Penguin Group (USA) LLC.

For information, address: The Berkley Publishing Group,
a division of Penguin Group (USA) LLC,
375 Hudson Street, New York, New York 10014.

ISBN: 978-0-425-25640-4

PUBLISHING HISTORY
Ace mass-market edition / October 2013

PRINTED IN THE UNITED STATES OF AMERICA

10 9 8 7 6 5 4 3 2 1

Cover illustration by Blake Morrow; texture © Allgusak/Shutterstock.
Cover design by Diana Kolsky.
Interior text design by Tiffany Estreicher.

ALWAYS LEARNING   PEARSON

To Benjamin and Julia, my future adventures—
you were always on my mind during the
writing of this particular adventure

Acknowledgments

Welcome, my dear book nerds, to the second book of The Spell-mason Chronicles. Much like Alexandra Belarus uncovering the arcane secrets of the Spellmasons, a book also needs others to make it happen.

Stonecast would not exist without the help of some pretty amazing people:

Each and every Penguin we keep in the penguin house at Penguin Group, especially my friends (and coworkers) in the paperback sales department; my editorial wizard, Jessica Wade (she may indeed be an actual wizard to make *my* words look good); production editor Michelle Kasper, assistant production editor Jamie Snider, and copy editors Sara and Bob Schwager; Judith Murello, Diana Kolsky, and Blake Morrow for a gorgeously creepy cover; Erica Martirano and her marketing and promo team; my publicity superstars, Rosanne Romanello, Jodi Rosoff, and Brad Brownson; my agent, Kristine Dahl, and Laura Neely at ICM; the League of Reluctant Adults for continued support and stocking of the bar; my family; and the *still*-elusive Orlycorn for her infinite patience with me when I disappear down the writing hole. And as always, dear reader, to you and your twisted little mind for venturing forth with me.

So without further ado, shall we?

For a charm of powerful trouble,
Like a hell-broth boil and bubble.

—*MACBETH* (IV, I, 18–19), SECOND WITCH

One

Alexandra

"For the record, I hate running," Marshall Blackmoore huffed, his shaggy brown mop of hair stuck to his forehead with sweat, covering part of his eyes. "Especially after creepy monsters."

Despite his tall, skinny Ichabod physique, my friend wheezed away like he was a three-hundred-pound fat-camp escapee chasing down an ice-cream truck. "There's a reason I opened a game store, you know. Lots . . . more . . . sitting."

I didn't have the energy to think about whatever my dear, nerdy friend was saying about Roll for Initiative. For me, running actually helped me concentrate, and in my new-found arcane life, focus was indeed a handy skill to have. Like now.

"I actually enjoy this," I said. "The running part."

"How do you feel about the chasing-a-rampaging-golem part of it?" my other friend Aurora Torres called over her shoulder as she ran by. Her short blue hair and black horn-rimmed glasses flew past me, her dancer's legs pumping hard as she easily pulled much farther ahead of Marshall and me. As she took the lead, her lean frame disappeared into the distance, the bounce of an artist's tube strapped across her back almost comical.

"Not so crazy about the rampaging," I said. "Especially given that it's *my* fault."

"Don't beat yourself up too bad," she called back. "Occupational hazard of being the one and only existing Spellmason."

Up ahead in the distance, the lumbering but still-speedy creature I had empowered continued on through the night, thankfully charging down one of the quieter side avenues near Manhattan's South Street Seaport.

The oversized human shape—comprised entirely of animated red bricks—moved gracelessly, crunching into anything and everything in its path: parked cars, tree trunks, low-hanging branches, hydrants—all of them coming away worse from their encounter.

"Don't beat *yourself* up," Marshall repeated, pointing at it. "You've got *that* thing to beat you up."

"Just be glad I chose to run these experiments late at night," I said. "We only have to deal with property damage and not, you know . . ."

"People damage . . . ?" Rory finished.

I nodded. "Exactly."

Rory turned back forward, pointing to a dark area up ahead that lay between two streetlamps. "It's heading for that alley!" she called out.

Not wanting to lose sight of it, I pushed myself harder, both physically and mentally. I pressed the power of my will out to it, fighting to regain the control I had lost over its form. I pulled at its spirit, but there was a resistance in the animated creature.

"No luck," I said, and the connection snapped shut as the brick monster vanished down the alley.

"I'll try to head it off," Rory called back, and sprinted farther off down the block, one hand already unscrewing the top of the art tube strapped across her back. By the time she had gone half the block, Rory had pulled two wooden shaft pieces free from it, coupling them together before affixing a third, longer, bladed piece to it.

"Not the most subtle weapon to cart around the city," I called back to Marshall, who I was steadily outpacing now.

"Says the woman who had a magical gargoyle as her weapon of choice," he said. "At least Rory can break her *glaive guisarme* down. Besides, there's no talking Ms. Torres out of something once she gets it in her head. She loves that thing."

"She does make it dance," I admitted.

"Surprising for a dancer!" Marshall added with a wheeze.

I didn't respond. The sheer act of talking winded me, so I shut my mouth as I headed into the alleyway after the creature. The darkness was worse here, and given the overturned cans and dented Dumpsters along the way, I slowed as I negotiated a path through it all.

Rory came into the alley farther up ahead of me from the side somewhere and, true to her calling in life, danced her way deftly after the creature, leaving me to feel all the more clumsy an oaf for slamming into everything as I went.

Cans rolled, and empty delivery pallets flew back and forth in the wake of the lumbering creature as it made its destructive way, but Rory managed to dodge them all with her natural grace and speed. Not wanting to leave my best friend since childhood to face the golem all alone, I secretly wished I had half her agility. When wishing didn't make me any more graceful—evidenced by the sudden sound of tearing fabric from my jeans as a stray pallet nail caught on them—I instead opted for focusing more on my immediate environment. I *needed* to pay attention. I wasn't going to be any use if I bled out right here.

Being more cautious slowed me, but it was a small comfort that I was *still* farther ahead than Marshall, whose every bump and crash behind me fell farther and farther away as I pushed myself harder down the alley.

"You doing okay back there, Marsh?" I asked, keeping my eyes glued to my path.

"Don't worry about me," he said. "Again, my bad for living the gamer's life. Just keep on them!"

I chanced a glance up. The alley turned left farther ahead, and Rory and the creature were no longer in sight. I pushed on, rounding the corner in time to catch the two of them roughly thirty feet straight ahead, where the alley dead-ended.

Trapped, the creature reached out to the brick wall in front of it, as if sensing that the wall was comprised of the same material it was made from. When it found no means of escape, though, it spun, its tall figure menacing Rory as I arrived by her side.

Despite the clear danger and its towering size, Rory didn't back down from it, extending her pole arm in front of her.

"Can you control it?" she asked. "You know, like you did for about, oh, twenty seconds back in Gramercy?"

"Shut it," I spat out. "You know that Hendrix didn't learn guitar in a day."

"True," Rory said, "but then again, a guitar doesn't threaten to kill you or crush you in quite the same way an animated pile of bricks does."

"Trying to concentrate here," I said, pressing my mind against the resistance of the creature once more. I latched onto it, but whatever was in there wasn't giving up control in any hurry.

Marshall arrived beside us, the sounds coming from him making me wonder if he was having an asthma attack. Between that thought and Rory's previous comments, my concentration was lost, and I snapped. "Yes, but at least Hendrix could go into a guitar shop and take lessons. He could go to guitar school. Hogwarts doesn't exist."

"Hey," she said, raking her blade in sparks against the brick golem. "We used to wish there to be magic in the world, and we *got* it."

"I'm not asking for much," I said. "Just some real instruction. A Dumbledore, a Snape . . . Hell, I'd even take a Trelawney right about now."

The creature knocked Rory's blade away, swinging its rough, thick hands.

"Don't say that," Rory said, backing up a little, scrunching up her face. "Don't *ever* say that. Trelawney, really?"

I shrugged. "In a pinch, sure. Not ideal, but—"

The air of the alley erupted into a flurry of tiny, leathery wings like those of a bat, but unlike a bat, these things had arms and legs to go with their sharp, tiny teeth.

"Stone biters," Marshall shouted.

"Not these guys again," Rory said, taking her pole arm and waving it about us in an attempt to drive the tiny creatures off.

Marshall, who smartly stood well out of harm's way from the golem, flipped open his blank book to a page where the winged creatures were already sketched out. "Your great-great-grandfather had them listed, and this appearance confirms it—they're drawn to magic in stone, not just stone itself." He made a quick note in his book.

As Rory continued waving her pole arm around, most of the swarm dispersed, save one especially flittery, shrieky one that dashed through the air in a tight circle around the golem. The tower of bricks seemed to be just as annoyed with our winged friend as we were. With the spirit in it distracted, my will found an opening into my creation's body, flooding forward into the brick as whatever resistant spirit within it vacated it.

"I have it!" I shouted, unable to contain my glee. Rory saved that kind of reaction for finding the sleekest, sexiest pair of shoes, and for Marshall, it was a decadent dessert, but my delight came from stopping brick monstrosities.

"Thankfully, the spirit realm hates whatever these winged things are as much as we do," I said.

The words were barely out of my mouth when Rory dashed forward and threw herself into the air toward the flying creature.

"Wait!" Marshall called out, but it was too late.

Rory's pole arm was already coming down fast on it, the tip of the blade driving straight through the center of its chest, pinning its tiny form to the wall of the alley. It let out a tiny screech that drove into the center of my brain, but in seconds, it was all over for the little beastie. Rory pulled her blade free from the wall, scraping the remains of the creature off the tip of her pole arm with the toe of one of her combat boots.

Marshall walked over to her, clutching his book against the pocket of his X-Men-logoed jacket. "Thanks," he said, annoyed, rolling the creature onto its back with his own shoe, his face losing what little color it had.

"Sorry," she said with a complete lack of sincerity, and walked back over to where I stood.

He flipped open the sketchbook once more and began drawing. "I wanted to get this creature right," he said. "And now—thanks to Miss Stabby here—I'll have to work around the damage she did to it."

"A simple 'thank-you' would suffice," Rory fired back. "Would you prefer it gouged one of our eyes out so you could get its good side? Why are you even doing this anyway? Half this stuff is already cataloged in Alexandra's great-great-grandfather's secret library."

Warm thoughts of the comfy couches on my favorite floor of the Belarus Building filled my head for a moment, until my arguing friends snapped me back into the moment.

Marshall looked up from the sketch, shooting his roommate a look. "A *Monster Manual* of my own will come in handy," he said, defensive. "Trust me."

"Easy, everyone," I said, speaking up, trying to hold the brick man in my sway.

Though Marshall and Rory excelled at fighting like a married couple, I didn't need them breaking the link I had just reestablished with my animated creation, but given the sudden, wobbly nature I felt radiating out from the brick man before me, I was already too late.

"Shit!" I said, fighting to hold it together. I rushed my will forward hard into it, which only made it more unstable at this point, and given the distraction, I could do little more than watch my creation fall apart brick by brick until there was nothing left but an inert pile of red bricks at my feet. "Dammit!"

"Sorry," Marshall offered. "But that's one way of stopping it before it could rampage any further." He flipped to the front of his book, making a note. "That's experiment 247. No *bueno*." After that, he flipped back through his book and started to sketch the dead creature.

Rory disassembled the pieces of her pole arm, wiping the blade down last, and when she was done, I helped her slide the pieces back into the art tube on her back.

"That went really well, Lexi," she said, turning to face me.

Given the results of our evening, I was poised to tell her to stop being a jerk, but there was actual sincerity in her eyes. "How can you be saying that? Look at it!"

Rory adjusted her glasses and pushed her blue bangs off her forehead as she caught her breath. "First of all, it was a full-human-sized creature," she said. "You've never done *anything* that big before."

"That's what she said . . . ?" Marshall snickered while still drawing away.

"Shut it," Rory said. "I'm trying to be constructive here."

I kicked one of the bricks, watching it topple off the pile. "I appreciate it," I said, "but it was still a failure."

"Also," Rory continued, not giving up, "it certainly stayed animated longer than anything else you've done." She pulled out her cell phone and checked the time. "It was nearly a half hour. Even if it wasn't in your control all that time, it still held together. Nothing's lasted that long except Bricksley."

I was ready to argue, but the mention of my little walking brick and his smiling drawn-on face brought a smile to my own face instead. "No fair invoking the cute," I said. "I only hope he's not tearing apart anything back in the art studio. We ran off in a hurry."

"Whatever," she said, slapping me on the shoulder, squeezing. "I'm chalking this up as a success."

"You do that," I conceded. "Still, none of my creations come even close to equaling—" In my frustration, I found I couldn't even say his name.

"Stanis," she said, sliding her arm fully over my shoulder. "I know. We'll get there. Slow and steady wins the race and all."

"You *still* haven't heard from him?" Marshall called over to us, his head still down in his notes.

Rory glared at him. "Marsh! Don't ask that."

He glanced up from his book, his eyes full of hurt. "What? I'm sorry I'm not up on all the details of your lives. I've got my own life. I've got the store, my games . . ." He pointed at the creature on the ground with his pen. "You know, this gross little thing to draw . . ."

"Just because Lexi hasn't heard from him in six months doesn't mean anything," Rory said as if I needed defending.

And maybe I did.

The last half year rushed to the front of my mind, over-whelming me. Life had erupted into chaos upon learning my great-great-grandfather Alexander Belarus had not just been an unparalleled architect and sculptor but also a prac-titioner of Spellmasonry—the arcane art of manipulating stonework to one's will.

That in itself would have been cool, except for the part where the servants of an ancient stone lord named Kejetan Ruthenia were intent on trying to kill us to reclaim said mystical secrets. If Alexander Belarus hadn't set the gar-goyle Stanis to secretly watch over our family centuries ago, I probably would have been dead by now.

No, I'd *definitely* be dead by now.

We had been losing *badly* when they invaded our family home on Gramercy Park. Our saving grace had been when Stanis discovered he had been killed and transformed by his father, Kejetan, centuries ago. Only by agreeing to go with the mad stone lord was he able to save the rest of us, leaving me with a parting message that we should prepare ourselves.

"It's okay," I said, giving her my best Bambi eyes. "I'm a big girl now. I can handle it." I turned to look at him. "No, Marsh, I haven't seen Stanis. The last you saw of him is the last time we *all* saw him. He did it to buy us time, and he has, all right?"

Marshall closed his notebook and crossed over to us. "So . . . where is he, then?"

I shrugged. "I don't know," I said, feeling the hollowness I had been trying to avoid within myself—the hollowness I had tried to fill with studying all I could in my great-great-grandfather's library on the subject of the Spellmasons. Not that I had come away with any such mastery of the subject. "Stanis told us to prepare. So that's what I'm doing."

The blaze of approaching sirens grew louder with each passing second, and Marshall snapped his book shut. "We need to go," he said. "Now."

"We've done pretty good of steering clear of the law so far," Rory said.

"Getting found out isn't going to help us," I said. "Marshall's right. We need to go. We need to prepare, more than just for evading the police."

I turned and headed back up the dead-end alley, an uneasy tension falling among the three of us. If I was being honest with myself, it had been there for months, really.

Prepare, Stanis had said. The implied threat behind Stanis's single word, the idea of a coming war for those arcane secrets between Kejetan Ruthenia—Kejetan *the Accursed* and us . . . It seemed a little less likely every day, given the way they had all but disappeared after getting Stanis back from us. The fact that my older brother, Devon, had given up his humanity all for the promise of eternal life only added to that bitter-to-swallow pill.

Add to that month after month of frustration with slowly learning the arcane familial legacy of Spellmasonry, and the fire had died down a little, but the questions that had haunted me for months were still there.

Where was Stanis? Was he alive? Dead? And why hadn't we heard from him, either in friendship or on behalf of Kejetan?

I couldn't help but hold him responsible for the awkwardness among me and my friends at that moment, but what I really hated him for just then was leaving me.

Two

𝄞 ☾

Stanis

There were times over the centuries when I missed the flesh of my once-human form, and as a metal spike drove through the tip of one of my wings, I experienced such a moment. Human flesh would have yielded with little resistance, but the arcane stonework of my wings was made from a higher quality of material.

Yes, there would have been pain, but none like that of my wings being torn through.

Still, feeling something was perhaps better than the nothing of the last few months, a time shrouded by total darkness—that of the mind and of the body with only a small circle of light shining down on me from somewhere above.

The weight of my heavy stone frame slammed down onto the steel of the ship's hull, ringing out with a dull echoing *thud*. I lay there, unwilling—*unable*—to move, my only movement that of my claws digging into the cool metal beneath me. The hum of the ship's mechanisms ran through my prone body, a different rhythm from that of the sway of waves against the freighter as it sailed on.

"Will the damage be permanent?" a deep and empty voice asked, that of my father.

I tilted my head to one side, seeking him out. Kejetan Ruthenia's inhuman form was barely perceptible in the darkness of the cargo hold, a distant, malformed shadow barely visible beyond the small circle of light that surrounded me.

He was not the human I had known centuries ago, no. This monstrosity bore more of a resemblance to a jagged pile of rocks, its crags and lumps held together in a mockery of the human form. For every carved bit of grotesque beauty that had gone into my maker's work, Kejetan's own arcane attempts had created an equally opposite abomination.

"Will the damage be permanent?" Kejetan asked again, his voice growling with impatience this time, waiting for an answer . . . but not from me.

"Nothing I can't fix," another voice replied from the darkness off to my right. The one who had driven the spike through my right wing, the one just outside my line of sight. I did not think I knew the voice, fairly certain I had not heard it before. By the tone and the fleeting glimpse I had of the figure off in the shadows, I knew him to be human, but that was all I had gathered. "You wanted answers . . . This should speed up the process considerably."

"Are you certain?" Kejetan asked.

"Honestly?" A short laugh barked out of the stranger. "I'm not sure. I've never done this to one of his kind. I'm not even sure if there *is* another of his kind."

"*We* are of his kind," my father snapped.

The stranger laughed again. "Have you looked in a mirror lately?" he asked. "No offense, but I wouldn't exactly call you cut from the same cloth . . . I mean, stone."

"You need not remind me," my father said, the tone of his voice becoming more measured, darker. "Of this I am well aware." His shadowy form turned away, looking across the dark cargo hold. "Devon!"

Another of the stone men walked over and stepped into my circle of light. This creature I recognized, its having only months ago still been human. This abomination in particular had once been the human Devon Belarus.

Kejetan joined him in front of me, the two stone men staring down at my prone form. "My son Stanis has claimed for months that the knowledge I seek has been stored—*built*—into him. Yet for months, we have not been able to extract it from him. You were once of the family who made him. Is what Stanis says true? Does he possess the secrets of the Spellmasons?"

Devon shifted from one jagged stone leg to the other as if uncomfortable with the question. If anyone here had a claim to discomfort, it was surely me, which made a grim laughter rise to my lips before I shut it down.

"You're asking the wrong Belarus for that," Devon said. "You want my sister, Alexandra."

At the mention of her name, a surge ran through my body, and I pushed myself up to the full extension of my arms until I could look first at him, then my father at the edge of the circle of light. "No!" I shouted, rising to my knees. "You promised to stay away from the Belarus family, and I told you I would give you the secrets that I hold. That was our pact, Father."

Kejetan stepped toward me. The rough stone of his hand grabbed at my face, jerking my head back until I was looking into the dark hollows where his eyes should be.

"Someone here has *not* lived up to his part of his bargain," he said. "So perhaps it is time we revisit your dear Alexandra."

Rage filled me at the very thought of it, but, weakened as I was, I could do nothing but stare back at him. "You *know* what will happen if you do," I said. "The information you seek has been locked away inside me, and if you break our pact, you will lose all of it. The rules set upon me by my maker will once fill me, forcing me to fight you, unrelenting, until I am torn apart. You will have lost both your son and the secrets of the Spellmasons."

I kept my eyes fixed on him, not daring to break contact or even hint that I was not exactly telling him the truth. It was, if I recalled Alexandra's word for it correctly, *bluffing*.

Kejetan stared at me a moment longer before letting go of my face. "Then we are at an impasse," my father said. He turned to the stranger. "Can nothing be done about this?"

The stranger, twirling a second spike just barely on the edge of my sight, stopped and sighed. "Possibly," he said, "but it will take time . . . and money. This one will cost a good chunk. You sure you can afford it?"

Kejetan stepped toward the figure, towering over him. "I did not cross oceans to bandy around about money or riches," he said with a bit of menace to it. "Just see to it."

"I'll need to do some research first," the stranger said.

My father moved away from him, taking a position directly in front of me again. "Don't you think you should finish stringing my *gargoyle* son up first?" Kejetan asked.

The word came off his jagged lips in a mix of disgust but also resentment. He wanted my form. He would *kill* for this form.

The stranger moved around behind me and pulled my left wing away from my body, stretching the stoneflesh of it out to its full extension. He raised the spike high overhead. "I said I need to research first," he repeated, but raised the spike high overhead anyway. "But still, I suppose it can't hurt to start breaking down this golem's will . . ."

As the spike pierced my other wing, the pain was far worse this time. All sensation had returned to me tenfold since Alexandra had restored my soul, and pain was no exception.

Was this what humans felt all the time? Was this what I had felt centuries ago when my father had accidentally taken my human life away from me? So white-hot in my thoughts was the pain this time that all other thoughts fell from my mind, and I once more collapsed to the floor.

"Not so fast, big fellah," the stranger whispered from behind, and he bent over me, affixing chains to both spikes. "You're not getting a reprieve just yet." The shadowy figure walked away toward the left of the cargo hold, the sound of chains pulling through fixtures high above us filling the hold. The slack on the lines attached to me pulled tight, my wings spreading out farther apart from each other with every passing second. When they could stretch no more, my body rose off the floor until I hung with the tips of my clawed feet just barely touching the steel below me.

The stranger stopped, but the resulting pain coursing through my stretched wings and body did not.

My father moved forward to me. "Will you reveal the secrets of the Spellmasons now?"

Dazed, I found it impossible to respond, my head hanging slack between my shoulder blades. I hung there for how long I knew not before Kejetan finally spoke again.

"Very well," he said, turning away from me to the other stone man. "What say you, Devon?"

"Sometimes you've got to blow up a safe to get to what's inside," he said.

Kejetan looked back at me, then to the human stranger off in the shadows. *"Break his will."*

"It's your dime," the stranger said, and there followed the sounds of his working with a tray of bottles, beakers, and vials I knew lay off on a table against the wall of the cargo hold.

"Now get ready, freak show," he said. "This is going to hurt me as . . . Well, actually this shouldn't hurt me one bit. You *will* be bent into servitude."

I could not imagine anything feeling worse than the pain I was feeling across my shoulders and extended wings, but as a shaft of bright, hot light appeared in front of me, I was proven wrong. Somewhere in front of me, a small, focused beam shot into my shoulder, the low hum of electricity thrumming behind it.

"Ultraviolet," I heard the man say although I knew not what the word meant until a second later.

Daylight.

The change in my body hit me, but only in the one spot and the area immediately surrounding it as the malleable surface of my stoneflesh turned to solid stone. My body seized up, the grinding of rock rising from the spot, and I could not help but let out a roar.

Can I endure? Can I take this pain, unbearable though it is?

Yes, if it means keeping the Belarus family safe, if it keeps Alexandra *safe.* Like the initial spike, there was a perverse pleasure in the pain. After centuries of being deprived of any sort of emotion or sensation, part of me welcomed feeling *something.* And if I was being honest with myself, *something* felt better than the nothingness I had experienced after ensuring Alexandra's safety by forcing her to break her bond with me.

I could only hope she had been using these months wisely. My father could not be held by my *bluff* or mutual impasse forever.

And, there was also the fear that, quite possibly, I would eventually break.

Three

C

Alexandra

It was amazing how a stupid pile of bricks could really bring a woman down.

Rory and Marshall had gone back to the apartment they shared down in the Village, but thoughts of tonight's failed experiment and Stanis filled my mind so completely that I was restless. Giving up on the idea of sleep, I instead stopped by the old Belarus Building to grab up Bricksley, stuffing him into my Coach backpack before heading out to Brooklyn. Sadly, it wasn't to party.

I let Bricksley loose on the docks along the Hudson, setting his tottering brick body off on wire legs and clay feet to the task of patrolling for any sign of Kejetan's freighter docked there. I knew it was in vain, but at least it felt like I was getting *something* accomplished, even if it was simply eliminating locations where it might return.

As the sun came up and the docks rose to a bustle of activity, I knew that Bricksley would freeze up the same way Stanis would in daylight, and I set off in search of him. Minutes later, I reclaimed the frozen, inert form of Bricksley from a pool of sunlight by the slip where the floating home

of Kejetan Ruthenia had once docked. I stood there longer
than usual as the world around me moved on, a small part
of me expecting the ancient cargo ship to just sail in after
its six-month absence, but when that little pipe dream didn't
come to pass, I gave up and headed back into the city.

A taxi dropped me off on the west side of Gramercy Park
in front of the half block where my family's building stood.
I stared up at my by-then-vacant home, admiring the one
bit of Gothic-inspired architecture on the whole park. I
hadn't felt too bad about self-condemning the place—both
for the safety of my parents as well as getting some more
alone time with the arcane library of my great-great-
grandfather. If I was lucky, I could manage several hours of
research work up in the art studio before the construction
crews arrived. Continued reinforcing of the underlying
structure of the catacombs was still going on—thanks to
the damage Kejetan, his men, and Devon had done—but
the art studio at the top should be fine for just little ol' me.

Could I have fixed much of the stonework myself? I wondered as I paid the taxi driver. Possibly, but I didn't want to
hang the entire structural integrity of our wholly unique
multigenerational building on my still-fledgling arcane
skills. No, I told myself, it was best to leave it to professional
builders and engineers, and thanks to years in the real-estate
business, my family knew the best of those around.

The cab pulled away as a I caught a sudden, swooping
figure out of the corner of my eye. I jumped back on the
thankfully quiet sidewalk just as one of those magic-craving
creatures from the night before dove through the space I had
just occupied. *Stone biters*, Marshall had called them.
Despite the faded and broken protections on the building,
it was comforting to know there was still enough magic
within it to draw the random passing monster, no matter
how tiny and annoying.

They truly were more nuisance than anything. It swooped
through the air around me, correcting its course and heading
straight for me. Its tiny claws and sharp teeth looked like

they could totally do some damage, so I treated it the way I had been treating a lot of things over the past few months— I was going to kill it.

Rory would be proud of my self-preservation instinct.

I didn't bother going for my backpack. I didn't need any of my notes or my great-great-grandfather's spell book to deal with this. I whispered out one of the most basic of phrases I had learned, reaching my will out into Gramercy Park. The sense of stone was everywhere within it, and I latched onto something that would be easy to replace—one of the cobblestones from the winding path within.

There was no resistance as I pulled it to me in a high arc over the street itself, bringing it straight down toward the creature. The little bastard was fast and dodged my first attempt at him, his tiny wings swirling him up and around the cobblestone. Since the cobblestone was close, and I had a good visual lock on it, the stone itself became easier to handle, bending more easily to my will. A few more practice swipes at the creature, and I had a good idea of its maneuverability. With each pass, I drove it closer and closer to the ground, giving it less room to shift its course, but by the time it realized it was running out of room, it was too late. I pressed pure hate and strength into the stone, feeding the darkest of my will into it, and the cobblestone slammed down on the creature, catching it dead center. The wings stuck out from under the stone, fluttering against the pavement for a moment before all life drained out of the creature, and they stopped.

Once I was sure the thing was dead, I checked the still-quiet street and lifted the cobblestone, arcing it back into the park, where I expertly fit it back into its spot along the path.

I looked down at the flattened, broken creature, almost feeling sorry for it despite the fact that it had been moments away from clawing my face off. Still, the sight of its twisted little body sent a shudder down my spine.

I couldn't just leave the thing there. It was daylight, and it had been risky enough using my powers as it was. I could hear the sound of people scattered elsewhere around

Gramercy, and it was just a matter of time before any one of them came this way. Using the toe of my boot, I nudged the broken body into the gutter of the street and reached for my backpack. I dug down deep into it, past my notebooks to the bottom, where my growing collection of tiny metal vials lay bunched together. Cool to the touch, I pulled a fistful of them free to examine my handwritten labels before finally selecting one.

Kimiya—one of the more all-purpose concoctions from my great-great-grandfather's mixes. Part of an ever-dwindling collection thanks to all the experiments I had been running.

Pouring it over the lifeless creature, I spoke my words of power, transforming the stonelike skin of the tiny monster. It cracked and flaked into a pile of pebbles as I pressed my will over it until the figure could no longer hold its form. When there was nothing more than a pile of dusty rock shards left, I scattered it with my foot, most of the remains going into the nearby sewer grate. Other than a small dark stain on the side-walk, it was like the creature had never been there.

Turning, I headed into our building's foyer, startling as the doors before me flew open. No one was supposed to be in there yet today. I jumped back, calling out to the stone around me, readying my will to defend myself . . . until I saw my foe, that is.

"Alexandra!" Desmond Locke exclaimed, raising his bushy black eyebrows in surprise. With thinning gray hair pulled back into a ponytail and a goatee, my father's spiritual adviser reminded me of Sean Connery from that movie Marshall had insisted we watch where all these immortals cut each other's heads off. Hadn't really been my thing, but Mr. Locke looked like a business-suited version of the actor nonetheless. Seeing him caused me to stand down from high alert despite the fact that he still creeped me out. I fought the niggling urge to drop the keystone of the vaulted arch of the foyer onto him, anyway.

Going with my better judgment, I let go of my will over the stone and quickly slipped the empty vial I was still holding in my hand into the pocket of my coat. Locke's eyes darted down, but I was pretty sure I had been fast enough.

"Mr. Locke," I said. "Nice to see you, but umm . . . what are you doing here? Everyone's been moved downtown to the new place on Saint Mark's while we're . . . renovating."

"Yes, yes, of course," he said, looking a bit out of sorts. "I must say, I find it more than passing strange that you have to vacate the entire premises simply for the sake of renovation."

Renovation had sounded a lot better than trying to explain to one of the "normals" that stone-men golems and a gargoyle had been the cause of all the damage.

"Just dealing with some structural things on the lower floors," I said. "You know old buildings. My great-great-grandfather was a fantastic architect and stonemason, but nothing lasts forever, right?"

"How right you are," he said, then crossed himself. "Except, of course, the Eternal."

"Right," I said after an all-too-long pause.

I didn't know what I believed in, more so after being exposed to the world of Spellmasonry, but I never liked broaching into theology with the man who had been guiding my father along what I considered a pretty weak divine path all these years. His oddness always left me feeling uneasy.

"Well . . ." I said. "I really should get inside. Just need to grab a couple of things."

I tried to step around Mr. Locke, but he stayed where he was, eyes lowered and raising a hand as if to grab my shoulder but stopping inches away from it.

"May I speak with you a moment about something personal?" he asked, keeping his hand hovering there.

I tried to think fast, but having just dispatched that creature and being stuck in this small space with him had me unnerved, and I came up short on excuses.

"Sure . . ." I said, shouldering my bag. "What's up?"

"Long have I cared for your father's spiritual well-being, and I would like to think that it extends to the rest of the Belarus kin as well. For instance, I would like to think your brother's soul was prepared for the afterlife at the time of his . . . accident."

I fought back a pained laugh, recalling the events earlier this year. Devon had been far from spiritual, and his death had been no accident. Hell, it hadn't even been his death. Kejetan's search for the Belarus family and the arcane secrets of our great-great-grandfather led the mad lord first to Devon. Devon—ever the pitchman and promising the secrets he eventually couldn't deliver—bargained his human life for that of an eternal stone one. The building collapse on Saint Mark's had merely proven the cover for ending his human life.

Still, I didn't think it was the time to broach that conversational hurdle.

"No offense to you and your beliefs, Mr. Locke, but I don't really think that was Devon's bag . . . or really my bag, either."

He gave a pressed-lip smile indicating the kind of patience one might have when dealing with a child. "Fair enough," he said. "Fair enough. That is perhaps a discussion for another day . . ."

Not if I can help it, I thought, literally biting my tongue to the point it hurt.

"But I wonder if I could discuss your father with you for a moment," he continued.

"Okay," I said, curiosity getting the better of me.

He paused, taking his time as if carefully trying to choose his words. "Have you noticed anything strange in his behavior lately?"

"You're going to have to be more specific," I said. "My dad is strange in a *lot* of ways."

"Spoken like a true daughter," he said with that smile again.

I once more resisted the urge to crush him with the keystone above us. "Have *you* noticed something strange?" I asked him back.

"I have simply noticed a change in our weekly discussions."

"What sort of change?"

"You know of his belief in angels, yes?"

I nodded, tensing a little. Everyone who had ever met my father knew about his belief in angels. Before he learned of Stanis only a few months back, he had met him as his "angel" decades ago when being pulled from the freezing water of the reservoir in Central Park. It had been the singular event that had turned him into a Holy Roller, and even after having met Stanis, knowing him for the *grotesque* he was, it somehow only further affirmed his belief in angels. The logic was rather circular, but there was no talking him out of it.

"As of late," Desmond Locke continued, "he seems more and more insistent on their existence."

"Don't you believe in angels?" I asked. "I mean, isn't that in your job description? Isn't it your thing?"

"Yes and no," he said. "Did you know that in Fatima, Portugal, up to one hundred thousand people witnessed unusual solar activity that took the shapes of Jesus, Mary, and several saints? Thirteen years later, the Roman Catholic Church accepted it as a genuine miracle from those reports. Then you have the people who claim to see statues of Jesus on the Cross weeping or see angels visit them in times of need. Do I believe those people? Well, I *do* believe their faith colors their world and that the human mind is a wonderful and powerful tool, but do I believe your father has empirical proof of angels, as he's been claiming lately? No, I am surprised to say, I do not. I do not believe He means for people to see actual proof of His divinity. Proof, after all, takes away faith, if you ask my opinion of it."

"What *has* my father said?" I asked, my stomach tightening. If the Church found out about our family legacy, I could only imagine some papal SWAT team taking over our home.

Mr. Locke shrugged, but his eyes stayed locked on me. "He hasn't said anything exact. He just seems more and more convinced of their physical manifestation. That isn't the focus of his belief. Faith does not require hard evidence; faith is believing for the sake of belief."

I was ready to start arguing what a load of crap that was,

that belief in anything should come from proof, but what good would that do? Politics, religion, and the series finale of *Lost* were just a few of the things it did no good talking about with someone who opposed the views you had.

The mischievous part of me wanted to take my great-great-grandfather's master tome out of my backpack and transform it from its stone form just to give Mr. Locke something that would shake his very foundation, but I thought better of it.

Again, what would the Church do with that kind of information? I imagined some kind of hotline phone in Mr. Locke's home that dialed straight to the Vatican. The Pope would answer it, and suddenly I'd be dragged in and kept on display in some vast underground papal prison. Or maybe burned as a witch, which I guess, technically, I was.

I pulled out my phone and checked the time. "I really should get moving," I said, stepping past him. "But I'll keep an eye on my father. In fact, I'll even keep two eyes on him."

He smiled, folding his hands together. "Very cute," he said. "I would greatly appreciate that. Thank you."

"No problem," I said, and keyed into the first-floor business-office lobby of our building. I headed for the elevators up to our empty living quarters, which included my great-great-grandfather's library and art studio at the very top.

"And Alexandra," Mr. Locke said from behind me, my name echoing in the empty hallway. I turned to see him holding the door open with one hand. "We really should have that talk one of these days."

I paused for a moment, then gave him a thumbs-up before turning and heading toward the elevators once more. The gesture was all I allowed myself—I was afraid of whatever words I might have let loose on the creep otherwise.

Four

Alexandra

I felt bad about how I had left things the other night with Rory and Marshall, so when I got back downtown, I texted them about swinging by the new place for dinner. When the buzzer rang, I ran down several flights of stairs to greet them at the door instead of just buzzing them in.

"Welcome to Belarus Building South!" I said, throwing my arms around the both of them. Rory had been here plenty of times already, but Marshall had been so busy lately, he hadn't had time. Rory fell instantly into the hug, but Marshall hesitated before joining it. After a moment he stepped back, looking up and down Saint Mark's Place.

"This looks a *lot* different than it did the last time I was here," he said.

"Yes," Rory said to him. "Much less collapsed building-y."

"At least it's probably not haunted," he said.

I cocked my head at him, screwing up my face. "That's an odd sort of compliment," I said.

"I mean, this is where your brother died," he said, emphasizing the last word with air quotes. "But since technically he's a villainous rock man instead, his spirit wouldn't be haunting the space. So see? Probably not haunted!"

Rory pushed him past me into the building. "In you go," she said, forcing him up the stairs. "Before we get un-invited."

"Is it livable now?" he asked, calling back down the stairs.

"It better be," I said, following them up. "I just moved my parents in the other day. Actually, just on the lower floors for now. I'm still deciding how to set up the top. I'd kind of like an art studio and library of my own."

"How are Doug and Julie handling the new digs?" Rory asked.

"They're adjusting," I said, pointing ahead to turn left at the next landing up, "but if I don't get them back into the Belarus Building soon, I might lose my mind. I've even set up their real-estate company on the first two floors here—high-speed Internet, the latest technology for their meetings and dealings, but they're used to doing things the way they do them on Gramercy. They miss their rut. In the meantime, I just need to not kill them."

"No one wants to have their parents as roommates," Marshall said, entering the kitchen, slowing as he took in the clean, modern style I had gone for. "And this is coming from a guy who spent maybe one or three too many years set up at home. But that was mostly so I didn't have to move my gaming stuff out of the basement."

Rory hopped on a stool behind the counter bar and simply stared at him.

"What?" he asked.

"Do you *not* even hear what you are saying sometimes?" she asked back. "On behalf of all women everywhere, I think my reproductive organs literally just crawled farther up inside me."

Marshall was on the verge of responding, but startled as he looked down at floor level.

"Bricksley!" he said with a nervous laugh. "You scared the crap out of me."

My tiny brick golem looked up at Marshall, his face ever the happy, painted-on smile and wide-eyed expression.

"Sorry," I said, heading to the ingredients I had laid out on the counter earlier. "I'm a sloppy cook and set him about Roomba-ing."

Rory joined me the way she used to when we took over the kitchen on Gramercy from my mother. As usual, it quickly turned into me fighting her on overspicing *everything*.

"It's my Latina heritage!" she protested, slamming her spoon-clenching fist against her chest.

"I like spice," I said, "but don't blame your heritage on the atrocity you're committing in my kitchen. You just have a bad palate and overdo it."

She started to argue, but she knew I was right, and gave in to the evening and just had fun with it.

After stowing Bricksley away, I invited my parents up from downstairs to join us for dinner, where we avoided talking about both the arcane and my run-in with my father's spiritual counselor. The former was a subject they were aware of but chose to avoid, and the latter simply gave me the wiggins that I simply didn't want to mention his name.

Marshall cleaned, claiming it was the least he could do although the least-that-could-be-done award went to my father, who headed back downstairs to attend to more of his business right after the meal. But Marshall's contribution was welcome.

The whole affair warmed me, reminding me of a simpler time—one before men of stone, mad cultists, and Rory's mastering medieval French weapons.

After my mother left, the three of us sat around the partially furnished living room enjoying each other's company, and, for a second, I felt normal, but eventually all spells must be broken, and all good things must come to an end.

"I've another surprise," I said. "I thought we might go over our notes from the last couple of outings. If I'm ever going to master Spellmasonry, I need to be able to not only control stone, I need to be able to do all the things that Alexander Belarus did. I still can't seem to control any stone creature larger than Bricksley, and I'm light-years away from figuring out how to build something like Stanis. There's something that I'm missing in the process. We just need to figure out what that is. And it wouldn't hurt to stumble across how to make a lot of Alexander's concoctions that we've been using up. The Kimiya is starting to look like a very finite supply these days. We need to step up our experimentation."

Rory sighed, sitting up in her chair. "You want to head up to Gramercy now?"

I shook my head.

"That's the surprise," I said. "I thought we might do it here."

"But what about the experiments and equipment?" Marshall asked. "What about your supplies?"

"We have a lot of the alchemical mixes on the premises," I said, "and I've been moving some of the other supplies down here. I thought it might be nice to have a change of venue."

Rory sat forward. "You mean . . . ?"

I nodded. "My great-great-grandfather's guild hall," I said. "I know how hard you've both been working on this with me. I appreciate it, but the idea of dragging the two of you back to the haunting emptiness of Gramercy again just seemed cruel. I thought a change of venue might help. It took a lot of doing. Clearing away the debris of the building collapse was fairly easy, but trying to build this place on top of Alexander's secret laboratory? I filed and refiled plans until I was blue in the face, changed construction companies at least half a dozen times. By the time it was done, I don't think anyone working on Belarus South knows what truly lies beneath this building."

"I am so jealous," Marshall said. "Think of the game setup I could do down there with all that creepy, dungeony, carved stone."

I smiled at Marshall. "If we can figure out how to create something like Stanis, you can throw your weekly games down here." A twinkle of approval lit up in his eyes, and I turned my head back to address both my friends. "So . . . we know that I can't sustain bringing anything larger than

Bricksley to life, but we know it's possible. How do we know it's possible? Stanis, wherever he is, is living proof that an autonomous creature of human proportions can be brought to life. I don't know how to unlock that level of power. My grandfather was clever about those arcane secrets."

I pulled my backpack closer to me from where it lay on the floor and reached for the solid stone book within it, finding Bricksley nestled in there. I took the book from under him, breathed out the words of power that transformed it to leather and paper, then pulled my own notebook out. "We've got his work and my own lame-ish start at a spell book of my own." I held up my own notebook. "We need to make this as powerful as his."

"There are too many missing pieces," Marshall said.

"That's why we compare notes, then," I said. "Do you think Einstein gave up just because he had too many questions?"

"This isn't science," argued Rory.

"Maybe it's more of a science than we think," I offered.

"Maybe it's more of a science than we *can* think," Marshall said.

I looked to see if he was mocking me, but he was serious.

"This hurts my brain," Rory said. "Can we go back to dinner conversation?"

"No," Marshall said. A second ago I wouldn't have thought him capable of it, but he looked riled up. "Lexi's right. We're all just frustrated, but that's no excuse. We need to continue to be analytical, keep experimenting, keep refining."

"Exactly," I said, standing. I gathered up my books and a few of the others I had been reading through. "Let me show you the cool stuff I've rigged up, then."

Rory stood, and we were halfway to the stairs when Marshall stopped.

"Go on without me," he said. "I'll be down to the Bat Cave in a couple minutes."

"Where's he going?" I asked, as Rory and I started down the steps.

"Excitement pee," she said, taking some of my books from me to carry. "He gets this way when he talks about Comic Con, too."

Five

Alexandra

Rory and I headed down to the finished basement of our new building, not wanting to wait around for Marshall while he hit the little boys' room. The sooner we got to work sorting through our comparative notes from the brick-man incident, the sooner I might get to sleep. Pillowy thoughts of slumber filled my head as we walked along the half-finished basement hall, following the series of bookcases off to my left.

"I'm glad you took Marshall's suggestion months ago when he tried to talk you into the library motif," Rory said.

I nodded, counting off the bookcases as I went. " 'Very Wayne Manor,' he had said. Apparently, Batman liked secret doors, too."

"I still don't get why you call it Alexander's guild hall, though," Rory said. "I mean, he was a guild of one."

"My guess is that Alexander built it in the hopes of using it for a higher purpose," I said. "For finding other Spellmasons, for educating others to his way, but I think having a madman hunting down that power made him think the better of it. Some things, it would seem, were better kept secret. Which, conversely, is why we're so busy playing arcane Nancy Drews."

We arrived at the bookcase that concealed the one thing that had survived the original building's collapse—my great-great-grandfather's old alchemical workshop.

I reached behind a copy of *The Hunchback of Notre Dame* on the top shelf to activate the pressure plate against the back wall, but, to my surprise, the bookcase was already clicked free from its swivel locking mechanism.

"This door shouldn't be open," I said. "That's the point of it being *secret*."

Rory looked at the unfinished section of the basement along the other wall. "Maybe one of the workers triggered it by accident?"

I shook my head. "I've changed enough workers in and out on this project. I switched them out every few weeks. No single one could have known enough about any one aspect of the project to open this door."

"Let's check it out," Rory said, dropping her dance bag on the floor. "Cautiously, of course."

I pressed against the bookcase, sliding it over to reveal the black stone door behind it, finding it ajar as well. I put my hand on it and willed the heavy stone to move as I breathed out the old country's words of power. It yielded, and the two of us entered the room beyond, the light spilling in behind us, allowing us to make our way easier as we went.

Carved-stone markings bearing the winged Belarus sigil adorned the walls of the cavernous circular space, rising up to a dome high above, but it was the lower part that sported tables, chairs, and counters built into the walls that we had to step through carefully. I checked the glass-covered cabinet built into the far side of the room, inventorying the array of my great-great-grandfather's alchemical mixes within it.

As Rory and I stepped to the center of the room, she stopped and pointed at the cobblestone floor beneath her. "You fixed it," she said. "That giant ball you summoned, protecting yourself from Alexander's defenses when we first found this place."

"Yeah," I said, recalling how I had needed Stanis's help to extract me from it. "I've been training myself to feel

Alexander's signature in his stonework. It helps that his magic in here had gone untouched for so long. It's still strong here, which made it easier to wrap my will around it."

"Aww," Rory said, all baby-voiced, "somebody's been giving magical hugs, wrapping their will around things again."

I pressed my sense out into the rest of the room, holding a finger up to my lips. "Somebody's definitely been in here," I whispered. "I can feel it."

I let my connection to the whole space take control, letting it run through me. Something felt . . . off. I moved around the room, reaching out with my will, seeking out whatever felt different, which led me toward the large glass case of alchemical mixes.

"What is it?" Rory said, joining me. "Has someone been stealing from the liquor cabinet?"

"Has," I said, focusing in on a dead spot on the wall just to the other side of Rory, standing by the glass cabinet. "And *is*."

Rory stepped in front of me to look at the spot, then turned back around to me. "Meaning what exactly?"

"Shh!" I said. "The walls have ears." I pressed my will toward the stone there, oddly finding no connection with the spot. I focused in, staring hard to find what my will could not. "Ears . . . *and* eyes."

"What?" Rory asked, starting to spin back around to it, but I was already reaching out to pull her away from the spot.

The stone did indeed have eyes then, and they went wide at my mention of them. A section of the wall impossibly peeled itself away from the rest, and although the stones kept their shape, the movements and outline of the figure rushing for the door were distinctly human.

I reached out to the stone creature with my will but found no connection to it. I pressed my power past the figure, grabbing at one of the stone tables along the wall, sliding it across the floor to block the creature's exit path. Unprepared, the figure slammed into the moving table, falling forward, then *over* it, landing on its back on the floor. Rory and I closed on it as the creature—burdened by its own weight—struggled like a turtle on its back to right itself.

"Shit," a male voice called out from it, and the stone of its skin began to transform. The rock seemed to melt away, fading to expose a twentysomething man with a mess of dirty blond hair and a knee-length brown coat. Now free of his stone form, the man righted himself, scurrying to his feet. He eyed the two of us with darting suspicion, then reached in his jacket and pulled a glass vial free from it, tossing it at our feet.

It shattered, and Rory danced out of its way, but I wasn't quite quick enough. The stone beneath my feet softened like clay, and I sunk into it, my boots slowly disappearing out of sight. Try as I might to pull them out, my feet would not come free.

Rory stood dumbstruck for a moment before shaking herself out of it and turning to our foe, her eyes dark. "Don't worry," she said to me out of the corner of her mouth. "I got this."

This drew a chuckle out of the stranger. "Do you, now?"

In response, Rory rushed him, jumping up onto the stone table that separated them and kicking him square in the chest. He fell back, tumbled over, and landed on his hands and knees, letting out a pained laugh.

"I guess you do at that," he said, struggling to stand up. "Fast, aren't ya?"

"The fastest," Rory said, jumping down from the table, keeping after him.

"We shall see about that," the man said, producing another vial, like a magician drawing his wand. He flicked the top off this one, causing Rory to instinctually jump back from him, but instead of throwing it at either of us, he chugged the dark yellow liquid within it. The man doubled over in pain, giving Rory an opportunity to close with him, but when she did, he was standing up straight again, waiting for her.

Rory grabbed for him, but the man—now moving with

more than human speed—evaded her, circling around behind her.

"Look out!" I called to her, but by the time Rory spun to face him, the man had raised a closed fist to swing at her. I waited for his flash of a blow to strike her, but it never came.

He swung, but the man stopped his fist mere inches from her face. "Nighty-night," he said. He opened the hand, palm facing up, and blew across it. A fine, white powder rose off it, engulfing Rory's entire head.

She sneezed from within the cloud, blinking with heavier and heavier lids until they closed, and she slumped to the floor of the guild hall, her head cracking against the stone.

"Rory!" I cried out, but there was no response.

The stranger blurred past me, heading back to the glass case.

"What did you do to her?" I asked him, afraid.

The man ignored me and helped himself to a variety of my great-great-grandfather's vials and tubes.

"What did you do to her?" I shouted this time as I lunged for him, but with my feet stuck as they were, all I managed to do was send a sharp pain through my right ankle.

"Don't worry," he said with the hint of a cocky smile on his lips. "She's not dead. Just sleeping."

That was a relief, but it didn't quell my desire to smack the smile off of his smug face. Realizing I was wasting my anger, I tried my power at the stone surrounding my feet again, but it remained unresponsive. I turned my frustration to something I could manipulate—the stone table I had slid across the room. Using my mind to pull it apart brick by brick, I fired them one after another at the man, but his speed helped him avoid my barrage as he continued pillaging the cabinet.

He turned to face me, waggling a fistful of tubes in my face.

"Thanks for the supplies," he said, and had the audacity to wink at me before turning and speeding out of the guild hall.

Outraged and trapped as I was, I jumped straight up,

hoping to at least come out of my sinking shoes, but only managed to send sharp pains through *both* my ankles this time, which also unbalanced me. I went down hard on my ass, and, despite what I perceived as a lot of padding to it, I felt the stone slam hard up against my bones, which took all the fire out of me.

Anger gave way to humiliation as I lay there, hurt, but all of that went away as my mind cleared and my thoughts turned to Rory, lying not more than ten feet from me, still unconscious. I needed to check on her . . . and where the hell was Marshall? With the stranger gone and my wits somewhat calmed, I reached out with my hands to the stone encasing my feet.

The stuff was impossible to grab ahold of, both solid and malleable at the same time, almost like trying to grab handfuls of quicksand. Using my will, I worked it around in my head, which also tried my patience in the process, and I once more felt my control over the stone returning as the effects of whatever the stranger had done to it faded. The rock gave way to my spell and thoughts, and I pulled my feet free, my boots covered in a thick black powder of stone.

I ran over to Rory, careful not to twist my ankle on any of the broken bricks of the floor as I went to her.

Movement in the doorway caught my attention.

"Don't start the party without me," Marshall sang out in a singsong voice. "Surprise!" He stepped into the room smiling, holding a large tray stuffed with an array of food. When he saw me kneeling beside Rory, the smile vanished from his face.

"Marshall!" I shouted at him. "What the hell took you so long?"

"I told you I had to pee," he said in a quiet voice, looking worried. "Then I thought I'd surprise you with some snacks while we went over our notes and stuff. So I raided your fridge. I washed my hands first . . ." His words trailed off for a moment as his mind worked to process what he was seeing, his eyes fixating on Rory's fallen form. "Is she okay? What happened?"

"Someone was down here," I said. "In here. Now help me."

Marshall dropped his tray, full of drinks and assorted snacks, on the main stone table at the center of the room and ran over to us. Falling to his knees. "Can we move her?" he asked.

"I'm not sure," I said. "I don't want to make anything worse."

The two of us quickly looked her over. There were no visible signs of damage, but that didn't mean jack.

Marshall moved closer to her, and I reached out a hand to push him back.

"I'm not going to touch her," he said, hurt. "I just want to try something."

I let go of him and nodded, waiting.

Marshall leaned forward, hovering over Rory's head, mere inches from her face. "Rory," he whispered. "I drank the last of the milk and used the last of the toilet paper . . ."

Our friend remained lying there, unmoving, and I was already reaching for my cell phone. I wasn't sure how I was going to explain to paramedics that my friend was under the influence of some kind of Sandman dust, but I could worry about that later.

Marshall grabbed my hand before I dialed, then leaned even closer to Rory's ear this time. "Aurora," he said, singing it out long and slow, like a nursery rhyme.

Rory's hand shot straight up, grabbing him by his neck meat, choking him. Surprised, I let out a small yelp and fell back from the two of them. Marshall tried to pull himself away, but Rory had him in a grip so tight he couldn't escape.

"*Don't*," she said, eyes still closed, "call me . . . Aurora."

Marshall's eyes turned to me, and he wrapped his hands around her arm. "Yeah," he croaked out. "She's fine."

When Marshall couldn't break her grip, he reached out to me and placed my hands around hers. Despite our joined effort, Rory's grip still held tight, but after a minute or two, we managed to pry her thumb away from the front of his throat, and Marshall managed to slip free, falling back on his ass.

He scrabbled to his feet as he cleared his throat and rubbed his neck, moving to the tray he'd brought in on the table at the center of the room. Rory, still out, lay there with her hand still up in the air as if still clutching Marshall.

"Awesome," he said, his voice raspy. He grabbed a bottle of seltzer off the table and took a deep swig, clearing his throat. "I think she's sleep strangling. Just what you want in a roommate." He walked back over to the two of us and stopped, just standing there looking down at me. "You've got my back, right?"

I nodded, but warily. "Sure. Why?"

"Just remember you said that," Marshall whispered, then upended the bottle of seltzer into Rory's face. It poured down on her, and her eyes shot open, her glasses doing little to protect them. Her mouth opened, too, and the carbonated water ran into it, causing her to choke and sputter.

Marshall was already stepping away from her, but Rory—prone though she was—launched in a defensive reactionary mode. Her legs whirled out toward him, catching Marshall behind his knees, knocking him back onto his ass. His head bounced off the stone floor once, and it was his turn to lie there, eyes open and groaning.

Rory sat up first, swallowing. Marshall was a bit slower, clutching the back of his head when he rose. "I think that's enough concussions for one day," he said, pulling his hand away and checking for blood. Luckily, it came away clean.

Rory hopped up onto her feet, staying squat. She wobbled forward, and I caught her before she could fall on her face.

"Easy, now," I said.

"Where is he?" she asked, looking around.

"Long gone," I said. "I mean, did you see how fast that guy was moving?"

Rory nodded and stepped away from the hold I had on her.

"Your intruder was superhuman?" Marshall asked from his place on the floor of the guild hall.

"Yeah," Rory said as she stared death at him. "And where were you, by the way? You might not have helped in a fight, but maybe I could have got the drop on him while he was beating on you."

Marshall pointed to the tray. "I was being a good friend," he snapped, looking back and forth between Rory and me. "I'm sorry, but I didn't expect you two to get attacked *in your own home*."

He had a point, and I did my best to let go of any anger I felt building up in me toward him.

"Sorry, Marsh," I said, offering him my hand, helping him up. "We're just a little on edge. There was a stranger in not only my home, but this space, which I consider sort of sacred."

"What did he look like?" Marshall asked.

"Stone," I said. "At first, anyway."

"Like Stanis?"

"Not quite," Rory chimed in. "When Lexi pulled me out of harm's way, the first good look I got of him, he was sort of . . . a chameleon."

I nodded. "Yeah. He was blended with the stone of the wall, but then he sort of . . . morphed."

"Blond hair, hipster-tousled, this long brown coat he kept pulling vials out of . . ." Rory trailed off, her eyes growing darker behind her glasses. "I really can't wait to hurt him."

"I need to ward this place," I said. "Ever since the building collapsed—when we thought Devon died—I suspected this new place might need it, but this clinches it."

"Can we at least do that later?" Marshall asked. "I brought snacks and my notes from the other night's experiment that we really should go over. I promise I'll help you ward the place later."

"Since when do you have magic powers?" Rory asked.

"I don't," Marshall said, holding up a single finger. "Yet. But I could learn."

"We'll see about that," I said, heading over to the tray on the stone table. I picked up one of those mini Pac-Man cheese wheels from its little net bag and peeled the wax off it. "But you're right. We should first do what we came down here to do. I also wouldn't mind plotting out some real defense around here."

As pissed as I was, I had to admit it was a little exciting to have met another person who—albeit under shifty circumstances—also had some prowess with alchemical transformation. Maybe after we beat him senseless for a bit, I might be able to talk shop with him. That is, if he dared show his face again.

It seemed likely. After all, as far as I knew, we were the only place in town he could "shop" for what he was coming here for in the first place.

The three of us settled in at the main stone table, arranging books from the old library as well as my notebooks and Marshall's *Monster Manual*, each of us working for a long while in silence as we snacked.

Eventually, Rory let out a sigh as she went through the pages of one of my great-great-grandfather's Moleskine notebooks.

"I miss having a gargoyle around," she said.

"Me too," I said, flipping through my notes to the ones I had made after the unstable brick-man incident the other night. If I judged my Spellmason prowess by that particularly calamitous experiment, I was a long way off from making any sort of animated stone army. And it was hard to imagine any of them replacing the singular soul-filled Stanis.

"Me three," added Marshall, and without another word, each of us set to our reading in the hopes of figuring just what the hell I was still doing wrong.

Six

Stanis

Living in constant pain as I simply hung from the two spikes driven through my wings had been difficult at first, but there had been the revelatory moment when the pain no longer mattered.

My body should have ached hanging from chains in the center of the cargo hold, left with just the tips of my clawed feet to support my weight, but all sensation had left my form by then. Even the shaft of light coming from the nearby machine—ultraviolet, they had called it—was barely noticeable, even though it continued to transform part of me into solid stone. When someone shut off the beam, the stone turned back to stoneflesh, the burning pain rousing me from my delirium.

A figure moved among the shadows beyond the light around me, unrecognizable until I heard the voice. The stranger had returned.

"How you holding up there, big fella?" the human asked.

"Holding up . . . ?" I replied, unsure of the expression. At best I guessed that it most likely was one of the "idioms" Alexandra and her friends had promised to teach me about long ago. "You are the one holding me up by the very spikes you personally drove through my wings."

"You'll be fine, golem," he said. "They can patch you up with a little quick-setting cement or something."

"I do not thing my father will be letting me down," I said. "I refuse to give him what he asks."

"I *know* this hurts you, creature," he said. "Even if you're just a construct. I've studied what little there is out there in the world about your kind."

"What could you possibly know of my kind?" I asked. "I *am* the only one of my kind."

"You'd be surprised," he said. "As far as what I *do* know . . ." The sound of the chain hanging off to my right rang out, and my right wing exploded with a fresh wave of pain as the spike pulled me farther up on one side only, leaving my left foot on the ground. I twisted and turned as I dangled there.

"I know you can be hurt," he continued. "They've paid me to hurt you. To get what they want. So why don't you save us both the time and trouble and give them what they ask for? They're going to get it anyway, thanks to me."

"You will not break me," I said, still swinging back and forth. "What makes you think you can?"

"I have a few tricks up my sleeve," he said, and stepped into the circle of light. A blond-haired human stared at me with a dark curiosity, his hand darting into the pocket of the long brown coat he wore. It came free holding an assortment of thin metal vials, reminding me of the kind my maker used to use.

Somewhere off in the darkened cargo hold, a door swung open, and the man turned away from me to see who it was.

I grabbed for him—for *them*—which only spun me around in place, missing the man completely.

"Now, now," my father's voice called from off across the hold, his steps ringing out as he crossed to us. "You would not start this without me, would you? I am paying, after all."

"Jesus," came another voice from off in my father's

direction. Alexandra's brother, Devon. "Save a piece for the boss, will ya?"

The human backed away from me, sliding the vials inside the folds of his coat. "I wouldn't dream of doing any of this without you," the stranger said. "Just continuing to wear down his will."

"Excellent," Kejetan said. "Do you have everything you need to extract the information I desire?"

"I think so," the stranger said. "Although it's getting harder and harder to get the supplies I need to do so."

"I am not concerned about how you procure them. Only that you do."

"I'm just saying." The stranger stepped out of the light, and moments later the full but dim lights of the hold came to life. A tray covered with vials, metal flasks, and an array of various stoppered containers sat against the near wall where the man stood. "Basic theories of economic supply and demand in play here, there might be a slight price increase on this job."

My father crossed to him. His deformed stone bulk stood towering over the man, who backed up against the wall, craning his head up to meet my father's face.

"Do not test me," Kejetan said. "While money is of little concern to me, do not think me the sort to be taken advantage of."

"I'm not taking advantage," the man said, sounding almost insulted.

His words were met with a silent stillness from my father. Even hanging where I was, I felt the intimidation of it.

The man's face fell, his eyes shifting away.

"Okay, maybe I'm taking a little advantage," he said. "But I'm not kidding about the supply. There's a risk factor, and the last time, I was nearly caught."

"Again, not my concern," my father said, stepping away from him to inspect me where I hung.

The man turned back to his table, placing his hands on several of the vials and flasks. "It *will* be your concern," he said, lifting them up one by one, "when the last of the vials is used, and there's nothing left. Everything I do relies on one master component, Kimiya, mixed with others. And right now, Kimiya is in short supply. No one's making it anymore. No one knows *how*. There's a finite supply available to me, and no offense, I have other clients and customers to think of as well as my own future."

Devon walked over to him, laying his own heavy, deformed stone hand on the man's shoulder. "Trust me, pal. If there's one thing I learned when I was human and doing business, it's that it's hard to think about the future if the deal you fuck up today gets you killed. You might want to play nice with his lordship there."

The fire in the man's eyes died. "Yeah, sure," he said. "No worries. Just wanted to make him aware of how hard I've been working to help him. No need to get excited."

Devon patted him, the man's face more pained with each jarring blow to his shoulder, fragile creature that these humans were.

"That's the spirit," Devon said, and walked to join my father in front of me.

"Hoist him up so he's even," the blond human said, and Devon crossed over to the left chain hanging from the ceiling. He pulled at it, a twinge of pain erupting all along my left wing until I had both feet lifted just off the ground and was hanging evenly.

The man came to me with one of the larger containers, pulling off the top of it, and began moving all around me. Consulting a notebook he pulled from his coat pocket, he walked around me, marking my stone body with his finger, the thick red liquid forming arcane symbols in a language I could not read. In the stretched pain of my body, the sensation was cooling, almost refreshing.

So close he was as he worked, yet I had not the fight in me to even lift a clawed hand to stop him. Nor did I wish to. Pain I could endure, if it meant that no harm would come to Alexandra and her friends. Her great-great-grandfather's rules—to protect the Belarus family—might have been expelled from my being, but the desire to do so had not been.

Whatever Kejetan and his men would do to me, I would endure.

After several more moments of this, the man stepped back from me, a pleased expression on his face.

"Is it ready?" my father asked him.

"Pretty much," the man said, reaching into one of the deep, outside pockets of his coat with the hand not holding the flask. "Now to bind it." He pulled free a battered black notebook, thick with well-worn pages, flipping through it until he found what he was seeking. His eyes met mine as he let out a long, slow breath, then he lifted the flask to his lips and drank.

His face twisted into a mask of displeasure, and for a moment he looked like he might fall over, but instead he forced his eyes open and looked to the notebook, reading from it. The words came out of his mouth in a soft, steady stream, and while I could not understand them, I did feel a connection snap to between the two of us, an invisible burning cord that stretched from his mind to mine.

The pain of it was far different from the physical one I had been contending with all this time.

This kind was far worse.

Only the distant memory of my human form being crushed to death centuries ago seemed even close to this excruciation. It was as if the very thoughts in my head burned. I opened my mouth to beg for it to stop, trying to fight it, but the only sound that came from my lips was a roar that echoed around the cargo hold, my father and Devon stepping back from it.

Although I thought that the violent sound coming from me would have torn a human apart, the man before me held his ground. He, too, looked pained, but his face was full of concentration, and it did not waver with even a hint of change.

Unbearable as it all was, I wanted to collapse but forced myself to stay awake through it all until, minutes later, the man stopped speaking, and the connection between the two of us broke.

My body—now free of the sensation—let out all its tension, and I fell slack, hanging from the two spikes driven through my wings. The man's body lost all its tension, and he collapsed to the floor. My father and Devon were already moving to him, but the human raised a weak hand, waving them away.

"Lower him," he said, his voice a mere whisper, and the two stone men moved to the chains. Together, they worked them until there was enough slack in the lines that I was able to collapse forward.

For several moments, I simply lay there, enjoying the lack of sound as well as the lack of pain. No one spoke until I pressed myself up to my knees.

"Is his will broken?" my father asked.

The human—still lying on the ground—rolled onto his back and slowly stood up. He brushed at and adjusted his coat and slid the notebook back into his pocket before speaking, running his fingers through his hair. "Let's find out. What do you want to know?"

My father contemplated for a moment as he moved closer to me, looking down into my face, where I lay on the floor of the cargo hold.

"I want to know the secrets," he said. "The ones the Spellmason Alexander Belarus stole from us."

I remained silent, once more not willing to give up any information that might betray Alexandra.

"Answer him," the man said. "Truthfully."

I started to answer "no," but the word would not come to my lips.

My mind screamed it, but somehow I could not. The harder I willed it, the more it would not come, and with each second that passed, my voice—my true voice—became quieter and quieter until it was barely a whisper at the back of my mind. Its former space was now filled with a foreign and dominant voice with but one desire—to answer my father with the truth.

"I cannot tell you those secrets," I said, trying to allow my true self to speak as cryptically as I could.

"You can and you *will*," my father shouted, full of rage. He turned on the man. "This was supposed to work."

The man seemed unaffected by my father's angered tone, holding up his hand to him as he stepped close to me.

"Hold on, now," he said, glancing back to my father and Devon. "You told me the secrets are locked away within him, yes? That's why you hired me, to get those out, right?"

My father nodded.

The man turned back to me. "The secrets of the Spellmasons are locked inside you, yes?"

"That is what I told my father," I said, speaking the truth while still fighting to hold back the details.

"I am giving you permission to unlock those secrets," the human said.

"I cannot."

"Why not?" the man asked, skeptical curiosity filling his eyes.

The small voice in the back of my head pressed forward, shouting for me not to tell him the truth, but just as quick as it had shouted, it was silenced by the new, dominant presence in my head.

"I am not in possession of the secrets," I said, a pained spike rising in my head. It throbbed, but my small true voice remained silent now.

"What?" my father shouted, pushing the man out of the way, his brute strength slamming the human into the wall, crumpling him to the floor.

"Easy," the man whispered in a pained breath.

"What do you mean, you are not in possession of those secrets?" my father shouted, gripping my face in his hand.

"I never was," I said. "I lied, '*bluffed*,' the humans call it . . . to protect them."

My father raged, lifting me into the air by my throat and throwing me. I tumbled end over end, chain and wings intertwining as I flew until I landed on the floor in a tangle.

"The time I have wasted," he said. "All on a false promise by my own kin." He turned to Devon. "Tell my men to head back to shore. We march on your family's building."

"What are you going to do?" the man asked, easing himself back onto his feet. There was fear in his voice, no doubt in fear for his life. "This alchemy is a work in progress. I just need some time to refine this . . ."

My father grabbed him by his arms, lifting him. The man screamed in pain, which stopped my father, but there was a current of rage underneath the restraint he was showing. "The only reason I am letting you live is because although you have proven a *failure* in extracting the information, you have at least exposed the truth of the matter."

"Yes!" the man said, earnest in agreement with my father. "Exactly! See? Some good *has* come from this. Let me continue my work . . ."

My father set the man on his feet. "I think not," he said.

The man paled. "So what are you going to do?"

"We tried your way," my father said, turning and walking toward me. "Now we will try mine." He looked to Devon, gesturing at the human. "Restrain him."

Devon went to the man, grabbing him at the shoulders in his giant fists. The man hissed in pain.

"Hey, now, easy," he said. "We can work something out. I'll cut my price—"

My father picked me back up by my throat again and lifted me until I was fully in the air again.

"What do you mean when you say you will try things 'your way' now?" I asked.

Kejetan's dark sockets stared into my eyes. "I spared those people of yours," he said, "because I thought that I was not only getting my son back but that I would get the arcane knowledge I had gathered back. I put my faith in *family* and a trust in your word, but you have broken with that. You disappoint, Stanis. You have made a mockery of me, and for that, I will make sure your humans suffer when I march against them and reclaim the secrets that are rightfully mine."

"You speak of *family* and *trust* as if those words mean something to you," I said.

"I have only ever thought of our legacy," he said. "Our desire to live forever!"

"*Your* desire," I corrected. "Not mine. And certainly not at the expense of the people you have and would kill in your mad pursuit of that power. Including me."

Kejetan shook his head, but there was no sadness in it for what he had done to me, only bitter resolve.

"Your death pained me, for centuries," he said. "Do you think I meant to strike down my only son? I had just cast off my human form, this stone one new to me. I had not mastered its strength yet."

"Your desire for longevity has blinded you," I said, "and that is what pains me most."

Kejetan shook his head, his words filled with bitterness when he spoke. "What pains me more is the man, the *creature* that you have become. Full of weakness, invested in these equally weak creatures."

"I see no weakness in them," I said. "Only strength."

"I will show you their weakness," he said, still holding me there. "Starting with the one you seem to favor most."

I struggled, a small amount of my strength returning to me at the very thought of harm coming to Alexandra, her family, or her friends. I raised my claws against my father, but he held me farther away from him so that all I could do was claw at his arms.

"Control him," he shouted out to the human.

"Can't right now," the man replied. "Kind of restrained over here by your second-in-command."

"Release him," my father said.

Devon did so, and the human stepped quickly away from him, rolling his shoulders as he went.

"Much better," he said, moving closer to me. "Now, then . . . *relax*."

My body went slack at the command, but part of my mind was still my own.

"You will leave Alexandra alone," I said.

"I think not," my father said, pulling me closer as he peered into my soul with those dark, dead sockets of his. "First, I will take from her that which her family has stolen from us. Then my people can be awakened from these hideous forms we now possess. Then . . . I will break her, as I did you. So fragile a thing like her must be. So many bones to crush . . ."

Although the dominant voice in my mind left me unable to react, the thought of Alexandra's going through the painful death I had gone through at my father's hand was too much to bear. The voice at the back of my head—my true voice—could not live with it and shot forward.

"You will leave Alexandra alone," I repeated, my own will rising and forcing itself into action.

"So much flesh to rip from her bones," my father continued, but I barely heard his words.

My entire focus became making sure that never happened. I raised my arms high overhead and brought them down against my father's. Bits of stone crumbled off the jagged rocks of his skin, and he screamed in shock, letting go.

I dropped to my feet, my knees buckling, but I remained standing. I rammed both my hands straight forward at my father, slamming into his chest and sending him flying back. Still tangled in chains, I pulled my wings close in around me, shaking loose what I could before sorting through the rest.

Devon was closing with me, but, with a flick of my wings, the attached chains spun out from me toward his legs, and he toppled forward in a tangle of his own.

I dug my clawed feet into the metal floor and stayed standing, Devon's struggles pulling the chains taut. Bringing my wings in around me with as much strength as I could muster, I placed my mouth over the chains still hanging from me and let my heavy stone fangs clamp down hard over them until they snapped off, leaving only a small amount still attached to the spikes.

I needed to leave this place. Now. The cargo-bay doors high overhead were the only barrier between me and what I hoped was the night sky, and I spread my wings, daring to fly for the first time in months.

The act itself was an excruciating burn through both wings, but it was also filled with the pleasure of liberation.

My feet left the ground, and I soared in small circles as I forced myself slowly upward like a bird learning to fly.

"Stop him," my father shouted, the words ringing over and over in my ear.

Down below, the stranger was quickly sorting through the inside folds of his jacket, pulling a vial of this and a vial of that free before placing them to his lips and drinking. I turned my attention back to my flight, circling ever higher to the doors above. With each bit of lift, my wings stayed spread longer, soaring higher, and, in seconds, my clawed hands dug into the seam of the cargo-bay doors.

There was nothing left except forcing them apart, which I set to. The metal did not want to give way, but slowly I forced the tips of my claws in between them and felt them begin to yield.

Chain wrapped around one of my feet, the surprise of it causing my grip to slip out of the small gap I had opened in the doors. Needing my wings once more to stay airborne, I dropped lower for a moment as I righted myself, but all that did was allow the chain around my foot to slacken, and, with a flick of the human's wrists, it looped around me again. It caught my other foot this time, binding them together as he pulled, but other than inconveniencing me, it was not really a problem. With my superior strength, I could easily lift the man into the air, chain and all. Once I got the doors back open, I'd be skyward-bound and able to fly. Then it would simply be a matter of time and puny human strength until his arms gave out and he fell into the water surrounding the freighter.

Except I never got a chance for that to happen. The man pulled at the chain, but instead of the weak human effort I expected, there was a powerful tug that sent me crashing into the floor. I landed on my side, dazed from the display of strength. The man stood over me, rolled me onto my back with a superhuman strength, and lowered himself until he was sitting on my chest. I raised my free arm to stop him, catching him on the side of his head, which should have ended him, but it did not. My hand connected with the flesh, but the flesh felt as solid as stone.

"Fall in line," he said, grabbing my arm, forcing it down under his leg, then raised his fists, bringing them down again and again on my head. Again, this would have been laughable under other circumstances, but the blows of his flesh hands felt just as heavy as those of my father or Devon. I fought to buck him off me, but it was no use.

"Fall in line!" he shouted with each shot he took at me.

With each passing blow, more and more of the fight went out of me until there was nothing left to do but take the abuse. My true voice subsided until I had no desire left in me.

I fell in line.

The quality of the blows changed, the stone of them quickly losing their weight, until the softness of flesh returned to them. The man stopped and stood up, wiping them against his pant legs. I remained lying where I was.

"Good gargoyle," he said.

"*Grotesque,*" I replied with what hint of mental fight there was left in me. "My maker called me his *grotesque.*"

"I'm sure he did," the man said, stepping back. Devon and my father joined him, the three of them staring down at me. "You see? I still have my uses. You shouldn't be so quick to dismiss me. And you really need to control your temper."

My father looked to him. "Like now," he said with a restrained tone.

"Exactly," the man said, turning away from him to concentrate on the supplies still on his table. "And as a reminder, I may be expensive, but you *do* get what you pay for."

"I paid to have our arcane secrets extracted from him," my father said.

"We can worry about the details of the old contract later," the man said. "You've gotten some very useful information out of this golem, I think. And thanks to my bringing him under control, you've got a great tool at your disposal to help you get the information back that you wanted, right?"

"So what now?" Devon asked.

Kejetan moved to stand over my prone, exhausted form. "Now?" he asked. "Now we take what is ours from the Belarus Building. That is not a problem, is it, Stanis?"

I thought about it. Other than the barely intelligible whisper of my true voice at the back of my mind, my dominant mind saw no reason to resist.

"As you wish," I said.

Seven

Alexandra

Despite all the time I spent trying to decipher the finer points of Spellmasonry, peace and quiet had reigned on the home front until last night. So it was with an angry and fearful heart the next morning that I set upon the dark and personal task of attempting my own arcane warding of the entrance to the guild hall.

If Alexander Belarus had protected the Belarus Building for several hundred years with the power of his wards, surely I could do a single room.

Or so I thought.

The alchemy of *how* to construct the safety measure was where I had the problem. If I already had prowess in any of this, I'm sure it would be as easy as following a recipe. Most recipes, however, didn't require you to imbue carved-stone markers with the power to grant or deny entrance to a space.

How the hell was I supposed to do that? I couldn't rightly "teach" stone how to read minds to determine intent or make judgment calls about anyone who tried to enter. And after several hours of tinkering, I settled instead on something that seemed an easier solution—enchanting the stone to activate and open by the invocation of simply speaking a password to allow safe entrance.

My stomach growled as I sat there satisfied with my work, and I set off upstairs in search of food, grabbing a quick sandwich before heading back down to the basement.

I nearly dropped my plate and soda when I saw a figure standing at the slid-back bookcase that hid the stone door, but, thankfully, it was only Rory, who was putting her key to the building back into her enormous dance bag.

She turned at the sound of my plate knocking against my water bottle, catching the surprise on my face.

"Sorry," Rory said. "I let myself in." She pushed against the stone door. "It's locked."

"After last night, I decided I needed to try my hand at upping security."

Rory looked around, her eyes looking low to the floor. She pulled a long, tall water bottle from her dance bag and brandished it like a club. "Am I about to be ambushed by an army of Bricksleys?"

"No," I said. "He's actually inside there. I left him putting away a bunch of the alchemy supplies I was mixing. Our supply of Kimiya is running lower than ever down here, thanks to our thief. There's more up at the Belarus Building, so I'll probably head up later to grab it, but even that's dwindling. If we don't figure out how to make it soon, I may have to back off our experiments."

Rory relaxed and turned back to the door. "Can you magic it open for us?"

I held up my sandwich and water bottle. "Sorry. Hands full here. You try."

She looked at me like I had two heads. "Be serious."

"I *am* being serious," I said. "You don't have to be all fancy magic pants to do it. It's like my laptop: password-protected. At least, I think it is. You're my first guinea pig."

Rory seemed wary, then glanced back at the door, striking a pose like a wizard readying for battle. "So what's the password?"

"I'll give you three guesses."

Rory thought for a moment, then, in her best Hermione Granger voice, said, "Wingardium Leviosa!"

Nothing happened. Rory looked to me, but I only shrugged at her.

She paced back and forth for a moment, then said, "A hint, please."

"Well," I said, thinking, "it has to be something all three of us could use, so consider Marshall in this, too."

Her eyes went wide, and she spun toward the door, shouting, "Friendship is magic!"

Again, nothing happened. Rory sighed.

"It's something Marshall *always* calls us," I offered. "Think *Lord of the Rings*."

The disappointment swept away from Rory's face as she did her best Gandalf—which wasn't very good at all. *"Mellon."*

The door clicked and opened into the room.

"Clever," Rory said, going in. "Now we just have to make sure we're not attacked by anyone speaking Elvish."

I shook my head as I marched to the table at the center of the room where I had been working. Bricksley had made short work of the mess I had left there, and I put my food down on the recently cleared space, attacking my sandwich.

I was three bites in before something hit me, and I pulled out my phone, checking the time.

"You're early," I said. "I wasn't expecting you for another couple of hours."

"Well, my dance card literally opened up for the day," Rory said. "One of the things that the Manhattan Conservatory of Dance frowns on is dizziness and vomiting in class."

"Rory!" I said, my mouth full of food, almost choking as I said her name. I swallowed. "You okay?"

She nodded, taking a long sip from her bottle of water.

"I will be," she said. "I guess I was a little more concussed than I thought. Our morning study was all textbook, history and such, which left me with a headache, but our late-morning session was practical. I got into maybe my tenth or eleventh *fouette* before I fell over and threw up."

She laid her dance bag by the table and sat down across from me, grabbing up one of the books she had been going through yesterday. "I'll try not to blow buckets of bile on any of your books."

"No," I said, taking the book from her. "No researching for you. Absolutely not."

Rory reached for the book but missed by a mile.

"I'm not going to vomit," she said, looking a little paler than I liked to see her. "Probably not, anyway."

I shook my head. "Rory, you must have hit your head last night harder than we thought," I said. "You need to see the doctor."

Rory leaned back in her chair, folding her arms across her chest. "That's where I spent the rest of my afternoon," she said, but nothing more.

"And . . . ?"

She sighed, running her fingers through her Cookie Monster blue hair. "She yelled at me for not coming in sooner," she said. "But not just because of the concussion. Under these clothes, my body is a rainbow of colors, going a bit heavy on the black-and-blue side."

"That's not from the dancer side of your life," I said, pained on her behalf.

"Dancers get injured, too," she said. "Do you know the shelf life of a dancer? It's almost as bad as that of a figure skater!"

"You need to take it easy," I said. "Go home and rest some more. I won't have you falling apart on my account."

"Lexi—"

I stood, pulling her up out of her chair. Her legs wobbled underneath her and gave out, but I caught her as she fell forward. It was an awkward grab, her forehead slamming into my chin, but when she looked up at me, the fight was gone from her eyes.

"Fine," she said. "But who's going to protect you if that guy comes back around here?"

I smiled. "Not this girl," I said, tapping her on her forehead. I scooped up her dance bag.

"At least let me sit here and do some puzzle solving in your great-great-grandfather's books," she insisted. "I feel so useless."

"Pretty sure you're supposed to cut back on the gymnastics both physical *and* mental," I said, walking her out of the guild hall. "And given the type of arcane stuff you might stumble across in Alexander's books, that's even more reason for you to steer clear for now. Don't worry about me. I'll be fine."

I led Rory all the way up and out to the front door, even hailing a cab and sliding her into it. She smiled up at me as I handed her the dance bag, but there was worry in her eyes.

"At least call Marshall," she said. "That would make me feel better about leaving you here all alone."

"Will do," I said, and, without another word, I shut the cab door, sending her on her way as the taxi pulled away from the curb.

I could have hugged her for her concern, worrying about me when she was the one who could barely keep her feet under her, but as I headed back into the building, I had no intention of calling Marshall.

Seeing Rory like that was more than I could stand. My body shook with the thought of my best friend since childhood coming to harm in my home over secrets that had been put upon my family generations ago. If she thought I was going to call Marshall in to watch over me and put *him* in harm's way, too . . .

Such fragile creatures.

Stanis's words came to me. In his gargoyle hands, the lives of human enemies would be in danger. What scared me more was that in my hands, the lives of my human friends were, too.

If I was going to keep them safe and out of harm's way, I needed to step up my research, and that meant doing it on my own. For that, I needed full access to everything at my great-great-grandfather's disposal.

I needed to be back in his library.

Eight

)

Stanis

Swooping down out of the night sky, I took in the Belarus Building, a welcome sight after all these months away from it. I had not known I could miss a place like this so much. With the new and dominant voice filling my head, I could only hope that Alexandra was not here even though I longed to see her after so long an absence.

I came down low over the trees of Gramercy Park, then arced up to land on the terrace that led into my maker's library and studio.

Show no mercy in your search for the stolen secrets until you have found them, Kejetan had instructed.

Tasked as I was, I approached the French doors leading in, tearing them off the hinges. I was relieved to see there was no response from within, which meant the Belarus family was safe from incurring any of the damage I was programmed to do. Curious though I was at the silence of the building as I entered, I was also relieved at the lack of human activity. It would make what I was about to do a bit easier.

Though my true voice called out for me to stop, I tore through shelf after shelf of the books there, knocking volumes of them onto the floor, my claws gouging out large chunks as I went. Pages flew free, drifting freely in the air like leaves on the wind as I hurried through my task.

Despite the outer cloud of destruction and chaos all round me, I felt nothing but sorrow on the inside. All of these were memories of the centuries I had known the family, watched over them.

Moving into the art studio lined with its puzzle boxes and statuary, my thoughts turned more toward my own creation, the years I had spent learning under Alexander Belarus—fundamental lessons in how I functioned, how I could learn, how I could *grow*.

And now? I had betrayed all that.

The small voice in my head begged for me to stop, but it was not the one in charge now. Destruction while searching was what my masters wanted, and that was what my body gave them.

After a long and violent sweep of the open floor of the building, I had ruined much but found nothing of use to those who now controlled me. I stood in the wreckage of it all, wondering just what I was meant to do next. Lessons in pure destruction had not been something that Alexander had ever thought to teach me even though I had done my fair share of dark deeds against those who had sought to harm the family Belarus.

I had followed my new master's rules, but I had nothing to show for it. My mind was slowly processing what my next step might be when the sound of footsteps came from somewhere at the back of the building, near the stairs leading down.

"Holy shit," a female voice cried out behind me, followed by a gasp of hitched breath. I froze where I stood, part habit in a world of humans but also out of shock. The sounds of cautious footsteps followed, the shift of rubble and debris following. "What the hell?"

The footsteps came to a halt when the woman no doubt spied my shape among the shadows, followed by a stifled cry.

"Stanis?"

It had been far too long since I heard my name uttered by anyone other than the my father's people, but just the sound of Alexandra's voice saying it calmed me, even among all the chaos I had just caused.

I turned, and there she stood, with her long black hair down over her shoulders, her eyes wide and glistening in the near darkness.

"Hello, my Alexandra," I said, my true voice coming forward. I did not move, but I did not need to.

She ran to me, throwing her arms around my body and squeezing tight. I returned the embrace, handling her human form with care, and foreign though it felt, I found great comfort in the gesture, even though the bond between us had been broken the night she had released me to my father.

We stood there in the darkness together for a long moment, neither of us willing to break the spell. When had I last touched her? Perhaps the night months ago when I had flown us to this very building to stave off my father's attack.

"You're here," she said, stepping back to look at me but keeping her hands on my arms. "You're actually here."

"That I am," I said.

"I've so many questions," she said. "Where have you been? Who did this? Did you see anyone?"

"Where I have been is a long tale," I said. "As to who did this . . . yes, I saw who it was. It was I."

The kindness in her eyes shifted, and I did not need a connection between us to see the confusion in her.

"*You* did this?" she asked, her voice becoming louder. "*Why?* Why would you do this?"

I tried to answer, but found it a struggle as my true voice fought with the dominant one that held control over me. As small as my own voice sounded in my mind, I needed it to rise, to fight, but it would not come.

When I did not answer, Alexandra shook her head. "I don't understand," she said. She started to shrug her backpack off her shoulders, but I grabbed her wrist, stopping her.

"No," I said, my true self fearing what was in it. "Do not."

Alexandra gave a dark and unsteady laugh, and I sensed her nerves and anger mixing beneath it.

"Why not?" she asked, hitching the straps back up onto her shoulders.

The dominant voice wanted the secrets of the Spellmasons, but my inner voice was determined to keep them from it. These were new rules set upon me, and like the old ones, I needed to choose my words carefully if I was going to bend the dominant voice away from harming Alexandra.

"I have been tasked to claim what is rightfully my father's from the Belarus Building," I said.

"So you tore the place up because Kejetan the Accursed told you to?" she asked. "Did you ever think, 'Hey, maybe I just won't do it and say that I did'?"

"I cannot do that," I said.

"Why the hell not?" she asked.

"Because I have been bound," I said, forcing my true voice to take control of the conversation for a moment. "I serve another. Listen to me *carefully*, Alexandra. I must do as I'm told. *Exactly* as I'm told, which is why I must ask you to keep your bag on your back."

Another wave of confusion filled Alexandra's eyes. "Why?"

"You must keep quiet for a moment, and you must keep your bag upon your back," I said with my true voice, choosing my words with care to keep the dominant one from stopping me. "I think I can guess what might be in that bag, but I do not *know* for sure. And for your own safety, do not tell me.

"As I said, I have been tasked to claim what is rightfully my father's from the Belarus Building. That would mean that *if* Alexander's master book of arcane knowledge *were* here, I would have to take it . . . by force, if necessary. I am bound to destroy anyone who interferes with that. But if I do not technically know the book is here, I cannot take it from the Belarus Building. Do you understand me?"

Alexandra nodded, but said nothing.

"So," I continued, "for both our sakes, I think it is best that the contents of your backpack remain a mystery to me."

Alexandra kept her hands on the strap of her backpack but did not move to take it off. "I see," she said when she finally spoke. "You're playing around with the rules."

I could not help but smile at that. "You taught me to bend the rules when and where I could."

The two of us stood there in the silence of the night, in the silence of the familiar building, simply looking at each other, taking a quiet comfort in that.

"So what now?" she asked.

"I must return to my masters," I said. "I must tell the Servants of Ruthenia that I did not find the book on the premises. That will not satisfy them, but it will buy us both some time."

All life and color ran out of Alexandra's face.

"No," she said, taking my hands. "Don't go back to them. Stay with me. I'm sure I can figure something out. We can work this out. It's been far too long. *Please.*"

The desperation in her voice pained me, but I shook my head. "I must return to my masters," I repeated, unsure of what else I could say. I stepped away from her, but she would not let go of my clawed hands.

"At least tell me where they are," she said.

The dominant voice rose in me, not allowing me to betray the location of Kejetan and the Servants of Ruthenia.

"Please let me help you," she pleaded.

I stepped back farther from her, pulling my hands away from her. "Do not do this. If you interfere, Alexandra, I will be forced to harm you. Do you remember the bargain that I made with my father the last night you and I were together?"

Alexandra nodded as she wiped away tears forming at the corners of her eyes. "Yes," she said. "You promised that you would go with him, to protect me."

"Correct," I said. "And what did I make you do?"

"You made me release you from my great-great-grandfather's rules. I released you from protecting my family."

"That is correct," I said. "But why?"

Alexandra thought for a moment, puzzling it out before answering. "If Kejetan had chosen to hurt us just then, bound by my great-great-grandfather's rules, you would have been forced to fight him. And you would have kept on fighting until you were destroyed."

"And the binding that holds sway over me now is much like that," I said. "Kejetan has set me a task, and I cannot violate his rules. If you interfere, you will push my hand, and I will . . . I will be forced to kill you."

I saw how the words stung her like a slap, and I felt the pain I caused her deep in my soul.

"Do you remember the last words I spoke to you?" I said, hoping to distract her with something more practical.

"Yes," she said. "You said, 'Prepare yourself. This does not end things.'"

"And have you done just that?"

Alexandra gave a grim smile, frustration radiating from her. "Rory and Marshall have been helping me."

I smiled at the mention of their names. "I am surprised to find I miss them," I said.

Alexandra gave a dark and pained laugh. "I'm sure they'll be thrilled to hear it."

"And how goes the preparation?"

"Somewhere between promising and impossible," she said. "You were the culmination of my great-great-grandfather's decades of arcane study. Spellmasonry isn't something mastered in a few months. Every time I think I'm making progress, I run up against a wall. I feel like I'm at a dead end. You remember Bricksley?"

"Of course," I said.

"*He's* still up and running. It's just when I try to do something more grand than that, things sort of . . . fall apart. Nothing stays bound together. I'm getting better at exerting my will over things, but what good does that do if I can't maintain it? I just end up with a pile of bricks or a poorly molded statue that shatters into a thousand pieces. The only thing that has gone right are the wards I've placed on the new building as the contractors work on the structural damage here down in the catacombs, so who knows if the building is even going to remain standing. We've got builders down there reinforcing everything, but we can't live here, really. I've moved the family down to—" She clapped her hand over her own mouth

For her safety, I needed to leave before she triggered the dominant voice in me any further. I stepped past Alexandra, heading back toward the torn-off doors of the terrace.

"I am sorry about your library," I said as I went. "Truly."

Alexandra ran along behind me, trying to catch up, climbing over the debris that I simply crashed through. "You're leaving? Now?"

"I must," I said. Once outside, I let the cool night air wash over me.

"Wait," she said, grabbing for my arm, but as much as I wanted to feel her touch, I did not think I could bear it. I stepped off the edge of the roof, my wings spreading to catch the wind. I spun back around to face her.

"When will I see you again?" she asked. "Seeing you like . . . *this*, I can't take it. I need to know."

"I am unsure," I said. "I am subject to the will of others and bound to return to them. This I cannot fight."

"Tell me what to do," she pleaded. "There's no one I can talk to about this, no one who even understands the power at work here. I need guidance."

"Nothing has changed since I first instructed you on this," I said, leaping into the air. I looked down at her trembling figure on the terrace below. "Learn what you can. For my part, I will try to do the same. But prepare."

"Prepare for *what*, though?" she shouted. "What does your father plan to do?"

"I am not sure," I said, working my wings to lift me higher into the night sky. Already the dominant voice was directing me back out over Manhattan, heading out to sea and the freighter. "The question is, will you be ready?"

Nine

☾

Alexandra

I'd had nightmares where the totality of my great-great-grandfather's knowledge was lost to me, destroyed, but no matter how horrific they had been, the reality of his tossed-around studio space felt far worse. The Belarus Building had been my home, but the library and art studio had been my heart, my inner sanctum all my life. To see it as a mass grave of books and art crushed that heart. Then to find Stanis the one responsible only drove a stake through what was left of it.

Seeing him tonight—cold though he was toward me—only reminded me how much I missed the warmth of his protection. Even though I was proving capable of watching out for myself, it had always been a comfort to know he had been watching my back. I missed it more and more in the face of his not being at—or *on*—my side now. I longed for the companionship of the old Stanis, but all that remained of him, unfortunately, was the destruction he had caused, still plentiful all around me.

Although I had promised myself to keep my friends out of harm's way, I needed to reach out to someone and called

Rory and Marshall. The danger had passed, the damage done, and I doubted this new, corrupted version of Stanis would return—at least not for a little while.

I couldn't just stand there amid the chaos of the broken room waiting for them. I'd go mad. I needed to feel productive somehow and grabbed up one of the mannequin forms and set about designing a new gargoyle from scratch. It was clear the current one wasn't going to prove very helpful to us, and the distraction of modeling a wire-and-clay frame for wings was very therapeutic just then.

I was still standing back from the figure, checking the symmetry of the wings, when I heard Rory and Marshall scurrying up the fire escape outside, still not quite able to take in the events of my evening.

"What in holy hell happened here?" Rory asked as she stepped with caution past the broken French doors.

"Are you all right?" Marshall whispered, grabbing me by the shoulders and looking me over.

I nodded. "Physically? Yeah. Emotionally, not so much."

"What happened?" Rory asked, dropping her dance bag.

I paused, trying to keep myself together before answering. "Stanis happened."

Rory's eyes went wide. "You saw him?!"

Marshall let go of me and spun around quick.

"Is he still here somewhere?" he said, whispering as he peered off into the darkness surrounding us.

I shook my head.

Rory leaned down and picked up one of the broken puzzle boxes at her feet. One of the drawers—once secret—slid out and fell onto a pile of books. "What the hell was he fighting that caused this much damage?"

"Stanis wasn't fighting anything," I said. "He did this all himself."

Rory stepped back, narrowing her eyes at me. "Lexi, do you know how *insane* that sounds?"

"I do," I said. "And I wish I had a different answer for you. But honestly, I don't. This was all Stanis."

"Why would he do this, especially to you?" Marshall

asked, flipping one of the upended couches back over before
collapsing onto it.

"We freed him," I said. "Now he serves a different master."
Just saying the words out loud sent a sharp pain through me.

"How?" Marshall called out.

I shrugged. "I don't know how they did it," I said. "I just
know they did."

Rory's eyes lit up, and she raised her voice in disbelief.
"Hold on," she said. "Stanis left—went with Kejetan—to
protect us . . . I mean, really *you*, right?" I nodded. "*This* is
how he does that?"

I looked at the couch to see Marshall shaking his head.

"We freed him," he contested, "so he didn't *have* to serve
anyone. That was the whole point!"

Rory looked around the room. She pulled the art tube off
her back, put together her pole arm, and scooped up a half-
torn book with the end of it. "And whoever did this to him
made him a dick," she said.

"Rory!" I scolded, more out of frustration than anger
with her. She was right.

Marshall stood. "So if Stanis is serving a new master,
and they put him up to this . . . did he actually get the secrets
he came for?"

"I think I have an answer for that," I said, going to the
spot where I had laid my backpack down earlier. I undid the
upper straps and pulled out the heavy stone book from
within. "No."

"That book right there is great power," Marshall said,
pointing to it. "Alexander knew it. It's why he hid it all away
from the world. You put that much power out there, and
people are going to *want* it; and not all of those who wish
to wield great power want the same thing. In your hands,
Lexi, and with your motivations, there's a chance you'd be
asked to join the Justice League. In another person's hands?
Totally Legion of Doom."

I nodded. "Stanis knew I had the book on me, but . . . he
went out of his way to stop me from talking about it."

"But why not just take it?" Rory asked.

"Because despite who or whatever is controlling him now," I said, "Stanis is still in there somewhere, trying to keep us from harm. He could have crushed me and taken the book, but he didn't. Stanis *is* in there with whatever else is in control, and he's fighting to find ways around it."

"So what do we do?" Marshall asked.

I shrugged. "I'm not sure. There's a good chance that if he sees me again, Stanis will be forced to take the book from me, or do something . . . worse."

"How do you take a gargoyle down?" Rory asked.

I glared at her. "Rory!"

She shrugged. "Sorry, Lexi. It's just . . . I know it's Stanis and all, but if it comes down to you or him, I'm always going to choose you."

Everyone was silent for a moment before Marshall spoke. "I'm afraid I'm with Rory on this one, Lexi."

"I don't care what anyone thinks about what the Servants of Ruthenia might force Stanis to do," I shouted. "I won't believe even then he would hurt me."

"Yeah, well, I don't want to find out the hard way," Rory said, just as loud, getting up in my face. "Lexi—"

"No," I said, interrupting. "I'm taking Stanis back. They made him like this, and I'm taking him back. He *won't* hurt me. I know it."

"I'm not willing to take that risk," Rory said, stamping her pole arm on the floor.

"Ladies," Marshall said, speaking up. "Stop it."

"No," I said. "Let's have this out. So this is how we operate now, Rory? At the first sign of trouble, we abandon our friend when he needs us?"

"You haven't seen him in months," Rory countered. "You don't know what's been going on or what's happened to him. For all you know, he's just as likely to snap your neck because his new master told him to do it. There may be Stanis's soul still in there somewhere, but someone else is calling the shots, and that body is still—what's Marshall's word . . . ?"

"A construct," he said, "but listen. We can't fight like this . . ."

"We don't abandon our own," I shouted back in Rory's face.

"Ladies," Marshall repeated.

"Stay out of this, Marsh," Rory added.

He ran to the two of us, pulling us close. "Wish I could," he said, lowering his voice. "But we've got a bigger problem."

"What?" I asked, the word coming out short, just as testy as I was feeling.

"I think I heard something," he said. "Something from *within* the building."

Like a campfire being doused with water, all the fight went out of me. Rory, too.

The three of us stopped, turning to listen, and when we heard sound coming from the back stairs of the building, we all spun to face it. Rory raised and readied her pole arm, but I put my hand over hers, forcing her to lower it, which she did, but only a little.

"Stay sharp," I whispered. "Just . . . you know, don't stab my parents if it's one of them."

Rory looked offended. "I think I can manage not stabbing Doug and Julie," she whispered back.

A shadow rose into view as it cleared the stairs leading up onto the floor, but it was not the shadow of my mother or father, which I was pretty sure I'd know by now. A lone figure advanced slowly into the room, unrecognizable until it stepped in a section of moonlight streaming in from one of the windows.

"Holy hell," Marshall whispered. "It's the ghost of Sean Connery."

"Not quite," I said, standing up, relaxing a bit. Seeing Desmond Locke was a relief compared to the myriad horrors I imagined shambling up those stairs—Kejetan's stone men or maybe something worse.

"Mr. Locke," I said, in turn startling him as his eyes darted our way.

"Well, well," he said, brushing off his pant legs as he stepped with care into the room, picking his way through the debris. "Have I caught you at a bad time, Miss Alexandra?"

I gave a weak but pained smile. "Not exactly the greatest timing, Mr. Locke," I said.

He glanced to the pole arm in Rory's hand, then over to Marshall.

"No?" he asked, a tight-lipped smile crossing his lips. "Would you care to tell me what happened to Alexander's library and studio, then?"

I looked to both Rory and Marshall, each of them staring back at me expectantly, no doubt curious what I was going to say. I was curious, too.

"I think we had a break-in," I said after a moment, which was, while technically true, the most vague answer I could give without lying. "Someone trashed the place."

"So I see," he said, not looking away from me, his eyes searching mine for answers.

I kept my own steady, refusing to give in to whatever type of intimidation the man hoped to use on me. It might work on my father given the religious sway Desmond Locke held over him, but it wasn't going to work with me.

"Pardon, sir," Marshall asked. "But what exactly are *you* doing here? This building is supposed to be closed for repairs and renovations, isn't it? And it's late."

Mr. Locke gave Marshall the simplest and most patronizing of smiles, which I wanted to smack off his face.

"I might ask the same of you three," he said. "As a point of fact, I believe I already have."

"This is my *home*," I reminded him, snapping. "I have every right to be here any damned time I wish. Which, Mr. Locke, is more than I can say for you. The only reason you've been allowed here before is due to my father's good graces."

Desmond Locke's smile faltered for half a second and he shifted his posture, turning his attention from Marshall back to me.

"Perhaps it's time we had that little talk I mentioned the other day when I ran into you down in the foyer," he said, his smile falling from his face.

"Are you *serious*?" I asked, his request flipping my bitch switch to full-on mode, unable to stop myself at his nerve.

"The last thing I want to hear about right now is your 'spiritual guidance' or its stranglehold over the rest of my family."

"Alexandra," he started, but I shut him down.

"I think you should leave. *Now.*"

Rory stepped forward, moving through the rubble toward him. "I'll show you out," she said.

Desmond Locke sighed. "I had hoped to avoid confrontation," he said, reaching into his coat. "But I'm afraid I will have to insist on that conversation now."

Even in the low light of the room, the gun in his hand caught the glint of the moonlight outside. Despite my dealing in a lot of arcane and crazy things, the purely mundane weapon set off another kind of panic in my heart.

Rory saw it, too, but ignored it and kept moving for him.

"Stop your little friend, Miss Belarus," Locke said, angling the gun toward her.

Rory was already raising her weapon, but I was pretty sure the gun could go off a lot faster than her closing with him, regardless of her prowess with the pole arm.

"Rory, don't!" I said, fighting to stay calm. This was exactly the type of danger I had hoped to keep both my friends out of, yet here we were, in it nonetheless.

Thankfully, Rory stopped, but she kept her weapon still raised.

"I've got this one," I said.

"You sure?" she said, remaining poised for action.

"Positive," I said, and breathed out one of my words of power. Broken bits of stone statuary were spread out all around us, littering the floor of the art space, and I called out to them with my will, the connection snapping to within me.

Reaching out with my mind's eye, I aimed the pieces at Desmond Locke and shot them through the air at him. The pieces responded in perfect unison, flying at the man, but just as they were about to hit their target, several of them shattered. The rest followed suit like stone bits of popcorn popping, forming a giant cloud of dust that hung in the air around Locke.

My friends and I backed away, all coughing, but within the cloud itself I could see there had been an invisible barrier surrounding the man, made visible now only due to our circumstance.

As the dust cleared, Locke stepped forward as calm as could be, his hand wrapped around something hanging from his neck. When he opened it, I saw a variety of lanyards and chains, talismans and charms hanging from them all.

Desmond Locke's eyes went first to Rory, her pole arm now hanging in her hand at her side. Gone were the kind, jovial eyes of the man who had come to visit my father in our home for years. His stare was dark, purposeful, his whole face deadly serious.

"Put that thing away," he said to Rory, pronouncing each word like an angry father talking to a child. "Before someone truly gets hurt around here."

Rory looked to me, her eyes full of reluctance, but I nodded. Moving slowly, she took apart the sections of her weapon and, with care, slid them back into their individual compartments within the art tube.

"Much better," he said, then added, "thank you."

"What is going on here, Mr. Locke?" I asked. Nothing made a lick of sense to me. Then again, it was hard processing anything sensible with a gun pointed at you. That and all the events of the night had my thoughts going a mile a minute, without hope of any actual destination or understanding.

Desmond Locke turned to face me, a modicum of his old self returning to his eyes, perhaps because no one else was brandishing a weapon in the room except for him. "As I said, I'd like to have that little chat now."

Marshall laughed, but it was short, nervous, and forced. "I say we let the man talk," he said, his hands up in the air like he was being robbed.

I remained standing, with my hands at my side, calm on the outside but screaming on the inside.

Months ago, when I was simply being chased on a regular basis by cultists serving Stanis's father, this type of interior panic would have sent Stanis to my rescue. *But now?* That time and bond was past, as was that kind of rescue. It formed an unsettled emptiness in me, mixed with genuine fear for my life. Not just mine but those of my friends as well.

I didn't dare try anything else with Desmond Locke, for fear of their lives more than mine. I raised my hands, slow, until I stood there like Marshall was.

"Fine," I said, not able to hide all of the bitter anger behind the word. "You want to talk? Talk."

Desmond Locke shook his head, looking around at the destruction in both the art studio and library halves of the entire floor.

"Not here," he said, cocking back the top part of his gun, something within it clicking. "Whatever did this might return."

"So where, then?" I asked, desperately hoping that the "whatever" that did all this would show his ass now.

"Come with me," he said, falling in behind Marshall, the gun pressed close to my friend's back. "And trust me, you don't want to find out what happens if you don't."

"Do we have a choice?" I asked, starting to pick my way toward the stairs leading down through the building, but Mr. Locke didn't respond, simply driving us down through the old building and out onto the street.

Hopefully, he wasn't leading us all to our death.

Ten

Alexandra

I never liked being down in the Wall Street area in the evenings. Once the suits and market makers had left, the neighborhood always became a bit of a ghost town. That night, however, it was a shame because as Desmond Locke's driver pulled up in front of an abandoned and dilapidated church that sat in the shadow of Trinity Church on Trinity Place, I would have loved there to be a crowd around so that the three of us might stand a chance of escaping into it.

Instead, Desmond Locke stepped out of the car first, then gestured us out of it with the business end of his gun.

I stared up at the old church in front of us, the building one of my great-great-grandfather's, but one that was relatively unfamiliar to me. It was more garish than his usual design, lacking the Gothic integrity of most of Alexander's work in Manhattan, which I suppose made it no surprise that the building looked completely abandoned.

Its heavy wooden doors were boarded over with a mish-mash of slats and boards, but despite their appearance, Locke guided us toward them. Once in the shadowy arch of the cruciform base of the church, he moved to the boards blocking the door. He grabbed at one of the solid beams, then easily lifted it on a hidden pivot point, which allowed him to swing open the mass of boards, revealing a cleverly disguised entrance into the building behind them. They swung away as one, and Locke, again gesturing with the gun in his hand, forced us in through them.

Once inside, he secured the door before he turned and motioned us forward through the entryway into the church proper.

I pushed through the inner doors, but what greeted me was nothing like what I expected. The large open nave I thought would be filled with rows and rows of pews and kneelers was instead bustling with activity that gave it more of an office-warehouse vibe. The left side of the enormous area was filled with office space and cubicles behind a half wall, and people working in there. The other side was stacked high with caged-off shelves crammed with boxes, books, and sundry other items I couldn't identify from where I stood.

I stepped into the space of the main aisle down the middle of the room, taking it all in as the four of us walked along.

"This doesn't exactly scream church to me," I said.

"Nor should it," he said, continuing on. "Let's just call this a different affiliation of mine."

I threw him a suspicious look. "I take it my father isn't part of this particular religious affiliation?"

Desmond Locke shook his head.

"I should say not," he said. "And I wouldn't exactly call the *Libra Concordia* a religious endeavor, although its roots *can* be traced back through various denominations of Christianity."

I stopped walking. "*Libra Concordia*?"

"Balance," said Marshall, stepping forward. "With one heart."

"Very good, Mr. Blackmoore," Locke said. "You know your Latin."

Marshall shrugged. "Dead languages and gaming go hand in hand."

Locke laughed at that. "Apparently, they do."

"What *is* this place?" I asked.

Rory stepped over to one of the open gates of the caged-off area and reached through it for one of the boxes on the shelves. "What is all this?"

Locke reached for her hand to stop her, but Rory's reflexes were quicker, and she pulled away before he could grab her.

"We call it the Hall of Mysteries," he said, "for lack of anything more imaginative, and it is just that."

"How did you accumulate it?" I asked.

"We've amassed a great many findings over the years, things the Church might look upon as . . . miracles."

"Or damnation," Marshall added. "If any part of this is what I think it is . . ."

Desmond Locke folded his hands together, the gun still in his right one, but lowered now. "And what do you think *this* is, Mr. Blackmoore?"

"I think you have a whole lot of what you say . . . mysteries. But if the Church caught wind of this collection of yours, it could go one of two ways."

"And those would be . . . ?" Locke smiled.

"If I go by history," Marshall continued, "one perception would be that anything of power could be seen to be tools of the Devil by your Church, the types of things that got people burned at the stake or flayed alive."

"What other way *would* the Church react?" Rory asked. "Going with that strategy seemed to get them through the Salem witch trials just fine."

Marshall stepped to the restricted area, raised his hands, and looped his fingers through the gate itself, eyes looking at the contents behind it. "Well, some might see all this and reckon it as definitive proof of God. Technically, everything 'magic' here *is* a miracle. Either way, I'm pretty sure the Church wouldn't want the world to know about any of this."

"Marsh, you're sounding conspiracy-crazy," Rory said. "Like tinfoil-hat territory."

Was it, though? I turned my attention back to Desmond

Locke, who was standing there looking like he was almost enjoying all of this.

"Who are your people?" I asked. "What is a *Libra Concordia*?"

"*We* are the *Libra Concordia*," he said, gesturing to indicate the entirety of the activity within the church. "Long ago, the Church decided in its wisdom that while much of its trade was invested in the idea of 'miracles,' there was much in the world that didn't fit with the Church itself that could also be called 'miraculous.'"

"Magic," I said.

"As clever as your friend here," Locke said with a nod. "So while some thought it best to burn witches and warlocks—their books, charms—there were also those in the fold who thought it best to keep track of such things instead of destroying them. Thus was the *Libra Concordia* born."

Rory laughed, but there was bitterness in it. "And the powers that be are just fine with all this? Doesn't it amount to blasphemy in their eyes?"

Desmond Locke gave a tight smile. "Let's just say that the ideology of some of our members does not fall in line with many of the current administrations; I hear we are quite unpopular in Vatican City."

"So you're outlaws," I said. "Tsk, tsk, Mr. Locke."

"Such an ugly word," he said. "The early members of the *Libra Concordia* set about going underground centuries ago, men and women with a more . . . long-term view of what may or may not be gained by having such arcane knowledge."

I smiled at that. I had always dismissed Desmond Locke as a religious fanatic, doing what he was told within the confines of the religion with which he held sway over my father, but it seemed there was more to him than just that. Desmond Locke was a freethinker and, in the eyes of his own religion, a bit of a heretic.

Locke raised his gun once again, but not at us, the barrel instead pointed straight up into the air. He wagged the firearm back and forth. "I trust I can dispense with this, Miss Belarus?"

"Preferably," I said.

"Good," he said, sliding the gun inside his jacket. "Dreadful things. Necessary at times, I suppose, but dreadful nonetheless." He turned away from us without looking back and once more started down the center aisle of the church.

I looked to Rory, then Marshall, who half looked like he was ready to run for the doors. I raised my hands out in front of me, palms down.

"Steady," I whispered. "Whatever these people are, we need to see this through."

Marshall made to argue, but Rory elbowed him.

"Relax," she said. "I've got your back."

"You didn't a second ago when there was a gun pointed at us," he grumbled.

Rory went to argue back, but I laid a hand on her shoulder. "Save the bickering for home," I said. "The gun's put away. That's a step in the right direction, yes?"

This seemed convincing enough for Marshall, and he walked off after Desmond Locke, Rory and I falling in behind him as quick as we could.

Marshall's eyes fixed on the rows and rows of shelves off to our right as we continued down the aisle.

"So is there, like, an Arc of the Covenant down here?" Marshall asked.

Mr. Locke turned to look back at him. "I'll have to check," he said, "but I doubt it."

Halfway down the waist-high wall of dark wood to our left, Locke swung open a hinged half door and ushered us into an area beyond it that was fill with a desk, several plush leather chairs, and a couch that sat to our right. He stepped behind the desk, gesturing to the empty chairs directly across from it. Marshall and I took the chairs while Rory sat on the edge of the couch, perched and ready for action at a moment's notice.

"So why *have* you brought us here?" I asked.

"Do you know how your father and I met?"

I shrugged. "Bible study camp?"

Locke laughed. "No, not that young, I'm afraid," he said. "I was already in my late twenties and working for this organization when we he and I met. I learned of him because the *Libra Concordia* keeps its ears to the ground when they hear rumors of strange things happening in the world."

"Like when the image of Christ appears in a tortilla out in New Mexico?" Marshall asked.

Locke nodded. "Or a weeping statue of Mary or any variety of such things reported to us, yes."

"Sounds tedious," I said.

"Truthfully?" he said. "It is. But if discovering the great mysteries of the world were easy, everyone would take to our calling. Sadly, our numbers are few."

"But why come after my father?" I asked, steering him back to the point of his original question.

"Ah, yes," he said. "Forgive me. I first came to New York decades ago, chasing down a particular story that was passing in hushed whispers throughout the churches here—that of a young boy who claimed he had seen an angel."

I tried to hide any reaction to his words. "My father's gone on and on about that all my life," I said. I left out the part where only this past year I learned it had been the work of Stanis saving him from Kejetan's cronies. Still, Locke definitely had my interest. What I needed to know was how much he and his *Libra Concordia* knew about the truth of it all. "Forgive me if I seem a bit bored hearing about my father's angel again."

"Your father was a persuasive man," he said. "More so back then. By the time I tracked him down, and he told me his tale, I knew I had met someone special."

"I won't argue that," I said. "Every girl thinks her daddy is special, after all."

"Naturally," he said with a patient smile. "But the Church's official stance on miracles such as a visitation by the divine is a bit dismissive. They know there are those among their flock who simply make up stories or, in their fervor, believe they have actually seen such things. The

Church doesn't usually move on something until a whole village has seen a weeping statue or some such thing. But with my grander interests, well . . . I like to give even the craziest of tales due diligence. See how they play out."

"You don't sound like you believe in miracles," I said.

Desmond Locke shrugged. "In my profession, you see proof of what falls in line with the arcane more than you do the divine."

"And you don't consider any of that miraculous?" I asked.

Locke shook his head.

Marshall cleared his throat and spoke. "Any sufficiently advanced technology is indistinguishable from magic," he said.

I turned to look at him. "Did you just make that up?"

"Afraid not," he said. "That honor belongs to Arthur C. Clarke."

"But Mr. Blackmoore is more or less correct," Locke pointed out.

"Care to explain?" I asked.

Marshall paused for a moment in thought before speaking. "Back in the good ole witch-burning days, people took the things they couldn't explain and called them magic. Eclipses, magnetism, earthquakes. But over time, as we've discovered the *how* and *why* of things through science, the magical mystery of it all is sort of rolled back."

"Precisely," Locke said. "To my way of thinking, magic is simply a science we have yet to fully understand."

"But what does that have to do with my father and angels?" I asked. "Angels still fall in the miracle category, right? Divine servants of God and all that?"

"And there's the thing," Locke said, leaning forward in his chair, whispering conspiratorially to me. "I don't think your father saw an angel. I think it might have been something else."

"Such as . . . ?" I said, holding on to the arms of my chair, my stomach clenching as I feared hearing Stanis's name come from his lips.

"Of that I am not quite sure," he said, sitting back in his chair. "That is where you come in."

"If you're so concerned about Alexandra's father and what he saw, why not ask him?" Rory asked.

"Religion is an easy way to find the unexplainable at times," Locke said. "I studied your father for years as we became friends. His belief in this divine angel was so strong that I was always reluctant to broach discussion of magic with him. I thought that if it was magic that was surely at hand, it would reveal itself over time, but your father never spoke of it."

I laughed at the idea of my father's having any working knowledge of the arcane world.

"*But then*," Locke continued, "strange things started happening around him. The death of your brother, Devon, in that building collapse, the damage to the burial site beneath your family home, the damage tonight in your great-great-grandfather's studio, and I thought to myself that perhaps your father wasn't the best person in the family to be asking questions to."

I shrugged and put on my best innocent face. "I know even less about my father and angels than you probably do," I replied.

Desmond Locke's eyes ran slowly over my face, no doubt looking for some hint of deception, but I didn't think he'd find one. Technically, I knew nothing of my father and an actual angel. Had Desmond Locke been asking specifically about a gargoyle, my face might have told a different story, but I simply stared back at the man.

"Really, now," he said. "I find it hard to believe that you, Alexandra—named for your great-great-grandfather—know nothing."

I held up a finger and smiled. "I didn't say I knew nothing."

"So . . . what *can* you tell me?"

I held my tongue. If one of the rules set upon Stanis centuries ago had been to keep his gargoyle form hidden from humanity, who was I to screw that up? It was impressive Stanis had managed to pull it off for all this time in a city of millions, with security cameras and iPhones.

At that point, I wasn't convinced that telling Desmond Locke or his *Libra Concordia* anything about the gargoyle was a smart idea. At least not on a first date.

Desmond Locke looked to Marshall, then to Rory, but as I suspected, neither of them was offering up anything either. He sighed.

"Very well," he said. "I can perhaps understand your reluctance. These are dark and important matters, not to be taken lightly. But think of this: Something destroyed your family's catacombs *and* your great-great-grandfather's studio. If you're as smart a girl as I think you to be, then you're probably smart enough to be scared. The *Libra Concordia* has ways to help you with that." He gestured to the caged-off area behind us. "We have the resources to help you, Alexandra, but you have to give me *something*."

"How can I trust you?" I asked. "You claim to be a man of God yet you pulled a gun on us. You also know about the arcane world. How can I believe you when you're a man of conflicting ideologies?"

He smiled across the desk at me. "You *can* be a man of God and believe in magic," he said. "Or, as your friend Marshall called it, a science we do not yet fully grasp. After all, who gave science to us *but* God?"

It made a sort of sense, and I wanted to believe him, especially if it meant he might be of some help in getting Stanis back.

"I need some time to think," I said. "I'm not the trusting sort."

"He could have already shot us," Rory whispered from behind me.

I spun around and glared at her over on the couch. "Not a compelling argument there, Ror."

"Perhaps this will help," Locke said, standing up. He walked to the edge of his office area and called out toward an area filled with other workers farther down the aisle. "Caleb!"

A figure rose from a shadowy corner of the offices farther along and stepped forward, heading down the aisle toward us. This Caleb stepped into a pool of light, revealing his muss of blond hair and long brown coat. They hadn't changed much since I had last seen him in my great-great-grandfather's guild hall.

The potion thief.

"You!" I shouted, only to get looks from the other people working around the office.

The strange man paused in the aisle, looking both sheepish and panicked at the same time. The hesitation lasted only for a second, but then he hurried down the aisle toward me, rolling his legs over the low wall and stepping into Locke's office space. Rory was on her feet in an instant, but Marshall was taking his time, not having actually seen the man that night.

Mr. Locke gave him a raised eyebrow. "You two know each other, Mr. Kennedy?"

"We've met," he shouted out before I could get an answer out. "Big fan of her great-grandfather's work."

He moved across the space quickly as he came to join us.

"Great-great-grandfather," I corrected.

"Yes, of course," he said, not missing a beat, laying his hands on my shoulders. "Great-great-grandfather. She and I met at the Metropolitan Museum of Art. We were both studying some of his statues there. So good to see you again."

Caleb Kennedy's eyes stayed with mine, locked, the smile on his face wide and forced, wavering slightly. His hands on my shoulders dug in hard, almost causing me to cry out, but I held it in, trying to read this man who—last time I had seen him—had knocked Rory unconscious.

Examining his face as best I could in our short reintroduction, I decided to play along. We were both of us in mixed company at the moment, and I doubted much could happen that was harmful this time, so I went along with whatever he was doing.

"Yes," I said. "Of course. I remember." I turned to my friends. "Rory, Marshall. This is . . ."

"Caleb," he said to them. The blond's face washed with relief, and he let go of my shoulders to vigorously shake hands with both my friends. Marshall, who had never seen him before, took Caleb's hand and shook first, but Rory only did so reluctantly, and when she did, there was a burning fire set deep in her eyes.

Caleb mouthed the word "sorry" to her, but it did nothing to change her expression, and he quickly dropped his hand away from her before stepping back toward Desmond Locke.

Locke eyed Caleb with a hint of suspicion, but the blond's face didn't falter. He simply stared at his boss, waiting.

"As a token of trust," Locke said, "I want you to help Miss Belarus here in one of the reference rooms with anything pertaining to her family."

Caleb's eyes went wide like those of a child. "Really?"

"You *can* handle that, can't you?"

"Absolutely," he said without hesitation, and turned. "Please follow me."

Rory, Marshall, and I fell in behind him, but Desmond Locke's words stopped us all.

"Just Miss Belarus," he said. "For now."

I looked over at him. "Why not all of us?" I asked.

Caleb stopped as well and turned back to Desmond Locke.

"The things we keep record of are precious to us," Locke said. "And since you're being a bit tight-lipped with me about your father's angel, Miss Belarus, I will do the same in return. As I said, this is a token of our trust, one that may turn into a mutually beneficial arrangement, but it is just that. *A token*. So for now, only Miss Belarus may have access to our records. If things go well, I promise your friends will be welcome in the future."

Rory shook her head and stepped up to Locke. "I'm not leaving Lexi alone with *him*," she said.

I laid a hand on her shoulder. "I'll be fine," I said, pulling her away from him, then lowered my voice. "Do you really think blondie's going to start trouble here?"

Rory didn't look convinced, but she relented and went to stand by Marshall.

Caleb turned and again started off down the main aisle of the converted church, and I followed him all the way to the back of it, leaving my friends and Desmond Locke behind us. I only hoped they would be safe with him.

Past the caged-off area to our right lay a series of doors, and Caleb headed for the one farthest back. I remained silent as we stepped in, and he shut the door behind us, which left the two of us alone in a stylish one-room book-lined library with a wide reading table at the center.

Locke's man smiled at me with such a level of smugness that I couldn't help but run to him and slam him up against the wall until I was pressing my forearm across his throat. "You want to tell me why you lied to Desmond Locke and his *Libra Concordia* about how we previously met?" I asked. "Or maybe why you attacked us?"

"I didn't mean to hurt anyone," he croaked out, already trying to struggle his way out from under my arm, but I wouldn't let up. He was probably stronger than me, but I was riled and pushed even harder as he tried to wrench my arm away from his throat.

"So that wasn't you who gave my good friend Rory a concussion, then?" I asked.

"Okay, fine, yes," he said. His hands slid between my arm and his throat, and he pried himself free with a mighty shove, forcing me back from him. He held his hands up in the air. "But I can explain!"

I walked away from him and leaned back on the reading table in the middle of the room, careful not to knock over one of the gorgeous green banker's lamps on it.

"This should be interesting," I said.

The man let out a long sigh and straightened his long brown coat while he collected himself. "I did break into your building," he said, "but that's not something I want the *Libra Concordia* to know."

"Oh no?"

He shook his head. "I'm not really part of them," he said. "I'm more of a freelancer. Yes, I do a lot of jobs here for them, but there's much I do on the side, some things I suspect the *Concordia* would *not* like to hear about. By the way, thank you for that save out there with Locke."

"Why wouldn't they like to hear about your other jobs?" I asked, ignoring his thanks. I wasn't quite sure whether or not I was going to regret that decision just yet.

Caleb paused, and I saw him struggling to find the right words.

"They would consider much of my life outside them a bit too proactive in the magic department," he said. "They're more of a watchdog group. They generally shy away from, you know, actually interacting with the arcane. Me? I'm much more of an . . . interacter."

"And Desmond Locke trusts *you*, a freelancer?"

Caleb held his hand out flat, moved it back and forth. "They trust me well enough," he said. "Locke and his people are not really fans of getting their hands dirty. So they hire freelancers when it comes to their more arcane or shady dealings."

"And breaking into my building *isn't* shady dealings?" I asked.

Caleb's face screwed up into a look of indecision. "It is, and it isn't," he said.

I folded my arms across my chest. "So tell me how breaking and entering both is and isn't shady."

Caleb walked past me to the other side of the table and settled himself into the large leather reading chair there. "It's all a matter of perspective, I suppose. Eight months ago, your family's lot on Saint Mark's was a pile of collapsed rubble, and before that it was a building no one had touched in decades. It was vacant. No one lived there, but there *was* something special to be had at that location for someone in my line of work."

"And what exactly *is* your line of work?" I asked.

He pulled open his coat, revealing tubes and vials lining it in a well-stitched array up and down both sides.

"Alchemy," he said.

Hearing the word actually gave me pause.

Many of the roots of Alexander's Spellmasonry were in alchemy. Despite Caleb's having been an intruder in my home, I couldn't help but soften a bit, focusing on the fact that I was dealing with a fellow practitioner of my solo endeavors in an arcane art. I couldn't help but smile at that.

"Is there a secret handshake I need to know?" I asked.

He smiled back.

"We could make one up, I suppose," he said, "but as far as I know? No." He closed his coat and leaned forward. "So here I am, a year ago, an alchemist who discovers an unguarded, unattended stash of one of the great lost alchemical properties in the world. Kimiya. Do you know what a find that was to an alchemist? It changed everything as far as my profit margin was concerned. It's a universal conductor in so much of a specific line of magic. Finding that stash of it on Saint Mark's made a lot of my freelance work child's play comparatively. Potent stuff, that."

"And in *limited* supply," I remind him. And *mine*, I thought to myself.

"And in limited supply," he repeated with a nod, leaning back in the chair. He crossed his hands over each other. "And here we are."

That smug look was back on his face, only this time I was more curious than angry. "So what now?" I asked.

Caleb shrugged. "Well, you heard Desmond Locke," he said. "He wants us to work together. He and the *Libra Concordia* are concerned with this 'angel' that watches over your family, but *we* both know that's no angel."

"It isn't?" I replied, not wanting to give anything up too willingly.

The man shook his head. "I've seen things in this city," he said. "I've seen your golem, your winged stone man. When your building collapsed on Saint Mark's months ago—cutting me off from my supply, by the way—I watched that site with a very vested curiosity for some time. I've seen you and your friends there, including that flying automaton of yours. Yes, I've seen him, too."

My heart jumped. He'd seen Stanis? I tried to keep my face reactionless. He stared at me in silence, and all I could do was meet his eyes, not talking. I still didn't trust this stranger. I already felt violated enough that we had been spied on.

When I offered him nothing, he sat up and spoke once more. "Look, I don't care about whatever that golem is to you," he said. "Frankly, I was glad he was around to help you clear all that rubble, which made it possible for me to once again access the Kimiya kept in that impervious room of yours. But I'm imagining right about now you and I share a very similar problem, alchemically speaking."

"Which is . . . ?"

"I haven't been able to figure out how to make Kimiya," he said. "And I bet you haven't, either. The *Concordia* has some notes on Alexander Belarus, but they are speculative, incomplete . . . They don't provide a recipe or the ingredients I need to create that elixir. I've thought about trying to reverse engineer it, but there are too many unknowns. Your great-great-grandfather has kept this secret well, Alexandra."

"The man loved him some puzzles," I said, a pained smile coming to my lips as I recalled the shattered statues and boxes back in the art studio.

"Between the two of us, I sense potential for some real genius happening," he said. "I've got access to a lot of information here at the *Concordia*, and I'm sure you've got some family knowledge, right? I can feed Locke some dead ends looking for this angel of his, and the two of us can find your great-great-grandfather's secret. Think about it. We won't have to rely on what little Kimiya is left in Alexander's legacy. I wasn't lying when I said I was a big fan of his work."

Part of Caleb's needs were the same as mine. I *was* going to need more Kimiya; Rory, Marshall, and I were going to need it if we were ever going to push through the arcane creative wall of creating other large-form animated statues. All we had was Bricksley to stand against Kejetan and the Servants of Ruthenia. Spirited though he was, I didn't think he was going to cut it as the "army" Stanis had instructed me to prepare in his time-buying absence. Trusting an admitted thief went against my grain, but Caleb might prove helpful both in figuring out how to produce Kimiya and in using it to move past our army of one.

"No more breaking and entering?" I asked.

Caleb shook his head. "Consider your home off-limits," he said, crossing his heart. "Besides, I'm pretty well stocked up right now."

The smile faltered on my face. "Don't remind me," I said.

He leaned over the table, lowering his voice. "And it's probably best if we don't let Desmond in on *any* part of this plan of ours."

I looked to the door, making sure it was still closed. "I would prefer he not know anything about our family's 'angel,'" I said. "For now, anyway."

"Locke is going to want *something* from you," Caleb said. "There ain't no such thing as a free lunch."

I nodded, conceding the point. "I figured that out when he pulled the gun on me earlier tonight," I said. "But there's some bones I can throw him, some leads in our family's private archives about actual angel statues that Alexander carved in Manhattan. That should keep him misdirected for a bit."

It felt strange choosing to trust the guy who had broken into my great-great-grandfather's guild hall. Still, it beat trusting the man who had brought me to this church at gunpoint.

Caleb was the first active practitioner of any kind of alchemy that I had met, and that went further in the trust department than a secret organization working clandestinely within the confines of organized religion to gather magic and keep it on a shelf.

"Let's get to work," I said. "Do you keep an alchemy lab here?"

Caleb rose and went to the door, checking to see if anyone was around. When he seemed confident we were alone, he turned back to me. "We can't set up here," he whispered. "They frown on actual magic use on the premises."

"So you don't you have a lab for all this?"

"I *had* a lab," he said, a bit testily, I thought. "But somebody made the building it was in collapse."

I thought about calling him a squatter in my family's building but decided to let it slide. Chastising could wait. We needed a place to set up, and although I trusted him more than I did Desmond Locke, I did not trust him enough that I wanted him back in my home again.

"Come with me," I said, heading over to him for the door. "I think I know a place."

Caleb pulled the door open with a low, gentlemanly bow. "After you, m'lady," he said.

I couldn't help but smile at that, continuing out into the church proper.

"Will it be safe?" Caleb asked, falling in step at my side.

"Based on my personal lack of prowess?" I said. "Probably not, but we can worry about that later. We've got enough to worry about *now.*"

"Why?" he asked. "What do we have to worry about now?"

"Right now?" I said, my mind still trying to absorb the totality of the evening's events so far. "Right now I need to convince Marshall that he won't need to take out an extra fire-insurance policy to cover us."

"Hope you're convincing," Caleb said.

"Hopefully, I can fake it."

Eleven

———— ☾ ————

Stanis

Days had passed within the darkness of the freighter. There were two voices in my head—my own suppressed true voice and what I had come to call the new dominant one. This new voice tried to discover what game my true mind was playing, but when it could not, its will to dominate me quieted to a steady truce with my true voice.

Despite the downpour of rain tonight, my true self even found a bit of pleasure in the freeing act of flight while the voice that dominated my mind saw it only as a means of accomplishing the tasks set upon me by the Servants of Ruthenia.

I flew over Manhattan in the singular pursuit of Kejetan's task at hand. The humans down below seemed to mind the falling rain, always running from it or covering their bodies against it, but I welcomed it.

Coolness overwhelmed my senses as I flew higher and higher through the night sky, the air and rain refreshing me in a way my mind could not. I was far too busy walling up the two sides of my thoughts, keeping the dominant voice in my head away from my first contact with Alexandra after long months away.

Given the control the new voice had in my head, I dared not let it put me back in proximity to her. It had been struggle enough that first meeting to bend the new rules set upon me. Who knew what harm might come to her if we should meet again?

Instead, I flew on in search of Kejetan's other objectives. The large park at the center of Manhattan spread out before me, and along its west side, I found what I needed on one of the buildings below. Spreading my wings as wide as they could go, I dove toward my target.

The skyline of Manhattan was *not* where one expected to find the depiction of an epic battle with a sea creature, but that was the stone tableau I found atop this particular building.

Swirls of tentacles rose from an enormous, carved monster that served as a base for my target. Perched on one of its thick tentacles was a *grotesque* similar to me, locked in battle with two of the lesser tentacles before it, its clawed hands midswing. As I closed with the statue, I could see the craftsmanship of the *grotesque* itself, strikingly similar to my own though its facial features were more demonic than mine.

I landed behind this familiar figure and pulled up on it from beneath the *grotesque*'s arms, testing the stone. Though it bore the familiar hand of my maker and was therefore strong, I needed to know I would not destroy it in the process of removing it. Finding the statue itself solid, I rocked the figure back and forth on top of the tentacle beneath it, praying it would come free with little damage.

The stone feet of the creature came free from their base with a loud crumble of stone, but even after I was done, the sound continued to grow, my feet slipping as the creature below me shifted into living stone.

The tentacles the *grotesque* had been combating groaned and flaked away bits of stone as they came alive—flaring up and whipping toward me. Shielding my body from their impact, I pulled my wings in close, but the tentacles were quicker and caught my legs and arms, coiling hard around them. My grip slipped from the slick wetness of the *grotesque* as I was pulled into the air away from it, my muscles screaming out as the tentacles stretched me to the extent of my reach.

Had I thought these tasks would be easy? No. These creatures were built by my maker's hands, to be sure. A certain complexity filled them, as it did me. Had I been human, my body would surely have been torn into separate pieces already. Had Alexander meant to protect this *grotesque* against the strength of another of its kind? I did not think so, hoping that, at best, the tentacled creature was meant to restrain nothing more powerful than a human.

I did not wish to harm it, but my body was giving out. I worked my wings—already spread wide—using the extra power they generated to pull me farther up and away from the monster. As I rose, I contracted my arms toward my body, using all my power. The stone tentacles wrapped around them held at first but then gave way to my superior strength and crumbled away in large, broken chunks.

Arms free, I raised my claws, slicing down hard on the tentacles still bound around my legs. I tore through them with ease, and they fell away, writhing on the rooftop; but more were rising to take their place.

I found it impossible to take further to the air, my wings failing to keep me in the sky, and I dropped, barely able to control my fall back onto the roof. I had my wings to slow my descent, but I still came down hard, driving one of my knees and one clawed foot forcibly into the stone below.

The roof shifted beneath me, and I leapt up as it gave way, caving into the building itself. Landing, I centered myself for battle and stood ready, minding the remaining tentacles whipping back and forth all around me. I needed to reduce their number.

Working my way across the rain-covered roof in a focused pattern, I let my claws loose on the tentacles, striking swiftly before moving along in haste. The pieces fell away, and the tentacles grew shorter and shorter as I went. The monster stilled, and what remained of its tentacles transformed once more to inert stone.

I moved for my hard-won prize—the *grotesque*. My claws stood at the ready should it also spring to life. Closing in on it swiftly, I wrapped my arms around it, ready for a struggle, but I was met by nothing more than an inert stone figure.

"Hey!" a voice called out from somewhere behind me. I turned, fearing that I had broken one of Alexander's old rules—that I remain hidden from humanity. Even though I was no longer bound to them, they still pulled at me after all this time. But looking around, there was no one else on the roof.

"Hey!" the voice called out again, and this time I homed in on where it came from—the hole in the roof. "Is anyone hurt up there?"

A beam of light shone up through the hole, catching the fall of rain in a glimmering cone. Despite the old rules no longer governing me, my need to leave before discovery took over.

I turned back to the *grotesque*, securing my arms around its chest. My wings strained hard as I forced them into action, pressing their limits in my effort to lift the extra weight. Burdened as I was, I rose into the night with part of my task complete, heading high over Central Park and away from Manhattan and out to sea.

I came down hard on the deck of the ship, using my claws to grab at the wet metal beneath my feet and steadying myself as I lowered the *grotesque*. It rang out with a dull echo, lost to the sounds of the heavy storm and waves of the ocean.

Kejetan, Devon, and the blond human met me on the deck, the one who had bound me immediately securing the new *grotesque* to the deck with chains.

His hair, once a spiked muss, lay plastered to his head, but he did not seem to mind working in the rain, unlike the other humans on board, who had made themselves scarce. They might be the Servants of Ruthenia, but only this lone human dared work on the open deck, my father watching.

When the man was done, he stepped away, and Devon walked over and gave me a rough slap on my shoulder.

"Good," Devon said. "Our dog can fetch."

I stood there, a silent sentinel. My true voice urged me to strike him for such an insult, but the new one kept me from doing so.

Kejetan circled the figure I had brought him. Even in his jagged form, I could sense an air of approval coming from him.

"Excellent," he said, further confirming my suspicion. "This will do." Halfway around the *grotesque*, he caught my eyes and stopped, shifting his focus to me. "And?"

"And what?" I asked back, unsure.

Kejetan stepped around the statue, heading for me, his face going dark. "What are you still doing here?"

"Where should I take myself?" I asked. "Back to the chains in your hold?"

We were face-to-face by then, the dark pits of his eyes meeting mine. "Are you mocking me?"

"I do not understand," I said.

Kejetan grabbed my shoulders and pressed me across the ship's deck before shoving me through the railings of the ship, snapping them like thin branches. My wings fought to take the air, but before I could, my father's hand closed hard around my throat, holding me in place out over the water.

Deep within me, my voice spoke up. It called out for me to fight back, but the dominant voice held it back.

"I ask you again," he said, the jagged rocks of his hand digging into the stone of my throat. "Are you mocking me? Where are the *rest*?"

I said nothing, still unsure of what he meant or what I was meant to say.

We stared at each other until the blond human approached us at the edge of the ship. He reached up and put his hands on Kejetan's arm.

"Easy, easy," he said, trying to press down on it, but there was no way the human could move him. "He's not doing *anything*. It's . . . it's my fault."

Kejetan turned to him, his eyes first going to the human's hands, which the man removed in an instant.

"Your fault?" Devon called out. "How?"

The man backed away from both the stone men, hands raised. "This isn't easy, you know? I'm forcing a new will upon the golem. His previous one is still in there, and it makes it harder to get him to do my bidding."

"But that is what we are paying you for," Devon argued.

"This isn't an exact science," the man said. "If it were, you'd be able to go and hire someone on every corner who can do this, but you *still* wouldn't find anyone better than me. I guarantee you that. I just need time to tweak how we handle your gargoyle here."

The human waved for Kejetan to pull me back onto the deck of the ship, which he did before dropping me. I slumped to the cold, wet metal.

"Fix him," he said, dismissive.

The human waited for me to stand before speaking directly to me. "Why did you only bring one?"

"Because that was the task set upon me," I said.

"Shit," the human said.

"What is it?" Devon asked.

The human sighed. "It's what I feared," he said. "I wasn't specific enough." He looked up into my eyes. "Do you understand what we're doing here?"

"You wanted a statue," I said.

"But *why*?"

"For Kejetan to inhabit."

"Correct," my father said, "but what about the rest of my people? The Servants of Ruthenia have long held their place at my side with the promise of a new form. We need more than just one. Do you understand?"

"Yes," I said, but my true self did not wish to do such a thing. I spread my wings.

"Hold on," the human said, undoing the chain around the other *grotesque*. "Hold on. Take this statue with you."

"Why?" Kejetan asked.

"Because I can't do what I need to do out here at sea,"

the human said. "This needs to be grounded to its element, set up on land. Find a discreet location that can hold the other gargoyle statues. Gather as many as you can."

"I know of a place suited for this," I said, the true voice speaking up from within, and the dominant one let it.

I grabbed the statue and once more forced myself into the night sky, the heft of it feeling much greater than before, but I did as I was told and set my sights on the far-off shore of Manhattan.

Twelve

☾

Alexandra

It took almost a week to convince Marshall to let me borrow the back room of his store for a meeting with Caleb. In the meantime, I kept feeding a steady diet of misdirection to Desmond Locke and his *Libra Concordia*. He seemed happy to see many of the private notes on the carved angels in Alexander's repertoire, but nothing I gave him had a thing to do with the Spellmasonry that went into making Stanis.

The rest of that week was spent focusing on two things: poring through the records on Alexander Belarus at the *Libra Concordia* and spending some alone time continuing to craft the gargoyle form I had started in the destroyed studio back at the Belarus Building.

The former left me with more questions about the Spellmasons, and the latter helped calm my mind and made me feel like I was actually making *some* kind of progress. Now, here in Marshall's store, it was time to see if any of the research Caleb and I had been doing was going to pay off.

The back room of Roll for Initiative was just as strange as it should be, stranger still with Marshall, Rory, and two alchemists in it. The surrounding shelves were full of games

I had never heard of, rows of tiny, painted figurines, and an odd assortment of nerd-world stuff that I thought maybe I had seen on one or another of Marshall's rotating array of geek shirts.

As odd as all that was, it still felt more odd that I had invited the man who had stolen from me and nearly head-traumaed Rory in the process to be there. She, at least, seemed to be handling it civilly enough. Her pole arm was put away, broken down into its component pieces in the art tube across her back, but more than anything I still worried about the look of mistrust in her eyes toward my fellow alchemist. I only hoped the pole arm stayed put away.

Marshall stood next to her, nervously wringing his hands together, while Caleb and I both watched with mutual concern.

"You sure this isn't a problem?" Caleb asked, looking from Marshall back to me.

"Don't mind Marshall," I said. "He's just worried about his toys."

Marshall looked like I had just slapped him—but I met his look with a steady gaze, and the offended wind went out of his sails.

"Just try not to destroy anything or set my store on fire," he said quietly.

"Relax," Caleb said, slapping him on the shoulder reassuringly. His eyes sparkled with a charm and confidence that none of us seemed to find fully convincing. The alchemist pulled a few glass vials from within his long brown coat, holding them up to the light, checking the colors within. "This is a science . . . sort of. And it's all in control. Mostly."

Marshall's face when white, and Rory clapped her roommate on the other shoulder. "Comforting, right, pal?" she asked.

"We need to test the version of Kimiya Caleb reverse engineered on his own," I said. "This is only going to be a small-scale experiment, okay? Just to see if it works so we have *some* jumping-in point if we're going to re-create it."

"And you're sure it's not explosive?" Marshall asked, still looking unconvinced.

"It's just my home brew," Caleb said. "My prototype version of the ever-dwindling concoction that Alexander Belarus mastered centuries ago."

"Your store's going to be fine," I said. "We're just going to test his version to snap an arcane connection all Spell-mason like. It's not explosive."

"*Probably* not," Caleb added. "Never say never."

I shot him a look but resisted the urge to bark at him. If he was half as punchy as I was from poring over the notes in the *Libra Concordia*, it was best to let it lie.

Marshall turned to me, grabbed my arm, and dragged me out through the heavy curtain that blocked the door into the customer side of the store. "You *are* taking responsibility for him, right?"

"He's not a pet," I said, easily pulling free from his nervous grasp.

"Just say it, then," he said. "If only to give me a little reassurance. Humor me."

"Fine," I said. "Caleb breaks it, I buy it. Fair enough?"

Marshall's face calmed a bit, but there was still worry in his eyes. "You couldn't do this at either one of your alchemy labs?" he asked.

I shook my head. "I've got the same trust issues that you and Rory both do," I said. "I didn't want us working at the *Libra Concordia*. Not the way Desmond Locke is pursuing his interest in Stanis. And until I have the feeling that I can trust this Caleb, I don't want him near either of my great-great-grandfather's workspaces."

Marshall sighed and gave a glance toward the small crowd gathered at the front of the store. "I just don't want any damage while I'm trying to run our Magic: The Gathering tournament."

I nodded even though I had zero idea what the last part of his sentence meant. From the group of people chattering away at the front of the store, it apparently involved consuming bucketloads of soda and a variety of snack foods while arranging colorful playing cards on tables.

"You go have fun," I said, pushing him off toward his people. "Go. Mingle. Get your nerd on."

Marshall started to protest just as Rory poked her head out of the back room through the curtain.

"Everything okay out here?" she asked.

"Do me a favor," I said, grabbing her arm and pulling her out from behind the curtain. "Go up front with Marshall, will you? Make sure he enjoys himself."

Rory shook her head and looked toward the back room. "And leave you alone with the guy who nearly gave me a concussion?" she said. "No way. What if *he* concusses *you*? I won't have you getting concussed on my watch."

"I'll be fine with Caleb Kennedy," I said, mustering as convincing a tone as I could. "I can handle myself."

Both of my friends met me with blank stares and raised eyebrows.

"Okay, fine, *sometimes* I can handle myself." I lowered my voice and pulled the two of them farther away from the curtain. "Listen. I *need* to work with this guy. He knows things I don't about Alexander and the arcane, and I *have* to access that knowledge. I'll be safe. Besides, do you really think he's going to start something here?"

"Yeah," they said in unison, which I couldn't help laughing at.

"I'll be fine," I said. "At the tiniest hint of trouble, I'll scream. All right?"

Marshall still didn't look entirely convinced, but Rory grabbed him by the shoulder and spun him toward the front of the store.

"Fine," she said, pushing him along. "I can hear the stubborn in your voice about this. Come on, Marsh. We'll wait for her scream while you play with your little nerdlings. We'll hear her, don't worry. I know she's good at it ever since our sixth-grade trip to Six Flags."

"Thank you, Rory," I said, singsonging, relaxing a bit as

relief filled me. "Yes, I can still scream, even if it's not motivated by roller-coaster panic. And for your information, I'm *much* better about heights now, thanks to our winged friend."

"Yeah, yeah," she called out over her shoulder, as Marshall finally gave in and walked with her on his own toward the crowd at the front of the store. "Hopefully, some of what you learn from blondie there will help you make our winged friend actually *friendly* again."

I hope so, too, I thought to myself, as they walked away.

The throng of alpha geek males and a few of the females turned their heads to check out Rory as she came down the center aisle of the store toward them. I turned away, going back through the curtain into the storeroom once more.

Caleb was squatting now by a long, low coffee table surrounded by an assortment of mismatched couches and chairs. A miniature stone maze lay on the table, and Caleb lifted a tiny metal figure out of it and rolled it around the palm of his hand. At my approach, he stood and turned to me.

"Sorry about that," I said. "I thought we might concentrate better if Rory and Marshall weren't watching over my shoulder."

His face shifted, his eyes narrowing at me with what I thought looked like an annoyed suspicion.

"What?" I asked.

Caleb stepped past me and ran his hand over the curtain across the doorway. "This *is* cloth, you know," he said, talking to me like I was a child. "And given its physical properties, it doesn't really block out sound all that well. I heard just about, oh, *everything.*"

I quickly went over what my friends and I had been discussing on the other side of it, and my face went crimson. After all, every last word *had* been about him.

"My friends are just concerned," I explained, trying not to sound overly defensive. "You *did* give Rory a good reason to be." I rubbed the spot on my head where Rory had hit the floor after his sleeping-dust trick.

Caleb started to protest, but his face fell into a crooked smile instead.

"I can't argue that," he said, then gave a nervous look around the back room. "Let's get to work shall, we? So . . . you want to regain control of your gargoyle, yes? Where do you want to start?"

"We'll get to that soon enough," I said, gesturing for him to slow down, "but first, I have some questions." My eyes met his, my own steady and unwavering.

How much control Desmond Locke did or didn't have over him remained to be seen, but I sure as hell wasn't going to be offering up too much on Stanis right out of the gate. And I knew that someone as clever as Caleb was wasn't going to be too willing to just hand over certain aspects of his arcane knowledge, but if we were going to establish any kind of trust, I needed him first to cooperate with the tone I was trying to set between us.

Uncertainty filled Caleb's face for a moment, but then he gave a reluctant nod. "Sure," he said. "Shoot. Although I do charge by the hour."

I stared at him, my eyes darkening. "Really, now?"

Nervous laughter escaped his lips, and he held up his hands in surrender. "Just a little freelancer humor," he said. "Consider this round a freebie."

His confidence and flip manner made me want to shake him, but I reined it in. I needed knowledge, and if I had to endure a little attitude in the process, so be it.

"So how *did* you come to know about my great-great-grandfather?" I asked, forcing myself back to the business at hand.

Caleb shifted from foot to foot as he thought for a moment before answering.

"I didn't really *know* about him," he said, "but this city is full of dark and mystical rumors. The legend of Alexander Belarus just turned out to be one of them." He looked down at his feet, his face reddening. "But once I was on the trail, I might have gone a bit stalkery concerning him."

"Way to keep it creepy," I said. "Define 'stalkery.'"

"I *might* have bartered and traded a few of my alchemical mixes for more and more of those tales," he said, "ones further involving Alexander. And they didn't come cheap, either. Talk of the lost secrets of the Spellmasons has always been a bit of a Holy Grail out there."

I turned to him, unable to hide the surprise on my face. "Wait," I said. "I thought what my great-great-grandfather did was a lost and secret art. There are people who *talk* of Spellmasonry?"

Caleb nodded. "Not just people," he said. "Whole arcane communities."

"Jesus," I said, sitting along the edge of one of the upright tables. "There's a whole community?"

Caleb laughed and looked at me with sincere curiosity on his face. "You *really* don't know, do you?" he asked. "Alexandra, there's a whole magical world out there. Just because Alexander Belarus chose to hide away the arcane art he knew doesn't mean there wasn't a world out there looking for them. The secrets that you hold are just the tip of a very large iceberg."

"Really?" My mind reeled at the idea. With the secrets at my family's disposal, I had always thought of this knowledge as *ours*, and all of a sudden to hear that there was a much larger world that sought those out . . .

"Really," he said. "I told you I was a freelancer, didn't I? That implies there's other magic out there to be had. Do you think I could make an arcane living without a client base? Much of arcana's written off by your average nonmagical person as quackery or old wives' tales, but arcana is a much bigger world out there than you know. And for me, it definitely pays the rent."

"Speaking of rent . . . where *do* you live?" I asked, curiosity getting the better of me. "Clearly you know where *I* live, breaking and entering aside."

Caleb held his hands up again, this time sounding a bit more defensive. "Baby steps, Miss Belarus, baby steps."

I backed down, letting a short silence fall between us as

Caleb placed the tiny figure back on the table before he
stepped away from it.

"There are lots of books on alchemy," Caleb continued,
taking off his coat. He turned it inside out before hanging
it on the back of one of the chairs around the table. The
lining was stuffed with sewn-in bandoliers that held all sorts
of vials, tubes, and metal flasks. I had a newfound respect
for the man, if only for his sewing and organizational skills.
He set about picking through the contents. "Not that there's
any all-encompassing tome written on alchemy, mind you."

"Why not?" I asked. "Surely, there's been research. My
family has hundreds of volumes dedicated to everything my
great-great-grandfather ever learned."

He stopped picking through the collection and looked up
at me, his face curious. "More than the *Libra Concordia* has?"

"It's all secure, don't worry," I said, in hindsight fearing
I might have offered up too much in mentioning it. "If you
know of Alexander's practices, it's heavily coded and cross-
referenced, so it's not like anyone could just read it and know
everything. Frankly, it's as much a pain in the ass as it is a
boon."

Caleb's grin went wide. "I'd like to see this boon."

It was my turn to hold my hands up. "Baby steps there,
Caleb. To borrow your words."

"As you wish," he said, and turned back to his coat, picking through it.

As you wish. The words Stanis always used when put to
task. I nearly fell over hearing the phrase. The sting of them
was as fresh as if Stanis himself—the kind one I knew,
anyway—had uttered them. As I tried to process my emotional reaction to them, I stayed silent and simply watched
Caleb as he continued selecting several of the items from
his coat, mixing them.

"Much of the magical world operates a bit differently
from Alexander's version of it," he said.

"How so?" I asked.

"Your great-great-grandfather was organized in way that

most magic I deal with isn't," he said. "He wrote it all down
in books, kept a library. He was smart enough to code them,
to hide that powerful information away. But the rest of
arcane knowledge isn't conveniently gathered together
like that."

"Why not?" I asked. "If it's a science, as you've said, why
wouldn't it be accumulated in the same manner?"

Caleb shrugged. "It's a science to a point," he said. "It's
still arcana, after all, and the people who practice it get
freaky proprietary over their secrets."

"What about all that stuff the *Libra Concordia* has gathered? That's more than enough to fill a library. It's enough
to fill that church downtown, at least."

Caleb shook his head. "The information caged off there
looks like a lot, yes," he said. "But it's nothing comprehen-
sive. All bits and pieces, really, accumulated over centuries,
only a fraction of the secret knowledge of the unknown
world. It's an impressive collection, sure, but consider the
mission of the *Libra Concordia*. They're trying to keep that
knowledge secret from the world. It's not like they have
enough knowledge to do anything with it. Unless, say, there
was an industrious freelancer willing to piece it all together
for themselves."

"And here I thought you were going to that church just
to do some community service for the Lord," I said.

Caleb gave me a get-real look, then set back to mixing
the contents of his vials. "There's a reason the magical world
wants to stay hidden, Alexandra," he said, "and it's done a
fair job of it, if you ask me. Think about it. It took the *Libra
Concordia* centuries to accumulate the small amount of
knowledge they *do* have, and that's only a tiny percentage
from around the *planet*."

"You've given this a lot of thought," I said, impressed.
"I've spent most of my time just trying to wrap my mind
around my family's legacy, which to you is just a small piece
of a grander puzzle, isn't it?"

Caleb nodded.

"Before I knew about the *Libra Concordia*," he said, "I

studied up on what I could find out about your great-great-grandfather, his work back in the old country.

"Several centuries ago, the world was a much bigger place, and it was easier to be hidden away in it. Scattered towns and villages, kingdoms that only talked to each other at wartime. And arcana was hidden *then* because religious zealotry would have condemned it. But reputations could be earned over time, especially if those arcane powers were put to good use for the *sake* of a village and its safety. Alexander Belarus was such a figure, and, yes, it did indeed earn him a reputation."

"Sadly, it also earned him the attention of a local lord mad for power," I said. "Kejetan the Accursed."

"Did it, now?" Caleb asked, a surprised smile on his face. "I hadn't read of that actual name."

I nodded.

"And *Accursed*?" he continued, his smile widening. He gave a pleasant laugh. "I mean, with a title like that, I guess you have to go into the mad lord business, right?"

"Don't be so flip," I said, anger suddenly rising in me. "Enslaving my great-great-grandfather ended up costing the lord his only son. Stanis is all that remains of him, and he is *not* cut from the same cloth as his father, believe me." I calmed myself for a moment before pointing to his hands. "Maybe we should get back to work."

"Oh, right," he said, and went back to the vials in his hands, mixing a drop here to a drop there, and every so often holding it up to the light once again to check its color.

Marshall had reorganized since last I had been here. When I couldn't find what I was looking for, I searched around the rest of the back room, checking shelf after shelf of painted miniature figures. Most looked to be about an inch or two high, either plastic or metal, but along one section of wall I finally found several of the troll-like creatures I had spied a while back that seemed to actually be carved from stone. I pulled one down.

"Only at a hard-core game store can you find everything for your wizarding and witching ways," I said.

Caleb resealed all but one of the vials before returning the rest to their slots inside his coat on the chair. He pulled another vial from the bandolier there, holding it out in front of me.

"Recognize it?" he asked.

Seeing the dark red liquid swirling around in the clear plastic tube, I raised my eyebrows and gave a tight-lipped smile. "Of course I do," I said. "I should, anyway. It probably came from my family's private stock."

"Kimiya," he said. "But no, you are incorrect. This isn't stolen. This is my attempt at the reverse-engineered home brew." He held up the other mixture. "And this—this is a bit of a transformative binding solution. Not all that much by itself, but . . ."

He pulled the stopper from the Kimiya, tipped it to the other vial, and let a single drop from it fall into the other. Caleb stoppered it back up, slipped it into his coat, then swirled the new mixture in the remaining vial. He held his hand out to me, and I passed the stone troll over to him.

Caleb laid the tiny stone monster on the empty chair his coat hung over and poured the concoction over the figure until it was saturated, the ritual beginning to look a bit like what I had gone through in creating Bricksley.

"I believe I know this part," I said, picking up the figure and lowering it into the maze spread out on Marshall's gaming table.

I raised my hand and stared down my arm at the wet figure standing there among the walls of what looked to be a fairly realistic miniature dungeon. I had no idea if sighting the figure between the pointer and pinky finger of my raised hand actually helped, but at the very least it gave me a focal point as I reached out with my will for control of the figure.

The connection snapped to—like holding the object in an invisible version of my hand—and I tried to will it to move through the maze on the table.

The tiny figure shot forward, slamming into the dungeon walls, knocking them so hard that one section fell from the table, and another flew into the air across the room before hitting the wall. The alchemical mix threw great power into even the simplest of my actions, the figure responding to the smallest amount of pressure I put on it, making it hard to use finesse in managing my control over it.

I forced the troll to stop near one of the metal figures in the maze, a short, bearded character with a stocky build carrying what looked like a giant hammer. A dwarf. I had to see if I could brew a little combat there.

My creature lifted its arms high over its head to smash the other one, and I brought them down on it. Rather than simply knocking the bearded figure over, my troll crushed the metal of it down into the faux stone floor of the maze, but the force of my will didn't end there. The sharp crack of wood came from beneath the dungeon. The coffee table split in two, the figures and stone maze collapsing in on themselves as its contents slid to the floor at the center of the break.

"Shit," I said, losing total control of the little figure, and it rampaged off through the rubble, crashing and smashing its way through the pile.

"I got this," Caleb said, sliding another vial from the coat. He dropped to his knees and held it over the still-swinging troll before pouring the contents onto it, then drank from the vial himself. His face drew up in concentration as he extended his hand out in front of the tiny stone troll. It continued on along its violent path, but it slowed as the stone of it seized up, toppling over inert into his palm.

Caleb got up off his knees, his eyes staying on the figure, and presented it to me.

I marveled at it. "You've got control of it now?"

"For the moment," he said.

I reached for the figure, but before I could take it from Caleb, its form began to shake and twist in his hand. It exploded as I was pulling my hand back from it, bits of stone shooting against my knuckles, but thankfully not breaking the skin.

Caleb clutched his hand with his other one.

"You said you had control of it!" I said, prying his fingers open to look at the damage. Luckily, Caleb had pulled away in time, and his hand remained in one piece.

"Controlling things are a bit more of a Spellmason thing than alchemy," he said.

I looked up at him. "What do you mean?"

Caleb pulled his hands away, dusting them off against each other. "With alchemy, I can affect the world by transforming things on an arcane level," he said, "but they're all momentary modifications."

"Like when you were turned to stone in my great-great-grandfather's guild hall," I offered.

"Exactly," he said. "Or I can transform other materials, but it's nothing more than chemicals, magic, and science. And much of it isn't permanent. I don't make or control things. But from what little I've been able to read from the notes the *Libra Concordia* have found from Alexander, I have been able to try my hand at what you'd probably call a rough version of Spellmasonry."

"That's still pretty impressive," I said. "I mean, given my resources and an entire library of books, the only stable creature I've been able to make is a glorified brick. You're a natural."

Caleb shook his head.

"I don't think so," he said. "I have a real handle on mixing and alchemy, but this? I don't have the finesse for it. It's like the stone is constantly fighting me with a will of its own."

"I know, right?" I exclaimed, way more excited than I expected myself to be finally talking shop with someone. "It happens to me *all* the time."

"If I had to guess," Caleb said, "Spellmasonry seems to be more of a contest of will over matter more so than the recipes and formulas of the magic-in-a-bottle of alchemy. It's why I have trouble dealing with the will of the stone."

I nodded. "I don't think it's a will all its own, though."

"No?"

I pulled out my notebook, flipping through to a section of research I'd been compiling.

"I've been having the worst time getting anything I try to control to stay living, anything that's larger than a brick, anyway. I can't seem to fill my creations with my will, and they stop working. There's a suggestion in Alexander's notes that there are lingering spirits in this world that want a body to occupy, and they don't care *what* form it is in. Again, my one success with it is brick-sized, so it's not like I'm a master of anything."

"You're one up on me," he said. "I haven't tried animating much of anything, just because the few times I have, it's been such a struggle to keep control, and I'm only dealing with a finite amount of time that I can keep it going before one of my concoctions run out. Besides, if it *did* actually work in any sustained way, I'm afraid of what might happen. Like if I left a construct active with something else 'steering the ship,' you know?"

I smiled, a wave of relief filling me just hearing I wasn't alone in my own struggles with this. "I *absolutely* know."

"Probably why I stick to alchemy," he said with a grim smile, looking down at the broken table between us.

The curtain across the door leading into the store flew open, and Marshall stormed into the back room. His eyes went immediately to the two pieces of the caved-in table on the floor, and he shook his head.

"I thought I heard a crash, followed by an explosion," he said, dropping to the ground by what remained of his gaming table. He scooped up tiny pieces of wall and figures from the pile there. "What the hell? Do you know how long it took me to build that dungeon?"

I gave a pained smile. "Sorry, Marsh."

Rory came through the curtain next and saw Marshall kneeling there. She turned to Caleb and me, her face annoyed, and she started a slow, measured clap.

"That didn't take long," she said. "Good thing I had bet on chaos ensuing in under half an hour."

"Things just . . . got out of control."

Caleb laughed. "You can say that again. So much for my reverse engineering of the Kimiya. If I had used it on myself, maybe I would have exploded, too."

"It's progress," I said.

"We'll figure it out," he said.

"Not just that," I said. "I've still got the issue of how to make and control an army of stone men to deal with Kejetan."

"We'll figure that out, too," he said, taking my hands in his, giving them a comforting squeeze. "Together."

It felt terribly reassuring coming from him. I wanted to believe him and was slowly convincing myself of it when Marshall *ahem*ed loudly next to us.

I turned to him. "I'm really sorry," I said, snapping out of my moment of hopefulness, once more taking in the destruction Caleb and I had caused. "I'll cover the damage."

"I'll hold you to it," he said, looking up at me, upset. "That was our deal, remember? Not even twenty minutes old! The ink would still be wet!" His eyes fell back to the pile in front of him and ran his hand along the wood sticking out from beneath the maze and figures.

"I said I'll cover it," I repeated.

"That's not the point," he said, snapping. "This was my *original* gaming table. I've had it since I was seven. My precious."

"I'm sorry," I said, but when no answer came from Marshall, I turned to Caleb. "Maybe this isn't the best place for this."

I hesitated for a moment as I pondered an alternative, walking over to the coat over the chair, grabbing it, and handing it to him.

"Maybe we should go somewhere a little more practical," I continued, looking down at Marshall still picking through the mess on the floor. "Can I help you clean up?" I asked.

"Just go," Marshall muttered. I didn't feel I could argue.

Caleb took his coat and slipped it on. Rory looked at the two of us in silence as I headed for the curtained door, grabbing my fellow alchemist by his hand and dragging him along behind me despite the reluctance I felt in him.

"Come on," I said to him. "I think Marshall may need a little time to mourn."

Thirteen

———— ☾ ————

Alexandra

Outside of Rory and Marshall, I hadn't really brought many people into the confines of my great-great-grandfather's art studio and library, and certainly not since any of the building's trashings.

It had always been my own sacred space, even now after suffering at the hands of the new and darker Stanis. It still brought me comfort, and after pissing off Rory and Marshall at Roll for Initiative, I definitely needed a hit of that. And while normally I would have felt strange taking someone there, I found escorting Caleb into the confines of the damaged Belarus Building surprisingly comforting as well.

We came up the fire escape as I had since I was a little girl, and I threw open what remained of the French doors leading in from the terrace. The right one twisted off its hinge and fell to the stone of the terrace, several of its glass panels shattering.

"Ta-da!" I said, weakly, going in before I could further embarrass myself.

"Where are we?" Caleb asked, coming in behind me, the crunch of his footfalls echoing in the open space. "It looks like you brought me to a condemned building. Is this a crack den?"

"Home, sweet home," I said, ignoring him and stepping across the library through the debris of broken statues and puzzle boxes. "What's left of it, anyway."

I slowed and turned to Caleb as he stopped in his tracks, realizing where he was.

"This is it," he said, marveling. "This is actually Alexander's library and studio."

"Give the man a kewpie doll," I said.

Caleb looked around, whistling.

"You really should clean more," he said, picking up the base of one of the broken statues. Part of whatever it had been still had the figure's legs attached to it. He ran his hand around the edge of its pedestal. "I recognize this."

"You do?" I asked. "For real? I couldn't identify that statue by just its legs, and I've studied my great-great-grandfather's work most of my life!"

"Not the statue as such," he said. Caleb held the base up, tracing the octagonal shape of it. The winged Belarus sigil with our initial was carved onto the bottom of the piece. "This design is stamped all over the guild hall."

"This is where my great-great-grandfather did the greater part of his art and architecture work," I said, "and this is the library where he accumulated much of his arcane knowledge."

Caleb was like a kid at Disney World, but all that stopped for a moment, his face becoming skeptical. "Why *did* you bring me here?" he asked.

"I would think you'd love to be here," I said.

"Well, yes," he said. "Of course. But it's awfully trusting of you, don't you think? I mean, I know me pretty well, and I certainly wouldn't trust me around all this."

"First of all, I think if push came to shove and you tried anything, I could probably take you," I said, meeting his eyes, my face serious.

"Oh really?" he asked, a half smile creeping on to his

face. "I don't know. As a freelancer, I do pride myself on the quality of my work."

"A fair point," I said. "But you *are* standing in Belarus Central, so I think I might have the advantage here. Besides, if I'm to take your promise to help me seriously, you and I have to start trusting one another, so this is me putting my best foot forward. Don't make me regret it."

"I'll try not to," he said.

I wanted to trust the sincerity in his eyes, but I knew that might simply be a tool of his trade, the easily told lies of someone who most days worked simply for the highest bidder.

Caleb moved to one of the overturned bookcases, running his hand along it.

"I'd hate for you to get my blood on any of this stuff," he said. "You know, you could have brought your bodyguard and Sir Nerdsalot."

I move to one of the still-upright stools by one of the art tables, sitting on it and spinning around, my hands resting on the front of the seat.

"It just seemed like this might be a better place for you and me to talk privately," I said. "I love Rory and Marshall, and they're a huge help—even though they don't have to help me at all. But they don't really get what I'm going through all the time. Outside of fighting the good fight and prepping for whatever's coming, Rory's got her dance, and Marshall's got his store. I've got . . . Well, I've got this. The family's true legacy. It's a singular focus, you know."

Caleb nodded. "Mastering any art is a commitment," he said.

I found comfort in his understanding of it.

"I thought maybe if I brought you here," I said, "we could get away from all that noise and maybe find ourselves in a place where we could each work with someone who's just as like-minded. Until meeting you, I hadn't really thought that there'd be others out there who dealt in the things Alexander practiced. As far as I knew, he had locked those secrets away as part of protecting not just his family but the rest of the world. When I began uncovering them, it just felt like my own family burden to bear. It's just, I don't know . . . *nice* to have someone to talk shop with . . . ? Does that come across as insane? Does that even sound normal?"

Caleb laughed. "As normal as that *can* sound, yes." His focus shifted past me. "May I ask what *that* is?"

I spun on my stool to face the draped drop cloth rising up in the middle of the far end of the art studio.

"Come with me," I said, taking his hand. He didn't resist my hand in his, holding tight as we crossed the room. I guided him carefully through the mess on the floor until we were standing by the draped cloth.

"Voila!" I shouted, pulling it free like a magician revealing his latest and greatest of tricks. The mannequin form stood there with the giant set of giant bat wings I had been sculpting onto it, impressively spanning nearly eight feet across.

"Holy shit," he said, running his hand along the interior side of the left one. "Are these stone?"

I laughed. "Hardly. If they were, given their size, I think they'd have snapped the dummy form in two and crashed through several stories of the building."

Caleb put one hand to either side of the form, slipped his fingers under the wing's lower edge, and lifted. "They're light."

"They should be," I said. "It's clay over chicken wire. They're hollow, but they hold their shape."

"You plan on going all Icarus?" he asked.

I laughed. "No," I said. "But sculpting comes hard to me, and if I'm ever going to master it for the sake of Spellmasonry, I need the practice. This is a study in building a gargoyle, working off the human form and adding to it. Once I figure out the right sense of proportion, I'll move the full statue carving over to stone."

"Could you animate these?" he asked, letting his hands trace over the arcs and ridges of the wings themselves. "If you attached them to a harness or something?"

"It's just a prototype," I reiterated. "An experiment. With

all this broken stuff around here and needing to step up my art game, I just wanted to model them first before ordering a freight elevator's worth of solid stone to go full dimension."

"I get that, but could you animate just these?" he asked again.

I thought a moment before answering.

"It's possible," I said. "I've used clay on parts of Bricksley for the hands and feet, and he seems to be operating just fine."

"What is a 'Bricksley'?" he asked.

"You'll probably meet him," I said with a smile. "In due time." I ran my hands over the top of the wings up to the sharpened claws I had modeled onto the tips, which gave them an extra-creepy Gothic touch. "In theory, I suppose I could animate these full-scale like this. It's a lot more clay than I'm used to exerting control over, but I think it could work. The minerals in clay are those of broken-down rock for the most part, so if I could enchant them . . . sure, why not?"

"These are truly fantastic," he said, his hands pressing against the faux-leathery texture I had tried to replicate in my sculpting of them.

"Thank you," I said, hoping that the dim light of the room hid my burning red face, but by the way Caleb was looking at me, it probably wasn't.

"You're blushing," he said.

I sighed. "It's one thing when my friends or family compliment my work, but it's uniquely refreshing to hear a compliment from someone who actually does what I do."

"I could never do something like this," he said, running his hand along the edge of the wings up to the clawed tips. "I mix and fill vials. I'm no artist—more of a bartender, really."

"Maybe not with stone or canvas," I said, "but from what you know of alchemy alone, you *are* an artist."

He smiled at me, then gave a deep bow. "Well, thank you."

"My pleasure," I said, meeting his smile with my own. Our eyes locked in the dimly lit studio, the moment lingering longer than I found comfortable. His shifted his eyes away for a second, no doubt in reaction to my discomfort. When he looked back at me, it was his turn to look uncomfortable because I was still staring at him, delighting in the discomfort I was causing *him*.

He stepped toward me, but I didn't move away, instead welcoming his advance as his hands slipped around my body, one to the base of my neck and the other to the small of my back. The strong press of his lips met mine. The scruff of his face rubbed hard against my cheek, and although the suddenness of it all caught me off my guard, I found myself wrapping my arms over his shoulders, welcoming all of it, meeting his passion.

My mind shut down all rational thought as I fell into the moment. Sharing more than just a mutual passion for the arcane felt more than right, and I would have gladly shared more given the reaction my body was having to him, but Caleb pushed away from me, showing a restraint I certainly wasn't. My eyes opened, but his were still closed a moment longer before they opened and a slow, deliberate smile overtook his face.

"Sorry," he said. "I needed to do that."

"Needed to, huh?" I smiled. "Was it a chore?"

"*Wanted* to," he corrected.

"That's better," I said, my smile widening, but I couldn't help but notice a bit of reluctance in his eyes now. "Is that not a good thing?"

"Oh no," he said. "Don't get me wrong. It was very good. But I needed to do that because . . . I'm not sure if I'm ever going to get to do it again."

My smile wavered. Was I that bad a kisser? It had been a while for me, sure, and I was definitely out of practice, but I wasn't *that* bad, was I?

"We could give it another chance," I suggested.

"That's not it," he said, looking down at the rubble around his feet. "Working with you this past week has been fantastic. And kissing you . . . Well, it's just that I'm afraid after what I have to tell you, you won't let me do it again."

"Awesome," I said, my heart already sinking. "That's what I get for living in the moment. Out with it. What is it?"

"You remember back at Roll for Initiative when you were talking about Stanis?"

I nodded. "Yeah, and . . . ?"

He stepped back from me, and held his hands up in front of him. "You sound irritated already," he said. "I don't think going into this irritated is going to help."

"You know what's even more irritating?" I asked, the pit of my stomach twisting up on me. "Being told not to be irritated."

"Fine, fine!" he rushed out, clasping his hands together as if in prayer. "It's just that I've seen him—Stanis. Like, recently."

I fell silent, making sure my jaw hadn't dropped open. "I'm sorry—what?"

"Stanis," he said. "Remember how Desmond Locke and I both told you I was a freelancer? Well, some of my projects outside the *Libra Concordia* are more freelance than others."

I stepped toward him, my tone rising. "Meaning what, exactly?"

"Look, Lexi . . ."

"Nuh-uh," I said. "*Alexandra*. 'Lexi' is reserved for my friends."

He smiled. "We were pretty friendly a moment ago," he said, trying to soften the situation, but I wasn't about to let that happen.

"Funny how that's gone away," I said, suddenly furious. "What do you know about Stanis?"

"Well, *Alexandra*," he started, choosing his words carefully now. "That's the thing. I didn't know *much* about him. From my side of the freelance experience, there wasn't too much to know. He was a job that came in."

"Caleb," I said, grabbing him by his shoulders. "What are you trying to tell me here?"

"As I said, he was one of my freelance jobs," he said, unable to meet my eyes, looking down at his feet instead.

"A lot of what I do isn't pretty. I was hired to help break down his will and gain control of him."

"Jesus, Caleb. Did you ever stop to consider what you might be doing or to whom?"

"The pay was good," he said with no pride in his word. "*Great*, actually, and when it's that high, you learn not to ask too many questions, all right? I did what they paid me for. I brought Stanis back in line with what my employer, Kejetan, wanted." Caleb broke away from me and stepped back, slipping on one of the broken statues, his arms pinwheeling before he righted himself.

"If you're working for Kejetan, then you've met Devon," I said.

"He's a charmer, that one," he said.

"My brother wasn't any more charming when he was alive, believe me," I said.

"I'm proud to say I don't see any family resemblance," he said.

I fell silent for a minute, going over everything he had said, my mind sticking on one point.

"What do you mean when you said 'brought in line'?" I asked, feeling sick.

Caleb paused before reluctantly answering. "When you're trying to bind something into servitude, you need to break down its natural resistances," he said. "Stone, being the strongest, is the most stubborn of materials when it comes to a golem. You need to hammer away at its natural strength, breaking what I thought was its base animal will, then replace it with another ruling will."

"You know what that sounds like?" I shouted at him, shaking. "That sounds like torture . . ."

"It was," he said, finally meeting my eye.

"So, what?" I asked. "You tortured his soul right out of his body? Is that why he's acting the way he is?"

Caleb shook his head. "No," he said. "He's in there still. You can't quite force something that strong to give up its form, but you can repress it."

STONECAST 121

"Who *are* you?" I said. "Does Desmond Locke approve of all this? He's watched over my father and this family for decades. He says it's to monitor us, to keep balance in the name of the *Libra Concordia*, which is supposedly a *good* thing if I'm supposed to believe him, but you—"

"The *Libra Concordia* has no idea of my other affairs," Caleb said quickly, his eyes full of worry. "A good freelancer learns not to let his activity with one group of clients get in the way of profiting off another. I would prefer that my other freelance work not be something the *Libra Concordia* take notice of. I'm trying to come clean here with you after wronging Stanis the way I have. Jesus."

"So you'll do just about *anything* for money?" I spat out.

Caleb's eyes sharpened, and he straightened up. "If I have to," he said. "Yes."

"Unbelievable," I said.

"Don't you judge me," he said, defensive. "I have a talent. A skill. So I get paid for using it. I'm sorry I don't have a guild hall downtown and a spare alchemical research library in Gramercy at my disposal."

"There are more honest ways of making a living than working for madmen," I suggested.

"Honesty is a luxury afforded to the rich," he said, his anger matching mine now. "Yes, I have a pride in the skills I have. I live for the challenge of answering the question *can I pull this arcane trick off?* Everything I earn goes into my *survival*. Supplies for what I do, the thrill of the next great job . . . *That's* where my money goes. I offer services most don't, that most *can't*, and sometimes those services go to those who pay the most. So, yes, I try not to ask too many questions because then that makes me a liability to my clients. One that might make them want me dead. But I keep it nice and clean. I go in, I do my job, and I get my money."

"It makes you an accomplice to their crimes," I said.

"When you don't have the luxury of taking the moral high road, it's better to think of it like this: If someone runs somebody over, you don't go after the guy who made the car, do you? No. It's simply a *thing*. How people use it is where it gets all ambiguous. So somebody comes to me wanting to be stronger or to cure something that ails them or whatever they want to do with what I can provide them, so I sell it to them. I don't ask what they plan to do with it."

"Oh that is *such* bullshit," I said. "You *know* what they're going to do with it. You just choose to turn a blind eye to it."

Caleb shrugged. "I won't deny that I've probably got a good idea sometimes, sure. In that case, I tend to charge a little higher to burden them more and maybe ease my conscience a little."

"So noble," I said, shaking my head.

"Nobility is for those who can afford it, too," he said. "I won't apologize for who I am or what I do, but I'm telling you all this because I *am* trying to help you here."

I resisted the urge to shake him or drop the ceiling on him. "How is *any* of this helpful? And why now?"

"Because helping you helps *me*," he said, his voice calming now. "Yes, I do jobs that I don't particularly like, okay? But knowing you and your friends . . . knowing what Stanis means to you all now . . . I can't do it anymore. If I can fix this, maybe I can not feel as shitty as I do right now about what I've done to Stanis. About what I am still doing."

"So you're just going to go back on your deal with the Servants of Ruthenia?" I asked. "Good luck with *that*."

Caleb shook his head.

"I know these people, this Kejetan," he said. "I can't just drop him and his rocky friends as clients. That would get me killed in a heartbeat, but I *can* find out some things that might help you out. There may be a way that I can help your Stanis without their knowing about it if I play this smart."

"I can help him myself," I said, bitterness in my voice. "I just need more information from you."

Caleb shook his head.

"I can't tell you anything more than I have just now," he

said. "You know how dangerous Kejetan and the Servants of Ruthenia can be. The less you know, the greater chance we all get out of this alive."

"How do I know you won't just turn around and give everything we've discovered together this week right over to Kejetan?"

Caleb thought for a moment. "Honestly, you don't," he said. "But if that were what I was going to do, why would I even bring any of this up to you?"

As frustrating as it was to admit, he had a point. He could have just kept his mouth shut. Still, I needed answers.

"Tell me where they are, Caleb," I pleaded.

"I can't," he said. "Not just yet. I don't need you exacting justice in your own special way. Not with the friends you have. Rory's got a temper. She'd want to meet them head-on, and right now, for your safety and *especially* for mine, I can't have that."

"I could beat it out of you," I threatened.

Caleb grabbed for the trim of his coat, pulling it back while his other hand poised over the vials within like a gunslinger over his gun.

"I don't think you want to do that," he said. "We know how that turned out the last time you tried to win against me."

The image of Rory unconscious on the floor of my great-great-grandfather's guild hall filled my mind's eye, as well as my pained helpless memory of the situation. "Maybe I'm willing to take that chance on a rematch."

"Easy, easy," he said, backing away another foot, his hands staying poised. "We were getting along so well, too."

I stood there for a moment longer, the two of us staring at each other in a game of chicken. Given the smile beneath his half-crazed eyes, I could tell the bastard was enjoying this just a bit too much, which only angered me.

Pissed as I was, I had to play this smart myself, so, breaking my gaze away from him as I slumped onto the stool behind me, I crossed my arms, then rubbed my eyes.

"So now what?" I asked.

Caleb let go of his coat and dropped his hands to his side, walking back over to me.

"I *could* have kept quiet," he reminded. "I could have kept pretending about who I am and what I know. You never would have known where Stanis is or the things I have done to him, but listen . . . that's not how I want this. Working with you these past few days . . . This makes so much sense to me, and I think you're of a similar mind, yes?"

"I still think you should tell me everything you can," I said.

"I can't," he said. "As it stands, it's bad enough that you know anything. And remember, you can't tell anyone at the *Libra Concordia* about this."

Despite the warm fuzzies I had been feeling a few moments ago, I had to shut all that down.

"If I even get a hint of your screwing me over, Caleb, Desmond Locke will be the first to hear of your extracurricular activities. I can promise you that."

"Believe me, I don't want any undue attention from either side of things," he said, backing away toward the rear of the studio. "I'd hate to get a bad rep for my bad rep."

"I don't give a damn about your bad reputation," I said.

"On no?" he asked. "Not you?"

I smiled at that, and instantly the old Joan Jett song filled my head, but I killed it immediately, try to stay focused.

"No more harm can come to Stanis," I said. "Do you understand me?"

Caleb held his hands up. "Not by these hands."

"And until we can figure out how to get him back, at least keep him from harm, Caleb," I said, stern this time.

He laughed, shaking his head. "I think you've got your sense of who's in danger messed up there. He's the strong, ancient stone guy. I'm the soft, fleshy creature. Just who exactly is capable of harming whom in this little scenario?"

"You . . . tortured him," I said, barely able to say the word for all the suffering it held in it. "Which means you have some formidable power if you did that."

"Actually," Caleb said. "To be fair, the gargoyle didn't put up a fight."

I stood, eyes wide. "He didn't?"

"Not at first," he said. Caleb looked to the ceiling shaking his head. "I really don't get that. I mean, what kind of creature like that doesn't even put up a fight?"

It was clear to me that a man of such questionable character as Caleb couldn't fathom it, but I could.

Stanis hadn't put up a fight because he was protecting me and my family. And what pained me more, it was at the cost of his own well-being, which pulled at my heart. It was even more impressive knowing that Stanis had chosen to give himself over to servitude after having been freed from my great-great-grandfather's sway, his sacrifice only making me feel doubly conflicted about having just kissed Caleb.

Not that anything of that sort could ever happen between Stanis and me . . .

"Go," I said, the word flat and lifeless on my lips, the sight of Caleb at once enticing and upsetting me.

Was that true, though? Or was I really more upset with myself for momentarily allowing myself to lose focus?

"If you think you can get Stanis back to our side," I said, "or break Kejetan's control over him, you need to do it."

Caleb sighed. "It's not that simple," he said. "Once I finished binding him, I gave control to Kejetan, which means I don't directly have the power to break that bind anymore."

"So it's hopeless," I said, not able to hide the frustration in my voice. "Great."

Caleb held up a finger and waggled it at me. "I didn't say that, now, did I? Do you think I would have brought all this up just to torment you if I didn't have a plan already forming in my head?"

"Well, whatever your plan is, get out of here and get on with it, will you? It's only a matter of time before Kejetan sets him more directly to the task of harming me, my family, and my friends in his search for Alexander's secrets. We need to be ready."

"We will be," he said, turning away toward the broken French doors leading out onto the terrace.

"How can you be so confident?"

Caleb spun back around, stopping. "Trust me," he said. "When you hear me sounding *this* confident, that just means my back's up against the wall, and I'm not particularly a huge fan of that. Luckily for you, it also puts my mind into panic mode, and that's when I tend to go a bit hypercreative. I don't have a full plan yet, but the wheels are turning."

"Please tell me they're not hamster wheels in there," I said, rubbing my temples in the hopes it would help dislodge the ice daggers his cheerful tone was plunging into my mind.

"We can use those wings," he said, pointing at my latest handiwork just behind me. "Keep working on them."

"Caleb," I said, stern as I could as I walked over to the statue. "Now is not the time for my fucking art project."

"And work on counting," he added.

"I *know* how to count," I said.

"Yes," he said. "But I want you to always be doing it in the back of your head, like keeping time with music."

"Why?"

"Just trust me," he said.

I wanted to, but it was hard to muster it for a man who for all intents and purposes was still a stranger to me, one who played both sides of the fence, always looking for an advantage.

"Right now, I trust you as far as I can throw you," I said. "Nonmagically speaking."

He held his hands up.

"I'm going," he said. "I'm going. You'll see. I'll show you I can fix this."

"Just go." I locked my eyes on his, refusing to look away. Eventually, he turned, made his way out onto the terrace, and disappeared over the edge of the building down the fire escape.

I collapsed against the wings, exhausted, leaning on the form that held them in place.

Knowing *why* Stanis was acting the way he was . . . it was the most promising bit of news I had, really. Caleb was close to reverse engineering Kimiya thanks to the week or so we had been comparing notes. I had no doubt we'd figure it out soon, but that was only the first step on our road to building an army to counter the Servants of Ruthenia. I still needed to unlock the arcane secrets of actually raising that army. The freelance alchemist had said he would help, but could I take Caleb at his word?

No, but I could work with and learn from him while also taking precautions to make sure I had a plan that extended beyond whatever he himself was concocting.

My thoughts were clouded as far as trust was concerned, more so due in part to what had been the pleasant sensation of Caleb's lips on mine.

I needed to clear my head, going for the stairs at the back of the building that led up to the roof. I pushed through the upper door, hoping that the night skyline might help me focus even if the familiar form of Stanis was not there waiting for me as it used to be not so long ago.

The spot where Stanis had once stood before waking every night was empty, as it had been these last few months, but the rest of the roof caused me to stop in my tracks, my breath catching in my throat.

Stanis wasn't there . . . but plenty of other statues *were*.

The inert forms of dozens of works—some on pedestals, some looking like they had been torn directly from the faces of buildings—covered the entirety of the roof. One thing stood out about them—they all bore the distinctive style of my great-great-grandfather's hand in their carving.

I should have known better than to have allowed myself a little happiness earlier, or even take a moment of pleasure from the kiss. Given my luck lately, letting my guard down for even a second should have been the perfect indicator that, of course, my life was surely going to get worse, and here I was with proof positive that something else strange was up.

Work on the wings. Caleb's voice sounded in my head.

I intended to, heading back down to the studio below. Carving was only a small part of the work. As I planned out my project, I set the back of my mind to Caleb's second task.

I began to count.

☾

Fourteen

Stanis

As I hung harnessed to the chains dangling from the cargo hold of the freighter, my inner voice demanded vengeance against Devon for the pain he had been inflicting on me for the last half hour. Blow after blow struck me, and my inner voice—my true self—wanted nothing more than to tear the deformed stone creature apart, but the dominant voice that held sway over me now allowed Devon's continuing punishment.

Kejetan stood watching. For the first twenty of the passing minutes, I thought perhaps Devon had simply been following my father's orders. For the rest of the time, however, it had moved beyond just a simple task for Devon, marked by the brutal enjoyment on his jagged stone face.

Kejetan dropped one of his thick stone hands on Devon's shoulder, causing a pause in the assault on me.

"Stanis, you have gathered what I asked for—Alexander Belarus's greatest stone creations—have you not?" he asked.

"I have," I responded, my two voices both allowing me to answer. There was no harm in stating the obvious course of my actions over the past week.

"And yet you still can neither find nor bring me the secrets of the Spellmason," he added.

My true voice held the dominant one silent by hiding the truth from it. How much longer I could keep secret the Spell-mason master tome Alexandra carried was the ongoing struggle for me. As I had instructed her in our one meeting, as long as Alexandra kept it physically hidden from me and did not reveal its whereabouts, I could continue to keep the dominant voice from acting out against her.

I only prayed Kejetan or his alchemist did not alter the phrasing of the orders they had set upon me, but for now both voices continued their silence on the matter, which, despite the immense amount of pain I was in at the moment, pleased me. The hint of a smile rose to my stone lips.

Devon shook Kejetan's hand off his shoulder and lunged at me.

"What allegiance do you owe my former sister?" he asked, barely able to associate himself with any of his old ties to his humanity. His arms renewed their furious motion as he resumed his attack on my battered body.

"What is it that makes her or the rest of the humans so special that you deny the Servants of Ruthenia the same form as yours?"

I did not need to answer with either voice. The voice that dominated me answered to only one creature, and that stone monster stood idly by, watching as Devon slammed his fists into me again and again.

As I hung there, attempting to ignore the pain, my mind drifted to what I thought was the point of hallucination and beyond. The far wall behind the two jagged stone men in front of me shimmered, a section of the metal there transforming. The area was vaguely human-shaped and moving, every step closer to us becoming more and more clear until I recognized the form of the blond human who had tortured me.

His face looked concerned this time, but when Devon and Kejetan turned to him, his face transformed, rivaling that of a man who had not a care in the world.

He looked to Devon, whose right arm was pulled back in midswing.

"Easy there, Scrappy," the human said, gesturing to my hanging form as I swayed on my chains with the motion of the ship. "You know, it might be more of a fair fight if you took him down off those spikes."

"I did not summon you," Kejetan said, his words dark.

"Yeah, I know," the human said, moving closer to me, looking my form over. "Let's just say I felt a disturbance in the Force."

"The Force?" I asked before anyone else could.

The human looked into my eyes and gave me a smile before lightly slapping his hand onto my cheek. "Never mind," he said.

My inner voice willed me to bite the hand from his wrist, but the more dominant one did not allow me to harm him, no doubt because he was the one who had forced me into this servitude.

The alchemist dropped his hand away and turned to Kejetan.

"Let's just say I have a heavy investment in my reputation out there," he said. "And I'd hate to see you or Rocky here damage my work before I can iron out all the kinks in it."

"I do not understand," Kejetan said. "But be quick in rectifying that. My patience grows thin."

"I've told you before that this isn't an *exact* science," the human said. "While I'm tweaking the alchemy here, I need you two to keep him in one piece."

"For someone so worried about his reputation," Devon said, "one would think you'd be a little quicker on the results."

"Don't like them?" the human asked, a bit of sting having come into his voice. "Try to hire someone else who can give you better."

Devon gave a throaty grumble, and the human turned to face him.

"I know you think that somehow you might beat him into submission," he said, "but that's not really how these things work. Were you in some kind of fight club?"

"Just working out some of my issues," Devon said. "Thought this might help bring him around to revealing the secrets my dear sister is keeping from us. It is clear your way isn't doing the trick."

Kejetan walked over to the human. "We already know that Stanis does not possess the knowledge I want," he said. "That is why I made you set him to his other tasks." He grabbed the man by his shoulder and pulled him closer. The human looked like all he wanted was to squirm away like a serpent. "He has not yet provided that which I seek. Do you think I am somehow pleased by this? I assure you I am not."

"Easy, boss, easy," the human said. "Baby steps. You wanted him in your service, he's in your service. Yes, he hasn't recovered the secrets you wanted yet, but I think I know why."

Kejetan did not move away from him. "I do pray you tell."

"I don't think the secrets of the Spellmasons are somewhere else," the human said. "I think they're still within this golem here."

Kejetan shook his head. "He has already confessed to not having them."

"*That's* part of the security that keeps the information locked away in him safe," the human said. "I mean, if you were going to hide something that valuable, what's the first thing you'd tell the gargoyle to say?"

Kejetan thought it over, but after too long a silence, Alexandra's brother spoke up.

"I'd teach it to say it didn't have the information," Devon offered.

"Exactly!" the human said. "Who's a smart but brutal chunk of rock?"

Devon moved to the alchemist, but Kejetan waved him away.

"So now I need to get in there and break down those defenses," the human said. "That's why I came tonight. Alchemy's tricky. These things take time to figure out."

I knew of no such system in place over me, having spent all these months doing what was called by the humans *bluffing* about any sort of secret arcane knowledge. Why did this man now come to them with this tale . . . ? Could he, too, be bluffing?

I watched and waited to see how my captors reacted.

Kejetan let the man go, crossing to me and grabbing my face, lifting me. "Is what he says true?" he asked, as the dead dark sockets of his eyes met my own. "Remember, you are bound to answer me with truth."

"I hold no secret knowledge," I said, freely speaking what both voices within me knew was true.

"See?" the human asked. "You need to let me work. I'll get it out of him."

I considered the man's words as I knew my father must also be doing.

What choice did he have, really? I was already in servitude to him, and if we were to take the alchemist at his word, he was still the best hope Kejetan had.

"Very well," Kejetan said, pulling Devon away from me. "See to it. I grow weary of this."

The human looked satisfied.

"Pardon my asking," he said. "But what's the point?"

"The point?" Kejetan asked.

"To all this," he said. "This endless hunt for this missing arcane knowledge. I mean, you seem to have a lot of bold ambitions. What do you want? Please don't tell me to rule the world, because if it is, a lot has changed since you were in power."

"Of this I am aware," my father said, choosing to engage the man instead of reacting with the anger I knew him capable of. "But your world does have leaders, yes? Why not my kind?"

The human laughed. "No offense, but your sense of perspective may be out of proportion with reality. I don't think the world is ready to be led by your kind. Not only are most not aware of you, but they can barely pick leaders among their own kind. At the risk of your swatting me across the cargo hold here, humanity isn't simply going to bow down and kneel before Zodd."

"Zodd . . . ?"

"Another famous despot of a ruler," the human said with a sigh.

"But some will look for leaders when the world changes," Kejetan said. "Alexander Belarus locked away some of the greatest secrets, and once those have been brought to light, others will look for a voice to guide them. And that voice shall be mine."

"Right," the human said, the word coming off his lips long and slow. It did not sound sincere to my ear, nor apparently to Kejetan, who stepped back in front of him, anger in his own voice.

"If you are unable to live up to the duties my people are paying you for, perhaps we should discuss that," my father said.

The human did not speak for a short time. "I'm up to the job," he said, the smile returning to his face. "I just wanted you to get a better idea of the whole picture there. Always like to see where the profit margin on the future is heading."

Devon laughed. "You *should* be more concerned about living through the day, pal," he said.

The human glanced at Alexandra's brother before stepping away to his table against the wall that held his mixtures and examining them.

"I kind of need him out of here," he said, pointing his thumb back over his shoulder to Devon. "Preferably, you, too."

"I do not take orders on my own ship," Kejetan said.

"Suit yourself," he said, removing the coat he wore. "This might get messy, though. I can't promise you won't get a little twisted up by what I'm about to throw down on Stanis here. Hard to keep some of this stone-affecting arcana one-directional. You want to hang in here, that's fine by me, but it's only fair warning you that you might accidentally get a little alchemical backlash on you."

Kejetan waved Devon out of the cargo hold, and Alexander's brother lumbered off without another word.

"I need results," Kejetan said.

"I understand," the human said without looking up from his work.

If there was one thing my father hated, it was being ignored, but he dared not disturb the alchemist. Holding his tongue, he turned and stormed off after Devon and out of the cargo hold, leaving the two of us alone.

I watched the man work in silence for several minutes. Without the sound of my father or Devon picking away at me, I enjoyed the reprieve from all the noise until the man turned from the table with a large vial in his hand and crossed the cargo hold to where I hung. He took my face in the cool of his hand, standing on his toes to meet my eyes.

"Listen, Stan," he said, searching my face as he raised the vial over the top of my head. "I know the real you is not fully at the wheel right now, but I know you're still in there."

He tilted his wrist, and the mixture poured from the vial onto me, cool and wet, as an electric charge slammed into my mind.

"This should help bring you out, if only for a little while."

The dominant presence that had ruled over me for days faded into the background, its panic at being suppressed quieting more and more every second that passed. My true self rose to the surface of my thoughts with only the edge of my mind still clouded. "What are you doing to me?"

"Just needed to talk to the old you for a few minutes," he said, lowering his voice and looking around to make sure the hold was still clear of others. "I don't think we've ever been properly introduced. My name's Caleb. Caleb Kennedy. Met a few friends of yours the other day. Nerdy guy, girl with a pointy-stick thing, and a hottie with a big stone book."

I could not help but smile, pained though it was to think of them, but it faded as quick as it came.

"How did you come to meet them?" I asked, worried.

"Can't really get into the finer details right now," he said.

"Just wanted you to know that everything I've done to you had been business. Nothing personal. I'm sorry to have put you through all this."

"Release me, then," I said, daring to allow myself a moment of hope.

The man stepped back from me, hesitant.

"I can't do that," he said.

With my own self at the front of my thoughts, anger filled me, and I roared, spreading my wings wide, but the chains through them held fast, and the human moved just out of my reach.

"Sorry," he continued. "But I'm in a bit of a tight spot here. If I do something like that, Kejetan would have me killed."

"I will take care of the man I once called father," I said.

Caleb shook his head at me. "No," he said. "You won't." He pulled back his sleeve and checked what I knew the humans called a *watch*. "Already, the concoction I gave you should be fading."

The other presence within picked away at me, rising once more. "Then hurry and let me loose to face him," I shouted. "I will destroy Kejetan for the situation he has brought on us all."

Caleb smiled at me. "You might be able to take him on; I have no doubt of that," he said. "But I don't think you would escape this ship facing off against the whole of his fellow stone men or his human servants. And—this is the most important part to me—I don't want to die or incur Kejetan's wrath in the process."

"You live your life as a coward," I said, feeling my true voice beginning to slip back behind the wall of the dominant one.

"That's not the first time I've been called that," he said, grim. "I prefer the term *self-preservationist*."

The struggle on my face must have been evident as the human looked on with concern. My wings relaxed on the chains, my body betraying me in service to the other presence rising in me.

"Why draw me out?" my inner voice cried out. "Why talk to me only to leave me here in Kejetan's servitude?"

"I pulled the *real* you forward, so I could tell you that I'm sorry."

"I will find a way to overcome this presence," I said, struggling against its domination. "While I must obey it, my true self has always remained, bowing to it only when it is forced to do so, but I've been fighting it, tricking it. And if I can trick it, I can beat it."

"There it is!" Caleb said, a dark smile taking over his face. "*Exactly* what I thought might be going on."

"What do you mean?"

"You see, I know that when your master has me assign tasks to you, I need to be *very* specific. I've been very lax about that to this point, running up the meter for the sake of my wallet, but things seem to be getting a bit crazy in my life as of late. And if I want to stay safe and living, I need to give Kejetan what he desires, what he really wants: results. I'm really in a bind here."

"No," I said, fearing whatever this human had to say next, fearing what specific task he meant to set upon me. "I beg of you . . . speak with care of what you will ask of me."

"Oh, I'll be careful," he said with a smile. "In fact, I'll name the exact time and place you can pry Alexander Belarus's master tome from the cold, dead hands of your biggest fan, Alexandra."

My inner voice was nearly shut down now, but at Caleb's words my rising anger forced it back to the surface. "If you harm her, I will find you and take your life," I said. "You have my word on that, human."

"I'm not going to kill her," he said, turning to pull several more vials from his coat. "I'll leave that up to the professionals. I'll leave that up to you. Kejetan's order."

My mouth opened to roar, but nothing came out. Once more, I was no longer the force in control of my actions. My true voice fell silent. The only hint of my anguish now lay in the screaming voice that dwelled deep in the center of

me, crushed as it was, like a bug under the heel of a boot,
by the dominant voice.

"As . . . you . . . wish," I said against my will, and waited
to learn the time and place where I would kill Alexandra.

Fifteen

☾

Alexandra

"You want to tell me why you have me counting all the time?" I asked Caleb, sitting across the table from me.

Caleb leaned back in his chair, looking around the bar he had brought me to, Eccentric Circles. I hadn't ever been there before, but it seemed popular enough that the place was crowded and loud. "Are you doing it now?"

"I'm not sure," I said, stopping to think about it, looking around the room.

"Focus," Caleb said. *"Why* aren't you sure?"

I sighed. "You told me to do it at the back of my mind," I said. "So it's not like I'm consciously thinking about it. I kind of have to—I don't know—mentally switch gears."

Caleb's eyes stayed locked with mine, unwilling to let up. "So . . . are you doing it or not?"

I reached out to that part of my mind, surprised to find I *was* counting, and nodded.

"Good," he said.

"That still doesn't tell me *why* I'm doing it," I said, my annoyance coming through in my words.

"Look around," he said, turning away from me to take in our surroundings. "Tell me what you see."

The bar was crowded with people at every booth and table, and it was standing room only by the bar itself. "I don't know," I said with a shrug. "People. Lots and lots of people . . . ?"

It was Caleb's turn to sigh. He leaned forward, knocking over his glass in the process. His drink spilled out across the table, but rather than soaking into the wood, the contents transformed into a wash of blue flame that danced high across the surface for several seconds before dying out. The table below remained unharmed.

I glanced around the room, but other than a few people who gave us a cursory glance, no one seemed all that interested in what had just happened.

"What the hell?" I said, surprised by the lack of reaction.

Caleb leaned in closer, and I noticed the vial in his hand as he discreetly slipped it back into his coat. "Are you still counting *now*?"

I switched my thoughts back over, finding the back of my mind a blank this time. "Shit," I said.

"I thought as much," he said. "I brought you here because you have to get used to distractions, Alexandra. All these people, spilling my drink, the flames on the table . . . You need to keep focused no matter what is going on around you."

"How is the counting supposed to help?" I said. "Why is it so damned important?"

"Let's start simple," he said. "I'm having you do it because that's how you're going to be able to fly with those wings you're building. The better a rhythm you can keep— without distraction—the easier it's going to be keeping yourself airborne. But the best reason you need to lock that rhythm off in the back of your mind is because the front of it is going to be occupied."

"With what?"

"Capturing your gargoyle," he said.

My heart caught in my throat. "Oh," I said, stunned.

"You're going to have your hands full," he said. "The last thing I want you worrying about is staying in the air. You need to learn how to split your mind. I think that's what's been keeping you from moving further forward with your arcane endeavors."

I cocked my head. "How do you know this?"

"That's the *other* reason I brought you here," he said. "When you look around this room, you just see a crowd of people."

I looked around, really only seeing a bar filled with customers and nothing more. "Well, what do *you* see?"

Caleb raised his hand in a subtle manner and began pointing around the room at various tables. "Witch, witch, druid, warlock—"

"How can you tell?"

"It's all in the details," he said. "To be fair, I've worked with or for a bunch of them before. But the details are what you need to start focusing on. Look at the first woman I pointed at. That medallion around her neck is a Wiccan symbol. The man across from her has a Green Man tattoo on his forearm, so I'm going with druid for him. That guy who just walked by you, the one in the knee-length leather coat—it caught on one of the chairs, and he had some kind of shiny, retractable bat hanging from his belt inside it. Probably silver."

I followed the movement of the man Caleb had just mentioned. "He looks familiar," I said. "I think he used to come in the Lovecraft Café all the time when I was still working there."

"Eccentric Circles attracts a certain type of crowd," Caleb said.

"Eccentrics," I said with a smile. "You sure this isn't a date?"

"Paranormals," he corrected. "*Focus.* It would serve you to learn your own kind."

"I'm sorry," I said, unable to take my eyes off the crowd all around us. "It's a lot to take in. The counting, finding a whole bar *filled* with our kind of people. It's distracting."

"Perhaps *too* distracting," he said, standing. He gestured toward the front of the bar. "Come on."

I stood, still marveling at the crowd. "Where are we going?"

"Back to your place," he said.

"Cheeky!"

"Still not a date," he said. "Trust me. I just need somewhere where we can concentrate. And maybe try a little practical magic."

Caleb refused to talk to me until he had me back at the Gramercy Belarus Building and had helped settle the stone wings I had been constructing on my shoulders.

"I still don't see how going to the bar is supposed to help with all this," I said, adjusting my balance so I wouldn't fall over from their weight. "What's that got to do with my learning to fly?"

"Tonight was bigger than just flying, Alexandra," he said. "It's about why you've been having trouble with the higher abilities you've been toying with as a Spellmason."

As he led me across the broken library out onto the terrace, I asked, "How so?"

"I've been asking some questions here and there," he said, ducking my wings through the hole where the French doors used to hang. "There's one thing most of the practitioners back in Eccentric Circles have in common. All of them possess an ability to split their mind, which I don't think is something I've seen mentioned in what you've shown me on Spellmasonry."

"And that's helpful how?"

"You spend your time trying to bring stone to life with your main focus," he said, pulling out a vial of Kimiya and rubbing it along the top edge of the wings, "but I think your arcane discipline demands you hold focus on several things at once. You have to be able to split that focus several different ways. It's not enough just to control stone; you also have to be able to finesse it in other ways. Bringing you someplace with a lot to concentrate on hopefully loosened you up to that a bit. At the very least, it should have helped you a bit with focusing your back mind on counting. Which is what I want to test now." He checked the inside lining of his coat. "I'm really starting to run low on the Kimiya. And my reverse engineering it is still likely to blow us both up, so that's still an issue, but right now we need to do two things: First, you need to practice with these wings."

"How?"

"By flying," he said.

I laughed, nerves behind it all. "Are you serious? Now?"

"No time like the present," he said with a smile.

"And what will *you* be doing?" I asked.

"Watching you," he said, "and also thinking about the second part of my plan for your flight. I have to come up with the best way to capture Stanis."

My stomach sank, knotting up. "So I'm . . . what? *Bait?*"

"That's such an ugly word," he said, pulling out his notebook and beginning to scribble in it. "I prefer to think of you as . . . motivational material."

No matter what Caleb called it, I still felt like a worm ready to be put on the end of the line. Still, I hated to be defeatist. Maybe I *could* keep myself in the air. Sure, failure *was* an option, but so was success.

I stood there, the wings feeling all the heavier now that we had moved out into the wind on the terrace. "So what do I do?"

"I want you to concentrate on bringing the stone to life, then using that rhythmic count, keeping it in time and using the tempo to lift yourself off the terrace."

I gave a grim smile. "You make it sound so simple," I said. "Dying is simple, too."

"Just go up a few feet and hold your position," he said. "We just need a proof of concept, not breaking the sound barrier or anything."

"Right," I said, and pushed images of my falling out of the night sky from my mind. I pressed my power out into the wings, grinding them to life as my connect set in. With the memory of Rory's *Swan Lake* audition piece in mind from our youth, I forced the wings into a quick and fluid pattern. Ignoring the press of their physical weight against my body, I pressed them harder and harder as I quickened my count. When my feet left the stone of the terrace, I pushed the count to the back of my mind, rising several feet into the air.

"I'm doing it," I said, unable to suppress a giddy laugh. "I'm actually doing it."

"Okay," Caleb said, looking up from his notes. "Now tell me about the people back at the bar."

I wavered in the air as my wings fell out of rhythm. "What? I'm flying!"

"Just do it!" he shouted with such force, I almost lost my rhythm again and banked closer to the edge of the terrace, veering toward the alley but pulling myself back up in time.

"You don't have to be so mean," I muttered.

"I'm not," he said, lowering his notebook but not really softening, "but if you can't do two things at once, or deal with a little surprise, then you might as well let Stanis tear you apart right now because that's what he'll do."

"I'm not going to have to outfly him, am I?" I said, counting. Always counting. "He's got centuries of practice."

"And you've got now," he said. "So I suggest you work at it. And no, you won't have to outfly him. At least, not for too long, anyway."

"Because you're going to capture him," I said. "How?"

Caleb held up his notebook, waving it at me. "I'm working on it," he said. "But by rough calculations, we may exhaust what remains of *both* our Kimiya supplies. Unless you want to try my home brew again, but that still has a 70 percent chance of blowing us up."

All of the remaining Kimiya? "What do you have planned?" I asked.

"You work on your part, and I'll work on mine," he said. "Now, tell me about the people you saw at the bar."

I thought back on earlier that evening, this time my wings staying at a constant rate, holding me in place about ten feet over the terrace. Now I needed to work on splitting my mind to recall the people in the crowd, not to mention that it was

already splitting away wondering how we were going to deal
with the Kimiya shortage . . . My wings wavered but I re-
focused my efforts, hoping this would help when it came to
flying against Stanis once Caleb's plan was ready.

"The warlock with the Green Man tattoo," I started, holding my position in the air, "the guy with the retractable bat
sticking out of his leather coat . . ."

Sixteen

C

Alexandra

The next morning, my knees were sore from landing hard on the stone terrace during our flight testing, so I slept in before hobbling downtown to the *Libra Concordia* in the old, abandoned church across from Trinity Church in the hopes of finding more information on either Kimiya production or this splitting of the mind Caleb was so keen on talking about.

Pleased with the angel-specific distractions I fed him, Desmond Locke had made good on his promise and granted Marshall and Rory access to the research room at the *Libra Concordia*. My friends' help in sorting through the books made the going much quicker, even despite their constant questioning. If there was information on how to master the production of Kimiya in what the *Libra Concordia* had on hand in their archives, we would find it. That was, if I could concentrate, what with Desmond Locke poking his head into the research room every half hour or so.

"You can't dodge him forever," Rory said, organizing her books where she sat across from me, with Marshall off to her left.

"I don't need to," I said, scribbling in my notebook. "I

just need to stay on his good side until we can find what I'm looking for."

"Eventually, he'll want to know about Stanis," Marshall said in a low whisper, his eyes on the door, "and what will you tell him?"

"I'm not going to tell him anything," I said. "He doesn't need to know about my family's secret legacy beyond whatever he's gleaned through his association with the *Libra Concordia*. And he certainly doesn't need to know what Stanis has been up to, gathering all those statues on top of the Belarus Building."

"It's creepy," Rory said. "It's like he's developing hoarder tendencies."

"I don't know what the purpose of it all is," I said. "But my best guess is he's amassing an army for Kejetan and his men. He's actually done us a favor, though."

"He has?" Marshall asked.

I nodded.

"Caleb and I have made progress on reverse engineering the formula," I said. "But it would help us perfect what we need if we can find my great-great-grandfather's 'recipe' spell book for it. I was working to build a statue to test it on, but now we've got plenty of Belarus-made test subjects gathered in one place."

Rory yawned. "I miss sleep," she said. "Dance classes by day, research and gargoyle experimentation by night."

"So much regular-world stuff to do during the day, fighting evil at night," Marshall said. "I don't know how Batman does it."

I took the conversation's turning to comics as my cue to get back to work and fell silent, thankful when Rory and Marshall did the same.

Looking through the histories of the late eighteen hundreds and early nineteen hundreds for clues to my great-great-grandfather's work was a slow and laborious chore, but if there was anything to be found outside of my family's library on the man, the *Libra Concordia* was the most likely of places for it.

"You're doing it again," Rory said, smacking me with one of the books from her side of the table.

"I am?" I asked. "Counting?"

"Yes!" Marshall confirmed it by hitting me with his own book.

"But I wasn't doing it out loud this time," I protested.

Rory pointed to the pen I had poised over my notebook. "You were tapping it out."

"Shit," I said, angry with myself more than anything. If I couldn't keep the count at the back of my mind without indicating it externally, I *still* wasn't doing it right.

"Can you at least tell us why you need to be counting all the time?" Marshall asked. "Does it have a higher purpose than just bothering us?"

"It's just this thing I've been working on with Caleb," I said, noticing the annoyed look on both their faces at my mentioning the alchemist's name.

"Counting," Rory said. "You and blondie are working on counting. Like in music?"

"Yes." I sighed.

"Are you starting a band?" Rory asked.

I considered just answering yes to that as well. It would be easier than explaining the whole of the events from the other night in the art studio.

"No," I said.

"Oh!" Marshall exclaimed in full-blown mockery. "Does it involve trying to destroy the rest of my store . . . ?"

"I paid for your damaged table," I reminded him. "*And* your little teeny town dungeon. Besides, Caleb and I both apologized for that. You should give the guy a chance. He's trying to help me."

The gap between us across the table couldn't have felt wider or more awkward than it did just then. I couldn't help but think it might be in part because they were sensing that I was leaving some things out of my story.

But why was I doing it? To protect them?

No. The truth was I wasn't sure how I felt about what was happening between Caleb and me. I didn't want to put my trust issues out there when I needed to get everyone on board with the idea of his working with us. Despite the potential embarrassment, I decided to woman up and put on my big-girl panties.

"You should give him a chance," I repeated, my voice lowering as I met their eyes, "because I'm giving him a chance. I kind of like the guy."

Rory laughed, then cocked her head at me when she saw I was serious. "Does he buy you flowers?" she asked, only half mocking now. "Or does he *bippity boppity boo* some mice and turn them into flowers for you?"

"We're not dating," I said, not liking the attitude I was getting after laying part of my feelings out there. "I don't know what to call it, so give it a rest."

"Fine," Rory said, leaning back in her chair, defeated.

Small victory though it was, I felt mighty triumphant about it. Still, why miss out on the opportunity to kick our conversation up a notch?

"Although," I said, drawing the word out, "we might have snogged for a bit over at the Belarus Building the other night."

Rory shot forward again, grabbing me across the table. "Shut *up!*"

Marshall sighed, leaning his head down into his hands. "Could you two maybe make all this a little less *Twilight*?"

"Jealous?" I asked.

Marshall hesitated, then looked up, cradling his face in his hands. "Maybe . . . ?" he said.

Rory and I fell back into our chairs, genuine laughter rising from both of us, refreshing after months and months of tension and failed experiments.

Marshall shook his head at the two of us. "How is it you get to make out with someone—a bit of a dick, by the way—and I can't even get a woman to hand me her real phone number?"

Rory shrugged. "Probably because you're busy throwing Magic: The Gathering tournaments . . . ?"

"Not now, Ror," he said, eyeing her with daggers. He turned to me. "I'm going to take this as a sign that you're definitely spending too much time with this alchemist."

"Take *what* as a sign?" I asked.

"I don't know," he said. "The tongue bathing you probably gave each other . . . ?"

"*That's* a pretty picture," I said.

"Almost as pretty as 'snogging,'" he said.

I couldn't argue.

"Well, that settles that," Rory said. "I mean, if a guy puts his tongue in you, he's totally trustworthy. Except, oh no, wait . . . He's a *guy*."

"I didn't say I trusted him," I said. "I only said I made out with him, which implies there's some sort of connection. Hopefully, that grows into trust, but I'm not stupid."

My instinct told me not to tell them anything about his freelance work with Kejetan. Eventually, I needed all three of them on my side working together, and to coin Caleb's phrase, I had to take baby steps toward building that foundation. Admitting intimacy between the two of us would get them to accept Caleb more readily while allowing me to use it in trying to figure out where his true loyalties lay. I only hoped I had given my friends enough information to get them not to make stink faces when I mentioned his name.

"Well?" I asked, looking for a reaction.

Marshall shrugged, having already voiced his discomfort over all this girl talk.

"Hope you know what you're doing," Rory said, falling back into the book in front of her.

This time I fell back to my own research, my mind freer than before thanks to my confession. It also seemed to do the trick in helping with my back mind counting because I went a half hour more with it without interruption until my phone vibrated on the table.

Caleb.

"Be right back," I said, standing, as Rory and Marshall looked up at me.

I snatched my phone off the table and ran to the door, throwing it open.

Outside the research room, the transformed church still held the air of authority, and I couldn't help but lower my voice to a whisper as I answered.

"Yeah?"

"You ready? Time to fly. For real."

"What?" I asked, looking around to make sure Desmond Locke wasn't anywhere close enough to hear. *"Now?"*

"There's no time like the present. Is that a problem?"

"No," I said, trying to hide my hesitation. "I just didn't expect to do this already. Are you ready on your end?"

"Yes," he said. "I'm broke from buying supplies, and I may have depleted much of your stash of Kimiya in the process, but I'm ready. Have you been practicing your counting?"

"Yes," I said, neglecting to leave out the part where I kept forgetting to keep it at the back of my mind.

"Then we shouldn't have an issue," he said. "Can we meet in, say, an hour?"

"Fine," I said. "Anything I should bring?"

"Just your Spellmasony little self," he said, and hung up.

I slid my phone into the back pocket of my jeans and hurried back to the room to gather my belongings into my backpack. Alexander's stone tome was still in it, and I slid my notebook in as I sorted through the books on top of the table.

"Gotta run," I said, trying to sound calm, but neither of them looked all too convinced.

"Everything all right?" Rory asked.

"Fine," I said, struggling with a quick response. "Just an . . . alchemy thing." I could endure the ridicule of confessing what Caleb and I had done the other night, but I didn't dare divulge the next part of our plan to them. Honesty was one thing, and sharing my intimate moment harmless in the grand scheme of things, but keeping this next part of the plan from them meant Rory and Marshall would be safe if it blew up in our faces.

I slid two of the more promising books I had pulled across the table to Rory. "Keep at it," I said. "We need to find Alexander's book."

Marshall grabbed one of them but eyed me with skepticism. "Sure this isn't a booty call?" he asked.

"No, it's not," I said, heading for the door leading out of the research room. "And please don't ever say *booty call* again. It doesn't work for you."

"Let me know how the alchemy of French kissing goes for you," Marshall called out after me.

I shot him a look that shut him down.

"Don't you stay out too late, young lady," Rory chided, as I opened the door leading out of the room.

I was already regretting being honest about that part of the other night. My only hope was that after tonight's plan, I still got to continue living to regret it.

Seventeen

———— ☾ ————

Alexandra

Nerves were a wonderful thing. They kept you on your toes, made you feel alive, especially when there was always a good chance of dying in the risky world of Spell-masonry. At least tonight there were some good nerves fill-ing my mind, and seeing Caleb reading through one of Alexander's books while waiting in my family's art studio filled me with an irresistible urge to kiss him. So I did.

For a second, he hesitated in surprise, but there was a hungry desperation in both of us that took over. All thoughts drifted from my mind for a moment, a welcome relief to everything going on, and I only broke away from Caleb when I realized I was still counting in the back of my head.

His smile was warm as he searched my eyes.

"Let me guess," he said, drumming a steady waltzlike cadence on his leg. *"One, two, three, four, one, two, three, four . . ."*

I bowed to him. "However did you guess?"

He gestured from my lips to his. "Does this mean you trust me now? Where are your friends?"

"I *have* to trust you at this point," I said, sobering as my momentary frivolity faded away. "Either you're going to help me release Stanis from Kejetan's sway or you're not. Keeping Rory and Marshall out of that for now is for their own safety."

Caleb stepped to the fully finished wings I had been working on, running his hands over them. The mannequin was already gone, and their expanse was simply held up by supports on either side.

"I've given them a final treatment," he said. "With what little Kimiya is left. You feeling confident about flying after our practice the other night?"

I nodded, hiding my uncertainty. I hadn't had to worry last night about anything like flying *and* dealing with several thousand pounds of gargoyle at the same time . . .

"Let me worry about the flying," I said. "You just better come through on your end. We either turn Stanis, or—"

Caleb was annoyed and already nodding when we were interrupted by the unmistakable sound of movement up on the roof.

I didn't need to finish my sentence. I was sick of thinking of Stanis as the enemy.

I stepped to the wings, pressing my back and shoulders up into the notch of the carved-out harness. The coolness of the stone came through my coat, a chill spiking down my spine. I shivered.

Caleb looked up at me while he adjusted the placement of the wings on my shoulders. "You okay?" he asked softly.

"I'm fine," I said, trying to find my center of balance. The wings were heavy, which I knew they would be, but I braced my legs under the weight of my new burden. "Pull the supports away."

Caleb ducked under the wing on my left as he moved to my back and put his hands along the stone stretching out to either side of me, lifting.

"On your toes," he said.

I pushed myself up into the air, the balls of both feet straining from the effort. Caleb pulled the supports free on both sides, and I lowered my feet, spreading my legs to take on the full, crushing weight. Despite my efforts, I wasn't perfectly centered, off-balance, and I stumbled to my left before correcting myself.

Caleb worked as my spotter, ready to grab the wings, but I shooed him away.

"You sure you can do this?" he asked. "I think our mutual frenemy up there might be a bit hostile tonight."

The thought of Stanis raging after me through the night sky drained the last of the color from my face. "How exactly did you get him here?"

"He needed motivation," Caleb said. "So I gave him one. He knows definitively that you have the book, and he can return it to his master tonight. By the rules Kejetan had me set upon the gargoyle, Stanis *had* to come, here and now."

"He had no choice," I said, my heart going out to the creature that would just as soon crush me in his claws. "Great."

"You *sure* you can do this?" Caleb repeated.

"I'm sure," I said, as anger and a bit of humiliation fueled me. I whispered the words of power over the stone and reached out with my will to either side of me, causing the wings to become malleable and fold in closer, which helped steady me and keep my balance.

I headed off toward the French doors leading onto the terrace. "You mind your part," I said. "I'm trusting you on this. Don't make me regret it."

"I won't," he said, sounding adamant. "Good luck, and try not to die."

I kept silent as I stepped out into the cool night air, focusing on the time I was already counting in my head. The roof proper lay a good fifteen feet above me, but the terrace seemed a much better place to try my takeoff. And if I fucked it up, it would only be a small drop, and I could attempt it again without Stanis's noticing.

I extended the back part of my counting mind out into my wings, establishing a rhythm, moving them the way Stanis worked his. The first few passes were clumsy, the wings not working fully in unison, but after a moment, I brought them into alignment.

On a pure physics level, it seemed unlikely that I could

work the massive stone wings into the night sky. Doubt overwhelmed me for a second, but I kept my count steady. I wasn't sure I would actually get the momentum I needed to do it until I felt my feet lift off the terrace. I cinched the stone of the harness tightly around me before pressing the wings to work harder to rise over the lip of the roof above.

The accumulated collection of statues had grown even more since I last looked up there, and there was Stanis below, moving one into place at the back row. The sight of him broke my concentration, my flight becoming a bit erratic as I rose higher and higher over the top of the Belarus Building. I needed to focus, to calm myself, and as I did, my flying steadied, and I flew higher until I was looking down over the entire roof and its landscape of silent, stone sentinels.

Now for the real work.

"Stanis!" I called down, drawing his attention. He pulled away from the statue, searching the skies until his eyes caught mine. "You care to explain any of this giant chess game you're arranging on my roof?"

I was ready for instant attack. Stanis poised himself on the brink of leaping into the air, but to my surprise, he lowered his arms to his side and pulled his wings in. Clearly some small part of him was struggling to maintain control. It gave me hope, but sadly for me, the kind gargoyle was not the one I needed to deal with if we were going to stand any chance of freeing him.

"Do not provoke me, Alexandra," he said. "I have warned you of the potential consequences."

I had watched Stanis bend his interpretation of my great-great-grandfather's rules, but at that moment I needed the power controlling him to leave not a spot of wiggle room.

"Caleb told you I have the secrets your new master is looking for," I said, slapping my hand onto the front pocket of my coat with my notebook sticking out of it. "And I do. But first? If you want them, you will have to take them from me yourself."

Stanis's face knotted with the struggle, but nonetheless, his wings spread wide.

"I know not why you would put yourself at such risk, Alexandra," he said, "but I will have what I have been sent to get."

The gargoyle leapt into the air with ferocity, whatever power was controlling him fully taking over.

Fear jumped up in my throat, but I did not want to find out how ferocious toward me Stanis could actually be.

I shot up into the night sky, stunned at my own speed, the count of *one, two, three, four* ever present at the back of my mind, going faster and faster with each repetition. I wasn't nearly as practiced as Stanis was in the art of flight, but I was ahead of him. That wouldn't last, but I sped away from the Belarus Building, hoping it would give Caleb the time he needed on the roof.

Despite my quiet panic, I found myself enjoying the chase. I was flying, after all, of my own volition. Part of me missed the gentle care with which Stanis had held me on our previous flights months ago, but to be flying by myself was a whole different experience, filled with a refreshing and powerful freedom I hadn't expected.

As I left Gramercy and hit the lower part of Midtown, I rose higher, soaring well above most buildings there except one: my target. The Empire State Building was awash in a dazzling bright white that night, brighter still at the angle from which I was coming at it. Its luminescence had been my guiding beacon, but it was also my turning point to head back home. I pulled my wings in close as I shot past the building, speeding into the bank of my loop around it, chancing a look back over my shoulder. I'd expected to find Stanis hot on my heels but was relieved to find I had pulled far enough ahead that he was out of sight. As far as speed was concerned, panic was doing an excellent job at keeping me motivated.

The changing of the wind as I hit the crosstown side of the building had my hair in my face. I wished I had at least brought a hair elastic with me. But with my wings doing all the work, my hands were free to clear my vision, and I banked around the Empire State Building heading back downtown.

I needed to keep my lead, and I once again sped up the count in my head. My concentration broke as movement rose in front of me, and I snapped my focus to the looming figure of an oncoming Stanis, claws out and wings pumping away with fury.

My wings faltered as I lost my count, but I willed them to close tight around me. Immediately I dropped like . . . well, a stone. Stanis flew through the space I'd occupied just seconds ago. His momentum was too much, and he crashed into the side of the building, glass shattering as chunks of stone exploded away from it as his figure vanished inside.

The debris plummeted down, catching in the netting meant for jumpers and dropped belongings—the reason I had picked the Empire State Building in the first place. The less damage on the ground, the less chance someone would get hurt.

It would take Stanis a second to right himself, caught within the confines of the building as he was, which thankfully bought me more time. I forced my wings back open, my torso screaming out in the stone harness as the inertia of my falling body met with the resistance of taking flight once more. I grunted as pain spread across the lower part of my rib cage, but I held my concentration and started heading back to the Belarus Building.

Moments later, the explosion of more glass and stone sounded behind me, but confidence filled me. My lead was greater now. As long as Caleb was ready, we should be good to go.

As Gramercy Park came into view on my horizon, I circled over the trees, angling back into the space above the Belarus Building. I scoured the rooftop for signs of Caleb, but in the darkness, I couldn't make him out. The fleeting thought that he might be double-crossing me filled my brain, but I pushed it away. Time would tell on that count, and just then unhelpful thoughts like that were nothing more than distracting.

Pain shot through me as I suddenly found myself tumbling across the sky, my wings thankfully absorbing much of an impact from behind. Without them, Stanis might have torn me in two, but the concussive force was enough to stun me. My wings fully locked and froze out to either side of me, the aerodynamics of that formation barely keeping me in the air.

Before I could compose myself, Stanis's wings and claws were all around me, grabbing me as he spun my body around in midair to face him. I forced my own wings back to life, pressing them between us, the tips driving against his shoulders.

Stanis's eyes met mine, and there was anger in them.

"Why would you do this?" he shouted. "I warned you against telling me *where* Alexander's secret lay. Now you force my hand to treat you like my enemy. I do not understand."

Hurt rose within me, and I used it to fuel my efforts, flexing my wings to break his hold on me. I don't think he expected such strength out of me, and, truthfully, I didn't either, but with my emotions running high, my will was strong, and I pushed away from him, his claws losing their purchase on me. With one giant swoop of my wings, I shot myself above Stanis.

"I can't stand seeing you like this," I said. "You're not yourself. I don't know who you have become, but I won't be afraid of you. I won't."

"But you should be," he said, rising to catch the tip of one of my wings in his clawed hand. Stanis flapped his own, sending the two of us spinning in a circle. He closed his fist into the structure of my wing, his claws sinking into it until the tip crumbled apart in his hands.

Broken but free, the centrifugal force of my damaged wing sent me spinning up and away from him. I fought to focus, dropping my count.

Keeping a steady rhythm wouldn't help me fly right at present. What I needed was stability, and up there that meant spreading my wings as far as they could go and steadying them. With the tip of one wing gone, I found myself, despite my efforts, slowly slipping into a descending arc back toward Stanis. The physics of flight were winning, whether it be magic-powered or no.

"Do you see the ease with which I can break you?" he shouted up at me. "You are far more delicate and fragile than that. Do not make me hurt you. Give me the secrets I have come for."

"Sorry," I said, pulling my wings in close to me, immediately plummeting toward him. "But I can't. And either I save you here and now, or I go down trying."

Stanis might have far more experience with flight, but what I hoped for was that he was far less equipped to deal with falling—especially since I was going to be the cause of it.

I dove straight for him, entirely giving up on controlling my flight and pressing my wings around me into a protective shell. I fell, and with the bulk of my wings sitting as deadweight, I fell *fast.* I slammed into Stanis. The impact had all the force of an auto accident, and despite bracing myself, my teeth came down hard on my tongue, the fresh and coppery taste of blood filling my mouth.

Focusing past that, I popped my wings open and entwined them with Stanis's own. The strength in Stanis's wings was superior; I felt that. In a slugfest, I'd probably be a smudged red spot on the side of a building already, but I had two things going for me.

Surprise was still on my side, first by using my new set of wings and actually engaging Stanis in aerial combat. There was no way he had been prepared for that.

The other was that at that moment, my basic knowledge of physics and gravity were my best friends. Even if Stanis *was* stronger than me, it didn't matter in midtumble. If he couldn't spread his wings, he couldn't fly, and as long as I concentrated on keeping mine tangled with his, the strength in his couldn't crush me like a bug.

The pride in my small bit of triumph, however, didn't have much of a shelf life. We were, after all, falling out of the night sky at an alarming and accelerating rate. I needed to act, and immediately.

We were locked together, tumbling, Stanis trying to force my wings away from his, his claws tearing larger and larger chunks out of them. I had to keep mine in motion swirling just out of Stanis's reach to minimize the damage, but there was another problem.

The roof was coming up fast, and I was relieved to see Caleb's now visible X in fresh orange spray paint marking the target zone. If I wasn't careful, I was going to be the one hitting it first, with Stanis's entire weight coming down on top of me.

The tips of my wings shot forward and wrapped themselves just behind Stanis's shoulders, near the base of his own wings. What I needed was leverage

Instead of wrestling with Stanis and fighting against his wings, I used his body as an anchor to shift my position around. Using the harness I wore as a focal point, I steered my body out of the danger zone by rolling to my left, pulling our tumble into another revolution. I shifted to my far right to compensate for the spin of our turn, so that Stanis would take the full brunt of the impact. Only in the last seconds did I attempt to disengage my wings from Stanis, hoping to catch a bit of air with them like an emergency parachute.

And while that seemed like a great plan, Stanis apparently had another, refusing to disengage his own wings from mine. I braced for impact with the rooftop. This wasn't going to be pretty, not at the speed we were falling.

Thankfully, Caleb had pulled off his part of the plan. Stanis and I hit the X, but instead of crashing against the roof, the stone gave way like freshly poured concrete.

Hitting the surface jarred my whole body with pain, but the roof was more trampoline-y than stone had any right to be. The worst of the blow came from the impact of my flesh scraping against the hard stone of Stanis's body, his wings finally going slack as the two of us sank down into the liquid stone.

The first time I had seen Caleb pull this arcane trick of his, I had lost a pair of boots in Alexander's guild hall. With its happening in large scale, I was happy to have it save my life.

I went to moan, only to find my nose and mouth weren't breathing air. This semiliquid stone went deeper than I had imagined it would, and my face had become submerged in its soupy, gluelike substance. Panicking, I struggled to pull myself out of it, praying that I wasn't still too firmly entwined with Stanis's wings.

My head broke the surface, my mouth gaping wide as I took my first free gulp of air, arms flailing. I fought to get my legs under me, pressing against Stanis's submerged body to help me stand, but it was like trying to get out of quicksand while wearing a burlap sack. My own wings only added to my troubles in finding balance and keeping my footing.

Fingers clamped down over my wrist, and I screamed.

"Easy," Caleb said, trying to pull me out of the liquid stone from where he stood safely on solid roof a foot or so away. "I don't want to get pulled into that."

"I'm covered in it," I said, barely moving. "Did you have to make so big a pool of it?"

"We only had one shot to catch Stanis," he said. He rocked himself back farther, and I started to move. "I didn't want to miss our opportunity, even if it meant depleting our remaining Kimiya."

I stopped and looked up at him, wiping the liquid stone away from my eyes. "We're out of it now?" I asked.

"Almost," he said. "I saved just enough to complete the rest of our plan, but essentially, yeah."

"Shit," I said, standing still knee deep in the liquid stone.

"You okay?"

"All things considered?" I said, doing a quick physical inventory, taking stock of the aches and pains of my body in all this. I nodded. "Yeah."

"Good," he said, and started pulling me out once again.

Slowly, I came free, the liquid stone running from my body and my damaged wings back into the pool below. I couldn't help but notice some of it was the color of my blood. My own set of wings, still partially intact, drooped against me as I concentrated on my footing. When I was finally out of the pool, I let go of Caleb's hand and turned to assess the situation.

The tips of Stanis's wings lay against solid roof on either side of the pool, the rest of him still submerged.

"I know he doesn't need to breathe," I said. "But still . . . Stanis . . . ?"

While I waited for Caleb to give me his thoughts on it, I was met instead by a flurry of explosive activity from the pool itself. Stanis's wings rose out of the liquid stone, their struggling flutter reminding me of birds caught in an oil spill. My heart ached to think of poor Stanis but was replaced by fear for my own safety when his claws broke the surface, struggling to find some kind of purchase.

"Shit," Caleb said, scrambling off to the right side of the pool, fishing his notebook out of his jacket pocket.

Stanis's wings twisted and turned, churning the liquid stone around him. One of them grazed Caleb, who was so caught up in his notes that he stumbled back with a grunt before looking over to me.

"We need to finish this," he said. "I need him a little more docile than this. Actually, a *lot* more."

"On it," I said, watching the roof beneath my feet as I stepped forward, wanting to remain on the solid part of it.

Stanis's head finally broke the surface of the liquid stone, letting out a monstrous roar. I wanted nothing more than to turn and run for the doors leading off the roof, but I held my ground. If I didn't deal with Stanis immediately, I thought my chances of ever helping him might vanish completely.

Truthfully, I wasn't sure how much help I would be in restraining him, but surely he was weakened from the fall.

The only solution seemed to be in the brute force of the

stone I still controlled. I extended what remained of my wings out full to my sides, then pushed all my will into them as I turned their purpose from beauty and flight to that of blunt objects of destruction. The right wing looked worse for wear, and I slammed it into Stanis, pinning him back down beneath the surface of the liquid stone. Then, as much as it tore me up, I slammed the heft of the left wing over and over again into Stanis's chest.

"Stay," I screamed, catching my breath between efforts, "down!"

Stanis raised his arms to defend himself against the brutality of my attack. My natural strength would never have stood a chance against his raw power, but at that moment in time, my magic was powered by my raging will, and the wings were actually having an effect. Stanis struggled to rise, but with him pinned securely beneath the one wing, it was impossible.

Chunks of my wings broke away as they slammed down on him. Blow after blow drove him further and further into submission, and when little remained of the left wing, I switched to the one pinning him and continued the onslaught with it.

Again.

"Alexandra!"

And again.

"Alexandra!"

And again.

"Lexi."

Hearing the familiar friendly form of my name, my mind snapped to, pulling myself out of my attack. Caleb's eyes were wide, switching from me to Stanis, now motionless in the liquid stone.

"Easy," he said. "I think he's down."

Not until I had stopped did I realize how crazed I was, teeth clenched, and my breath coming out in a raspy hitch. I needed to calm myself.

"Sorry," I said. "Did I . . . ?" I couldn't finish my sentence.

"I don't think so," he said. "But we need to finish this. Can you lift him?"

I looked at the torn and tattered remains of my wings.

"Maybe," I said.

"I just need you to for a minute," he said. "I need him standing."

I moved closer to where Stanis lay submerged, then lowered the wings into the pool, bits and pieces of them crumbling away as I searched. I slipped their broken tips under his arms and raised him until he was standing knee deep in the pool, unconscious.

Caleb went to the edge of it and knelt, pouring the entire contents of the vial in his hand into it. Like watching sped-up footage of a lake in winter, the stone froze, once more becoming solid.

I lowered Stanis until he was lying back, bent at the knees with his legs trapped in the by-then-solid roof. I stepped away, unable to take my eyes from him.

"He's not moving," I said.

"I know," Caleb said, already flipping through his notes.

"Will he be his old self?" I asked.

"Only time will tell," he said, moving to an assortment of containers that lay near the door leading off the roof. "I need to work on that still."

I stood in silence, watching Stanis for several minutes before I felt Caleb's hand on my shoulder, squeezing gently.

"This may take a while," he said. "Also, you might want to clean yourself up. You're sort of soaked in some of that liquid stone, and it's starting to seize up."

I lifted my arm, the stiffness in it making it almost impossible to move. Chunks of my hardening coat broke away, but in another couple of minutes I was going to be in trouble if I didn't get clean. I touched a spot of the stone I felt solidifying near my mouth.

"At least it stopped some of my bleeding," I said, hobbling away toward the door.

I don't think Caleb even heard me. He was already mixing various containers together and moving them into place around the still-lifeless Stanis. Just then, I wasn't sure what more I'd have to say anyway.

As Caleb said, time would tell as far as Stanis was concerned.

I planned to use that time wisely—a hot shower in my old room, a change of clothes that hopefully wouldn't involve a jackhammer, and a call I needed to make.

Judging by the strange mix of confused emotions creeping over me at present, I wasn't sure I was ready to deal with both Caleb and Stanis by myself just yet.

Eighteen

☾

Stanis

I awoke with my wings spread out beneath me, my head clouded with thoughts, many of which were not my own. As I stared up at the night sky, my true voice fought to make sense through the madness of the dominant one within, but when it could not, I instead drew my focus to the world around me, the location feeling familiar.

I attempted to rise, but the only movement I found possible was to sit up, and when I did, I discovered the reason for my lack of mobility.

The lower halves of my legs were encased within the stone of a roof I had known for centuries, the one where I had once stood a lone sentinel, watching over the family Belarus. No amount of struggle would release me, strong was the stonework of Alexander, even now, and as I fought to recall how I came here, the sensation of being watched overcame me.

The alchemist Caleb stood well back from the limited arc of my reach, his fingers wrapped around a still-sealed vial. He held my eye a moment longer, but when I didn't speak or make any attempt to move, he slid the vial back within his coat and walked off to a vast array of alchemical equipment I did not recognize.

How had I come here? I could not recall. So lost in my own thought was I that it took a moment to once again feel the alchemist's eyes upon me, and I looked to find him kneeling by his equipment, facing me.

Flame rose from a single match in his hand, and he lowered it to the rooftop. A small, thin trail of blazing green fire burned its way toward me before breaking into two and encircling the spot where I stood trapped. Small pots along the circle released a thick cloud of smoke that rose over me until I could not see anything but darkness.

The once-dominant other voice in my head cried out for action, but I was surprised to find myself able to ignore its pleas. My true self rose more and more to the front of my mind with each passing moment, until I no longer felt even the slightest trace of the other.

Fanning my wings, the cloud broke, and the night sky once again filled my sight, its clarity as sharp as that of my mind. How long I had been within the cloud, I did not know, but it had been long enough that I had drawn a crowd since its passing. My Alexandra stood near the alchemist as the doorway leading down into the building filled with familiar faces. Her friends—and mine—Marshall and Aurora paused there when they saw me.

Alexandra looked to Caleb. "Is he . . . ?" she asked.

"Am I what, Alexandra?" I asked back. "I am quite capable of answering for myself."

She smiled at that, awakening a lightness in me that I had long thought gone.

Marshall crept forward out of the doorway toward me, caution in his every move, but Aurora stayed there. The cylinder was already off her back, the pieces of her weapon already in her hand as she slipped the pole arm together.

"Hello, Marshall," I said, my words causing him to stop. "Aurora."

"It's okay," Caleb said, going back to work on a table near him full of vials and potions. "I think he's back to normal. Although, truthfully, I'm not sure what passes for normal in gargoyle terms."

"I prefer the term *grotesque*," I said. "It is what Alexander called me."

The blond human shrugged, then set about moving around the roof to pick up the assorted clay pots surrounding me. "Suit yourself," he said.

Aurora came out of the doorway, pushing past him before stopping in front of me, her pole arm raised. She looked to the alchemist.

"How do we know he's not in your control?" she asked.

"No, please, don't all rush to thank me," Caleb said, his voice flat.

"The lady makes a valid point," I said. "How can they know that you are not the one in control of me now?"

Caleb shrugged once more.

"I guess they don't," he said.

Alexandra stepped to him, putting her hand on his arm. There was something tender in the gesture, something I found I did not care for.

"Caleb, please," she said. "A little patience, please. They've got every right to be wary."

Given my last encounter with the alchemist on the freighter, Caleb should be grateful I could not reach him at the moment.

He pulled his arm away from Alexandra and fell silent, returning to his work.

Aurora struck the roof that encased my feet with the blunt end of her weapon.

Alexandra's eyes went to it.

"We need to release him," she said.

Caleb looked through the interior of his coat. "That's going to take a few minutes," he said, picking among the contents there. "I used most of the mixture up in creating the trap to capture him in the first place. I need to whip some more up."

"I can do that," Marshall said. "I mean, I'm a quick study with what I've been able to read at the *Libra Concordia* on alchemy."

Caleb turned and stared at him, unmoving.

"Or if you just jot it down for me . . . ?" Marshall said, some of his confidence fading.

"Alchemy and you?" Aurora asked. "*That* sounds like a lethal combination. Just let blondie here do it and be done with it."

"No," Marshall said, the single word filled with a sudden and surprising anger.

"I may still be able to free myself," I said, attempting once again to move my legs within the solid stone. "It may take some doing, but I will try."

"No," Marshall repeated, turning to Alexandra. "I can do this! Lexi, look . . . I'm no good at what you do, right? I simply don't possess the talent for it. As far as casting spells, I don't have Rory's level of precise movement or your level of determined will to drive it. But what Caleb here does . . . That's like . . . cooking. It's recipes, nothing more."

"Nice," Caleb said back to him. "Let's downplay my skill set. Yes, Mr. Blackmoore, it's *just* like cooking. *Anyone* can do it, right? Just ask any cook who's gone up against an Iron Chef. Simple!"

"You're no Morimoto," Aurora said, leaving me to wonder what a "morimoto" was.

Caleb went to the table, slamming several vials down from out of his coat next to another group already on the table.

"Fine," he said, pulling his notebook from his side pocket. "You want to try? Be my guest. But go easy on the Kimiya. That's pretty much the last of it."

The alchemist wrote with haste upon one of the pages, walked over to Marshall in front of me, then tore it free and handed it to him. "There you go, padawan. Try not to blow anything or anyone up, okay?"

Marshall paused before taking the page from him. "Is . . . that a possibility?" he asked, his voice quiet now.

Caleb shrugged. "Guess you'll find out the hard way."

Something about both the gesture and his voice set me on edge. Perhaps it was reminiscent of the tone he had taken with me while I was in captivity, and I could not help but react to it.

Trapped as I was, I could not reach out with my claws and grab him as I wished. My wings, however, covered a much greater span than my reach. I scooped them forward, catching Caleb between them and pulling him to me. I spun him, my claws digging into his shoulders through his coat, and I raised his face to mine.

"When last we met, you sent me here bound by Kejetan's rules," I said, growling. "You sent me here, putting Alexandra directly in harm's way from me. You said I would take the secrets of Alexander from her cold, dead hands."

The alchemist gave a nervous glance to Alexandra.

She came forward, circling to stand next to me in order to face Caleb.

"You said that . . . ?" she asked, her voice a mix of anger and pain.

My claws dug in at that, and Caleb hissed in my grip.

"I *had* to if this was going to work," he fired out. "We were on Kejetan's ship, and Stanis was *entirely* under his control. If I had told Stanis our plan, Kejetan would have found out. The dominant power that controlled Stanis would have blown everything if I had let your gargoyle in on it." He met my eye. "You know it's true."

But was it?

"I cannot deny your claim," I said.

My true voice had simply been a passenger to the dominant one. If Caleb had set me to any other task less specific than seeking out Alexandra to retrieve her secrets, it was quite possible I could have ignored it by circumventing Kejetan's rules. Worse, I would still be hanging in the cargo hold as a prisoner. It was also quite possible that had he told me of the rescue plan, the dominant voice would have kept me from ever reaching them, and it might have forced me to reveal it to Kejetan.

"You see?" he said, craning his head around to meet everyone's eye. "I'm not in with the bad guys."

This was harder to see the truth in. Flashes of the torture I had endured at his hand tore through my thoughts. Every pain. Every injustice. Every moment that had kept me from Alexandra.

"Do you put these people in jeopardy?" I asked in a low growl, my claws digging even harder into his shoulders. "It was one matter to torture me, to break me . . . It is quite another to put these humans in harm's way. I will not stand for it."

He hissed again, but to his credit, the man's head turned back to me, and his eyes stayed locked with mine. I would have taken him for fearless if not for the nervous laughter that followed.

"Relax, big guy," he grunted out. "Rest assured that Alexandra's safety is my paramount concern in this world. And Rory? I'm pretty sure she can handle herself with that pigsticker of hers." He turned his head to Marshall over at the table, who was already sorting through a handful of vials. "And Marshall? I'm not going to leave him with anything he can lose his hands with." His eyes came back to rest on me. "Trust me."

My eyes stayed locked with his a moment longer before setting him back down on the roof.

"Very well," I said, some of my anger dying down.

Caleb moved with swift steps beyond the reach of both my arms and wings before turning to face me. "I mean, Marshall might be able to do some damage to himself if he, like, drinks whatever he mixes." He looked to Marshall at the table. "You're not stupid enough to drink any of those, are you?"

"*You're* stupid enough to drink some of them," Alexandra said, still at my side.

"Ouch," he said, raising his hand over his heart, then turned to Marshall. "But seriously, try not to blow yourself up."

"Are humans always this confusing?" I whispered to Alexandra.

To my surprise, her face was burning crimson, her eyes

fixed straight ahead. "Don't get me started," she said, then leaned her head against me. "Good to have you back."

"It is good to be back," I said. "But I fear my freedom does not change much. When I went with my father months ago, it was to buy you time. Have you spent it well?"

Alexandra stepped away from me. "That's a debatable point," she said. "We're certainly making progress. But you know Alexander. All codes and enigma!"

"Speaking of Alexander," Aurora said, no longer keeping her pole arm ready for action. "I think we found something useful in the books at the *Libra Concordia*."

"That would be a pleasant surprise," Alexandra said.

"*Libra Concordia*?" I asked, unsure of the term.

"Just another group I freelance for," Caleb said, joining us.

"They'd love to get their hands on you," Alexandra said. "They've been looking for you since you rescued my father as a boy, when he had his whole religious conversion."

I looked to Aurora. "What did you find?" I asked.

Aurora handed Alexandra a notebook filled with writing.

"Marshall and I started comparing notes from the books of Alexander Belarus that the *Libra Concordia* have," she said. She pointed to a specific grouping of lines on the page.

Marshall called over from the table, busy reading the labels of several vials that filled his hands. "Your great-great-grandfather keeps referencing the Holy Trinity over and over in multiple books," he said to Alexandra. "He talks about the secrets of the Holy Trinity again and again. We thought there might be some significance to that. It shows up too much in the books the *Libra Concordia* has acquired to be a coincidence."

"Forgive me," I said, all of the humans turning to me, "but Alexander was not a man of religion."

"Stanis is right," Alexandra said.

Aurora's excitement died, replaced with confusion. "But he built all those churches," she said.

"He built a lot of things," Alexandra said. "Building

office buildings doesn't make him a businessman any more than building churches made him religious."

Aurora smiled. "Then it's even stranger he kept referencing the Holy Trinity, isn't it?"

Alexandra returned her smile, which I did not understand.

"Why do you take pleasure in this knowledge?" I asked.

"Because," she said, "if my great-great-grandfather wasn't a religious man, then the Holy Trinity and its secrets most likely refer to something else. And I think I know what it is."

Aurora stepped back from the notebook and looked up at her friend. "You do?"

Alexandra nodded. "I do," she said. "At least, I think I do. Many of the books Locke has gathered reference the secrets of the Holy Trinity, you say. Now, maybe it's just a coincidence, but I find it quite interesting that the *Libra Concordia* just happened to acquire one of Alexander's long-abandoned churches, and that it just happens to be located on Trinity Place across from Trinity Church."

Aurora's eyes widened. "Alexander has some of his secrets there?"

Alexandra turned to Caleb. "What do you think?" she asked.

"It's possible," Caleb said. "It is one of Alexander Belarus's buildings. And I agree with your theory about why they bought the church in the first place. A church would be a perfect hiding place. No one tears churches down these days."

"We need to search that building," Alexandra said. "But we won't get too far with Desmond Locke watching us like a hawk every time we step out of the research room. If we're lucky, there will be more than just the secrets to Kimiya. I'm hoping we'll find out the deeper secrets of the Spellmasons, so I can raise our own army of stone fighting men."

"Desmond Locke?" I said. "Your father's spiritual adviser?"

Alexandra laughed. "It's been a long six months. We've a lot to catch up on."

Marshall came to us, a small glass container full of liquid in his hands. "I think I'm ready," he said.

Caleb looked down at it. "Ready?" he asked. "I don't think so. That's not nearly enough."

Marshall's eyes went to the mixture and stayed there. "I—I think it is," he stammered, a lack of confidence. "Besides, there was barely enough Kimiya to make this. It will have to do."

Caleb laughed, but there was derision it. "You can try," he said, "but you're not going to free him, I'm telling you. There's no way you're going to affect the stone of the roof deep enough to get Stanis loose."

The tone of his voice awoke something hostile in me, and I brought my clawed hand down on his shoulder. "Let Marshall try," I said, squeezing.

Caleb hissed. "Suit yourself," he said, and pulled himself away from the rest of the group.

Alexandra looked to Marshall. "You sure you're up for this?" she asked.

He nodded and looked up at me, but his eyes were uncertain.

"You can do this, Marshall," I said. "I have faith."

He did not respond but instead circled around me as he judged the amount in the container and began pouring it.

"That's not nearly wide enough," Caleb said, crossing his arms. "You're not going to free him that way."

"Shush," Rory shouted out at him.

Caleb shrugged. "Just trying to help," he muttered under his breath.

Marshall was on his knees by then, pouring in a tight circle around me.

"I don't need to go wide," he said. "I need to go deep. I only need to free up the area around him."

The stone around my legs began to transform. It loosened around the lower part of my legs to the point where I could move them. Stretching, I pulled one foot free, stepping up and onto the solid part of the roof. The other foot, however, was still stuck in solid stone. Marshall's concoction had not gone deep enough indeed.

Still, I did not wish to give Caleb the satisfaction of being right, so with all my strength, I put all my weight on my freed foot and pulled. The stone immediately around my trapped foot did not give, but the rest of the roof did. My foot came up and out of the liquid stone with a chunk of jagged rooftop surrounding it. Marshall gave a victorious cry, and he and Aurora slapped their hands together. I stepped onto the roof, walking away from the hole and bringing my foot down hard enough over and over that the rest of the stone fell away piece by piece.

Alexandra rushed over, throwing her arms around me. As the heat of her skin against me set in, the world and everything around us seemed to melt away. My stone arms wrapped around her, the jagged rise and fall of her chest beating against mine as I felt her tears hit the coolness of my carved skin.

"You have been missed," she said.

"It has been far too long since I have been myself," I said, pushing her back so I could look into her eyes.

We stood, simply staring at each other, lost in the moment. It felt longer than the centuries my existence had, but suddenly felt all too short when the sound of the alchemist Caleb clearing his throat rang out.

Alexandra turned her head to him, her head falling back for a moment to rest on my chest.

"We need to find Alexander's work," Caleb said. "May I remind you we're so out of Kimiya it's not even funny?" He pointed to the statues all along the rest of the rooftop. "And we've got an army up here we need it for if we can also find the secrets you need to bring them to life. Let's hope whatever Alexander's hidden away there helps you unlock the Spellmason secret to your splitting your mind more easily for casting. Either way, we need to act fast."

"He's right," Alexandra said, pushing herself away from me with reluctance.

"You and I should go," Caleb said to her. "The church is full of special-access areas and secret alcoves . . . stuff that only I among the group of us has access to."

"I can tear that church apart looking for Alexander's secrets," I said.

Caleb shook his head. "We can do this discreetly."

"I'm all for discretion," Alexandra said, her eyes locked with mine, hesitation in them. When she spoke again, her voice sounded more like she was trying to convince herself into going. "Having a Belarus there might get more answers than not. My family's legacy has been one big game of hide-and-seek. What's one church more?"

I said nothing. Alexandra needed to go, but I was not going to let it come from my lips. There was a selfishness in it, I knew, but I could not let my own words be the ones that sent her away again.

Especially with him.

Caleb looked out across the statue-covered roof of the Belarus Building, gesturing at them. "We've practically got an army up here, and if we can find a way to mass-produce enough Kimiya to bring them to life, we can oppose Kejetan."

"Aren't you worried about him complaining to the free-lancers' union?" Aurora asked him.

Caleb sighed. "Such a snarky, angry bunch," he said. "You sure you're the good guys?"

"That is the trouble with playing both sides," I said with a growl. "You run the risk of angering twice as many people."

"Don't remind me," he said, then gave me a smile. "But then again, the higher the risk, the greater my reward. I figure helping raise this army here should be worth something."

"Nuh-uh," Aurora said, scolding him. "You're doing this act out of the goodness of your little black heart."

Caleb spun around to her. "I am?"

"Yes," Alexandra said, walking to me and laying a hand on my chest as she looked at Caleb. "You are. You've got a lot of bad blood to work off here, remember? You've spent months wronging our good friend here, so consider this payback."

"Unless you'd rather I beat it out of you," Aurora said, poking the nonbladed end of her pole arm at him.

Marshall gestured to the hole in the roof. "Rory and I will work on patching this up," he said.

"Aurora's beating would be the least of your concerns," I said to Caleb. "There is still Kejetan for you to think of. My father will kill you for your betrayal."

What color was left in the man's face went away, his amused look disappearing.

"Yeah, I know," Caleb said, turning away and heading for the doorway. "Don't think that's not on my mind twenty-four/ seven now. That's why we need to make more of your kind. That's why we need to go back to the *Libra Concordia*."

"I'll grab my library card," Alexandra said, going for her backpack, patting her hand against the stone spell book sticking out of it. "Maybe it grants me special access to the off-limits areas."

Alexandra ran to me and threw her arms around me again, and I did the same back. She looked up at me, her eyes unwavering.

"I'll be back," she said. "I promise. Look after Marshall and Rory, okay?"

"As you wish," I said, causing her to smile.

She lingered a moment longer before turning and walking slowly away.

"Don't hold your breath about gaining special access at the *Libra Concordia*," Caleb said as he hit the stairs heading down into the building. "There's off-limits, then there's *really* off-limits."

As I watched Alexandra run off to catch up with him, something deep within me twinged with pain.

"You okay there, Stanis?" Aurora asked.

"I do not like this ease and familiarity between the two of them," I said, fighting my sudden urge to tear apart the man who had tortured me for months. Caleb had told me that he had not known I was a living creature, but even with that knowledge, I found it hard to just let it go.

"It takes some getting used to," Marshall admitted as he held up a clear tube full of a dark green bubbling liquid.

"I think I understand what you're getting at," Aurora said with a smile. She leaned in closer. "I don't trust him either. But I'd hold out on any desires to crush his head in just yet."

"That is unfortunate to hear," I said, leaping into the air and taking to the night sky. "I would like nothing more."

The confusion of fighting the dominant other voice in my head was gone, but I still felt the need to take to the sky to clear my thoughts. There was still the problem of my father and the Servants of Ruthenia to contend with, and Alexandra and the alchemist, but for now the only peace I could find was flying as a free creature after so many months of servitude. Head crushing could wait.

For the moment, at least.

Nineteen

◗

Alexandra

When Caleb had said there were a multitude of secret alcoves and such throughout the *Libra Concordia*, he wasn't kidding. My head still spun from earlier. I went through the boarded-up hidden doors of the church, planning to systematically work my way down the main aisle, but Caleb grabbed me before I could and instead dragged me off through the maze of the space in search of my great-great-grandfather's secrets.

The sounds of people working echoed throughout the area, but thanks to Caleb's sneaky ways, we didn't cross paths with a single one of them in our initial pass of the main floor. Despite our clandestine lurking about the church looking for Alexander's secrets, we still had nothing to show for it except frustration, and Caleb dragged me into our usual research room before I could scream.

"Fruitless," I said, once he had shut the door behind him.

"Don't sound so disappointed," Caleb said. "I didn't really expect to find anything on the first pass, did you?"

"Truthfully?" I said. "No. But it would have been nice."

Caleb laughed and shook his head. "Nice doesn't enter into the dark, magical secrets business. Sorry."

"Maybe it's carved in runes on the outside of the building or something," I said. "We should come back during daylight to check it out."

"And miss checking out what the basement here has to offer us?" Caleb clicked his tongue at me. "You know that caged area up here?"

I nodded. "That's where they keep all the stuff they've recovered."

"Partially," he said. "It's the area where they keep the cataloged stuff. Most of it is written up in their ledgers, and if you had the time to sit back and read them, they're endlessly fascinating. Luckily, they let me bill by the hour for that. I make lawyers look like they're undercharging."

"And yet you were squatting in my old family's building on Saint Mark's before it collapsed," I said.

"My costs for supplies are high," he reminded me, then pointed down at the floor. "Let's stay focused, all right? There's an area or two here in the church that I'm not allowed into. Probably because I'm a freelancer . . . or a heathen. None of what's kept down there is on the record up here."

"Then how do *you* know about it?" I asked.

"I'm the curious sort," he said.

I smiled. "I bet you are," I said. "Didn't turn out well for the cat."

"Nor did it for me," he said, frowning. "The stairs leading down to it are protected. I was back in the *apse*, and next thing I knew, the railings flew off the side of the stairs and wrapped around my arms. Desmond didn't seem particularly thrilled to find me trying to venture downstairs, but I talked my way out of it, making it seem like nothing more than an honest accident."

"You *can* be very convincing even if you're lying," I said, filling the words with a darker bite than I meant to, surprising myself.

Caleb stepped back from me as if I had slapped him. "What's *that* about?" he asked.

"Sorry," I said. "It's nothing."

I hadn't meant to lash out, and I wasn't sure I wanted to

explain it to Caleb even if I could. With Caleb's having
returned Stanis to his former self, I knew I could trust him,
but at the same time I was discovering that having the gargoyle back conflicted with my growing fondness for Caleb.
Now was not the time to get into it. "You were saying about
this restricted area . . . ?"

" 'It's nothing' . . . ?" he repeated, narrowing his eyes at
me. "All right, well, you just tell me when you want to talk
about this nothing, then."

"Caleb . . ."

He held his hands out in front of him and pretended to
let go of something heavy.

"This is me dropping it," he said.

He wiped his hands together as if cleaning them off.

"As I was about to say, my money is on the restricted
area."

"We just need a different way in, then," I said. "Unless
you think we could take on a set of enchanted stairs?"

"I think that might draw a little attention," he said, moving to the table at the center of the room. He reached into
his pocket, pulled out his notebook, and laid it down, taking
a seat. He gestured to the chair across from him. "Maybe
we should compare notes on your spells and my concoctions,
see what we can come up with that might help us get down
into the lower parts of this church."

With no better plan, I sat down opposite Caleb and set
to work looking through my own notes, also pulling out
Alexander's stone spell book and transforming it into read-
able pages. After twenty minutes, I slammed both books
shut.

"This is ridiculous," I said, standing up and stepping
away from the table. "I don't have half of the things I want
here to do most of this."

"Me either," Caleb said, in the middle of inventorying
the left-side contents of his coat's hidden bandoliers.

"And even if I did, we can't just walk out into the main
room and hope not to cause a commotion."

"There's got to be another way down there," he said.

"There is," I said, stepping farther back from the table. "We're just overthinking it."

Caleb stood, looking where I was at the spot in the center of the room.

The church, despite its current life as a secret society's storehouse, was still an old-world piece of architecture, which meant the touches my great-great-grandfather had applied in building it were a luxurious mirror of the time period. And being the man that he was, his attention to the stonework was impeccable, including the large slabs of stone floor where we stood.

Caleb was already fumbling through the insides of his coat, but I shook my head.

"No," I said. "We don't want to damage anything if we don't have to. No one knows we're here, and if we do it my way, hopefully no one *will* know."

"Good point," he said, and let his hands drop to pick up his notebook instead.

I slid my master tome into my backpack and snatched up my notes, breathing out the words of power into the large stone square at the center of the room. No doubt it was cosmetic, with others beneath it, but it was a start.

My will connected with it, and I guided it with my right arm as I forced it up and out of its slot, the dust of ages falling from the cracks around it. It wavered unsteadily at my command, but I managed to set it down without a sound before realizing I was clenching my teeth from the effort. I rubbed my jaw.

"You're going to hurt yourself doing it like that," he said. "Stop looking at the stone like the heft of it truly matters. Your mind is tricking you into compensating for the weight it thinks you should be lifting."

"Yes, Professor," I said, turning back to the hole I had just created. The stones beneath were rougher but only half the size of the one above. I reached out to the one on the left, and grabbed it with only my will. Maybe Caleb was onto something because although it was more firmly wedged into the foundation, when it came free I did notice a sizable difference in handling it if I tried to ignore the stone's actual size.

The two of us moved to the edge of the hole I had made. A dim light filled the area below, but I had the Maglite that Boy Scout Marshall had given me and shined its light down below. The lower levels of the church weren't quite as finely finished as the main floor, but they still looked in good shape.

"About fifteen feet or so," I said. "Damned old-world luxury and high, religious ceilings."

"We're getting down this way," he said. "But I don't think it's the way we're coming back up."

Marshall's voice screamed at the back of my mind reminding me on the importance of rope. Sadly, I had none.

"Normally I'd say ladies before gentlemen," Caleb said, lowering himself in to his waist, his hands spread out on the floor to either side of him. "But somehow I don't think letting you plummet into trouble first would be chivalrous."

Before I could respond, he pulled his arms in tight and dropped through, landing on his feet with a hushed *thud*. He waved for me to jump down, and before I could start worrying about breaking an ankle or hitting my head on a rock, I sat on the floor, scootched forward, and let go.

I needn't have worried about damaging myself on the floor below. Caleb caught me in his arms, lowering me to the ground.

"Thanks," I said, welcoming the closeness.

"That's two chivalry points," he said with a smile.

The walls and ceiling there were nothing like those on the main floor. No ornamentation or detailing beyond the plain, carved stones fit together and the vaulted arches supporting the structure. Not that there was much to see in the narrow corridor we found ourselves in. The entire lighting consisted of bare bulbs that had been pegged into the stone walls too far apart to actually give off much light.

"Come on," Caleb said, turning right down the corridor.

The space echoed with our movement as we walked through arch after arch, coming to a final one barred by a thick iron gate that ran from floor to ceiling. Beyond it, in the shadows, lay the outlines of what looked like shelves similar to those in the gated area upstairs.

"Now, see, *this* says restricted area," Caleb said in a triumphant whisper as he pressed his face up against the gate, looking through. "Don't you think?"

"I particularly like the bars," I said. "Nice touch."

Caleb stepped back and wrapped his hands around the gate, pulling then pushing them, but they didn't move.

"So how do we get in?" I asked.

Caleb took my light from me and set to examining the gate and the arch.

"Maybe you need a secret decoder ring from the Pope," he said. "I don't know. All I do know is that we need to find a way in." He continued his investigation, his face inches from the wall where the arch met the gate. "Oh great."

"What is it?" I asked, straining to notice what he might be looking at but failing to see jack.

"Mr. Locke might not let your average Joe down here, and it seems he's had some extra precautions installed."

"Like . . . ?" I moved closer, watching Caleb as his fingers traced along the surface of the stone wall.

"I'm not sure, exactly," he said. He reached out and took my hand in his. If I weren't already panicked about being discovered, I might have taken a moment to enjoy it, but the desire passed as Caleb raised my hand and pressed it to the stone. He placed his hand over mine and guided my fingers along the stones of the archway.

"Feel that?" he asked.

I nodded, pulling my hand away and focusing on the spot as my eyes finally tuned in to what I hadn't seen at first.

"It looks like a language," I said.

"Runes," he corrected. "More specifically: runes of warding. Meant to keep us out."

Both my eyebrows raised. "Did Locke do this?"

Caleb snickered. "These religious types don't like to dirty their hands dabbling in magic," he said. "Too above it all, but you know what they're not above? Hiring freelancers to do their dirty work. I'm just a little hurt he didn't ask me."

"Do you know *how* it's meant to keep us out?"

"Not exactly," he said, "but by the style of the carving, I can pin who did it. The Witch and Bitch Society. You know, like the Stitch and Bitch knitters."

"O . . . kay."

Caleb let out a long sigh. "I wish I could say it was just a clever take on a sewing circle name, but I've had a run-in or two with them. Not all that fond of their work, mostly because they cut into my profit margin in competitive freelancing."

"But can you break this ward?" I asked. "Can you get us in?"

"Maybe," he said, and started poking through the contents of his jacket.

Nerves getting the better of me, I couldn't stand waiting, and as a thought occurred to me, I pressed past Caleb toward the gate. I grabbed the latch, which he had completely ignored, feeling resistance, but more of the kind that came with aged metal. I jerked the latch upward, and the gate swung freely into the room beyond.

"Look at me," I whisper shouted. "I'm a wizard!"

"Or we could try that approach, sure."

Triumphant but still full of nerves, I pressed on into the room beyond. Much like the gated area above, rows of shelves filled the room, a large maze of books and artifacts stacked high on each of them. Row after row continued down the line, and at the end against the back wall lay a small, carved basin set half in the floor and half into the wall.

"A well?" Caleb asked.

"It's a stoup," I said. "It's a Roman Catholic architectural thing. The more ornate ones are set at the front of the church by the doors, but I'm thinking the *Libra Concordia* is keeping a ready supply in case they have to deal with any of the nasty toys they might have gathered here."

"Is it holy water?" Caleb asked, stepping back from it.

"Afraid you might get burned?" I asked.

Caleb ignored me and set off down one of the aisles. I picked another and headed into it. If my great-great-grandfather's secrets were somewhere in the church as the notes had said, this had to be the place.

There was little hope in determining the point and purpose of much that was here, not without some kind of reference material, but I slogged on through the aisles for half
an hour or so before something on the shelves caught my eye.

"Caleb!" I called out to the next aisle as quietly as I could,
and he came running.

"Find something?" he asked.

I raised my light, shining it on the small, sculpted building that sat on the shelf.

Caleb reached for it, pulling it from under several books
that were leaning against it.

"This is where we are," he said. "It's a scale model of
this very church."

"This isn't a scale model of this church," I said, taking
it from him.

Caleb eyed me with suspicion. "It looks like one to me,"
he said.

"It's a puzzle box," I corrected. "One of my great-great-
grandfather's, to be precise. What it is doing here apart from
the rest we kept at the Belarus Building is a mystery."

"Maybe Desmond Locke took it," he said.

"I've never seen it before. It must have gone missing from
the collection before I was born."

"It's pretty elaborate," Caleb said, still staring at the miniature in wonder.

I looked up at him, a little perturbed. "All Alexander
Belarus knew how to make were elaborate things. You've
met Stanis, right?"

"I'm just saying," he said. "As far as nonmagical things
go, if that's a puzzle box, it's also an amazing miniature
architectural wonder."

I ignored him, continuing to look it over. By its heft
alone, I could judge that the miniature of the church was
itself actually comprised of stone. I doubted that simply
trying to smash it on the ground was going to make it
divulge its secrets to us.

"We had lots of these in his art studio," I said. "Nothing
quite like this, mind you, but I had worked my way through

all those puzzles over time, so hopefully this one won't take me too long to figure out."

As I set to examining the miniature church closer, Caleb moved past me back out into the main aisle, looking around.

"The sooner, the better," he said. "Not sure how long we have before someone discovers we're down here."

"Puzzling as fast as I can," I said, and turned the church over and over in my hands.

Alexander might have been a Spellmason, but the core of that practice was his artistry and, in this specific case, his flair for architecture. The real trick of his work was in knowing what to look for. My great-great-grandfather was a logical man, and if you paid attention to the things he had created—arcane or not—there was a sense to them. With that in mind, I set the church back down on the shelf to ponder its mysteries.

I tapped at it on all sides, hoping to hear a hollow part, but the damned thing seemed as solid a piece of stone as it looked.

"Damn Alexander and his old-world craftsmanship," Caleb said, shaking his fist at the miniature church.

Think, Lexi, think!

"Craftsmanship . . ." I repeated, the word striking a chord in me. "Whether in miniature or not, the principles of architecture should hold true."

"Principles of architecture?"

"Things such as the classical-ideals stuff that sprung out of the Roman Empire, like the arch." I pointed at the one over the door of the tiny church. "What's the most foundational item in supporting a structure like this church? If you wanted to build something tall out of stone, it had to be sturdy." I spun the model around and pointed to another arch. "Tensile stress of open space is taken up by compressional stress."

"Compressional?"

I spun the model again, pointing to another arch, dragging my finger to the top of it, pointing at the stone there.

"Keystones," I said, turning the church back to its front face. I ran my thumb over the keystone above the main doors of the church and it felt solid to my touch, but when I pressed hard against it, the tiny keystone slid inward with a *click*. I rotated the church, moving from arch to arch, activating all the rest of the keystones I could find. The last two were along the top of the steeple, and once pressed, the base of the model came free, sliding out and away from under it.

"Got it?" Caleb asked.

"Maybe," I said, examining it. I pried the top of the base open from a notch at its center, finding what I was looking for, the familiar scrolled Belarus *B* etched into the cover of the book.

Caleb reached past me and grabbed the book from within the base, struggling to lift it in one hand. "Heavy," he said. "It's stone."

"To keep it safe from the ravages of time," I said, grabbing it back from him. "Like my great-great-grandfather's master spell book. I can take care of that later."

"We should go," he said.

I agreed, fixing the by-then-empty base back under the church until I felt it lock into place. I slid it back on the shelf, leaning the books against it as best I remembered them, hoping I was leaving it the way we had found it.

Caleb grabbed my hand and pulled me down the aisle after him, gaining speed. Now that we had had the luck of finding what we had come for, neither of us wanted to press it further by staying a moment longer than we had to. Halfway up the main aisle, the gates ahead slammed shut of their own accord. I ran to them, pulling once more at the iron handle, but it wouldn't budge.

"Is there a password to this?" I asked.

"Probably," Caleb said, looking around. "Damned if I know it, though."

"Do something!" I shouted. I shook the gate, the rattling of it echoing through the basement of the church. I didn't care about the noise it made now, but only because another sound caught my ear—the burbling of water behind us. I turned and looked back past Caleb in time to see the stoup along the back wall erupt in an explosion of water.

Caleb spun around. "Oh hell," he said. "I *really* hate those Witch and Bitch hags."

What I thought must be a geyser bubbled up out of the stoup all the way to the ceiling before I realized it was something more than just that. An actual form took shape within it, resembling something that reminded me of one of those Chinese parade dragons. "What *is* that?"

"Not sure," Caleb said, grabbing my arm as the creature charged us. He pulled me away from the gate after him as he darted down one of the other aisles. "Let's not find out, shall we?"

I agreed wholeheartedly, running after him just as the creature hit the iron gate. It slowed as it passed through it, the solidity of its body working its way around the bars, but its head was already rearing around to come back through for a return trip. Caleb jerked my arm as he turned down a side aisle, and the creature fell out of my line of sight.

"We need another way out," he said, coming to a stop. I slammed into him, turning to find ourselves at the back wall once more, with the broken stoup in front of us. The creature's telltale sloshing noise, coming from somewhere behind us, grew louder with each passing second.

Was I supposed to fight the damn thing? How the hell did you fight water?

And I didn't dare defend myself in the bowels of this unfamiliar church by rearranging any parts of the walls or ceiling to protect us. We were in the basement now—most of the architectural structures around us were probably crucial to keeping the building standing. The last thing I wanted to do was magic the wrong stone out of place and pull the entire building down on top of us.

The floor near the stoup, however, was another story. If there was water coming in, there was also a source for it, one that might be a way out. A mass of pipes leading away from the stoup drilled down into the floor, and I set my will against several floor slabs that lay just in front of them.

I breathed out the words of power once more, the weight of the ancient stones straining my will as I forced them up and out of the floor where they had sat joined for centuries. I rolled the bunch of them off to the side as I pushed my will into the stones beneath those, feeling the shift and grind of the ground beneath us as I did so. Dust and dirt fell away from the stones as they came fully free, and I tore them up out of the earth, feeling a bit of hope when a waft of air rose up out of the open hole.

"Get in," I said, peering down into the darkness below. Light danced along a hint of water below, but the noxious smell of trash and something more foul arose, driving Caleb back as he approached.

"Is that . . . ?"

"Don't argue," I shouted. "Just get in!"

Caleb still looked hesitant, but the sound of the water creature was closer than ever. I didn't bother to turn around, opting instead for shoving Caleb down into the hole before jumping in after him.

Once through, the light was not nearly as bad as I thought, allowing me to see Caleb crumple into the stream of sewage below us right before I landed on him. My boots caught him in the middle of his back, driving him fully underwater, which on the plus side allowed me to keep standing. I stepped off him onto the floor of the tunnel and stumbled away as Caleb resurfaced.

His hair was matted to his head, and he gasped for breath, using all of his energy to stand as quickly as he could, but even so, he was drenched in sewage. He looked ill, his eyes wide, and his mouth fighting not to gag.

"Are you kidding me?" he shouted. "Are you *kidding* me?"

"I'm *sorry!*" I shouted back. "What did you want me to do?"

"Not dump me into a river of *sewage*, for starters—"

Caleb didn't get to finish his sentence.

The water creature poured down through the hole above us like a concentrated tidal wave. It splashed beneath the surface of the murky water and disappeared, the only movement that of the running sewage.

"I don't know about you," Caleb said, "but I don't plan

on drowning in a river of shit. You might want to get your spell book out."

Caleb didn't have to ask twice; my hands were already fumbling for my notebook as the stream of sewage erupted with the splash of the rising, swirling creature. The clear form of its body was now a dark and chunky mix, which I didn't care to think about, but I'd be damned if I'd let that thing get ahold of me, especially in *that* form. The real question was what was I supposed to do?

"A little help here," I called out while looking for anything helpful in my notes. "Liquid really isn't my forte."

The creature lunged for Caleb, and rather than trying to avoid it, he pushed forward, lunging *through* it. There was resistance in its body, but Caleb came through the other side of it wet but otherwise unharmed. The same could not be said of the creature, which fell into two pieces. As the two pieces of the monster fought to rejoin themselves, Caleb held up a vial filled with something gray.

"Liquid isn't really your forte?" he asked, repeating me while upending the vial, the powdery concoction pouring out of it into the creature. "Unless it's liquid *stone.*"

The color of its form shifted from its addition, and when I reached out with my power, I felt it connect to the writhing creature in front of me. The monster lunged, but I could feel the presence of stone growing within it as the gray of its form grew darker and darker. My will lashed out, and what had become a stone creature fell to my command, and I slowed it, and to my surprise, the mass solidified, crashing into the bottom of the tunnel. It shattered into several sections as it settled there, the twisted, tortured features of its solid face sticking up out of the sewage at me.

Caleb held up the emptied vial, tapping the last few flakes out of it.

"What *was* that?" I asked, unable to suppress a shiver.

"Mostly just concrete," he said.

I looked at the broken length of the twisted creature. "That vial didn't hold *that* much concrete."

Caleb slipped the empty vial inside his coat and shook

his head in disappointment at me. When he spoke, there was anger in his words. "See? It's *just* that kind of linear, literal thinking just like upstairs with the stone that is holding you back," he said. "Sure, I get it. You carve things. They're finite, tangible . . . but alchemy isn't about size or proportion all the time. *You* see a single vial of concrete. You know what I see as an alchemist? A bit of concrete mixed with some quick-spreading Kimiya that accelerates growth." He shook his head, then slapped me on the shoulder as he walked past me. "You need to get that kind of thinking out of your head."

Despite what I had just accomplished, I felt tremendously stupid. I stared at the stone-still creature a moment longer as the sounds of Caleb's splashing away down the tunnel rose behind me. Turning, I ran to catch up, careful not to fall.

"I'm still learning," I protested. "Caleb, you have to understand. So much of what I can do is literally textbook— notes from Alexander—but there's no school for this. You're the only other practitioner I know!"

"Lucky me," he said, softening a bit. "And look at all this quality time we're getting to spend together reeking of sewage."

"Maybe this Witch and Bitch club can help us with making another gargoyle," I suggested, trying to ignore the smells all around us. "They're freelancers, after all. They did some work for Desmond Locke. Why not us?"

Caleb stopped and spun around to face me. "No!" he shouted.

"Well, why *not*?"

Caleb looked like he was biting his tongue as he composed himself, and I waited, with more patience than I expected to have considering I was knee deep in a river of filth.

"First of all," he said, "*I'm* the freelancer you need to be working with. Do you really want to work with some group whose security system you just defeated?"

"That was more you than me," I said.

Caleb sighed, running his fingers through his hair before

he realized how gross it was and gave up. "It was *both* of us," he said. "We work well together. I don't want to bring in outsiders when I know we can do this ourselves. You'll learn quickly that the fewer people you get involved in something, the less chance of other people's messing it up."

All this talk of us working together, it was almost romantic. Again, if not for where we were standing.

"Okay," I said, holding up my newfound secret book of Alexander's. "We have this to work from and a bunch of test gargoyle subjects to animate and all that, so no witches for now."

I started sloshing my way toward him. "But I would like to know more about this Witch and Bitch club," I added. "We might have defeated their sentry, but we didn't have an easy time of it."

Caleb looked down at his clothes in disgust and turned away, heading off down the sewer tunnel.

"Oh, I plan on seeing them again," he said. "And when I do? I'm going to *really* give them something to bitch about."

"Tough words for a guy covered in shit," I said, hoping this tunnel actually led the hell out of the sewer system before I found myself having to fight mutant turtles of the teenage variety.

Caleb did not seem amused by my comment. "If we succeed in animating another gargoyle, I may have to borrow it for a bit," he said. "Call it a vengeance loaner."

"We'll see about that," I said. I couldn't muster the strength for vengeance just then. I wasn't even sure if I could muster it to shower before collapsing from exhaustion.

I just hoped I didn't collapse while I was still down here.

Twenty

◖

Stanis

Time had not always been kind to the copper of the large female statue that stood towering over what the humans called Liberty Island. Now, standing atop it, it was clear that at some point the humans had intervened to preserve her form, which gave me immense satisfaction, even amid my own current turmoil. I found her constant vigil over the city I had come to love soothing, her presence helpful in centering my thoughts.

I always gave thanks for her presence, even during the years of her restoration, when she was inaccessible and surrounded by scaffolding. At the moment it was most especially welcome as I attempted to sort out the mix of sensations that overwhelmed my mind. I always found a sadness in its face that matched my own. If only it, too, could come to life, I would gladly have welcomed discourse with it.

My newfound freedom had come at a price. Alexandra now worked with the very man who had tortured me at Kejetan's command. I wasn't sure what to do now that I was free, but I reasoned that my presence would be missed by my father if I should not return from the work he had tasked me with.

Worse, I imagined that Alexandra might then become a more specific target of Kejetan. In order to ensure her safety, I knew what I had to do and leapt into the night sky, heading out to sea.

It always took some navigation to find the freighter, but the farther out I flew, the higher I went, the sense of perspective making it easier to spy the ship in the darkness of the sea. I spiraled down toward its deck, alive with a handful of stone men and human Servants of Ruthenia, but it was not their activity that caught my eye. A familiar face lurked among the shadows of the shipping containers stacked on the deck of the ship.

Correcting my course, I aimed for the figure, and, before he could notice my approach, I had the alchemist's head in one of my hands, lifting. Doubling the speed of my wings, I rose into the air as Caleb wrapped both his arms around the one holding his head, clinging on for his fragile human life. I came down on one of the more deserted upper decks of the ship, throwing open the door that led into one of the empty storage compartments there, then closing it behind us once we were inside.

"What are you doing here?" I asked, still holding him. "And where is Alexandra? She was with you when last I saw her."

"Ow, ow, ow," he said, pounding his fists against arm and clawed hand. "Let go of my head, and I'll tell you."

I unclenched my fist from around his skull and lowered my arm.

"Alexandra's fine," he said.

Now that we were no longer moving, a noxious odor filled the air around us and I stepped back from him. "What is that smell?"

"That would be me," he said, raising his hand. "The oh-so-pleasant and hard-to-get-out scent of raw sewage."

I leaned over him, my voice a growl. "You took Alexandra to the sewers?"

The alchemist raised his hands between the two of us and backed away.

"Technically, *she* took me," he said. "But long story

short, we found the spells we needed. She went home to sleep and study up on them, so that maybe we can build you a girlfriend or whatever, but she's fine."

"I am not in need of a girlfriend," I said. "I am in need of allies."

"*I'm* an ally," he said.

"Are you?" I asked, unsure. "Back to my question, Caleb. Why exactly did you come back here?"

The alchemist shifted in place, full of nerves behind the bravado he was trying to convince me he had.

"I'm just trying to tie up some loose ends," he said, rubbing the sides of his face where my claws had been digging in. "I've got unfinished business here that needs some discussion with the big man. I planned to cover my ass. What are *you* doing here?"

"Protecting Alexandra," I said.

"Shit," he said. "Can I change my answer? That sounds a lot less selfish than mine."

"You *are* selfish," I said.

"Yeah, yeah," he said, dismissing it. "Hey, my plan was going to cover yours, too. Now I answered you, so you answer me. What are *you* doing here? What do you even mean by 'protecting Alexandra'?"

"I had thought to make an appearance," I said. "Kejetan would think it strange if neither of us showed ourselves around here anymore. I wanted him to believe that, as you humans say, it is busy-ness as usual."

Caleb laughed. "Close enough. You really think you're up for pulling one over on Kejetan the Accursed? You're pretty easy to read. Your wings betray you. Right now, they're twitching, meaning I'm annoying you. If I can see through you, maybe you should fly away now while you still can. I don't need your ruining this."

His attitude over the last few minutes, mixed with his laughter, struck a chord in me, one of anger. "And do you think you will do any better manipulating my father?"

"Don't think I don't know what this is all about," he said, wagging a finger in my face.

"I do not know what you mean."

"Bullshit," he said. "If you had your way, you'd actually crush my head."

It was true the desire was strong in me, but I did not wish to give the human satisfaction.

"I wish no such thing," I said. "But would it be such a stretch, human? You *did* torture me."

Caleb sighed. "I told you I didn't even think there was a lick of humanity to you," he said, throwing his arms up the air, his voice filled with exasperation.

I knew that particular feeling all too well and stepped up to him, staring down into his eyes.

"That does not change the fact that it happened."

The human looked ready to burst, but he had no immediate answer for that and fell silent for a moment. It was a petty victory, but a victory nonetheless. The sensation felt most gratifying.

Caleb walked off in silence and moved about ten feet away before turning back to me. He looked around the empty hold, making sure we were alone.

"You know what?" he said. "I don't think any of this is about what I did to you."

My wings fluttered in reaction, and I cursed myself for it, but his words caught me off guard. "No?"

"No," he said, marching back up to me. "I think this is all about Lexi. She spoke about the connection you two once shared when you were bound to her family. I think you want that back, and it kills you a little to see her wrapped up in me."

It was strange to hear this person I knew so little of speak of private matters that were only the business of the Belarus bloodline, and I raised my voice.

"The affairs of this family are none of your concern."

"Lexi's *made* them my concern," he said, rapping his knuckles against the stone of my chest, scraping them against it until the skin tore and a hint of blood rose to the surface. He held his bloody fingers up to my face. "And, really, what can you offer her? Abrasions? A skinned knee?"

The sight of human flesh torn due to me in any capacity

filled my thoughts of Alexandra coming to harm from contact with me, and I forced myself to keep control of the darkness rising within me. "You know nothing of the bond between Alexandra and me."

"I know it's broken," he said. "What she feels for me is there because it happened naturally, *not* because someone wove a spell over me to make that connection happen."

My arm shot out as I grabbed him by the edges of his coat and lifted him.

"Perhaps you have woven your magic over her," I said. "Perhaps you poisoned Alexandra's better judgment with your elixirs, your potions, your magic that lives in your tiny bottles. But its power never lasts too long, does it? It is only a matter of time before she sees you as you truly are."

Anger coursed through me, but was it because he was antagonizing me or because he spoke the truth about a jealousy I had of mortal man? I stared at Caleb in contemplation of this, raging within, but the eyes that met mine had become calm.

"Let's face facts," he said bluntly. "The lovely Miss Belarus prefers my company to yours. You're nothing more than a family heirloom."

His words stung, but I put him down and turned away before I did something impulsive. Regardless of the truth of the matter, I needed to keep my calm aboard Kejetan's freighter.

Caleb straightened the edges of his coat, tugging the fabric into place until it was once more smooth against his form.

"And even if there was something more between you and her," he said, circling around to meet my eye, "what could there ever truly be between the two of you? Think about it. She's human. What kind of a life would that be with her? With me she stands a chance of being a part of humanity, of actually being happy."

As much as I did not want to admit it, the alchemist had a point, but that did not mean it sat well within me. I fumed over it in silence until he shook his head and headed for the door out of the room.

"Where are you going?" I asked, blocking his way.

He met my eye, his gaze unwavering. "Move, Stanis," he said. "There is work to be done here on this ship. I need to talk to Kejetan if I'm going to keep him unaware that his stone 'Dobbie' is a free gargoyle now."

I did not know what this Dobbie was, but I stayed in front of the door, unmoving. "I can handle that myself," I said.

Caleb sighed. "No, you can't," he said, stuffing his hands down into the pockets of his coats. "You don't have the practice at lying that I do. Trust me. You go in to your father, in front of your own kin—"

"He is *not* my kin," I growled.

Caleb stepped back and pointed at me with both hands. "You see? You get so agitated at even the mention of him, and *that's* what's going to ruin it. You don't stand a chance of convincing that mad pile of rocks that you're still under his sway gathering statues for him. Go home, Stanis. Go back to the Belarus Building and let me handle this."

I could not argue with him and stepped aside, though it hurt my soul to give this man anything. "You will never have the bond that Alexandra and I share."

Caleb did not look back. He simply walked out the door. "Get out of here, Stan," he said, his voice flat. "Leave the lying to the professionals."

The alchemist turned out of sight, and by the time I went out through the same door moments later, he had already disappeared into the freighter.

I flew off, frustrated, but knowing the human had probably been right in handling the situation himself. I could have stayed and argued, but I had not, choosing instead the chill of the night against my body as I shot across the night sky.

The heaviest question that lay across my heart, however, was not about dealing with my father.

Was I fighting with this Caleb to keep Alexandra safe or was it because of his connection with her? And what if Caleb was correct, saying that my bond to her had only existed because the last practicing Spellmason from centuries ago had put it there?

It left a hole within me that, for the moment, I could only fill with the joy that flight brought me, but the question still lingered.

How could I trust that my feelings were my own?

Twenty-one

Alexandra

The threat of rain hung in the night air as the group of us worked atop my family's building. Caleb had moved his mixing station from the other night just inside the covered doorway leading back downstairs. In his hands, colorful concoctions flew from one vial to another while flasks and beakers foamed with other mixtures. Very mad-scientist. All the while, Caleb consulted his notes, adjusted volumes with a care and precision that boggled my mind. He had even been set up and hard at work before the rest of us got here.

The ever-wary Rory leaned on the wall next to him, arms crossed, watching, while Marshall played lab assistant, applying the last batch of Caleb's home brew to the one statue I was going to attempt to animate. Going over my notes next to Caleb, I noticed Alexander's newfound book lying closed on the worktable.

"How do you know what you need to do to prepare the statue for tonight?" I asked. "You're not even consulting the book."

Caleb kept his face down in his work, producing a tiny vial from within the shoulder bag he wore that night, pouring it into a large beaker on the table.

"I told you I was a Spellmason fan," he said. "I'm an avid reader when it comes to it."

I looked down at my notebook in my hands. "I took a ton of notes," I said. "I couldn't memorize anything that quick."

Caleb smiled. "Trust me. When you end up ingesting as many of these alchemical elixirs and potions as I do, you learn to pay attention very quickly."

"Let's hope you finish all this without accidentally killing yourself," Rory said, drawing a look from him. She gave a pained smile.

I was finding both her and Marshall's mistrust of Caleb a bit unfounded lately, but then again, they hadn't been working as closely as I had with him. I chalked it up to maybe a bit of jealousy that there was someone around who I needed more than them right now, but that was a discussion for another time.

"I don't plan on drinking this," Caleb said, looking up to her. "You don't have to watch over me, you know."

"Yes," she said, not moving. "Yes, I do."

Caleb took a moment, kept silent, then turned back to his work. He grabbed a reddish brown jug of our own attempt of Alexander's Kimiya recipe and added some of it to the flask in his hand, filling it with about three inches of the mixture. He put the jug down with care, then slowly stirred the contents of the flask with a glass rod.

Marshall came back over to us from the statue, a brush in one hand and an emptied beaker in the other.

"Ready for another," he said, a little damp from the few drops of rain that had begun to fall. He wiped his forehead with the forearm of his left sleeve. "I didn't realize there would be so much arts and crafts. How am I supposed to learn what you're mixing there?"

Caleb smiled but didn't look up. "Consider this the hazing part of your education," he said. "You get the grunt work."

"Great," Marshall said with a long, slow sigh. "Just like high school. Yay."

"Here come the traumatic flashbacks," Rory added.

Caleb lifted the beaker with care, but when Marshall reached out for it, he shook his head.

"I'd better do this one," Caleb said.

"Why?" Marshall asked, looking a little hurt. "Is it my painting? Am I not leaving the right brushstrokes?"

Caleb held up the beaker with painstaking slowness.

"This mixture here is what I call *active*," he said. "Right now, it's a volatile liquid. And no offense, I still don't know you that well, so I'm going to trust *me* not to kill anyone with it over *you*. Is that a suitable enough answer for you?"

Marshall's face fell, and he raised his arm slowly, holding up the brush. "Sure," he said, stammering. "No problem. You take this one. I'll just watch, and, you know, not blow my hands off or anything."

"Great," Caleb said, grabbing the brush from Marshall's hand. "A little goes a long way."

The skies opened up, the fall of rain growing heavier every second.

"Won't that wash off?" I asked.

Caleb shook his head. "It's viscous," he said. "You'd need a scrub brush and a couple of hours to make a dent in it. Don't worry about the rain."

He walked off, and Rory, ever vigilant, followed him, leaving Marshall and me to walk over to Stanis, perched at the edge of the building and watching it all. Whether it was real or I was imagining it, his silence felt more pronounced than ever since his return to us.

"You ready to see if we can make you some allies?" I asked.

Stanis looked down at me. "I do not know how to answer that," he said, his words heavy. "I have never known another of my kind. If they are anything like the Servants of Ruthenia, perhaps I am not ready."

"Relax," I said. "I'm only going to try this on one of the figures first. If it works and goes well, then we'll move on activating the rest."

Marshall looked uncertain. "How's this going to work exactly?"

"Somewhat like Bricksley," I said. "Only on a much grander scale. The act of binding life to stone is different than manipulating it, which comparatively has been easier. The effort I put into getting Bricksley working was draining. It's weaving spirit to stone, animating the material and allowing the spirit in."

"And what if we get an asshole in there?" Marshall asked.

"We force it out," I said. "In theory, anyway. But if it *does* work on this one, we'll be able to create enough of an army to take care of Kejetan and the rest of his servants." I looked up at Stanis, catching his eyes. "I'm not compromising this time. I did that last time when I released you and let you go with them, and look where that got us."

"I am sorry," Stanis said. "I could think of no other way that would have kept you safe."

"And it did," I said, my heart breaking with the memory of it. "You bought us time, but at your expense, and I won't have that again. We end this together or not at all."

Stanis turned to watch Caleb prepping the statue. "And *he* is a part of us now," he said.

"You don't trust him," I said, more of a statement than a question.

"I cannot help it," he said, his mood growing darker. "After all, it was he who bound me to my father's will."

"And the one who released you from it," I reminded him.

This seemed to satisfy him for the moment, which was good because I needed to go over the notes I had written out about the ritual.

Caleb came over to us, empty container in hand, checking the time on his watch. "Ready?"

I closed my notebook and slid it into my pocket. "As ready as one can be for creating life," I said, and crossed the roof to the lone statue. Marshall and Rory came with me, moving off among the other statues at what I hoped was a safe distance.

Caleb came over and squeezed my hand.

"It's your show now," he said.

I squeezed his back and let go. I needed to focus, which

was hard enough in the rain without thinking about him. I breathed out one long, slow breath, then set about the ritual.

With the skill of Rory when she danced, I moved through the gestures, speaking my family's words of power as I went. The burst of connection to the stone of the statue rolled throughout me stronger than I would have imagined, but I forced myself to ignore my surprise and concentrated on the spell.

This was more than just connecting with the stone the statue was made of. This was bonding with the actual *grotesque* form of it. Every part of me felt its wings, its arms, its legs, its hands, its fingers, the claws at the tip of them. My mind readied the statue to be more than it was, readied it to be an open vessel to fill its form. The words of my spell tore away the last barrier to it, releasing the will with which I was controlling it and setting the animated stone free to receive whatever spirit it drew. Drained, I stumbled back, pulling out of the spell's narrow focus, finally able to once more take in my surroundings on the rooftop.

A lot had changed in the minutes I had been under the thrall of my spell.

The rain had turned into a full-blown storm all around us, and Rory was grabbing at Marshall from where they stood among the other statues, spinning him around to her.

"What's wrong?" I shouted, weakened now, my words lost in the storm.

Rory pulled her hand back from one of the surrounding statues. "Why are these like this?" she shouted out.

"Like what?" Marshall called back.

"It's wet," she said.

"It's *raining*," he said.

She held her hand up in front of his face. "It's *coated* . . . in the same stuff you two were putting on that one statue."

I stumbled to one of the other statues nearby, slapping my hands on it. "They're *all* coated," I said. My eyes landed on an unfamiliar piece of jagged stone sitting on the base of the statue, but I didn't have the time to process what it might be.

"Shut it down!" Marshall said, grabbing me by my shoulders, which almost toppled me over in my weakened state.

"How do you stop it?" Rory asked, joining him at my side.

"You don't," Caleb called out from where he stood at the side of the building. He looked down over the edge at something below. "It's happening now!"

"Stanis!" I shouted, looking around to find him still perched on the edge of the roof. "What is it?"

The gargoyle spun around and looked down. "Trucks," he said. "Like the ones at the shipyards."

Oh no, I thought. The massive kind that could carry heavy cargo coming in from a ship, or in this case, a more sinister payload.

The door leading into the building came free of its hinges, shooting across the roof as it tumbled away. The jagged stone form of my former brother took up most of the doorway, powering through it as he came.

"Devon!" I shouted. "What is this?"

"Just call it reclaiming my family birthright," he said.

Kejetan stormed through the door after him, a steady stream of stone followers pouring onto the roof behind him.

Stanis flew past me, slamming hard into their leader, knocking him back. The two tumbled over, locked in combat, Stanis attacking with a ferocity I hadn't seen in him previously. Pieces of Kejetan's stone form chipped away from him as Stanis landed blow after blow, flying across the roof.

One of them struck my foot, and I looked down at it, dawning realization hitting me. They looked just like the jagged piece I had seen laid out on the bases of the other statue.

Markers. Kejetan's plan suddenly made sense to me. He and his servants weren't here to fight us; they meant to cast off their jagged stone forms and have their spirits take over those of my great-great-grandfather's statues instead. The pieces of stone—the markers—on the bases of the statues were meant to lead each of the Servants of Ruthenia to their new bodies, thanks to the treachery of Caleb, it seemed.

Caleb was running among the statues, touching a vial to

about half the ones on the roof as I realized he was activating the Kimiya on them. Each of them bore a piece of one of the stone men at their base.

Rory and Marshall chased after Caleb through the pounding rain, but it was too late.

"Whose side are you on?" I shouted at him over the noise of the storm.

"My own," he said, stopping finally, letting the vial fall to the roof.

Stanis landed another blow to Kejetan, but as my spell and Caleb's alchemy took effect, the rocks that made up the mad lord's body flew apart with the impact of Stanis's fist.

All around us, the jagged stone forms of Devon and the rest of the Servants crashed to the rooftop, lifeless, the spirits within leaving them for the more sophisticated forms of my great-great-grandfather's statues. The component parts of their stone bodies came apart, and what had once been vaguely humanoid forms dissolved into piles of rough rock all along the roof.

Against the pouring rain, the invisible shapes of their searching spirits swirled through the air, the only telltale sign of their existence that of displaced rainwater as they flew. I followed the apparition that rose from the pile of rocks that had once been Devon and watched as it went to one of the stone-marked gargoyles in his attempt to be reborn into its form.

I ran to the statue, but by the time I got there, the swirling aerial shape had vanished into it, the stone of the gargoyle there changing in front of me. A roar of pain—my brother's voice—cried out from the demonic-looking creature's mouth as it reared its head to the sky. The rest of the body came to life as well in an uncontrolled flailing of limbs and wings, my brother's spirit trying to gain control of it. Its feet tore free from the statue's base, and the gargoyle fell to the ground on all fours, twitching.

"Devon . . . ?" I asked, moving to touch the cool, rain-covered stone of the gargoyle's skin.

The wings flew open, the tip of one catching me in the

stomach and sending me flying across the roof. I landed hard against one of the untreated statues and slumped to the ground, the wind knocked out of me as a sore spot spread out along my entire right side from the impact. Fighting the pain, I forced myself to stand as I took in the chaos of dozens of other statues coming to life all over the roof.

I did my best to ignore them, concentrating still on my brother, who by then had worked his way back to his feet, though he was unsteady still.

"It worked . . ." I said, sad to see the efforts of my spell wasted on him.

"That it did," he replied, his smile revealing a set of stone fangs that rivaled those of Stanis.

Stanis.

I turned to find my gargoyle, but with all the activity of other stone figures on the roof, for once he didn't stand out. Only when I listened for signs of conflict did I spot him fighting his way toward Caleb through an increasing number of other living gargoyles.

Marshall and Rory already had the alchemist by his arms, but Stanis grabbed him at his throat, and lifted. Caleb's feet were well off the ground by the time I stumbled my way over to them, spit flying from the alchemist's mouth, gagging.

"You betrayed us," Stanis said.

"Wait," Caleb managed to croak out. "Not . . . finished."

Both his hands were wrapped around Stanis's arm to keep himself from choking completely, but he managed to let go and leave just one in place. The other darted into his jacket and came out with a thin plastic vial that he slammed against Stanis's arm. The plastic of the vial cracked, a dark gray liquid seeping out of it.

Part of Stanis's arm transformed back to its solid state, and he grunted with pain but did not let go. The man's own hand froze like stone as well, but he managed to pry it free, leaving him hanging by his neck only. He sputtered, but managed to reach down into the shoulder bag he wore, producing what looked like a giant glass egg filled with a swirling pink liquid. He threw it high overhead behind him toward the group of statues that were still inert.

Volatile liquid, Caleb had said earlier when he had been mixing things. His voice screamed the words in my head. Whatever explosive effect it might have, I needed to stop it.

My will took control of the by-then-empty pedestal my brother had stepped off of, and I guided it into the air, directing it at the glass ball. The base wobbled as I fought to hold control of it with any level of precision, but I was determined to hit my mark.

True to my aim, the base hit its fragile target high in the air, shattering the glass on impact. The contents of it rained down over the crowd of statues, but that wasn't all it did. As the pink tendrils and cloudy mist fell through the rain, the water all around it lit up with thousands and thousands of tiny sparks.

Defying gravity, the reaction lifted higher and higher into the night sky, jumping and arcing through the rain all around us and out over the city.

I closed my eyes as the wave of it rolled toward me, and I flinched. A tingle of sensation washed over me, through me, then disappeared as quickly as it had hit. Marshall and Rory were already examining themselves, none of us seeming the worse for having been caught up in it, but once I stopped focusing on myself, I saw the larger problem.

Every statue on top of the building was now twisting to life.

Some struggled with the change, others immediately taking flight, and yet others fell to fighting among themselves.

Rory pulled the art tube from her back, going for her weapon, but I waved her down.

"No!" I shouted. Did she really think she could fight this madness? "Inside. All of you! Now."

Marshall didn't need to be asked twice and was running for the stairs before I barely had the words out. Rory went next, and I was already in motion.

"Alexandra," Stanis called out to me. I spun to see him

still standing there, with Caleb still hanging in place from his hand.

"Bring him," I said, turning and running for the door as a pairs of passing wings swung dangerously close. "But by all means, there's no need to be gentle."

Twenty-two

C

Stanis

The feel of Caleb's thin, fleshy throat in my clawed hand filled me with a great and terrible satisfaction as his weak little form attempted to break free. The sound of conflict on the roof above filled my ears, and the desire simply to close my hand shut until my fingers met in the middle of his neck was strong, but since retreating to the art studio, Alexandra had been quite clear that she did not wish it done.

"Forgive me, Alexandra," I said, pressing my fingers in with a slight pressure, causing the blond human to struggle further to free himself, a dark joy filling me, "but why should I not just crush his head for his betrayal?"

Alexandra grabbed onto the arm I held Caleb with, pulling at it, but I would not yield.

"Because we're not those kind of people," she said, anger and concern in her voice. "Not just yet, anyway."

She tried again to lower my arm, but her effort proved to be in vain, her physical strength no match for my own.

She met my eyes, and her voice changed, softening. "We all saw what he just did," she said, "and I understand you have issues of your own with him. And after all you've been through, I would not dare order you to do anything, but please . . . I'm asking you not to harm him. We need answers."

Aurora also put her hand on the stone skin of my arm.

"Don't worry, big guy," she said, brandishing her pole arm with her other hand. "I'll keep an eye on him, without crushing his head. I've got a little more finesse with taking someone down without actually killing them if they act up. No offense."

True choice had rarely been an option when I still lived by Alexander's rules. Until Alexandra had freed me from them, I had not even known what it meant to choose of my own free will. For that, I would always be in Alexandra's debt, and as I held this fragile human in my hand for wronging us, I did not take his life out of respect for her wish.

"Very well," I said, lowering Caleb to the floor, my eyes burning into the wide, white pools of his. "But make no mistake, human. I will not hesitate to act at the hint of any further treachery."

Free of my grip, Caleb stumbled onto the art studio's debris-covered floor before finally righting himself. He straightened the coat he wore, wiping water from both it and his hair, all the while backing himself up against one of the half-empty broken bookcases.

"I'm sorry," he said, holding up a hand as his eyes darted around. "But none of you will understand. I *had* to do that."

"Did you, now?" Alexandra asked, the calm she had exhibited melting away as she charged him. With nowhere to turn, he held his hands up by the sides of his head and made no move to stop her. Alexandra slammed up against him, grabbing the edge of his coat.

"Did you really?" she asked again, but before Caleb could answer, she let go of his coat with her right hand, pulled her arm back, and shot it forward into his midsection while making a fist.

The air went out of the man, and he crumpled to the floor. I could not help but let a small smile creep onto my face. Clearly, I was not the only danger here.

"Well, I guess that I just *had* to do *that* then, too," she said, and stepped away from him.

Aurora leaned closer to me. "Looks like we can both stand down," she said.

I looked down at her, cocking my head. "Stand down . . . ?"

She smiled and shook her head. "I'll explain it later."

Something about the man lying there stirred anger in me, and I grabbed him by the back of his coat and pulled him onto his feet, letting go. He fell against the bookcase and stood there, fighting for each breath. "Okay," he managed to get out. "I deserved that."

Marshall walked over to him, his finger pointed to the roof above us. "What the hell just happened up there?"

"That," the man said, "was me saving my life."

Alexandra looked at each of us before turning back to Caleb. "It's not looking so good down here for you, pal. I've got to be honest."

"You don't understand," he said. "I tried to get out of working for them. I even went back after freeing Stanis to make it seem like business as usual, to not arouse their suspicion. I can prove it. Stanis was on the boat. He can confirm it. He saw me there."

"I thought you had a change of heart," Alexandra snapped. "I thought after you helped me free Stanis, you were all Team Gargoyle."

"I *am*," he said. "But those creatures had hired me for a job, and you don't get to back out of something like that. I tried to. I really did. I even recommended other freelancers, which I *never* do, but Kejetan left me between him and a hard place. If I didn't at least give them the refined gargoyle statue forms they asked for, they *were* going to kill me. Worse, Kejetan was resolved to come after you. They wanted you and your friends dead. Kejetan told me himself when I went back to their ship trying to negotiate my way out of my contract. Just ask your gargoyle here. Stanis saw me. He can back me up!"

Alexandra turned to me. "Is this true?" she asked.

"I do not know," I said. "I was not in on any private conversations Caleb had with my father."

"But you actually went to the boat?" she asked. "Why, Stanis? Did I free you for nothing?"

"For the same reasons Caleb has stated. This 'business as usual.' My freedom means nothing if Kejetan becomes aware of it."

She turned back to Caleb, shaking her head at him. "We could have protected you," Alexandra said.

The man looked over at me. "No offense, but your team's only got one stone man to their dozens. I'll play the odds for my safety, thanks. Besides . . . I'm not used to having backup. I did what I *always* do—try to take care of things myself."

At an impasse, silence fell among us for several minutes, with only the sounds of continued struggle on the roof filling my ears.

"Umm . . . what about the rest?" Marshall asked, finally breaking the silence.

"Rest?" Aurora asked.

"Of the statues," he said. "Kejetan only had a couple of dozen stone men with him. There were far more statues that came to life on the roof than that. What happened with the rest?"

Caleb let loose a sigh.

"That was *supposed* to be my backup plan," the man said, looking to Alexandra. "Although thanks to *everyone's* interference, it worked a little too well."

"Meaning what?" Alexandra asked, wary.

"Like I said, I was in between a rock and a hard place," he said. "Kejetan and the Servants of Ruthenia got what they wanted. They all got to cast off their crude stone form and take over many of Alexander's statues up on the roof. Kejetan can fly around the city on his own pair of wings and be a happy little gargoyle now. But bringing the remaining statues to life . . . that was my ace in the hole that hopefully would have kept them from exacting vengeance on you."

"You do not know Kejetan, then," I said. "He did not earn the moniker *the Accursed* for his charity."

"Giving Kejetan the gargoyle body that he wanted . . . well, that should have ended my deal with him, guaranteeing my safety. My hope was that activating the *rest* of those statues would let whatever random spirits haunt New York

City find them and fight it out, maybe reduce the number of Kejetan's new gargoyle army."

Aurora laughed. "*That* was your genius plan?"

"Okay," he said with anger in the word. "What would you have done, then? My life was on the line, and it seemed to be my best chance for living. If a few of Kejetan's men died in the process of dealing with the other animated statues, then all the better."

"Back up a little bit there," Alexandra said. "What did you mean by 'it worked too well'?"

"My plan *was* actually working," he said, pointing at her, "until *you* interfered. That globe I threw with the mixture in it . . . It was meant to hit the roof and spread out among the remaining statues, activating them. It would have created the same type of potion cloud like the one I used when we captured Stanis and freed him. But you smashed the globe before it could properly land. That's when everything went a bit off the rails. The mixture wasn't supposed to go *that* airborne. It had a reaction I didn't suspect, mixing and amplified with the power of the storm."

"The sky went awash with that pink haze," I said.

"That wasn't supposed to happen?" Marshall asked.

The alchemist shook his head.

"The rain must have acted like a current carrier when the object released prematurely," he said.

"Is that bad?" Marshall asked, wrapping his arms around his body. He turned to me. "That's bad, right?"

"I do not know," I said, then turned to Caleb. "Is it?"

"It's not good," the human confessed. "It became far more powerful than I would have imagined. The way it was spreading . . . I'm not sure how big a radius it covered, but it was more than just over your building here."

Alexandra leaned back against one of the art-studio tables that still stood. "Meaning you *might* have animated an entire city's worth of statuary," she said. "Who knows how many more of Alexander's statues around Manhattan have come to life? And what's occupying all of them? More than just the Servants of Ruthenia, that's for sure."

"It's possible," he said. "I'm not sure. My plan was local-ized until you messed it up."

"Do *not* put this one me," Alexandra shouted, shaking her head. "If you had been up front about your plan . . . If you had trusted us . . . If we can't trust you, we don't want your help. Not after this fiasco."

The humans fell to arguing, and with Aurora and Mar-shall joining in with the shouting, the flow of their words moved too fast for me to follow. One thing, however, became very clear to me.

"Silence!" I roared after I confirmed my suspicion. All of them turned to me, their words dying on their lips.

"What is it, Stanis?" Alexandra asked, her voice calming.

"If you would stop fighting among yourselves for a moment, there is something I *must* point out."

I waited to hear if anyone was going to say anything more.

"So . . . ?" Caleb started. "What is it?"

"What do you hear, now that you are not fighting with each other?"

He listened for a moment. All the humans listened.

Caleb shrugged. "I don't hear anything," he said.

"Exactly."

The humans ran for the stairs leading to the roof, and I followed, stepping out onto it. Empty pedestals marked the entirety of the roof, and the broken forms of far too few gargoyles littered the area. Every other living creature was gone, the night sky filled with dark shadows and the flapping of wings.

"I believe the days of keeping secret the existence of gargoyles may be at an end," I said.

Twenty-three

C

Alexandra

Sleep was good. In fact, I might have called it my best friend. A night of ignoring calls from Caleb and not having to think about the events of the previous night was blissful. Sleep even gave me the false hope that maybe I had been dreaming the events of the past few days. But when the door buzzed over and over for a good ten minutes, I finally gave in to waking and checked it out, only to find Desmond Locke at the door, his face full of curiosity.

"Is your father in?" he asked. "I would like to speak with him."

"No," I said. "If he wasn't in the offices here, then I don't know where he is."

"Pity," he said, extending his open palm into the building. "May I?"

Not having seen him since before Caleb and I had liberated my great-great-grandfather's book, I wasn't sure I wanted to be talking to a man whose church I had broken into, but compared to the events of last night, it almost felt like a welcome distraction.

I headed upstairs to the kitchen to make myself some

coffee but made no effort to offer him any. I sat down at the breakfast bar, leaving him standing.

"What can I do for you, Mr. Locke?" I asked, taking my first sip, coming a bit more alive with it.

"I wonder if you've been watching the news," he said.

My stomach sank. "No," I said. "I've been holed up in bed all morning. Bit under the weather and all."

"Interesting reporting this morning," he said. "They say overnight there were many sightings and reporting of angels and demons throughout the city sky. There were hundreds of incidents reported. Even footage on the Internet."

"Really, now," I said, a bit of curiosity winning out over my growing fear. "And what do you make of all this?"

"What with all the reports of angel and demon sightings," he said, "one would think we are seeing the End of Days."

"Isn't the Rapture something someone in your line of work is supposed to look forward to?"

"In theory, yes," he said, "but I am not as dogmatic as most. We both know there are strange things in the world, Miss Belarus. And I think the regular world is catching on to that now because of the meddling of certain people who do not know any better."

Given the air of superiority coming from him, I resisted the urge to throw my coffee in his face. "And what would be better?" I asked.

"The world would be a better place if these things were kept in check," he said. "Or at least used on the side of God."

"Ah, there we have it," I said. "No one wants to just take this power and put it on the shelf. Maybe that's what your *Libra Concordia* thinks to do in theory, but the truth is that theory doesn't work. There are always men and women who seek power, no matter how altruistic they claim to be."

"There are those better suited to judge those needs than others," he spat out.

I walked up to him, tugging on the thick ropes of medallions and talismans he wore around his neck. "No offense, but I find it hard to trust your judgment when I see you wearing and using the very objects you swear to keep out of the hands of others."

"Sometimes it is better to be forearmed," he said. "What is going on, Miss Belarus?"

It was true that this man had shared some of his knowledge about my great-great-grandfather with me, but it had all started only after he had a gun in his hand. I was sick of people trying to push me this way and that. I was tired of feeling used. "I don't think I have anything I want to share with you, Mr. Locke," I said.

"Oh no?" he said. "I think you have taken advantage for far too long of my goodwill, allowing you to do research at the *Libra Concordia*."

"If what you say about the news is true, why not just head out into the streets?" I asked. "I'm sure you could have your pick of whatever's out there."

Desmond Locke shook his head, his voice becoming sharper now. "The thing about these creatures is that I do not care about them at the moment," he said. "What I am interested in—what I have *always* been interested in— would be the angel that watches over your family."

"Why is that one so important?" I asked.

"Because before all this other nonsense erupted, it was the singular mystery that brought me to this city, and I have spent much of my life seeking it out." A bit of madness had entered his voice. "Other mysteries within the *Concordia* have come after it, but it is the singular thing that has eluded me, and I will not be denied. I will rein this angel in, or I will bend it to my will."

"There is no angel," I said, not even hesitating. It was the truth, after all.

Desmond Locke's voice calmed, but his eyes danced with fire. "Miss Belarus, please. I have offered you my hospitality as a guest at the *Libra Concordia* in the hope that you would get the answers you seek."

"And I thank you for that," I said.

"But that *does* come with a price," he said. "A little

give-and-take, and I do mean to take. I have more than earned it."

"You have earned *nothing* where my family is concerned," I said. "You watch over us under false pretenses yet dare call my father 'friend.' I find it repulsive."

"I am simply a curious man," he said, changing tactics yet again. "I like knowing things, and for the sake of my organization, this is the sort of knowledge and creation that we would like to keep in balance."

"You expect me to trust you? I think you should leave."

"You talk about trust," he said. "Perhaps I should not have trusted you."

"What do you mean by that?" I asked, my anger growing.

"It seems we have had a break-in at the *Libra Concordia*," he said with his eyes searching my face for a reaction.

I gave him none even though my heart leapt up into my throat. "And what does that have to do with me?"

"I'm not sure," he said. "But there are signs of both breaking in and breaking out, though we cannot determine if anything was taken. But I'm *sure* you know nothing about that, do you?"

I shook my head. "Sorry," I said.

"No matter," he said. "We will get to the bottom of it, I am sure. Your lack of cooperation here will be something I consider when we question Mr. Kennedy once more."

"So you've spoken to him already about it?" I asked.

Desmond nodded.

After dismissing Caleb on trust issues the night before, I could only imagine how fast he'd sell me out for his safety. "What did Caleb say?"

"He says he knows nothing about what happened the night of the break-in," Desmond said. "But I am not sure I believe him."

"Why not?"

"Just a hunch," he said. "He is a freelancer, after all. Not to be trusted. They are profound liars for the right price."

Was Desmond Locke admitting to some knowledge of Caleb's working both sides of the good-and-evil fence? Or was he simply trying to draw me out, getting me to make an emotion-driven mistake?

I couldn't be sure, and in doubt, I held my tongue. When I didn't answer after a full minute of silence, Desmond Locke gave a pressed-lip smile.

"If I find he had anything to do with the break-in, it will go poorly for him," he said, heading for the stairs leading back down to the door. "And given your lack of cooperation here with other matters, it will be doubly so."

I wanted to rage as I watched him go, and I followed him down the stairs until I could shut and lock the door behind him. All the while I kept silent because any other reaction might betray something to him—be it Stanis, the secrets of the Spellmasons, or even something that might get Caleb killed. Yes, I had driven him off and ignored all his calls, but did I want him killed at the hands of a secret society?

I needed to do something with this energy and confusion, so I ran down the basement stairs, heading for the guild hall. I wanted nothing more than to get into my great-great-grandfather's inner sanctum and, at the very least, get out a good scream.

The secret door was once again propped on its hidden hinges, sitting ajar, despite the warding password I had put upon it. I threw it open, focusing my will to take down whoever had dared enter my family's sacred space.

Storming in, I quickly surveyed the room. The scattered books I had been reading on the center table of the great hall were now piled in a single tower almost three feet tall. At the top of it sat a small wooden box with ornate, arcane carving on it.

What the hell was it?

A weird prank left by Desmond?

It didn't seem likely as he had been with me the entire time. I knew of only one person who had the guts to break in here.

I ran to the box, taking it from the top of the stack and

laying it down on the table. It was no larger than a cigar box, but there was both weight to it and the sensation of fluid movement from within. Furious at yet another violation of my space, I flipped the lid open, not caring if it was a trick or not.

A large glass orb sat in the middle of a cushioned insert, its contents a swirling mass of liquid. Even as I stood there looking down at it, the liquid maintained its motion, almost hypnotic. Tucked into the lids were several sheets of note-book paper in Caleb's clean script. One sheet spelled out in detail the use of the concoction, the same mixture he sup-posedly used to control Stanis while on the payroll for Kejetan Ruthenia.

The other bore a far more simple but ominous message.

Watch your back.—C
PS. Sorry.

Twenty-four

Stanis

My pained transformation to living stone upon the setting of the sun was a welcome one. Even after centuries, it struck me fresh every time, a constant reminder that it was a miracle I was a living creature. I minded the burning sensation even less that night because I awoke on the edge of the roof where I had stood for centuries. I was home, even if my home was littered with the remains of broken *grotesques* and the lifeless stones that had previously housed the souls of Kejetan's closest Servants of Ruthenia.

I walked to the edge of the roof, the awakening sensation already fading, and dropped down to the terrace below. It did my soul good to find Alexandra in her great-great-grandfather's studio, even in the condition I had previously left it in. As I came through the open hole where the doors should be, the floor crunched with the sound of stone and wood, drawing Alexandra's attention.

She turned, for a second wide-eyed with concern until she saw me standing there and relaxed. That did my soul good as well, and I crossed to her as she returned to working on a mound of clay sitting on a table in front of her. To her left

stood a large, solid block of stone taller than I was, which had
not been in the space when last I had been there.

"Where are your companions?" I asked. "This building
is not safe, not after the events of the other night."

"Kejetan and his people got what they wanted," she said,
painful as it was for her to admit. "They're probably off
flying the friendly skies or doing a victory lap. As for Rory
and Marshall, they've got lives. Me? I've got work to do.
Between cultists and religious fanatics threatening my family, I need to get creating."

"What about *him*?" I asked, not sure I wanted to hear her
answer.

"Caleb?" she said. She wiped her hands off on a piece of
cloth and reached into her bag, pulling out a decorative box
I would have expected Kejetan or one of his lords to have
owned in life. "He's out of the club. After the other night,
I'm not at all sure I can trust him. *But* he did send me this
as a peace offering." She lifted the lid to reveal a small
sphere filled with a glittering gold liquid.

"Is it true as it was in my century that women love to
receive that which shines?"

She smiled at that.

"That we do," she said. "I prefer the kind I can wear,
personally, but it's a start."

I watched the liquid dance within the sphere. "What
is it?"

She lowered the lid and slid it back into her bag.

"Let's just say if you develop any other personality dis-
orders, I should be able to cope with it on my own. It's what
he mixed when he freed you. It even came with instruc-
tions."

"Let us hope it does not come to that," I said.

"Let's hope," she said, crossing her fingers. As she went
back to the clay she was working, the box she had just held
out slid out of her bag.

"What the hell?" she said, tentatively pushing it back in,
but finding resistance.

I moved closer, wings involuntarily spreading as I worried, but when Alexandra's tiny brick creature crawled out from behind the box out of the bag, I lowered my wings.

"Hey, Bricksley!" she said. "I wondered where you had gone off to." She picked him up and set him down on the floor. "Not now, buddy. Mama needs her time to get her creative art on. Can't beat the baddies without some goodies, and since New York is crawling with every other Belarus statue in motion right now, looks like I'm back at square one crafting my own."

I could not help but watch the little animated brick as it moved around the room, its wire arms and clay hands moving about freely, set to no actual task that I could make sense of.

"I wonder if perhaps your charge should have wings," I said after watching him stumble around for a few more minutes.

Alexandra turned from her work and looked down to the floor at him. "Who? Bricksley?" She shook her head. "Not sure a flying brick is such a great idea."

"It is a shame."

My maker's kin stopped working and turned to me. "Is it?"

"You have flown, Alexandra," I said. "Both with me and of your own accord." I picked up the miniature brick man and looked him over as he squirmed in my hands. Painted eyes and a smiling mouth stared up at me, unmoving. "Seeing him earthbound as he is, I feel . . . sorry for him."

Alexandra walked over and took him from me, placing Bricksley on the table next to her. "Don't," she said. "He's got a pretty good life. And look how happy he looks!"

"His face is painted on," I said. "Of course he would seem that way."

She leaned forward, looking him over.

"I'll consider it," she said, setting back to work on the mound of clay next to him. In silence, she sculpted it as I stood there watching, marveling at the *grotesque* figure that began to emerge before my eyes.

I could have stood watching her work for a century if my guilt over the sad state of my creator's studio had not taken over, so I set about undoing what damage I could. Even the creature known as Bricksley moved about the space, returning randomly scattered books to the shelves in the library. Only when the heavy thump of footsteps on the roof sounded did I stop.

Alexandra looked up, then turned to me.

"Continue," I said, heading off to the terrace, barely needing to retract my wings as I went out through the opening. "I will see to whoever is distracting us."

"Thanks," she said.

I nodded and took to the sky, rising just high enough to come down on the roof above.

A lone carved figure stood among the broken ruins of other *grotesques*, its body lean and serpentine features on its face. Its wings were wide, flapping in a nervous rhythm, betraying its mood. The stone itself was finer than mine, more of a textured yellow marble, and despite the new and strange feeling it still was to see others like myself, I could not help but feel my anger rise toward the intruder.

What business it had here was a mystery, but it was one I meant to solve.

Months of frustration, servitude, and not being able to crush Caleb's head the other night had left me wanting conflict. I ran for the other *grotesque*, but was only halfway across the rooftop when it spied me and leapt into the air, taking flight.

I took off after it as I had Alexandra the other night, the *grotesque* even heading uptown the same way, but its flight was not nearly as stable. Its wings fought to strike a steady beat, the creature's flying only improving when it forced itself into a glide. I was determined not to be outdone by a *grotesque* that was at best days old. Centuries should give me the upper hand here, and I fought to push myself through the sky even faster in pursuit.

The distance closed between us with every block, but even then it took minutes to catch up, and we were halfway over Central Park before the *grotesque* was nearly in my grasp.

When the *grotesque* looked back to find me so close, it dropped lower over the park, hoping perhaps to lose me under the cover of the trees, and that was its crucial mistake. The centuries had taught me how to maneuver through this city, its parks as well, and I dove after the creature, gliding with little effort between the branches and boughs that it struggled to get through.

Only its strength and claws kept its path clear, but even that was enough to slow it down. I pushed my wings harder in flight, closing the gap, and the closer my prey, the more fury I pushed into my pursuit of it. With a final burst, I pulled my wings in close to maximize my speed, slamming into the *grotesque* and wrapping my arms around it.

We fell from the sky into the park, our bodies and wings tearing through limbs until the two of us hit the ground in a tumble. A wide swath of dirt opened from our impact, the cut of it growing larger and longer as we went. I used the momentum of our roll to give me the advantage when we finally came to a stop, the spread and motion of my wings pushing me into position on top of my prey.

"Which of my father's men are you?" I shouted at it. With its wings pinned underneath my knees, I balled my hands together and raised them high over my head, ready to unleash my fury upon the creature.

"Please don't hurt me!" the voice cried out, that of a woman, and I faltered in my downward swing, stopping myself.

"You serve Kejetan Ruthenia, do you not?"

"Yes," the *grotesque* shouted, but the voice was an unfamiliar one.

I had known most of the people who had served my father in his human life, the ones who had earned a place as Servants of Ruthenia, but I could not place this one.

"You are not of my father's kind," I said, unable to hide the surprise and curiosity in my voice.

The *grotesque* looked up at me with fear and confusion on its face. "I—I don't understand," she said.

"You serve him," I said, "but yet you are not one of them, not of the Servants of Ruthenia."

"Please!" she pleaded. "I don't understand any of this. They told me they'd take me in, that they'd care for me. I don't understand *what* has happened to me!" The creature looked at the sharp claws at the tips of her fingers. "Why do I look like this?"

I lowered my arms but did not release her. "Who *are* you, then?"

The creature's face struggled as she thought, but her body relaxed. "Emily Hoffert," she said. "My name is Emily Hoffert."

"Listen to me, Emily," I said. "The men who made these promises to you are liars."

"No," she said, shaking her head in earnest. "They've taken many of us in already."

I cocked my head. "Us . . . ?"

She nodded. "Yes," she said. "There are others like me. Lost, confused . . ."

Of course, I thought, remembering the night Kejetan and his men had come to claim their new forms on top of the Belarus Building. There had been far more statues than necessary for the Servants of Ruthenia to occupy.

"How old are you, Emily?" I asked.

Again, she paused in thought. "Twenty-three."

"And what year is this?"

"It's 1963," she said with no hesitation.

"I do not understand how it happened, Emily," I said, "but it would seem your spirit found this form as its new home." I stood, freeing her and offering her my hand. She took it and rose, her wings fluttering behind her, but I held her eye, and they calmed after a moment.

"We are going to have to have a long discussion about a few things, Emily," I said. "But first you must tell me: What did Kejetan promise you when you found yourself in this form the other night?"

"It wasn't him exactly," she said. "It was the one called

Devon. He offered me safety. He said they had a ship where I would be safe."

I cringed at hearing the name of Alexandra's brother. "The Servants of Ruthenia do not make promises lightly."

"Who *are* the Servants of Ruthenia?" she asked. "I had not even heard of them until I awoke in this form the other night, when they offered their protection."

"What price did Devon set for such protection?"

"There was no price," she said. "He only asked one favor."

My wings fell against my back, a sinking sensation overwhelming me. "And what was that favor?"

"He told me all I had to do was look for the building on Gramercy Park with all the broken statues on it and if another *grotesque* should try to talk to me there, I should fly as fast as I could away from it."

"That," I said with growing dread, "is what we call a diversion tactic."

I spread my wings and leapt into the sky.

"Wait!" she cried out. "Don't leave me here!"

"We will meet again, Emily Hoffert," I said, already shooting straight up into the night sky. "Seek me out where we met at a later time. Let us hope then, however, I am not as foolish as I was just now."

Twenty-five

———————— ☾ ————————

Alexandra

Our building on Gramercy Park was close enough to the subway that I was used to feeling its rumblings, so with my focus entirely on the clay sculpture I was working, that was what I took the initial shaking for.

When it persisted and grew in intensity, my mind shifted to only the most paranoid New Yorker's fear—the fault lines under Manhattan were finally giving. Books fell from the half-broken shelves of the library as the light fixtures swayed and smashed up against the ceiling.

I didn't wait to see what else would happen. I scooped up Bricksley and shoved him in my bag with my other belongings and ran for the back of the art studio as my ears erupted with a cacophony of sound.

I spun around in time to catch much of the terrace outside the French doors fall away, followed by the entire exterior wall on the front of the building. My favorite sofa over in the library tilted and slid out of sight as the wood of the flooring twisted and snapped apart, looking like a nightmarish set of wooden teeth.

I turned to the stairs, ready to run, but I could do nothing more than watch as more and more of the art studio got eaten away by a great cloud of dust rising from the crumbling building. The area of the studio just over my old bedroom crumbled away and disappeared down into the cloud. I wished that the old sympathetic connection between Stanis and me still existed in the hopes that he'd fly in to rescue me, but alas, that had died the night I granted him his freedom.

The shaking lessened, dying down, a good third of the art studio/library gone. Coughing, I covered my mouth with the sleeve of my sweater as the cloud rolled over me. The earthquake was over, but as I moved toward a still-intact set of windows to my left, something strange struck me.

All the rest of the buildings surrounding Gramercy Park seemed fine, the only damage being to my family's building. The dust was already settling, and as I stepped to the edge of the damage, the cloud before me parted with a mighty gust of air as the shadowy form of a gargoyle came through it.

To my shock, it was not Stanis, as I had hoped, but one I knew nonetheless.

"Dear sister," Devon said as he landed in what remained of the room.

The shapes of other winged creatures off in the distance danced through the dusty cloud behind him, but none of them came into the building.

Angry tears ran down my face, making tiny rivers in the dust already caked there. "Where's your master?" I asked, shock filling me.

"Not here," he said, closing his wings. "Oh no. This is family business."

"This was your *home*," I said. "You grew up here. How . . . *Why* would you do this?"

"Any sentimentality I had died with my human form," he said, then he folded his wings and stepped forward. "While the old mad lord has been willing to wait for what he seeks, I am not. Kejetan is weak. He's willing to take his time waiting for his monster-son to reveal Alexander's Spellmason secrets. As if somehow the boy he killed forever ago would somehow forgive him. Dude's got issues. He's thinking

Stanis might see the light and join Kejetan at his side. The way I see it, Kejetan's wasted *months* while that idiot potion maker of his kept promising he can make Stanis give up the secrets of the Spellmasons and rule by his side. Me? I'm not tied so much to all that family sentimentality."

"Then that makes you worse than your master," I said, shaking with rage.

"Kejetan is a fool," he said.

"This coming from you . . ."

"He's wasting his time trying to control every last one of these gargoyles," he said. "His Servants of Ruthenia and the rest that were created. Rather than simply enjoy our new forms! He wants to lead, but I say why lead when you can just live by your own rule, doing what pleases you? Want something? Take it. Someone tries to stop you? End them."

"Have you forgotten your humanity so completely?" I asked.

"All that is behind me now," he said. Devon spread his wings and arms. "Look at me. Do you see even a hint of my old form?"

"No," I said. "And that is the problem. Whatever and whoever you once were is lost."

"Flesh is a *weakness*," he spat out at me.

I shook my head. "Feeling a little mad with power, are we?"

"Don't believe me?" he asked, crunching over the rubble toward me. "Let me show you how weak it can be."

Halfway across what remained of the room he stopped, raised his hands over head, and brought them down onto the art studio's floor, again and again. The old boards beneath my feet tore apart as the foundation beneath gave way, and my entire section of floor tilted out into the open air, falling away.

Devon spread his wings to keep airborne, but I tumbled down through the air as the broken section of the floor started to drift away from me.

I needed to get control of it and get it back under me if I was going to live. The piece of floor moved farther below me, crashing and rolling down the landslide of debris that was all that remained of one side of our building.

Determined not to end up underneath it all, I lashed out with my will for the stone foundation of the floor piece beneath me, bending it to my control. I twisted it around until the piece lay horizontal enough for me to land on it, and I slammed into it with both knees, grabbing on, scraping my palms on its jagged edges.

Holding on for dear life, I could do little more than control its fall, riding it like a sled, forcing all my will to keep it from rolling over and crushing me. It bounced and sparked off the caved-in part of the building, a rain of broken but recognizable belongings flying by me as I went until the chunk came to a stop on at least a story's worth of piled wreckage.

I stood, exhausted, staring up at my family's building. By my best guess, I was roughly where our main living floor used to be. I felt overwhelmed by a nightmarish burst of the surrealness of it all. The damage to my great-great-grandfather's work had my soul in torment, and when my brother's winged form landed behind me, I spun around to face him, a newfound fury building in me.

"Give me the book, Alexandra," he said, holding out a clawed hand.

"After what you've done?" I shouted. "I'd rather die."

Devon let out a disappointed sigh. "So be it," he said. "What's one more dead human anyway?"

His wings stretched out, and his sharp stone claws came up as he charged. Stanis's roar sounded out of the sky above as it erupted with the sound of combat. The crash of stone on stone filled the air like thunder, and seconds later, the broken form of one of Devon's gargoyle cronies slammed out of the sky into the wreckage of the building. The sound of battle raged on above.

Stanis had definitely arrived, but given the battle above, I was on my own against my brother.

A primal snarl arose from Devon as he closed, gaining speed as he came, my mind becoming a mix of fear and

fury. I braced for the impact as my will whipped out into
the debris all around me, and by the time Devon would have
crashed into me, there was a wall of broken stone, which
took most of the blow, standing between us.

Most, but not all.

Chunks of it fell away as I stumbled back, driving me
into the open floor of the building. I tumbled over a couch
in what used to be our living room and landed hard on bits
of broken furniture.

Devon reeled from the impact, sliding partway down the
ever-shifting mound of building debris.

I didn't waste a second. I rolled off the upturned couch
and ran for the edge of the living room where the damage
began. Picking my way carefully to the still-stumbling
Devon below, I called out to the stone all around me. It
responded with ease, having been crafted by the master
Spellmason, after all. Like pieces of a puzzle, I brought it
close to my body, fitting it over my form as I went. By the
time I arrived at Devon, I looked roughly like one of the
jagged stone men he and Kejetan had once been.

"What could you possibly hope to do to me?" he shouted.
"Kill me? It's not in your nature, Alexandra."

He swung at me, his claws slamming into my right side.
Pieces of stone chipped away, the pain of the blow cutting
into me, but it was lessened by my stone suit.

"That's the great thing about nature," I said. "It allows
for evolution."

My mind and body worked as one. When I swung my arm,
so too swung the stone of my suit. While my own physical
strength stood little chance against my brother, each of my
blows was stronger than that, powered instead by my will.

My fists hammered into Devon, driving him back as he
fought to strike, but he could not keep up. His own attempts
to combat me turned defensive as he curled his wings around
him in a ball—but I would not let up. The pain of everything
he'd done was too great for me to relent. I smashed at him
till his wings fell open, and I brought both hands swinging
from left to right at his head, the blow knocking him over.

His body slid down the pile, and I went to him, my rational mind taking over. What was I truly prepared to do? Devon was barely moving by then, just looking up at me, sensing my hesitation and managing to get out a weak laugh.

"You sure have toughened up since I used to torment you down in the family crypt," he said, and while the words stung, I shook my head.

"Don't," I said. "You're preying on my humanity, my sympathy for who you were. Don't you dare try to pretend like there's any kind of connection between us now."

"But there *is*," he said, anger rising in him. "You've got your precious memories, your weak humanity, your flesh that makes you hesitate right now. You're not going to kill me, Alexandra, and even if you did, my spirit has already occupied two stone vessels. I'll just find another."

Damn him, but he was right. While I felt like I could end this creature that had once been my brother, there was always a chance he might find a way back. The pack on my back squirmed against me, and I let the stone suit around me fall away, the pieces rolling off onto the pile of debris.

"That's a smart girl," he said. "Showing your compassion, even for your annoying older brother."

"You're not my brother," I said, removing my backpack once the last of the stone suit dropped away.

"Of course I am," Devon said, struggling to get off his back, pressing his wings up to get some leverage.

I unzipped the pack. Bricksley was squished in there with several of my other items. Alexander's stone spell book, my own spell notebook . . . but it was the box from Caleb that Bricksley's tiny clay hands tapped against.

"You're not my brother," I repeated, sliding the box out and opening it. I plucked the orb from within and held it in the palm of my hand, the elixir which Caleb had used to control Stanis swirling around like a miniature tempest within it.

Devon looked up at it from where he knelt before me, wary. "What is that?"

I hesitated, and this time I was glad for that most human

of sensations. To do what I was about to do *without* hesitation would mean I, too, was as monstrous as Devon.

"An insurance policy," I said, and smashed the orb down on his head. The liquid oozed over him, a fine mist rising up from it until the air around him became a thick, noxious, gray cloud.

Devon screamed, falling back to the ground.

The sounds of combat overhead had stopped, and the graceful form of Stanis descended out of the air, a stark contrast to the writhing, mewling mass before me that was Devon.

"Forgive my lateness," Stanis said. "I believe I was what you call *tricked*."

"No worries," I said with a dark smile. "Happens to the best of us."

When the last of the arcane smoke cleared, Devon rose to his feet, his face a mask of confusion as his eyes darted back and forth between the two of us.

"I'm sorry," I said, reaching out for the connection over Devon as I forced my will into him. "I truly am. But the last piece of my brother died the night his flesh did on Saint Mark's."

"What are you doing to me?" he cried out in panic, clutching the sides of his head as if that could somehow stop my intrusion.

"The same thing you and Kejetan did to Stanis," I said.

"You think you can control me?" he shouted. "Force your mind upon my own and hold it down as a slave?"

Devon thrashed about as if wrestling with something I could not see, but I knew his struggle was internal, and he had no way to contend with what I was doing. My brother had been an opportunist, even a slick businessman, but in a contest of spirit and will, he was not my match. Certainly not after all that had happened. To him. And to me.

I pushed my will further upon him, feeling his spirit being crushed beneath the power of mine.

"No, I'm not looking to control you," I said. "That would mean taking responsibility for you in this form. But what I will do is drive you down so far into the background of this creature that you won't have the ability to even blink on its behalf. Then? I'm shutting it down. With you inside it."

"No!" he cried out. "Please, take pity."

"I am taking pity," I said, stepping to him, inches from his face now as I met his eyes. "On humanity. You? I couldn't give a shit about."

I wondered if Stanis would approve of this, having gone through it himself, but if he had any problems with it, he did not voice them. I wasn't sure I would have stopped even if he had.

Devon tried to speak, but I refused to let him, shutting down any ability he had to control the gargoyle. I could feel his last desperate attempts to struggle, allowing them to surface for just a moment, the gargoyle's face becoming a mask of twisted pain as I silenced Devon and shut the creature down. The gargoyle's muscles tensed as the stone skin turned to solid stone, bits and pieces of it crumbling off until the figure stilled completely.

Stanis and I stood there for a moment, staring down at the unmoving form.

"Is it done?" he asked.

"For the most part," I said, feeling no remorse.

"I am sorry for your loss, Alexandra."

"I'm not," I said, as my mind began hatching a plan. I slid my backpack back on, leaving Bricksley sticking out of the top. I grabbed the arms of the broken gargoyle that had once been my brother, and using every last bit of my strength and little help from my powers, I started dragging him down the remains of the Belarus Building as the sound of approaching sirens filled the air. "Devon may prove far more useful to me in death than he did in life."

Twenty-six

C

Alexandra

While I could appreciate the artistry of the architecture that went into the building of a church, I always found the statuary within them a bit on the morose side, more so when I was the one dragging it into the damned place.

The staff all around the *Libra Concordia* watched with curiosity as I pulled the cowering, twisted form of my former brother down the main aisle, letting it drop with an echoing *thud* in front of the half-walled partition of Desmond Locke's office.

Locke rose from his desk, peering over the wall as he crossed his space and pushed through the half door to it, joining me in the aisle.

"Miss Belarus," he said with a tight-lipped smile. "This is an interesting surprise."

Several of the other workers stopped what they were doing to rise from their own desks farther back in the church; my heart caught in my throat when I spied Caleb among them. I hadn't talked to him since the fiasco on the roof of the Belarus Building, yet a small, dark part of me had secretly hoped I would find him at the church. Still, it was not the main reason why I had come.

I turned my focus back to Desmond Locke.

"Is this a present?" he asked, holding his hand to his chest. "For me? I am flattered."

"You know, I've never particularly liked you," I said. "Always creeping around my family. Then these past few weeks, finding out what you were *really* all about . . . I used to think maybe I hated religion, but I think the truth of the matter is maybe I just hate you."

Locke circled around the tormented, broken form of the gargoyle until he was standing opposite me. The rest of the crowd kept their distance, all except Caleb, who moved away from the bull pen he had been working in to come down the aisle toward us.

"Why do you bring me this?" Desmond asked, looking up at me for a moment.

"You wanted my father's 'angel,' " I said. "This is what remains of him. This is the creature that watched over our family for centuries. Stanis."

Desmond stared down at the broken gargoyle. "And why bring him to me now, when he is broken?"

"I want an end to all this," I said. It was true. Years of my family's being influenced by this man, the fact that there was a secret society keeping tabs on us . . . the creep factor was off the charts. The lie that the remains on the floor of the church were actually Stanis's was one easily told for the freedom it might bring me.

"There's a new world order starting out there," I continued. "The skies over Manhattan are full of his kind now. You shouldn't have any trouble finding another to fixate on."

Desmond stood there, examining the broken gargoyle at me feet. "This is not Stanis," he said.

I didn't react, fearing any reaction might betray me. "What makes you say that?"

"I know this piece," Desmond said, squatting down next to it, running his fingers against the stone of it.

"You do?"

"Yes," he said, bitterness in the single word. "Of course I do. It comes from one of Alexander Belarus's churches. If there's one area of architecture I *do* know, it is most certainly the churches of Manhattan. I believe this one belonged to one of the closed ones that is now a nightclub or some such monstrosity. Dreadful treatment of the divine, if you ask me." His hand lingered on the face. "Funny. I do not recall the face looking so tortured from my memory of it."

A twinge of pain shot through my chest at having been the cause of that torture, regardless of the fact I was perfectly justified in my actions.

Desmond stood. "Why do you bring this lie before me?" he spat out.

"It was worth a shot," I said, shrugging. "I had hoped to do this the easy way."

His eyes filled with wariness, and he stepped back from me. "And what is the hard way?"

I didn't respond, my mind and will already reaching out beyond the confines of the church, allowing an old connection to familiar stone to call out. In response, the enormous stained-glass panel to my left erupted, shards of it crashing down into the room as a familiar figure came through it.

Stanis's wings were spread wide, catching the air as he gently glided down into the gap between me and Desmond Locke.

"I know you," Stanis said to him. "You are the one who has kept watch over Alexandra's father all these years."

A fascination crept over Desmond's face, his eyes sparkling like those of a child on Christmas Day.

"Yes," he said, addressing Stanis. "And the *Libra Concordia* will *always* be watching."

"No," I interrupted, his face falling at the word. "They won't. I want you to call your people off of researching the Belarus legacy, and I want you, specifically, to stay the hell away from my family."

My words had little of the desired effect I had hoped they would, and Desmond turned back to Stanis, continuing to marvel at him.

"Stay away from the Belarus family and their delicious secrets?" he asked. "Oh, I think not. Not after seeing this glorious creature."

"You will," I said. "You'll hand over what you have about my family, about my great-great-grandfather, or I will have 'this glorious creature' kick your ass."

Nearby, Caleb coughed into his hand.

"You might want to do what the lady asks, sir," he said.

Desmond spoke, his tone a bit darker now. His hand went quick into his coat, coming out with his gun. He waved it at me. "But I've dedicated my life and work in the search of him."

"Find a new hobby," I said, more angered than scared as I stared down the barrel of the weapon. "My family is off-limits."

Locke shook his head. "My organization is more than just me," he said, a hint of desperation in his words now. "The *Libra Concordia* is long-lived."

Stanis stepped in front of the gun, looking down at Desmond Locke no more than a few inches away from him.

"And so am I," he said, his voice lowering into a growl. "The dedication of your entire life to this pursuit is but a small moment in time to me. What is the waste of one lifetime such as yours? I have watched over four generations of this family. I have stood looking over this Manhattan as people withered to their years and were buried, over and over. I will outlast your *Libra Concordia*, and the Belarus family will always be under my watch."

The gun shook in Desmond's hand, then tumbled from his fingers, clattering among the broken glass on the floor. He rose and grasped the many talismans hanging around his neck.

"You cannot hope to harm me," he said.

Stanis smiled, revealing his fangs. "I can try."

"Maybe you should bring him closer to God," I said.

Stanis grabbed the man by both arms, his claws tearing through the cloth of the suit. Desmond did not seem pained, but kept staring into Stanis's eyes, shaking. Stanis's wings opened to their full extent, and with one great leap, the two of them were airborne. They rose like a shot up through the church, passing out through what remained of the stained-glass windows. I covered my eyes as a few fresh pieces came loose and fell to the floor.

Caleb walked over to me, his eyes fixed on the broken stained glass. "Is he going to . . . ?" He smashed his fists against each other several times.

I laughed.

"No," I said. "Just wanted to put a healthy dose of fear in the man, so he'll back off. I've pretty much had it with people trying to manipulate me."

Caleb nodded and fell silent.

As one of the people who *had* actually manipulated me, the best he could muster was a sheepish half smile, but words themselves seemed to fail him.

The rest of the workers of the *Libra Concordia* still seemed in a panic, the gargoyle at my feet causing those who were fleeing to give Caleb and me a wide berth.

"Anyway," I said, finally breaking the silence, "I just wanted to thank you."

Caleb's eyebrows raised. "For . . . ?"

"That gift box you sent," I said, looking down at Devon's body at my feet. "It proved . . . useful. A real lifesaver, in fact, quite literally."

"Good," he said, managing a small smile. "Great, in fact."

I managed a small smile of my own. "I keep expecting to find an invoice in the mail."

"Lexi," he said, souring, but I didn't want to let him off the hook just yet.

"Don't tell me you didn't consider it."

"That gift was just the first along the way of making many an apology," he said. "What Stanis said that night about playing both sides of the fence . . . he was right. I never knew who or when to trust. I've been doing this so long on my own that I couldn't think straight. I was so busy trying to get you to trust me, I didn't think to trust you. I fucked up. I'm sorry."

"It's not all bad," I said. "That potion bomb you set off . . . You changed the world. There have been sightings, videos on YouTube . . . People are talking. They don't understand what they're talking *about*, but it's a start. They're awakening to the idea that there's more to this world than what they can actually see."

"I know some witches and other clients out there who might not be as ready to come out of the broom closet yet," he said. "A gaggle of gargoyles may prove a bigger hassle to them than not."

It felt good to have even the slightest hint of our easy rapport once more. And, more important, I sensed his total sincerity at the heart of his apology this time.

"I could use a hand in bringing the situation under control," I said, by way of a peace offering. "I'll hire you if I have to."

"Not necessary," he said, running back to his workspace and gathering his things into a messenger bag before slipping it over his shoulder and coming back to me. "If it's the client I think it is, I'll be happy to do this one on the house. I only hope we can get to him before he can post any one-star reviews of my freelance services online."

"Let the *Libra Concordia* find shelf space for *that*," I said as I stepped around Devon's gargoyle, leaving it behind me. I stopped and looked at Caleb. "Is that really a thing? One-star review on some kind of arcane Yelp Web site?"

"Give the changes going on out there in the world, with the media reporting all these gargoyle sightings these days?" he asked, taking my hand in his and walking for the door leading out of the *Libra Concordia*. "It probably will be soon enough."

─────── ☾ ───────

Twenty-seven

Stanis

After truly convincing Desmond Locke I was no angel, my instinct was to fly back to the Belarus Building, but that was not my destination. At Alexandra's request, I sought out another.

I had not been by their building by Saint Mark's Church since before my disappearance late last year, and there was little chance I would recognize it. Last I had seen the location, it was a ruined pile of bricks that had been the death of Alexandra's brother. The first time, that was. I did not know what I would find in the ruined building's place, only that Alexandra said I would recognize it when I saw it.

She, of course, was right.

As I flew uptown from the church of the *Libra Concordia*, I thought perhaps I had overshot my mark in the East Village. Before me lay the park at Gramercy, confusion setting in until I realized it was not exactly the same.

To begin with, the "park" sat atop the roof of the building. I spied Alexandra reading by gaslight on one of the benches along its cobblestone paths, and I came down in front of her, descending slowly as I tried to absorb my strange and wonderful surroundings.

Alexandra shut her great-great-grandfather's book of arcana when she heard me land and stood.

"Is it done?" she asked.

I nodded.

She laid the book on the bench and came to me. "How did he react?"

I could not repress a smile. "Desmond Locke might wish to seek out the mysteries of the heavens, but given his reaction, he does not wish to *visit* them," I said.

Alexandra laughed, the sound pleasing to me. "He's afraid of flying?"

"I believe so," I said. "Although I would also like to think that the fear on his face was due in some part to the show I put on."

"Show?"

I bared my fangs and twisted my features to appear as demonic as I could. "You told me we needed to convince him he needed to back off from your family," I said. "He is convinced now."

"Excellent," she said, and threw her arms around me. "Thank you for that performance."

"Of course," I said, and looked around the roof. My surroundings here were much different from the rooftop at the Belarus Building. The stonework was exquisite and purposeful up here, not the flat and lifeless slabs I was used to seeing atop the buildings of the city.

Alexandra stepped back. "You like?"

"This place," I said. "What is it?"

"It's yours," Alexandra said. "I designed it with you in mind when the building was going up. I always hoped you'd return to us one day."

"This looks familiar."

"It should," I said. "It's based on Gramercy. It even has a little river running through it."

I moved around the space among the trees and walkways, Alexandra at my side.

"I do not know what to say."

"You don't have to say anything," she said. "I figured you

must not get a lot of opportunity simply to enjoy the things I get to enjoy on the streets, so I had this installed. That way, you can use it anytime you like."

I did not know how long we walked, my mind too taken with the surrounding beauty of it all, but eventually Alexandra stopped and turned to me.

"I've been giving this a lot of thought," she said, "and perhaps we should go back to the way things once were."

"How do you mean?" I asked.

"The bond we had," she said. "I was thinking maybe I could restore it. I'm not exactly sure how to do that just yet, but I'd like to."

The offer aroused something within me, but I did not see the sense in such a thing. "Why would you want this?"

"Because I miss that connection," she said, looking away from me. "At first I thought I was being selfish, that I simply wanted to know you'd come to my rescue as soon as I felt in danger, but I realized that wasn't it. I want the bond back because when you disappeared for nearly half a year, and I had no idea where you were . . . that nearly killed me."

"I was protecting you," I said.

"Yes, I know, but it was like you were dead. I'd rather have that full connection than no connection at all."

I thought about her words—her desire—before answering. "I miss it as well," I said. "When shall we do it?"

Alexandra shook her head. "I need to work out a few things about the ritual," she said, "but soon."

I looked out over the park again and smiled at her. "Thank you for this, Alexandra."

She returned my smile, but there was a darkness in her eyes that I could not quite fathom.

"Don't thank me just yet," she said, grabbing my clawed hand. Alexandra pulled me toward the doorway discreetly built into the back of one of the stone pillars along the path. "There are things we still have to do."

Alexandra led me down through the new building, and I followed her until we reached the bottom floor. I was surprised to see a library there much like the one at Alexander's studio, and I finally oriented myself to where I was when we went in through the doorway leading into her great-great-grandfather's guild hall.

Doubly surprising was the fact that the blond-haired alchemist was there as well.

I stopped in the doorway, my wings fluttering with my annoyance. The center table of the room was filled with a variety of glass containers and racks of vials, most of which were being used by Caleb.

"What is *he* doing here?" I asked.

"Nice to see you, too," Caleb said, only looking up from his work long enough to catch my eye before getting back to it.

Alexandra turned to me and pressed her hands against my chest. "Don't freak out on me, okay?" she said.

"He betrayed us," I said. "He betrayed *you.*"

"I was trying to save my own ass so I could be of *help* to you later on," Caleb said. "You stone types really don't think about the long game, do you?"

"Caleb . . ."

It did my heart good to hear Alexandra chastising him, but I could not stop myself from attempting to march over to him.

Alexandra tried to stop me, but her strength was no match for mine, and she slid across the floor with her arms held out straight against me. "Stanis . . . *don't.*"

"I am not like those others," I said. "I can promise you that."

"Can you two stop fighting?" she asked. "There's too much to do."

I began to respond, but the sound of activity out in the hallway drew my attention. The voices of Aurora and Marshall arguing filled my ears, and as they came into the guild hall, I saw that their clatter came from both of their arms being overburdened by buckets, plastic containers, hoses, and a host of other implements whose nature I did not fully comprehend.

Marshall stumbled to the far side of the room, crashing along awkwardly as he went.

"Bless the Home Depot on Twenty-third Street," he said, laying down the equipment.

Aurora followed, laying her armful of equipment down next to his.

"Seriously," she said, pulling a list from her pocket. "They had everything you asked for, Lexi." As she handed the note back to Alexandra, her eyes fell on Caleb, standing at the table. "What's *he* doing here?"

"I asked the same question," I said. "In the same tone, even. So far, I have not been given a good enough answer."

"Everyone relax," Alexandra said. "*I* asked him to join us."

"Why?" Marshall asked.

Caleb continued mixing several vials together, not stopping his work but looking over to Marshall.

"Because I can do more than be sent on shopping errands . . . ?" Caleb said.

Alexandra turned to him, which caused the alchemist to close his mouth, effectively shutting him down.

"Because," Alexandra said, "we're going to need his help if we're going to stand a chance against Kejetan. We've got what we need to reproduce as much Kimiya as we want, but I need his alchemical expertise in this."

"Fine," Aurora said, but it did not seem she meant the word. She stepped to the wall near where her pole arm rested and leaned back.

Marshall looked at the massive amount of equipment they had come in with, then back to Alexandra.

"This is great and all," Marshall said, "but what are we supposed to do? I mean, we don't have an army. Kejetan and his men took most of the statues that were left. I don't care how many buckets of this stuff we make. We've got nothing to use it on."

"We don't need statues," Caleb said.

"Oh no?" I said.

"*This* is our army," Alexandra said, gesturing to all of us. "Caleb's right. We don't need statues . . . present company excluded, of course."

"Thank you," I said, unconvinced. "But I would feel far more positive about our endeavor if there were more of my kind on our side."

"I'm sure you would," Caleb said. "But we don't need that."

"We don't?"

"No," Alexandra said. "Having statues wouldn't change anything. Kejetan has always ruled by brute force. And I doubt we could have matched his even before he and his servants took their new forms. I've been so fixated on handling brutality with brutality that I hadn't considered much else in the way of handling them."

"You want to share how five of us are supposed to take on a freighter full of baddies?" Aurora asked.

I, too, was curious to hear an answer to this question. I was also curious what baddies were, but I thought I could figure that one out on my own.

"We don't need to beat them with strength," Alexandra said. "We'll do it with what we've got."

Aurora picked up her pole arm and swung it through the air with such grace, she appeared to be dancing with it.

"I'll go with what I know, thanks," she said.

"Don't be like that, Rory," Marshall said. He went to the center of the room, where Caleb was working, and began sorting through the glassware there. "Between the five of us, we've probably got a pretty good brain."

Aurora looked at him over the top of her glasses.

"We *can* outsmart them," Alexandra said, her voice stern.

"I don't know, Lexi," Aurora said, still not convinced.

"Aurora may have a point," I offered.

Alexandra turned to me, a look of shock on her face. "Don't tell me you're on Rory's side, too."

"I do not know how you will fare against my father," I said. "He has not lasted this long by being a foolish creature."

"Enough infighting!" Alexandra shouted.

Everyone stopped their tasks and looked to her.

Alexandra looked to Marshall, then to Aurora.

"I know I've put a lot on you by asking you to help me

here," she said to her friends, the words quick from her lips in anger, "and I know I've kept a lot from you. But I need you to trust me on this."

Marshall set down the vials in his hand. "Why *have* you been keeping things from us? Maybe Caleb was right . . . Are we just your shopping team?"

Alexandra sighed, then pointed to Aurora. "When Rory got knocked out . . . it made me realize how serious it was that I was putting both of you in danger. More and more. I couldn't take that. I thought maybe I could do it all. So if there was danger involved, I turned to Caleb. It didn't matter what happened to him."

"Gee, thanks," Caleb said, returning to his mixing.

"You know what I mean," she said, exasperation in her voice now. "You were a stranger. Arcane things are what you deal in, what you freelance in. You've chosen the dangerous life. Marshall and Rory? This was all forced upon them."

"First of all, nobody forces us to do anything," Aurora said. "We do things because we want to . . . or in Marshall's case, because *I* tell him to."

"You don't understand," Alexandra said. "It's not just the danger. There are certain things that I don't want you to have to do."

"Like what?" Aurora asked, the girl getting heated herself.

I stepped forward. "Like Alexandra's having to take the life of her brother," I said.

Alexandra and Aurora both went quiet for a moment, then Aurora spoke. "Is it true?" she asked.

Alexandra nodded. "I killed Devon," she said.

"No," I said. "You killed what had once been your brother."

Alexandra looked serious. "I did what needed to be done. For the safety of all of us."

Much of the anger fell away from Aurora, and she walked to Alexandra. "So you just beat him down?" she asked, impressed.

"Not quite," Alexandra said. "I had a little help."

Marshall and Aurora both turned to me, but I shook my head. "It was not I," I said.

Slowly, they turned to Caleb, who took a moment to wave, the smile on his face causing me to feel a desire to remove it from his face.

"In all fairness," he said, "all I did was leave her a little gift. *She's* the one who decided to use it."

"Okay," Alexandra said. "So technically it was Bricksley who reminded me I had the damn thing on me, but I'm glad it was I who did it and not any of you. If I'm going to be a part of this life, I need to be ready to do such things. I know that now. It's why I've dealt with Devon and Desmond Locke, and now there's only one other person I need to contend with."

"Kejetan," I said.

"And his followers," I said. "I'm sick of living in fear."

"Don't worry," Marshall said. "I've got plenty enough to go around for all of us."

"You should be scared," Alexandra said, going to the table. She reached into her coat pocket, threw her notebook down next to a stack of books and mixing vats. "This isn't going to be easy, but if we play this smart, we can end this . . . tonight. Putting Devon out of his misery was difficult. But Kejetan and his men?" She pointed to the empty containers that Aurora and Marshall had brought with them. "We're going to have to do a lot of alchemy first."

Twenty-eight

C

Alexandra

The calm of the ocean all around me should have been soothing. Given the plan fixing itself in my brain, however, I found that the silence only creeped me out.

Stanis stood a silent sentinel at the bow of the small boat, his eyes fixed on the dark horizon where the shape of the distant but familiar freighter steadily grew larger at our approach.

I shivered and pulled out my notebook to go over the spells Caleb and I had worked out.

"This quiet is killing me," I said to him. This far out at sea, away from the city and other ships . . . Then it struck me. Something about how the boat was moving seemed . . . off. I turned to look at the back of the boat, where Marshall and Rory were. "You're not actually running the motor engines, are you?"

He smiled. "I don't have to," he said. "The biggest problem with working for the Servants of Ruthenia was their having a floating home—the freighter. It's never in one place at the same time."

Rory laughed from where she stood by several air tanks and stacks of bucket-sized containers. Her pole arm rested against the boat's wheelhouse as she pounded the palm of her hand around the lid of one of the containers, securing it.

"Of course their ship is always on the move," she said. "Those Ruthenians wouldn't dare return to their docks. Not after the trouble we caused for them last fall."

"Trouble?" Caleb said with a smile. "Do tell."

"We had tracked them to a slip out in Brooklyn," I said. "Rory might have gotten a little . . . kicky . . . with some of them."

"And," Marshall spoke up from where he was looking over the back of the boat at the silent engine, "I got a few of them myself."

"You?" Caleb asked, unable to stifle his laugh. "Rory's a dancer with a pole arm. What's you're weapon of choice?"

"I . . ." Marshall looked defensive, but it fell away and his voice went quiet. "I hit a bunch of them with books I was throwing, thank you very much. I even drew blood. Those corners can be pointy and lethal at high speeds, you know."

Caleb's face was full of suspicious doubt.

"It was actually quiet impressive," I whispered, leaning in to him.

Marshall went back to peering over the side of the boat. "So if you're not running the engine, and you don't know where to go," he said, "how is this boat taking us there?"

Caleb lowered his notebook. "Kejetan's freighter is never in the same place twice, so in order for me to get there, I had to get creative. I'm friendly with a few of the Village witches who owe me a favor or two after a job I did for them, so I incorporated some of what they could teach me into creating an arcane binding that's also alchemical."

"Like when Alexander bound Stanis to my family?" I asked, looking at the front of the ship to the stone-still gargoyle in question. "He set up rules when he created him. I set up a few simple ones to keep Bricksley from destroying the house when I'm gone, but that's about all I really grasp of binding. So tell me, how the hell do you set rules to bind a *boat*?"

Caleb shook his head. "This kind of binding is sort of

the same idea," he said, "but a different principle. Think of it like the relationship of a magnet and a piece of steel. Drawn together like that, with this boat acting as a magnet being pulled to the ship. Except to make it work in the witches' case, I needed *this* boat and the freighter to share something in common. They call it sympathetic magic."

I thought it over for a second, but it didn't make sense. "How do you make the two objects sympathetic?"

Alexander pulled off his coat and started rolling up his right sleeve.

"Oh no," I said with dawning realization. "You didn't."

Caleb pulled the sleeve all the way up to his elbow, revealing a relatively fresh scar running across his inner arm near his elbow joint.

"A bit of blood magic," he said. "I bound myself in blood to both of the ships."

Marshall had stopped looking over the railing and came up to us, his face pale. I was pretty sure it wasn't due to seasickness.

"And how does *that* work?" he asked.

"Lexi here isn't the only artist," Caleb said, pushing his sleeve back down over the scar. "I do a little painting myself. I mixed my blood with some seaworthy paint and coated the bow of this boat with it. I did the same with a small section of the freighter, too. So when I step on board this small craft, I drink a little something down, my connection to both ships snaps to, and *voila*! We're under way."

"Blood magic," Stanis said from behind me, suddenly so close that I jumped. I hadn't heard him join us, but his voice was practically in my ear now. "The work of necromancers. Dark work."

Caleb hesitated, then gave a reluctant nod. "Maybe several hundred years ago, sure, but don't forget . . . magic has changed with the times. Yes, a lot of it has been lost to legend or locked away by men who thought it too great a power for the world to know—"

"Like Alexander," I said.

"Yes," Caleb said. "But the magic that *has* remained has

been adapted. 'Blood magic: not just for necromancers anymore!' "

Marshall's eyes narrowed. "So let me get this straight: You willingly cut yourself, drained your blood, then painted two separate ships with it?"

Caleb nodded.

"There has *got* to be some kind of great alchemical insurance coverage out there," Marshall said.

"Not as such, no," Caleb admitted, "but given what Kejetan *had* been paying me, I would have considered maybe sacrificing a complete limb."

"It is amazing the trust one criminal puts in another," Stanis said, frustration oozing out in every word. "Once my father was done with you, your life would have been forfeit even before you betrayed him by joining in Alexandra's cause."

"Hey!" Rory said, stamping her pole arm on the deck of the ship. "It's *all* our cause."

"That it may be," Stanis said, not looking away from Caleb, "but this human sullies himself with such darkness. Alexander would not have approved of such arcana."

I stepped back, finding pain in Stanis's words. Hearing his opinion of how my great-great-grandfather might have reacted—especially when it was contrary to my own feelings about Caleb—struck a nerve.

"I understand your concern," I said. "However Caleb has worked this, it *is* working. This gets us to Kejetan and his followers. We're going to stick with our plan. Okay?"

Silent nods came from everyone except the gargoyle. "Stanis?"

"As you wish," he said, turning back to the bow of the ship.

I looked to the horizon, surprised to see the freighter less than half a mile away, already looming menacingly higher than our tiny boat.

With our craft being the David to its Goliath, the stark reality of our situation sunk in.

Kejetan's floating homeland was a singular island on an empty sea. There was no shore in sight, only the distant lights of New York somewhere off in the fog behind us. We wouldn't have to worry about innocent bystanders out here, but if we failed, there was no one to hear our cries for help, either.

Judging by the drumming in my chest, my heart was already opting for panic, but I tried to calm it, telling myself to focus.

"This can work," I said, for my own reassurance more than anyone else's. "If everyone does their part." Our boat was angling in toward a small dock that rose and fell with the waterline, the side halfway up the ship marked with a dark circle that could only have been Caleb's blood.

"Don't head for that landing zone," I said. "We need to board somewhere with cover, and I suspect there might be people watching the docking section. I know I would be if it were my ship."

"Right," Caleb said. He turned away from the freighter for a second, shaking himself to break his focus. It seemed to kill the connection to both ships as we fell into a drift. Caleb turned back around, and our small boat curved off its course, the sensation of being pulled by some sort of tractor beam now gone.

"You *do* have oars around here somewhere?" I asked, and started to look among all the cluttered tanks and buckets we had brought with us.

"*Somewhere* around here," he said, joining in as he picked his way among the cargo nearest him.

"Allow me," Stanis spoke up, once again perched on the very bow of the boat itself. He pushed his wings up and over the front of the boat, dipping them into the water on either side. The stoneskin membrane of his batlike wings worked as massive oars, propelling us forward and keeping us parallel to the ship.

My eyes searched the deck high above us for a good place to board, and when the familiar sight of multicolored cargo containers caught them, I pointed below where they were stacked.

"There," I said.

Stanis corrected our course with his left wing, bringing us in at the spot, while Caleb moved up next to him at the bow. Caleb's eyes searched the side of the ship while he squatted and hefted a massive wrap of chain in his arms. Once he had found what he was looking for, Caleb maneuvered past Stanis and secured the chain through a metal loop on the side of the freighter.

"Don't want to have our only means of escape drift away, now, do we?" Caleb said as he walked back to me.

I nodded. "Ready, everyone?" I asked, trying to whisper with as much authority as I could.

"As ready as I suppose we can be," Rory said, sliding her collapsed-down pole arm into the artist's tube across her back. She slapped her hand on the large, steel pump canisters sitting between her and Marshall.

"Suit up," I told them, then turned back around to Stanis. "We need all this equipment up on deck, out of sight."

He nodded, grabbing several containers at once before leaping straight up into the air, pumping his wings with ferocity. In a second, he was gone into the night sky.

Everyone on the deck set themselves in motion. Marshall helped Rory strap one of the large canisters to her back before pulling on one of his own.

I consulted my notebook once again as I went over my spell modifications for the evening, laughing when I saw Caleb standing across from me in a mirror image, holding his own notebook. His eyes met mine, and the two of us both embraced the lightness of the moment and held on to it in silence as the last tranquil seconds of our night ticked away.

"Promise me no blood magic tonight, okay?" I asked, only half joking. "I don't need you bleeding out in the middle of all this."

"Don't worry," he said. "Blood magic's really not my thing. When I bound these two ships together, trying to get blood out of these veins was near impossible. Had a little trouble even breaking my skin, and that was with a witch-sanctioned sacrificial dagger. Apparently, there *are* some good side effects to all this self-alchemy."

I laughed. "All kidding aside," I said, composing myself. "I can't do this alone."

"You're not alone," Caleb reminded me, stepping closer. "You've got your big, bad, bat man there, Marshall, Rory . . ."

"And you," I said, finding it hard not to smile, unable to stop myself from stepping closer to him. This was more than just the comfort of having a fellow alchemist to talk to.

The deck shook as Stanis came down hard next to us, and I stumbled forward . . . into Caleb's arms, naturally. I went to push myself back to standing, but Caleb's arms held me in place for a few seconds longer before releasing me.

Stanis couldn't have landed more than a few inches from us, and given his posture—wings spread out behind him—it had been no accident. Was the gargoyle actually pea-cocking?

I wasn't entirely sure, but now was not the time to call him out on it. Of course, it *also* wasn't the time for me to be locking eyes with my fellow alchemist, either, but I decided to let that one slide.

I looked up into Stanis's stoic face.

"Those were the last of the supplies," he said, his voice plain, betraying no hint of any emotions he might be feeling.

I looked back at the mostly empty deck of our small craft.

"Good," I said, turning away with only the slightest twinge of guilt. I instead looked up the long expanse of the side of the ship. "Now for us."

"As you wish," Stanis said.

One by one, Stanis flew each of us up to the edge of the deck, dropping us behind the empty shipping containers where our piled-up supplies lay before finally landing there himself.

Something didn't feel quite right. I looked around and did a quick head count, coming up one short.

"Where's Caleb?" I asked.

Stanis stood still and silent. I walked up to him. He didn't

answer, so I brushed past him to look back over the railing.
Caleb stood on the tiny deck of the transport boat staring
up at me, confused but waving.

"Stanis!" I whispered. "Get . . . him."

"We do not need him," he said, stoic as ever. "He has
done his part in bringing us here."

"And he has *more* to do for us," I said. "Just get him."

Stanis said nothing more but simply turned and leapt
over the railing, swirling down to the small craft below in
ever-growing circles. The gargoyle was not gentle scooping
up Caleb, and an audible *oof* escaped Caleb's lips as Stanis
grabbed ahold of him. Their return flight was a fast, straight
shot inches away from the side of the ship. Stanis shot past,
dropping Caleb in front of me from high enough that the
alchemist's legs buckled under him as he absorbed the shock
of the landing. He stumbled, then righted himself as he
smoothed his coat down.

"What's up with the attitude?" Caleb asked me, as Stanis
came down on the deck next to him.

I had an idea, but I wasn't sure that it was the time to get
into it. Still, I needed both of them at my side in this.
"What's the deal, Stan?" I asked.

The gargoyle cocked his head at me. "Deal?"

Although Stanis was ignoring him, Caleb got up in front
of him. "What's up with all the flight turbulence?"

Stanis didn't engage him, stepping to me instead. "He
says he is a new man, Alexandra, but he *has* worked for my
father. How do we not know this is not some part of Kejetan's
mad plan? How do we not know that Caleb here will not
just hand us over to him?"

I stood there, silent. I didn't have a good answer for him.
Truth was, I wasn't entirely sure. I *wanted* Caleb to be on
Team Belarus now, but as I knew, wanting something didn't
necessarily make it so.

"Way to have my back," Caleb said, shaking his head at
me, then turned to Stanis. "I can answer for myself. Frankly,
it looks like I'll have to. First of all, I need you to *think*—if
you're capable of it in that big chunk of rock of yours. Do

you know your father to be a forgiving man, Stanis? You *really* think he'd even let me on his team now after I freed you and took away his chances of learning the Spellmason secrets?"

Stanis stared as him for a moment in thought, but Caleb didn't look away.

"You perhaps have a point," Stanis said, his voice softer now.

"Great," Caleb said, testy. "I've been paid well by the Servants, *and* a good part of it in advance before they froze the rest. Kejetan is a determined pile of rocks, and he doesn't take kindly to being slighted. *But* . . . he's also mad with pride. He'll never expect us to bring the fight right to him, which, of course, is why we have. So you wonder where my loyalties lie? Yes, I'm selfish. And yes, I hope this puts an end to a series of fanatical flying madmen coming after me. I'd like a little less of that in my life. I've already got enough regular enemies out there, thanks."

Marshall *ahem*ed loudly and we all turned to look at him. "Are we done determining who's going to be on our side tonight?" He threw one of his hands up over his shoulder to slap the tank strapped to his back. "This thing isn't getting any lighter."

Rory sighed. "You want me to carry you?" she asked, patting her own tank. "On top of my rig?"

"Let's get focused," I said, going over my spell notes. "Everyone clear on what they're doing?"

Rory, Caleb, and Marshall nodded, but Stanis did not. I met his eyes.

"You're with me and Caleb," I said to him. "We're going to go in all stealthy-like."

Caleb leaned over to him and put a hand on his shoulder. "Think small and quiet thoughts."

"Will that help?" Stanis asked with sincerity, missing the point.

"Just try to keep quiet," I said, then turned to Marshall and Rory. "Head for Kejetan's throne room when you're done. And try not to get seen."

Marshall smiled. "Don't worry," he said. "I've got a little something for that."

I paused. "Like what?"

"You'll see," he said, pressing a single finger to his lips. "Shh! It's a surprise."

"You know," Caleb said, "historically speaking, the words *surprise* and *plan* aren't considered great bedfellows."

"Trust me," Marshall said. "You'll like this. I promise."

"All right," I said, smiling. "Let's do it."

I did trust Marshall, and if he had a surprise in store, not knowing what it was might be helpful, especially given the distinct possibility that we might be failing miserably at any second.

Marshall and Rory disappeared around the side of the shipping container, each carrying two sealed buckets in addition to the tanks on their backs. We waited several minutes, then made sure the deck was clear before setting off in a run across it, headed for the interior depths of the freighter itself.

Stanis and Caleb took the lead since they knew the way. I was happy to follow along, readying the spells in my head as my own memories of the path to the throne room below had faded somewhat. Stanis's preternatural hearing always caught the approach of any of the gargoyles or human Servants of Ruthenia in time for us to hide ourselves as we went.

The way to Kejetan's throne room was far more crowded than last I had seen it, what with all the additional gargoyles on board. It was easy to differentiate which were true Servants of Ruthenia by how they carried themselves, while the outsiders moved with more modern mannerisms or exhibited signs of meek confusion.

Surrounded and crowded by other gargoyles, Stanis abandoned any pretense of hiding and instead powered his way through the confusion until he burst into the throne room, wings fully spread, with Caleb and me at his side.

Kejetan sat upon his throne, and upon seeing us flew to his feet, his own set of batlike wings extending wide.

"My people," he called out, and the assembled crowd

turned to take notice of us. "A plague has come upon my great hall." He pointed to the three of us, going down the line, starting with Caleb. "First it weaved its way into those in my service, then my son, and now a woman brings her family name here, one that has been cursed these centuries by all who serve me."

"Belarus," I said, unable to contain the swell of pride and power I felt behind the simple word. I turned to the crowd. "Curse it if you will, but no one is to blame for your long suffering except the man you call your lord."

I sensed division among the ranks there, open hostility on the face of some, while others looked on in confusion.

"Followers of Kejetan, hear me," I continued. "There are those of you who have long been with him. I doubt my words will appeal to any sense of reason in you. But for those of you who find yourself new and afraid in your service to this mad lord, know this: This is not your fight. Your lives may be spared if you turn from the false promises of this man. Mark me, I will only offer you this option once."

The room erupted in conversation and shouting, some of the crowd attempting to disengage from it. Caleb grabbed my arm and dragged me behind Stanis's wings.

"Laying it on a bit thick, don't you think?"

I shook my head. "Remember, we don't have to beat them; we don't even have to fight them. We just have to keep them engaged."

"Right," Caleb said.

Before either of us could move, Stanis stepped away from us toward his father.

"What is the matter, son?" Kejetan said to him. "No longer feeling special in a roomful of your fellow creatures?"

"Do not call me your son," Stanis said. "You lost that right centuries ago."

"And you lost any chance you had to rule by my side when you choose to stand with *their* kind," Kejetan shouted, pointing at Caleb and me.

The alchemist moved closer to me, whispering.

"What part of not engaging them did that hunk of stone not understand?" he asked.

I ignored him, trying to draw the focus of Kejetan back to me.

"Really hating on humanity," I shouted, before Stanis could escalate this any further. "Do you forget where you come from, Kejetan? Do you forget how you were created?"

"I have no need for humanity," he said. "Except as servants to my higher form. When I was stuck in that jagged stone body for centuries, all I could do was sit and watch your kind squander their lives, toiling in this world with the mundane. There is no nobility in you."

"If *you're* the paragon of nobility," I said, "I think I'll pass."

Kejetan waved his hand, and the circle of gargoyles closest to his throne broke away and ran toward us, but Stanis dashed in front of them, blocking their way. Their claws and fists rained down on him as the shouts of the scared and confused filled the room.

I had hoped to avoid this, but all I could do was watch in horror as the fight in Stanis slowly went out of him because of the superior numbers of his attackers. Many of the newborn gargoyles ran off in horror, leaving only the most dedicated human and gargoyle Servants of Ruthenia remaining. The ones surrounding Stanis grabbed at him with their clawed hands, restraining him.

"If humanity has nothing, what do you have?" I asked Kejetan. "Followers, dedicated only because of the promise of eternal life. A promise that you have failed on yet again, and without that, what do you *really* have? Empty dreams filled with empty promises."

Kejetan stepped down from his throne, eyeing me as he crossed the floor to his son. He grabbed Stanis's face in his clawed hand. "And what do you offer us, Miss Belarus?"

I didn't truthfully know what to say that wouldn't get Stanis's head crushed in, but luckily I didn't have to speak.

"What does she offer you?" Rory's voice spoke up out of nowhere. "How about us?"

The entire room turned to the empty space off to my right. Ten feet away, the air shimmered like I was looking underwater. Rory's shape appeared, slowly coming into focus like a film projection.

I looked off to the door behind her, wondering if Marshall was coming through it. Or maybe he was inside already.

"We good?" I shouted out to her.

"We're good," Marshall's voice called out from the far end of the throne room. I focused on the sounds coming from the only exit other than the ones behind Rory and me. Marshall came into focus by the door, a vial raised to his lips with one hand, the other one holding the spray nozzle attached to the container on his back.

"Nice touch with the invisibility," I said, looking over to Caleb.

He nodded. "It was. But it wasn't mine."

Rory came over to us, holding up an empty vial of her own.

"Courtesy of Mr. Blackmoore," she said.

I smiled as Marshall ran over to join us, spraying the ground behind him as he came. "Surprise!"

"Somebody's been doing his homework," I said.

He blushed.

"I'd have to turn in my Dungeon Master's Screen if I didn't figure out how to at least mix an invisibility spell," he said.

I started to laugh, but a much darker laughter filled the room, booming over mine.

"So this is what you have to offer as opposition?" Kejetan asked, letting go of Stanis's head. The rest of the mad lord's pack still held their grip on him, but Stanis kept his head up with a grim determination on his face. "You mean to stand against me with whom?" He looked to Caleb. "First, a traitor to me, his greatest benefactor. Who will line your pockets now?" Kejetan turned to the rest of us. "And three other humans . . . ? A shopkeep, a dancer, and a stoneworker. Did you really expect to come here and challenge us with only one gargoyle against my multitudes? Did you hope to beat us down one by one?"

"Oh please," I said. "Give me some credit. I am of the Belarus blood, after all."

"And don't worry about my pockets," Caleb said. " 'You never know when one well will run dry' . . . especially one so foul. It's practically a freelancer's motto. I'll be fine. Which is more than I can say for you."

"You dare—"

"Oh, we dare," I said, the anger rising hot within me. "You've prolonged your life, but every last piece of your existence is driven by fear. The fear you strike in others. The fear you strike in *yourself.* It's so all-consuming that you've spent centuries hiding away, chasing after revenge and power, but never living, never learning."

"And why should I not have vengeance?" Kejetan asked, wrapping his hand around Stanis's throat this time. The secrets your family stole were still mine, and they have been denied to me far too long."

"No," I corrected. If we were going to pull off getting out of here alive, I needed to turn Kejetan's anger against him. "The arcane and the alchemical are not something *you* made. They're things you accumulated, gained through intimidation and murder. Alexander's child, your own son. And you wonder why my father took them from you? You wonder how your son chose to love Alexander more than *you*?"

My words had the effect I desired. Kejetan's face became monstrous with rage, and he lunged for me across the throne room.

The sudden opening of his wings struck terror in me, but this was what I had wanted—him away from Stanis.

Caleb's hand went into his coat and from within he pulled a clear vial filled with purple liquid. He unstoppered it and let a single drop fall to the ground on the spot Marshall had sprayed on his way over to us. I only hoped he and Rory had covered as much of the ship as they could have with the amount of Kimiya we had made. The rest relied on Caleb's transformative mixture.

My mind and arcane will were already reaching out, searching for the one thing I needed to isolate in this freighter and finding it—my arcane connection to stone . . . and it grew every passing second as the steel of the ship began to transform all along the path of Marshall and Rory's trails. I breathed out my words of power, the rest of my will and energy bridging the newfound connection.

Kejetan was in a full-on run toward me by then, and the deep part of my primal brain wanted to flee, but I stood my ground, focusing on the gargoyle's feet as they hit the floor of the ship. As his right claw came down, I rushed my will into the spot below it, what had become a stone floor itself rising up around his foot, twisting over it, encasing it.

Kejetan stumbled, and when his other foot came down, I caught that one in another swirl of malleable floor, hardening them both in place.

The momentum of his charge sent him tumbling forward, but Kejetan caught himself with his wings to remain standing. Immediately, he used their clawed tips to free himself from where his feet were trapped, but it did him no good.

Caleb laughed. "Now, you see, maybe if you worked smarter and not just meaner, you might have stood a chance."

Kejetan looked down at his feet, then caught my eye, confusion in his voice now.

"How?" he asked. "How are you using the steel of my ship to do this? Your bloodline's arcane skill is only with *stone*!"

"Technically," I said, "I *am* working with stone here."

"But *how*?" Kejetan shouted, still struggling in vain to free himself.

"Allotropy," Caleb said, holding the purple vial up. "You hired me, Kejetan, because you needed an alchemist, and what is alchemy really but a science most people don't understand. For instance, take allotropy. An allotrope allows for elementary substances in material matter, like say those found in steel, to exist in other forms, such as stone. Superman crushes a piece of coal; the allotropes help it become a diamond. Same principles at work here. Steel, meet stone!"

"This fight was only the distraction," I said, "keeping you and your men occupied down here in the depths of the ship."

Marshall held up his spray container. "There's a lot more where this came from," he said. He shook the container, the contents of it sloshing around. "Actually, there's not much more of it left. Almost all of it is coating your ship, sadly."

Kejetan shook his head.

"Tricks," he said, struggling. "Your potions and concoctions are limited in their uses, alchemist, offering nothing more than a delay."

"You'd be surprised," Caleb said, stoppering the vial. He slid it back inside his coat. "A little goes a long way, and it doesn't take much for the structural modifications of the elements to spread. Just a jump to the left. You hired me because I was good, remember?" Caleb turned to me, giving a deep bow. "My lady, the ship is yours."

I began to thank him, but Kejetan would not let me speak.

"It is not hers," he shouted. "It is *mine*. Or would you rather have my men tear your dear Stanis apart as you watch?"

Kejetan had charged me before, but his men had stayed their ground, Stanis still strung up among them, caught in their grasp.

"It seems, Miss Belarus—much like when I stole Stanis away from you the first time—that we are at an impasse. Harm me, and my men will have no other choice but to end Stanis. I no longer care for the miserable cur. It has become more than clear that he is no longer one of my kin."

"Nor would I ever wish to be," Stanis said. My heart went out to him, stretched out in submission among the other gargoyles.

I looked to Rory, who had already assembled her pole arm. A vial of her own appeared out of her coat, and she applied its contents liberally to the bladed end.

"You sure that's going to help?" I whispered to Caleb, and he nodded in response. Her blade hadn't always been the best weapon against stone, but this concoction was supposedly going to change all that. Now I just had to make sure I had the power to pull off the rest of this.

I turned my attention away from all other things back to Kejetan.

"Release me, and you can have my worthless son once more as yours," he said, a nervousness behind his attempts to bargain with me.

"I don't think so," I said. "We've done this dance before, remember?" I pulled my own notebook from my pocket, letting my anger grow as I turned to the spell I had marked out in detail there. "You broke into my home last year, *threatening my family*. Stanis gave his own freedom over to protect us, to take you away from us, but, no, *that* wasn't a permanent enough solution. All that did was buy us time, and right about now, I think a more permanent solution is in order."

At my command, Rory leapt forward, winging her pole arm at the gargoyle closest to her. The blade came down as the creature raised its claws to block it, catching it between two of its fingers. Like a hot knife through butter there was barely any resistance, and the blade slid down through its hand and the center of its arm. Everything below the gargoyle's elbow fell away in two pieces, which crumbled when they hit the floor.

However, even with that advantage, their numbers were too many, and I needed to act fast if we were going to keep from getting overwhelmed.

Already, the rest of the other gargoyles began pulling Stanis's limbs in four different directions. The strength of his wings knocked some of them back from him, but not enough were falling away in the struggle.

"Your men aren't going to hurt Stanis anymore," I said, pushing my will further out into the immediate surroundings of the throne room and the changing steel-stone of the ship. My body began to thrum with the almost overwhelming connection to it. "Your men have bigger fish to fry."

"Meaning what exactly?" Kejetan asked, lashing forward with his wings in a last, desperate attempt to attack, but he was still not able to reach any of us.

"Oh right, I forgot," I said, reaching out with my mind to slam shut the two other doors leading out of the room, the once-metallic clang of them sounding like a stone coffin sliding shut. "You ancient types have trouble with idioms like 'bigger fish to fry.' It means Stanis isn't their biggest problem right now."

The only door left for escape was the one behind me and my friends, and Marshall was already running for it as he unscrewed the top of the spray canister and spilled its remaining contents along our path out of the throne room.

"*This*," I continued, letting my will loose on all the steel-stone spread out in front of me, "is their biggest problem. First, I'm going to crush this room in around you like a balled-up prison, so you can't escape. Then I'll fold the rest of this ship in around you until it sinks to the bottom of the ocean."

The floor and walls were alive to me by then, the connection complete. I reached out to it, and it responded to my command. The floor beneath the gargoyles began to twist and buckle, the wrenching sound of metal fatigue and the grinding of stone filling the room as the walls pulled in to surround Kejetan and his men.

Many of the gargoyles holding Stanis broke away and began scattering around the room to push back against the walls that were pushing in, but several of them were still on him. With the numbers of captors thinned, Stanis struggled to break free, his wings thrashing about him.

"Stand still!" Rory called out to him, poised for action, holding her pole arm over her head, hesitant to take a swing with it. "Stanis, I'm serious!"

I lent her a hand, steadying the buckling floor directly beneath Stanis for a moment, allowing the gargoyle a bit more control of his movement. Instead of struggling, he pulled his wings in tight around him, making his body as small a target as he could.

Rory's blade made quick work of removing the arms of the gargoyle to Stanis's right, which freed his other arm enough that he lashed out with his claws at the remaining ones on his left. Roars of pain echoed throughout the room. But, in the end, Stanis was free.

Instead of coming to us, he turned, stepping toward his father.

"I do not know what you truly hoped," he said to Kejetan. "We stopped being family centuries ago when you killed Alexander's son and forced him into your servitude and when you ended my own life. I was willing to be taken into servitude by you as well, to protect them and to buy them time, hoping I could dissuade you from your madness, but the truth is that a man such as you will *never* be satisfied. You would try to bend this modern world to your will, never giving up on obtaining the knowledge you do not justly deserve to have."

"We could have lived as gods to them," Kejetan said.

"And that is your true failing," Stanis said. "We are still human born. No better than they. What you consider your calling, I consider madness."

"Stanis," I called out, feeling the use of my will beginning to take its toll as it drained me. "We need to go. Like, now."

More and more of the ship was crushing in behind them, and it was taking every last part of me to keep it from adding Stanis to it all.

"Kill me, then," Kejetan said, turning to me.

"No," I shouted. "Back away, Stanis." At my word, the gargoyle stepped away from Kejetan and toward me, his eyes still fixed on his father. When Stanis stood by my side, I spoke again. "I will not give you the dignity of death. Truthfully, I'm not sure if I *could* kill you. I might simply destroy this form you sought so hard to get all these centuries, but what of your spirit? Would it find another vessel?"

There was nothing but pure disgust on Kejetan's face now. "Your lack of commitment will leave you undone," he said.

"For generations, my family has either been hunted or suffered by your hand," I said. I pressed my will into the steel-stone at his feet, crumpling the floor up over the lower half of his body, encasing him further. "And now, for generations it will be yours to suffer instead. You finally have the physical form you desire, but it will do you *nothing*." I turned to Stanis. "You don't technically breathe, correct?"

"This is true," he said. "I do not."

"Good." I stepped toward Kejetan, still keeping well out of the reach of his wings, which were already partially trapped beneath the metal of the collapsing room.

"Do you have any idea how cold and dark it is at the bottom of the ocean?" I asked, watching his eyes widen but not waiting for an actual answer. "No sound, no one to rule . . . losing all freedom of movement, the ability to fly. No control, whatsoever."

"No!" he shouted, his usual air of authority finally replaced with open fear.

"You've had more than a lifetime to choose your course," I said. "The only 'good' to come from you was Stanis. Now you'll have a lifetime to contemplate those choices. At the bottom of the sea."

I expected rage. I expected pleading, screaming. I did not expect silence, which almost caused me to lose my angered emotional hold on my spell. Faltering for a second, I let the thoughts of what Kejetan might have wrought on this world fuel me. The corpses of my friends, the shattered remains of Stanis, and yes, even Caleb's lying dead at my feet. All those images filled my mind's eye, sticking my conviction to the spell.

"Lexi!" Rory called out from the doorway behind us. "Out, now or never!"

"Go," I whispered to Stanis through gritted teeth.

"Farewell, Kejetan the Accursed," he said to the man who had once been his father. Without another word, he turned and walked past me to Rory.

With the room clear of my friends, I backed my way out of it, rolling my will over it, trapping Kejetan and his fellow gargoyles in twists of crumpled steel-stone. I focused all my will to compress it in as tight as I could. Soon, the sight of anyone in the room was lost to me, but I kept compressing bit after bit of steel in on itself. My legs shook with the effort, the press of my nails digging into my palms, my body on the edge of collapse.

As I passed through the doorway of the throne room out

into the rest of the ship, stone arms scooped me up into a carry.

"I have you," Stanis said. "Do what you must."

The five of us backed through the rest of the freighter while I continued collapsing everything that was in our wake.

Rory and Caleb took on any stragglers we came across, although at this point the bulk of those belowdecks still seemed to be of the human-servant variety, the newborn gargoyles having had at least the smarts to leave a sinking ship.

The freighter continued to collapse, and I fought to block out thoughts of the enormity of the task, as Caleb had so often instructed me.

And he had been right, too, about how a little of his alchemical mixes went a long way. I had been worried we hadn't mixed enough Kimiya to affect the whole of the ship, but every time I thought the connection to the balled-up steel-stone would give out, I felt more of it come to life as the alchemical process continued to spread, like a virus, throughout the entire ship. I folded deck after deck in on itself as we worked ourselves higher and higher through the freighter, until we emerged on the ship's already tilting top deck.

"Holy crapballs," Marshall called out behind me.

"What?"

"Just . . . *look.*"

I turned my head. The deck of the ship was pure chaos. Human Servants of Ruthenia scrambled around, looking for some way off the ship. There were even a few gargoyles left, some not knowing what to do while others struggled to take off from the deck. With so many humans latching on to them, however, their winged forms could not get airborne.

"The diehards stayed with their master," I said, "but the rats are fleeing a sinking ship."

"So what now?" Rory asked. "The deck is swarming!"

"Here," Caleb said, handing her a flask. "Take a sip and pass it around."

Rory looked unsure. "What is it?"

"You might remember it from the night at the guild hall

when I first fought you and Alexandra," he said. "When I sped myself up."

It was no doubt an unpleasant memory for Rory, but she drank from the flask nonetheless and passed it to Marshall. I followed, then handed it back to Caleb, who in turn drank from it and offered it to Stanis.

He shook his head. "I do not believe such a thing would work on me," he said.

Caleb nodded and recapped the flask.

"Run for our ship over the side," I said. "You should be speedy enough now to avoid conflict. Stanis and I will meet you there."

Stanis didn't wait for an answer, and with me still in his arms, he leapt into the air, arcing high above the madness below.

My friends sped across the deck of the ship below at their accelerated rate and I watched their progress as the two of us flew.

"I can take you to the safety of land," Stanis said.

"No," I said. "To our boat. We came here together, and we're leaving together."

"As you wish," he said. The words, as always, comforted me, but I pushed comfort away.

I still needed my anger. After all, there was so much more of the freighter for me to collapse in on itself.

Twenty-nine

Stanis

There was a singular happiness in carrying my Alexandra. Had she asked, I might have been able to carry all four of them into the sky, but I thought perhaps trying to get airborne amid all the chaos on the freighter would have proved difficult.

I rose high above before swinging down and around to land on the small boat tethered to the side of the ship. Some of Kejetan's men had discovered it already in their haste to find any means of escape, a dozen already having boarded it. I slowed our descent by spreading my wings as we dropped onto the still-empty back of the boat and lowered Alexandra.

"First to the party," she said, still concentrating on the freighter behind me. "Feel free to mop the deck. I need to keep working this spell." Her voice dropped to a low whisper as the arcane words of the Spellmasons spilled from them.

Standing between her and the fleeing Servants of Ruthenia, I set to work on them, using wings and claws to knock them away. The more I handled, however, the more seemed to board to take their place. The deck of the pitched freighter high overhead was filled with men who, spying our vessel, were quick to jump into the waters all around us.

"Incoming!" I heard Marshall's voice cry out before spotting him among the jumpers. He hesitated, but Aurora pushed him out over the edge, catching him by surprise.

Aurora followed after him, but the alchemist did not jump.

Caleb drank a vial of an elixir before climbing like a spider down the side of the freighter, losing his grip on it about ten feet above me.

"Damn," he said, crashing down next to me at the front of the boat. "Thought that one would last longer."

Before he had a chance to lament it any further, one of the cultists grabbed his leg as he attempted to climb out of the water. Caleb spun and kicked at him, driving the man back.

"We need to leave," he said.

"No," Aurora said from the water. She pulled herself up on the vessel after throwing her pole arm onto it. She rolled forward, grabbed the weapon, and came up standing and swinging for more of the men, driving them back from her. "First we need to clear the deck."

Marshall came on board with much less grace than Aurora had.

"I'll work on the leaving part," he said, heading for the steering wheel at the back of the vessel.

With Alexandra concentrating on crumpling the freighter and Aurora and Caleb by my side, it should not take long to get under way.

Or so I thought. What had Alexandra called them back on the freighter's deck? Rats fleeing a ship?

Yes, that seemed appropriate. Our ship was teeming with these Servants of Ruthenia.

"This isn't working," Marshall called out from the back of the ship, and I turned. The lean human was locked in combat with several of Kejetan's men, all of them wrestling for control of the wheel. Lashing out behind me as I continued the fight in front of me, I used my wings to brush two of Marshall's attackers away. The two fell over the edge of the small boat into the water, but two more ran forward to replace them.

Caleb fought the men closest to the bow, his strength augmented and currently the match of my own as his attackers flew through the air with each of his blows that connected with them. He looked up and backed into me as several more cultists landed in the spot he had occupied a second ago.

"Shit," he said, ducking under one of my wings. He headed back to Alexandra, who was still concentrating on collapsing the freighter.

"What do you want?" Alexandra asked, keeping her eyes focused on the freighter. She ignored him even though the blond man was already inches from her face.

"This," he said, and moved even closer.

His lips met with hers, her eyes fluttering for a moment before sliding shut, the two of them locked together. Although I could not recall from my human life centuries ago ever experiencing that gesture myself, I had seen it many a time among the humans I had observed over the years. I knew it to be a sign of affection, and while I had no such ability in such matters, something dark and uncomfortable inside me stirred.

Unable to process fully what it was, I took my frustration with it out on one of my attackers, dashing my claws at him with such ferocity that his upper half fell away from his lower, both pieces sliding over the front railing of the ship into the ocean all around us.

By the time I moved on to the next of my foes, Alexandra and Caleb had parted once more.

"I wish there was more time for that," Caleb said, taking her hands in his. "It's the least I could do, what with you saving all of us."

"Don't thank me yet," she said, pointing to Rory. We all watched as she pushed two men over the edge of the boat with the dull end of her pole arm.

"It takes a village, after all," Alexandra continued. "And besides, I wouldn't exactly call this being saved at the moment."

"Not yet, anyway," Caleb said. He pushed farther from her, his hands dropping away. "Hopefully, I can change that."

Just as quickly as he had gone to her, he fought his way back to the bow of the ship to join me again.

Still unable to process the strange and dark sensation inside me, I resisted the urge to push him into the ocean, possibly in more than two pieces.

"Need your help, big fella," he said, looking up at the deck high above us.

"You do?" I said, the request catching me off my guard.

Caleb nodded and pointed up to the deck of the freighter. "The freighter is sinking too slow; too many of the Servants of Ruthenia are overrunning our tiny ship here, making it impossible to escape. We'll be overmatched and over-whelmed by them soon if I don't do something to give you all a chance to escape." He looked up at the deck of the ship far above us, more and more men attempting to jump down to our escape vessel every passing second. "I need to get up there."

I pushed away several more of the cultists, but more scrabbled forward, not necessarily to fight but at least to try to take control of our boat.

"I cannot fly you up there now," I said. "The others would not be safe."

"Looks like we'll have to do this the hard way, then," Caleb said, spreading his arms straight out to his side. "Hope you've got a good pitching arm, then."

"Pitching . . . ?"

"Never mind," Caleb said. "I need you to throw me. Just, you know, not into the side of the ship. I can't help anyone with a broken neck."

I grabbed him under his shoulders, lifting him with ease, his head raised to the sky. The dark part spoke up again inside me. It would be so easy to just squeeze until my hands met somewhere in the middle of his chest.

Caleb looked down, his eyes face-to-face with mine.

"Watch out for her," he said, his words full of concern.

"Watch out for them all, but her most of all. This isn't me ordering you . . . This is me asking you."

"I know," I said, some of the dangerous new sensation dying in me. "And I shall."

"Good," he said, and turned his head back up to the deck above us.

As more men climbed onto our deck by the moment, I took aim and threw the alchemist. Judging the distance in the heat of combat proved difficult; Caleb's body half hit the deck above, leaving much of him dangling over the side of the freighter.

Caleb pulled himself onto the deck and out of sight, and I found myself with a new problem. With one less person on our side, I was being overrun. Kejetan's men surrounded me on every side. Their hands pulled my wings and limbs in every direction. I worked my wings, the added weight of those hanging on making it much more difficult a process, but I forced them into motion. Careful not to hit any of my human friends, I extended them, sending the Servants of Ruthenia still holding on into the ocean as they lost their grip on me.

I turned to Alexandra, whose eyes were on the deck of the ship above.

The alchemist stood at the edge, his hands flashing in and out of his coat as he mixed the contents of several vials together.

"Go!" Caleb shouted down at us with a vial clenched in his mouth.

"We're not leaving without you," Alexandra called out to him.

"Yes, you are," he said. The alchemist tilted his head, which poured the contents of the vial into a larger one in his hand before spitting the empty container free. "Stanis, the chain!"

The cultist in front of me blocked my view of where I knew we were still tethered to the ship. My claws sunk into his shoulder as I tore into him, throwing him out of the way and into the hull of the freighter. My other claw came down hard on the chain, slicing through it and sending it sinking into the water.

Fresh hands came down on my arm, and I spun to knock away my new opponent, only to find Alexandra at my side.

"Get him," she said. *"Please."*

Already, men on the deck of the freighter were swarming Caleb while others still attempted to jump down to our boat.

Caleb struggled against the men pulling at him, but kept his footing while he continued working.

"Get them out of here, Stanis," he said, then looked to Alexandra. "We'll talk again. If not in this life, then the next."

"Are you sure about that?" Alexandra screamed to him.

He smiled despite the chaos all around him. "As sure as I am about anything."

I pushed off the hull of the freighter, our boat launching away from it.

"No!" Alexandra called out, the desperation in the tone of her voice sending a bitter pain straight through me.

"I am sorry," I said. "But we must go."

"Get him! Please!" she shouted at me.

I shook my head. Caleb had told me to look after them, and with the boat still being boarded by Kejetan's men, I needed to secure the ship.

"Concentrate on your spell," I said.

Nothing was going to save the freighter now even if she let it go. Already the prow was lifting into the air as the bulk of it descended beneath the waves.

I turned away and moved to help Marshall, who was wresting the controls back from two of the cultists.

"Screw my spell—" Alexandra started, but the words died in her mouth as a massive explosion wracked the last of the freighter that was still above water.

As I dropped the two men overboard, I watched flame shoot out across what remained of the deck and up into the sky. The reds and yellows mixed with a green light, and although the explosion had been sudden, my eyes had caught the point of its origins.

It had caught Alexandra's eye as well.

"Caleb!" she screamed.

But the only answer came as the roar of fire mixed with the sounds of the violent waves and our drowning enemies all around us as we headed back to shore and the lights of Manhattan.

Thirty

———— ☾ ————

Alexandra

"Lexi," a voice called out to me, but I didn't respond. That was the nice thing about shock. Nobody really expected you to answer while your brain shut down to take a rest from everything that had happened. Well, not completely shut down. Images of the evening flooded my mind, flashes of the crumpling freighter, stone wings, the column of flame amid an ocean of water . . .

And Caleb at the center of it all. *Caleb*.

"Dead," I said, simply to acknowledge the fact out loud to myself.

"Lexi!" the voice called out, sharper this time, accompanied by the sensation of someone grabbing my shoulder and shaking me. Rory.

I lifted my head and opened my eyes, and, to my surprise, we were not on the small boat anymore. The rooftop garden of my new building on Saint Mark's greeted me. I had no idea how I had gotten there, but I was comforted in my grief to see Rory and Marshall to either side of me on one of the park benches there.

"Caleb's dead," I said.

"We know," Stanis said, and I looked up to find him standing ten feet away on the pathway. "Are you unharmed?"

I turned my attention to myself for a moment as I took his question in. "I . . . I think so." I looked to Rory. "Caleb's dead."

She nodded and squeezed my shoulder.

Marshall's hand fell on my other one. "But not in vain," he said. "He saved us."

I stood on shaky legs and walked to Stanis. "You could have saved him," I said.

"I could not," he said. "I was honoring Caleb's actions. As well as honoring his request to watch over you."

I searched his face, but Stanis was as grave and silent a sentinel as ever. "I hate this," I said. "Not being able to read you."

"I am truly sorry," he said.

"Don't worry," I said. "When I restore our connection, it won't matter. Everything will be as it should." I looked up into Stanis's eyes. "Do you think it's over?"

"The threat from my family, yes," he said.

"Good," I said, and grief took me over. I collapsed against the smooth cool stone of his chest and lay there, unmoving.

"Lexi," Rory cried out, pointing up into the air.

Marshall was staring up at the sky as well. "I think you may have called it a little too early on being over," he said. "Incoming gargoyles!"

All around the rooftop park, branches swayed and shook as wave after wave of gargoyles came down out of the night sky. Although each was terrifying in its own unique way, one stood out among the rest as it landed on the roof and dropped the inert, burned form of Caleb Kennedy at its feet.

I turned my eyes away before I could take in the full extent of the damage to him, turning my fury on the creature who had dared to bring him before us. Had it not, I thought, been enough to watch him engulfed in flames upon the ship's deck without having to look at his corpse?

As the other gargoyles came down in their clumsy attempts to land, tree limbs snapped and cracked, falling from their trunks. I'd already had one home destroyed, and even though we were outnumbered, I'd be damned if I wasn't going to fight for my new one.

Stanis went for the same lead gargoyle I was heading for, but the reach of my power was closer and quicker, lashing out to the stone surrounding the figure, the bricks of the pathway responding to my command and rising.

The gargoyle stopped, raising its clawed hands against the bricks, and stepped back.

"Please, no!" it said. No, *she* said, looking to my *grotesque*. "You told me to seek you out."

Stanis paused in his advance, his face unsure. I ran to his side, but I held the bricks under my control in the air surrounding the figure.

"Emily . . . ?" Stanis said. "Hoffert."

"You know this one?" I asked.

He nodded. "We met . . . briefly. She was your brother's diversionary tactic."

I looked the slender creature over, its features more bat-like than those of Stanis. "You worked for my brother?" I asked, anger rising against my will. The bricks wavered, inching forward around her.

"No!" she said, fear in her voice. "Stanis, please . . ."

My *grotesque* looked around the roof at the others. "Why did you bring our enemies here to our home?" Stanis demanded.

"They're not your enemies," she pleaded. "They're the same as I . . . confused, scared, unsure."

I stepped toward her. "You expect me to believe you're not our enemies when you dare lay our dead friend at your feet?" I shouted. I could contain my rage and sorrow no longer. I hurled one of the bricks through the air at her, but she swiped her claw at it, causing the stone to shatter into fragments.

I expected her to attack in retaliation, but she simply stayed where she stood and lowered her arms. When she spoke, her voice was less fearful but still quiet.

"Your friend," she said. "He is not dead."

Of course he is, I thought to myself. I looked down at him once more, examining the burned body I had been so quick to look away from. The tattered remains of Caleb's clothes were charred with soot—still smoking—but Caleb himself looked untouched except for the few remaining pieces of singed hair that were flaking away.

Even though his eyes were closed and his face unresponsive, the sight of his chest rising and falling caused my legs to give out beneath me. I fell by his side, grabbing him up in my arms, and the bricks under my control fell back to the pathway.

"You're alive!" I said, pressing him close against me, feeling his heartbeat strengthen as his head stirred against my chest.

"You . . . sure about that . . . ?" he said, his voice weak. The last word was barely out of his mouth when he fell into a fit of coughing that ended with him spitting out a thick black liquid onto the roof.

"Pretty," Rory said as she joined us, Marshall at her side.

I pushed away from him, holding his weakened body away from me at arm's length so I could look him over. "How? How is it possible?"

"We watched you go *kaboom*," Marshall added.

"I'm not sure," Caleb said. "I watched me go *kaboom*, too." He went quiet for a moment, lost in his own thoughts before speaking again. "Do you remember when I told you about the spell I used to bind myself to the two ships? How I had trouble driving a blade into my own skin when I needed the blood for the binding?"

I nodded.

He marveled at the smooth but unharmed skin of his arms and hands. "Years of ingesting alchemical mixes must have had more of an effect on me than I thought," he said. "I guess my body is a bit more resilient than I previously would have imagined."

Caleb ran his hand along the burned edge of what remained of his right pant leg, which was cut off just above his knee.

"You look like the Incredible Hulk after he changes back into Bruce Banner," Marshall said.

"After surviving that explosion," he said, "I *feel* like the Hulk."

I hugged him hard, but not too hard. I'd hate for him to have survived an explosion only to break his ribs in my overzealousness at finding him alive still.

As I released Caleb, Rory caught him as he lay back down.

I stood, turning to this new gargoyle. "If you aren't here to cause trouble, why *are* you here?"

Her wings flitted with nerves, and though she looked on the verge of taking to the sky once more, she held her ground. "Stanis told me to find him," she said.

"I did indeed tell you to seek me out, Emily," Stanis said. "But who are these others?"

Although this other creature was a gargoyle, her body moved like that of an uncomfortable young woman, something I was all too familiar with.

"Many of these others were promised the same safety that Devon promised for allegiance to him," she said. "And others were like me . . . alone, scared, confused. So when you told me to seek you out, I did. When I saw the ship ablaze, I rescued this man you had been working with and followed you and your friends back to the city." The gargoyle turned to me, looking down into my eyes. "I am sorry to intrude, but I—and many others—have questions we *need* answered."

I could not help but smile. "It is no worry, Emily," I said. "A polite gargoyle is welcome here anytime, unlike the kind you first aligned yourself with."

"There is much to discuss," Stanis said, "but you must forgive me a moment, Emily. I must speak with my maker's kin privately."

Emily nodded, and now it was my turn to be confused as Stanis took me gently by the arm and walked me away from my friends and the gathering crowd of gargoyles. He stopped when we were well away from all the others.

"What is it, Stanis?"

"I have been thinking," he said. "Even after these many months of no longer being bound by Alexander's rules, I still find it a novel thing to do."

"What about?" I asked.

Stanis stood silent, staring up into the night sky before finally looking down to meet my eyes.

"I do not think it would be wise to reestablish our bond," he said.

The words hit hard, as if Stanis had actually slapped me, and I stepped back.

"Why not?" I asked, confused. "The timing is perfect now. We're out of danger and can take the time to do it right."

"There are others who need me more," he said. "And I do not think restoring that connection would help me in doing what is right for them." My *grotesque* looked over to the assembly on the rooftop. "I have a people now. A confused people with the need for some sort of leader. They need the person Alexander always wanted me to become."

"What about what I need?" I asked, feeling stupid and greedy the second the words were out of my mouth, but my heart could not keep quiet. "What am I supposed to do without that connection? I miss it, Stanis. What if I'm in peril?"

Stanis turned to my group of friends, his eyes staying on Caleb, who by that time was standing.

"You have more than enough people interested in your well-being," he said. "You will be fine. I cannot, however, say the same for these others. They need me more."

Loath though I was to admit it at first, Stanis was absolutely right. There was no room for my selfishness in all this. All I could do was nod and head back to my friends, leaving Stanis behind me.

Rory and Marshall had Caleb stretched out between them and I took him from them, wrapping my right arm around his waist for support.

"What's going on?" Rory asked.

"I'm not entirely sure," I said. "I thought things would go back to the way they were once things were over between us and Kejetan, but it just seems to get more complicated."

Caleb gave a pained laugh that erupted into a fit of coughing. "Life has a way of doing that," he said. "At least these gargoyles didn't want to tear me to pieces."

"Not yet anyway," Marshall said, nervous, looking at the gathered crowd of winged creatures.

Caleb leaned his head against mine, his skin burning hot to the touch. "I don't think I have the strength in me right now if we did have to fight them," he said. "But if they wanted trouble, I doubt they would have brought me here."

I watched as Stanis walked back to the gargoyle who had brought Caleb to us.

"Just because they don't want trouble doesn't mean they haven't brought it," I said.

I walked toward them, helping Caleb along as I went, happy to have him by my side despite the madness of the past few minutes.

"What is it you want from us?" I asked her.

"I don't know," she said. "I only know that Stanis told me to seek him out. I guess I—we—want answers."

"We can provide those," I said. "As best we can, anyway."

"You've got an actual alchemist as your service," Marshall added, jerking his thumb toward Caleb.

"No," Caleb said, clapping Marshall on the shoulder. "You've got two."

Marshall blushed. "I'm still learning what I can," he said. "More of an apprentice, really."

"But if we can help, we will," added Rory.

"Thank you," the gargoyle said, then looked back to me. "I do not mean to take advantage of your kindness."

"You're not," I admitted, softening to the creature's sincerity. "We're just not used to being around creatures of your kind without their trying to tear us to shreds."

The gargoyle's face registered shock, one of its hands flying to its mouth in surprise. The gesture looked almost comical on it as it exclaimed, "Oh my!"

"I will help as I can," I said.

Stanis cleared his throat, and my friends and I turned to him.

"Forgive me," he said, "your help is welcome, but I fear this may require the finesse of one more learned in the ways of the *grotesque*, the way of the gargoyle."

It both pained me and gave me great pride to see the creature my great-great-grandfather had first taught to speak so earnestly offering to help.

"Are you sure?" I asked.

Stanis bowed his head to me. "These are . . . for lack of a better expression, my *people*."

"There are others out there," the female gargoyle said. "Beyond the ones who have chosen to follow me here. Others who do not wish well toward us or humankind. We have already fallen victim to some of them."

"We can help," I said.

"No," Stanis said.

"Excuse me?" I asked.

"*I* will deal with them," Stanis said. He looked out over the assembly on our roof. "And I will teach you how to deal with them as well."

He turned to me. "Do you mind?" he asked.

The very fact that he was asking brought an unexpected joy to me. I shook my head. How could I say no to that most human level of concern for my feelings in this?

"Come," he said to the crowd. "I have much to tell you about the family whom you have to thank for your existence." Stanis shot up into the air over the roof, hovering high above as he waited for the others to take flight, leaving the four humans standing there.

The night skies over Manhattan would be forever changed. So, too, it seemed, was my relationship to Stanis. Whether either would prove for the better or worse remained to be seen, but as I stood there among my friends and Caleb, one thing was both clear and bittersweet.

Stanis no longer belonged to just me.

The strongest bonds are set in stone...

FROM
ANTON STROUT

Alchemystic

BOOK ONE OF
The Spellmason Chronicles

🌙

Alexandra Belarus is a struggling artist living in New York City until she's forced into her family's real estate empire, which includes a towering Gothic Gramercy Park building built by her great-great-grandfather. But the truth of her bloodline is revealed when she is attacked on the street and saved by an inhumanly powerful winged figure.

Lexi's great-great-grandfather was a Spellmason—an artisan who could work magic on stone. But in his day, dark forces conspired against him, so he left a spell of protection on his family. Now that Lexi is in danger, her ancestor's magic has awoken his most trusted and fearsome creation: a gargoyle named Stanis.

PRAISE FOR THE NOVELS OF ANTON STROUT

"Like being the pinball in an especially antic game, but it's well worth the wear and tear."
—Charlaine Harris, #1 *New York Times* bestselling author

"Make room on the shelf, 'cause you're going to want to keep this one!" —Rachel Vincent, *New York Times* bestselling author

antonstrout.com
twitter.com/AntonStrout
facebook.com/ProjectParanormalBooks
penguin.com

M1324T0513

About the Author

ANTON STROUT was born in the Berkshire Hills mere miles from writing heavyweights Nathaniel Hawthorne and Herman Melville. He currently lives outside New York City in the haunted corn maze that is New Jersey (where nothing paranormal ever really happens, he assures you).

His writing has appeared in several DAW anthologies—some of which feature Simon Canderous tie-in stories—including: *The Dimension Next Door*, *Spells of the City*, and *Zombie Raccoons & Killer Bunnies*.

In his scant spare time, he is an always writer, sometimes actor, sometimes musician, occasional RPGer, and the world's most casual and controller-smashing video gamer. He now works in the exciting world of publishing, and yes, it is as glamorous as it sounds.

He is currently hard at work on his next book and can be found lurking the darkened hallways of www.antonstrout.com.